NERVE ATTACK

— A Kolya Petrov Thriller —

Paperback ISBN 13: 978-1-64599-195-3
Hardcover ISBN 13: 978-1-64599-196-0
E-book ISBN 13: 978-1-64599-197-7
Kindle ISBN 13: 978-1-64599-198-4

Editor: Cynthia Brackett-Vincent
Cover design by Deirdre Wait
Cover photographs © Getty Images

Published by:

Encircle Publications
PO Box 187
Farmington, ME 04938

info@encirclepub.com
http://encirclepub.com

Printed in U.S.A.

NERVE ATTACK

— A Kolya Petrov Thriller —

S. LEE MANNING

Encircle Publications
Farmington, Maine, U.S.A.

To Jim. With love.

Acknowledgments

FIRST AND FOREMOST, I want to thank Encircle Publications for taking Kolya Petrov and company from the confines of my imagination and my computer to the pages of my critically acclaimed novel, *Trojan Horse*, and now to the pages of this sequel, *Nerve Attack*. Thank you as well to the Encircle author community, for welcoming me into your midst. It is an honor and a privilege to be one of you.

Thank you to my wonderful readers/editors who contributed so much to crafting of *Nerve Attack*: to James Manning for patience, encouragement, and insights through multiple drafts; to Jenny Manning, whose suggestions on story and character were invaluable; to Joseph Yuan for his perceptive notes on story and PTSD.

Thank you: to Dean Manning and Marcia Wagner for talking me through the symptoms and treatment for PTSD; to Kyle Patel at Monarch Air Group for an informative discussion on the procedures for hiring a private jet; to Kay Kendall for reading a very early version of this novel and authenticating the Russian scenes.

And thank you, once again, to my family, Jim, Jenny, Joseph, and Dean for all your encouragement, support, and love. It's been a hell of a ride.

PART I

1

THE SWIRLED MULTICOLORED DOMES of St. Basil's and the Kremlin glowed in the early darkness of the Russian winter, and at the far end of Red Square, skaters twirled on an ice rink in the lightly falling snow. A Christmas card perfect scene—if one just went by appearances, but, as Kolya Petrov knew, appearances could be deceptive. Nothing in Moscow was ever as it seemed. Still, if he were a tourist, Kolya might have enjoyed the sights as well as the music, Mussorgsky's *Pictures at an Exhibition*, blaring over the rink's loudspeakers. While his musical passion was for jazz, both playing and listening, he also liked classical—even if the Mussorgsky piece seemed a bit of an odd choice for skating music. It was only an idle thought. He wasn't a tourist or a visiting musician. Nor was he from Belarus visiting relatives—as his fake passport claimed and as he'd casually mentioned at the hotel. He was an American intelligence operative.

An older woman in a shabby coat stood in a booth with an electric heater, renting skates to those who hadn't brought their own. He told her his size, peeled off the requisite bills, and she handed over a pair of brown hockey skates with rusty blades. He carried them to a nearby bench, kicked off his shoes and tried them. They fit, a little looser than he would have liked—not great if he'd wanted to play hockey or figure skate, but good enough for today's purposes.

He was dressed warmly, a wool cap covering his blond hair and three layers—long sleeve shirt, wool sweater, blue ski jacket, but it was still cold. He estimated the temperature at maybe five degrees. Colder

1

than Washington D.C. where he currently lived—but not as cold as he remembered from his last experience of January in Russia.

The skating rink, small by Moscow standards, was in front of the GUM, the state department store during the days of the Soviet Union, now a luxury shopping mall, filled with designer stores. Open December to March, the rink was well lit, and dozens of warmly bundled skaters of all ages circled the ice.

While tightening his skates, he assessed the small crowd around the rink. One man in a sheepskin hat, late middle age with a hard face, stood on the far side of the rink, hands in pockets. He seemed to have no connection with any of the skaters—nor did he seem interested in skating.

Sheepskin Hat, a little less surreptitiously than Kolya, was checking out the crowd around the rink, but his attention focused on a woman with red hair skating with a dark-haired teenage girl. Did Sheepskin Hat know that the red-haired woman was about to pass something off to American intelligence—or was he just routinely assigned because of who she was: Maria Andropov, mistress and accountant to the President of the Russian Federation—and Kolya's contact?

Or maybe nothing was going on. The man could just be enjoying the sight of the skaters or maybe watching a friend or a relative.

Kolya's instincts said no, and he hadn't survived seven years on the job by ignoring his instincts. Sheepskin Hat had the look and feel of a professional on the job. Kolya suspected he was FSB—the state security organization that had replaced the KGB.

Kolya saw no one else that looked suspicious. Then again, someone with good tradecraft probably wouldn't draw attention to himself. The mere fact that Kolya'd noticed Sheepskin Hat either meant that he was there to divert attention from whoever might be the real threat—or that Maria was considered low priority, and they'd assigned someone who wasn't all that good.

He hoped it was the latter, but he had to be prepared for anything.

Moscow rules. Trust no one. Trust nothing.

Working with no official cover (NOC) meant he had no diplomatic immunity. If he were caught, the American government wouldn't admit that he worked for them. As a former Russian national, he'd be deemed not just a spy but a traitor. Being a Jewish former Russian national would just increase the abuse he'd suffer. He'd wind up in a concrete cell in the basement of the Lubyanka, where a guard would put a bullet through his brain—after months of physical torment. And he wouldn't be the only person executed.

The red-headed woman and her child would be shot along with him.

He could walk away, but there were no backup arrangements. Besides, if Maria was under surveillance, all the more reason to act quickly—before anyone found evidence of her betrayal—and she was arrested.

Everything was in place, and this was the best chance.

He wobbled from the bench to the edge of the ice and entered the rink. Muscle memory kicked in. Although he hadn't skated in years, he remembered the feel and the moves from when he had played hockey as a child. But the trick was to look like a novice.

He waved his arms as if trying to keep his balance and stumbled into an old man, who said two rude words. Kolya apologized.

He made it halfway around the rink before tripping and falling, landing on his knees and the palms of his hands. The ice stung. After a minute, he pulled himself up, took two tentative strokes on the ice, lost his balance again, and grabbed onto a young woman. She was startled but put out a hand to steady him.

"Lean forward," she said. "Bend your knees."

"*Spacibo*," he thanked her. But he needed to appear clumsy. He shuffled forward, tiny steps on the ice, resisting the urge to glide.

Two minutes later, the red-haired woman passed on his left. He stumbled again, grabbing onto her to get his balance. While holding on to her, he whispered a sentence into her ear.

Her response was indignant. "Idiot. Let go of me. If you can't skate, get off the ice." Her tone was in contrast to the fear in her deep blue eyes. Not just for herself. For her daughter. The President of Russia murdered people for much less than what she was doing.

"*Izvinite.*" He pronounced the Russian apology.

She shoved him.

"What an asshole." Blissfully unaware, the teenage girl shot him a withering look.

Then the two of them skated away. He made his way to the edge of the rink and continued to circle, falling, bumping into strangers, and apologizing for another forty minutes, twenty minutes after Maria and her daughter had left the ice. Then he exited the ice, changed back into his shoes, and returned the skates.

The thumb drive that Maria had slipped into his hand was safe in his pocket. His next destination would be the mall, where he'd pass the drive on to another operative who would get it out of the country. By evening, the information on the accounts, a number of which were located inside the United States, that the Russian President used to hide billions he'd stolen, would be in the hands of the Executive Covert Agency, otherwise known as the ECA, the Executive Covert Agency, the intelligence agency that employed Kolya.

Next, the more dangerous operation: getting Maria and her daughter safely out of Russia.

He looked for the man in the sheepskin hat—but he was gone as well.

2

WEDNESDAY EVENING, MOSCOW, RUSSIA

KOLYA GOT OFF A bus and strolled through the park known as the Patriarch's Ponds, famous for an appearance by the devil in a novel by Mikhail Bulgakov. *Appropriate. Demons could be lurking anywhere.* Metaphorical demons. FSB agents were much more frightening than the witty Satan or his black cat minion in Bulgakov's novel.

He pulled his mind away from contemplating the novel, an amusing story with religious elements woven into a satire on life in the Soviet Union. *Focus on the business at hand.*

He'd changed into a black cashmere coat, a red scarf, and a black fur hat, which felt ridiculous in its extravagance. It was nothing that he would have chosen to wear on his own, nothing that he could have afforded either, but a complete change of style might avoid his being recognized as the awkward skater from earlier in the day.

He strode past the ice-covered pond and down snowy paths, and then satisfied that he was not under surveillance, headed towards the bustling cafés and restaurants two blocks away.

Despite the cold, the sidewalks teemed with people patronizing the bars and the restaurants clustered around the intersection of *Spiridonevsy* and *Bolshoy Kozikhinsky.* The crowds made it both safer and more dangerous. Safer—because it would be less likely that Kolya would be noticed. More dangerous—because it would be harder to spot a tail.

Cars were lined up along the curb. Illegal and legal taxis, and Ubers.

Kolya slowed to take out his phone and a man behind him shoved Kolya in the middle of his back. He stepped aside, muttering the polite

5

"*Izvinite.*" Kolya returned to the phone, purchased on his arrival in Russia. He checked for messages and then sent one of his own over the encrypted app. *Here. You?*

The response from his friend and partner, Jonathan Egan. *Here. Silver Rav4, first in line. Are they?*

Jonathan had papers identifying Maria and her daughter as his wife and child, and he would drive the two north to the border with Finland. The southern border was closer, but with less friendly countries on the other side. The longer route was safer. Kolya would make his way separately out of Russia. Splitting up reduced the risk.

Moscow rules. Trust no one.

Kolya texted back: *Not yet.*

Exactly nine o'clock. Where were they? The phone gave him an excuse to linger for a few minutes—but in this cold, most people would be hurrying to get inside.

He thumbed through the phone while watching the time tick down. *One minute late. Two minutes.*

He was nervous, not for himself, but for the two people he was charged with protecting.

He'd whispered the time and place into her ear when he'd pretended to fall at the rink. He reminded himself that Maria wasn't a professional—that she might not be as aware of the importance of precision as an intelligence operative.

But she was the one in greatest danger—she and her daughter—and that alone should have prompted her to be on time.

Five minutes. Where the hell were they?

His phone buzzed with a new text, but he ignored it. There was nothing to tell Jonathan, except to wait, and silence would say the same thing.

Six minutes.

If she were caught, she could give Kolya up. He had a fleeting thought of the basement of the Lubyanka and the bullet in the back of his head, but Maria—and her daughter—were his main concern.

If she'd been caught, the FSB would already be here, wouldn't they?

The phone buzzed again. *Abort?*

This time he answered. *Five minutes more.*

Then he saw the flash of red hair under a scarf—Maria and her daughter—exiting Uilliams's, a popular restaurant, and his tension eased.

They were a little late, but safe. For now. The danger wouldn't end until they were out of Russia.

He pocketed his phone and pulled out a cigarette, patting his pockets as if looking for a light. He stopped in front of Maria.

"Do you have a light?"

"Yes, certainly." Her eyes were still frightened, but her voice was calm. She pulled out a matchbook and handed it to him. "Smoking's bad for your health, you know."

"I know. It's the Russian curse. That and vodka." He lit the cigarette. Then more quietly: "Silver Rav4. First in line."

The daughter, on her own phone, didn't look up and showed no sign that she'd heard nor did she show any sign of recognition.

Maria smiled at him, and she seemed almost to be relaxing. Then to her daughter. "Vera, we're taking an Uber instead of the Metro. The silver car over there."

The daughter looked puzzled but shrugged, not knowing that she was about to leave Russia forever. Kolya felt for her. She'd had no preparation, no chance to say goodbye to friends, and she would have to adjust to a new identity in a strange land where she didn't speak the language.

He'd done so himself—and it had been difficult. He had missed his friends. There were still many things about Russian culture and language that he loved. But he'd been thrilled to escape the abuse and anti-Semitism of the boys' home where he'd lived for five years and move to America. He suspected that Vera would be less eager, especially with the restrictions that would be on her forever.

At least she'd be alive.

The two of them walked away, and Kolya smoked his cigarette. It was a dirty habit, and he disliked it, but it was a useful tool. He could linger until Maria and her daughter were safely in the car. Smoking was the perfect loitering excuse.

In the reflection of a store window, he watched as the car door opened, and Maria and Vera slid into the back.

But his momentary relief evaporated. The man in the sheepskin hat from the ice rink strode past, his attention on Maria and her daughter.

Just Sheepskin Hat. No one else.

Kolya tossed the cigarette on the sidewalk, turned, and followed,

7

close enough to hear Sheepskin Hat speaking on his phone. "They're getting into a car. License number—one minute—and I'll send it."

He couldn't let the man send a photo of the car's license plate.

Kolya kicked Sheepskin Hat in the back of his right knee and he went down, dropping the phone. Kolya stomped on the phone as the man groped inside his coat, pulled out a gun, and aimed at the car that was pulling away from the curb. He fired as Kolya grabbed the man's gun hand.

The man shouted. "FSB. Help me."

No one came, and the sidewalk was suddenly empty as people ran from the scene.

Still, there were cameras and police everywhere. Backup would be there within minutes.

The man's eyes widened in recognition. "You were at the ice rink. Spy." He hissed the words, then shouted again for help.

Minutes. Maybe seconds.

If reinforcements arrived, he was dead. Maria and her daughter too.

They struggled for control of the gun. Kolya, younger and stronger, bent the man's wrists until the gun pointed at Sheepskin Hat's chest. Then he pushed the man's finger on the trigger, and the gun fired.

Kolya stood and ran. No one followed. He turned one corner, ran to the next street, turned again, and slowed to a walk. His heart thudded, from adrenaline and fear, as much as from the exertion. He had been exposed. His picture would be everywhere. Maybe the hat and the scarf had hid his face enough that he wouldn't be recognizable, but taking a plane or train was now risky. The authorities would be on alert at the airport and on trains, and he stood a good chance of being stopped and interrogated. His previous escape plan had just evaporated.

The phone buzzed.

Meet us. We'll all get out through Finland.

Jonathan sent the name of a metro stop on the outskirts of Moscow. Kolya texted that he'd be there in half an hour. If he were lucky.

A block further, he tossed his hat into a garbage can, and in the next block he discarded the scarf. In another two blocks, he descended stairs to the Metro, found a bathroom, and entered a stall. Inside, he hung the cashmere coat on a hook and waited a few minutes for his heart to stop racing and his breathing to calm.

Thoughts of the FSB agent he'd just killed flashed through his mind. It wasn't Kolya's first kill, but killing wasn't something he enjoyed. Did the man have a wife? Children?

But it had been necessary. If Sheepskin Hat had completed his call, the FSB could have picked up Jonathan and Maria and her daughter. All of them, Kolya included, would have been dead. That had been the choice—their lives or the life of the FSB agent.

He walked out of the stall wearing jeans and the ski jacket from earlier in the day that he'd worn under the oversized cashmere coat. After washing his hands and face, he checked the restroom. No one. They might find the coat eventually, but he'd be far gone by then.

He boarded the first train to arrive, changed twice, finally exiting the train and the Metro at the arranged spot on the outskirts of Moscow.

The Silver Rav4 waited across from the Metro entrance. He opened the car door and slid into the front passenger seat. They weren't safe yet, but being out of the center of Moscow was an improvement. A step at a time. It would become more dangerous closer to the border with Finland—but he'd worry about that when they got there.

Hopefully, the documents should hold up long enough to get out.

The teenage girl, in the back seat, huddled against her mother, looked up.

"You." Then she turned to her mother. "What the hell is going on, Mama?"

"I'm sorry," Maria said.

Kolya again felt a pang of sympathy for the daughter. She was a little older than he'd been—but unlike him, she didn't have a reason to be happy to leave Russia. Well, she did, she just didn't know what Yuri Bykovsky would do to her and her mother if they stayed. And he wouldn't tell her either.

Jonathan put the car into gear and pulled out.

3

"I WANT YOU TO find them." Muscular, built more like an American linebacker than a marathon runner, dark haired with gray just starting at his temples, Yuri Petrovich Bykovsky, President of the Russian Federation and Supreme Commander of the Armed Forces, glared across the oak desk in the ornate, cavernous room that was his office in the Kremlin. In direct line of displeasure: a short thin man with glasses, dignified with a shock of white hair, the current Director of the FSB. Also in the room were the Director of the SVR, a nondescript man who could fade into the background, and Yuri's subservient Chief of Staff. "I want you to find all of them. Maria. Her daughter. And the man who helped them get away."

He tossed on the desk the picture of a young man, around six feet tall, face partially obscured by a fur hat and a red scarf.

"It won't be easy." The Director of the FSB cleared his throat. "The Americans are good at hiding people. Maria and her daughter will be in some remote town, somewhere in the Midwest, maybe. It's a big country. And as for the spy... from what I understand, he spoke Russian without an accent."

"He must have been born here and then moved to the United States."

"Well, that narrows it down," the Director of the SVR said. "To maybe a million people."

Yuri narrowed his eyes, suspicious that he was being mocked, but then decided not to push it. "There can't be that many native Russians in the CIA."

10

"You don't know he was CIA. There are nineteen intelligence agencies in the United States."

"I don't care what fucking agency he works for. I don't care how long it takes. I just want them found. All of them. Do you know what Maria did? The bitch gave them all my accounts, accounts in the United States and in the Cayman Islands—and they've frozen ten billion dollars of MY money." Money that he'd used periodically to fund rebels in countries around the world—and money that belonged to him, no one else.

She'd shared his bed and more importantly, his secrets, and she'd done this to him. Why? He wouldn't say that he'd loved her—but he'd had as close to love for her as he'd ever had for any woman. But things had changed. Her attitude had changed. Not that she'd said anything, but he'd noticed her pulling back. She'd continued to sleep with him, continued to be his accountant. But there had been a change.

All dating back to when he'd made some remark about how her daughter was turning out to be a sexy young woman, as if it were his fault that her daughter was attractive. Stupid woman. He hadn't touched the girl—yet—but even if he did, it wasn't as if he'd hurt her. He'd taken care of all the women he'd ever slept with.

Maybe it was just jealousy—that Maria was afraid of being supplanted by her own child.

Whatever the reason, he didn't care. She'd betrayed him, and he wanted her to pay for it.

"I did know that."

"Do you understand that I trusted her?"

"And trust violated is a terrible thing." The FSB Director adjusted his glasses. "We can't allow that to go unpunished. Nor can we allow the killing of an FSB officer without seeking revenge."

"And yet they got away."

"So it seems."

For the second time, Yuri noted the Director's tone. He'd been wondering about the Director for a while—wondering whether he was insubordinate.

"How did they get out of the country?"

"I don't know for sure. This man," he nodded at the picture, "had help. Someone driving the Rav4. But we haven't traced them beyond Moscow."

"Find out. I want to know what idiot let them across the border."

"They could have taken a boat. We don't know. We do know that it was an elaborate plot by the Americans—that Maria had contacted them months ago. We tracked that much down."

Yuri glared at him. Maybe it was time to make a change at the FSB. How could this idiot have let Maria—and an American spy—several American spies, maybe—get out of the country?

The Chief of Staff cleared his throat. "We could make a formal protest."

Yuri turned to him, ready to unload his full fury, but the Chief wasn't done.

"We make a formal protest about an American agent operating on Russian soil and we let it go. The Americans will think we're done. And we will be. Until we have enough information to locate both Maria and this man."

Yuri laughed and slapped his hand on his desk. "I like that. Let's lull them into complacency. All of them. Maria. This man. And American intelligence services. Then we act. Cold revenge is always the best."

PART II

4

ON THE NIGHT OF his last trip, Jean Claude Gautier drove his pickup a mile under the speed limit past a line of shops just north of the Canadian border. He neither knew nor cared what might happen with his cargo once it reached the United States. His wipers beat rhythmically against a heavy downpour. Driving, he drummed his fingers on the steering wheel to the music of Bruce Springsteen. He turned left onto a two-lane street of homes. Through the storm, he saw the lights of the crossing station ahead on his right. He was still in Quebec, but if he pulled into a driveway on the right, he'd be in Vermont. As long as he didn't stop, the U.S. authorities wouldn't bother him.

He continued, just below the speed limit. There were few other cars. Despite the night and the pelting rain, flags decorated with stars and stripes waved in cold gusts of wind in the front yards of the Vermont homes, while across the street, flags bearing the maple leaf of Canada whipped back and forth.

Night and rain: the flags shouldn't be outside. He remembered that from school—but he couldn't remember the last time the flags hadn't been displayed. *Sometime before 9-11*, he thought. *Sometime before everything changed.*

He'd grown up here in Beebe Plains, on this odd street that divided two nations. Back then he'd cross the street to play with American kids, and they'd cross to play with him in Canada. In his teens, he'd dated an American girl he'd met in a library in Stanstead, where a black line down the building's center marked the border, the front door in Vermont, and the parking lot in Canada. Back then, everyone smuggled a little. It was easy. Walk into Vermont and return with a backpack full of cheaper American goods. Groceries. Blue jeans. American CDs. Sometimes marijuana. And sometimes harder drugs.

But now cameras watched over the streets, and if you crossed over for a cup of coffee with a neighbor, the border patrol would show up within minutes. And smuggling had become harder. Casual smugglers dropped out, leaving the business to a handful of professionals who knew the locations of cameras and sensors and the best times to get past them.

Unfortunately, the best time was at night during a storm. Especially a storm like this one, with high winds and driving sheets of water that at best could knock out electricity for the substation that monitored the sensors and cameras and at least, would obscure the views. And the storm made it easier to evade patrols. The night was perfect for what he needed to do—even if it was unpleasantly cold for late May.

He was getting old for this. Forty-eight, with five kids. It was dangerous these days, and the arthritis in his knees protested the treks in the rain. He'd waited for this moment, for one last big haul, to retire. He had a new business planned—taking visitors from Montreal boating or fishing on Lake Memphremagog.

First, he had to finish the run.

Two blocks farther, he turned into a driveway, steered the pickup past a closed shop and then around to the rear where granite tombstones lay on the ground. It was deserted, dark, and isolated, with direct access to the biking path that would take him to the safest spot to cross into the United States.

Jean Claude killed the lights. With his customary caution he kept watch as he buttoned up his black slicker and put on his brimmed hat. He reached for the backpack on the seat next to him. It had appeared inside his truck in the afternoon after the forecast predicted evening thunderstorms. It wasn't that heavy, so carrying it the few miles across the border shouldn't be a problem.

What was inside? Other smugglers ripped off their clients from time to time, but he'd never been tempted. It didn't make for repeat business. It could also negatively affect longevity.

Still, he was curious.

He unsnapped the two hooks, unzipped the bag, and stared at two metal spherical containers with caps so closely milled that the seams where the caps locked on were almost invisible, and, carefully swaddled in bubble wrap, three crystal blue bottles of what looked like perfume. He considered unwrapping one of the bottles to examine it closer but decided against it. Charlie, his client, would not appreciate his goods being inspected, and thanks to Charlie, this would be his last trip. *Finish the job and collect the money.* Zipping the bag shut, he pushed down his curiosity. The money was all that mattered.

Turning off the interior light, he opened the door. A gust of wind drenched him. With a sigh, he shouldered the pack and hurried along the path, skirting the parking lot and the rear yards of houses and stores. The deep lugs on his boots minimized any slipping on the path that had turned muddy with the downpour.

After a mile, the houses ended, and open fields and patches of trees spread before him. He continued until there was only forest on both sides of the road. The border was no longer in the middle of the street but across the street in the woods.

The rain became a torrent. *Good.* The rain worked to his benefit.

His nervousness increased. This was the critical moment, when he was most vulnerable. Everyone worried about terrorism. Anyone who spotted him could alert the Americans or the Canadians, even if he hadn't done anything illegal. *Yet.*

Reaching his favorite crossing place, he paused inside the woods. Through gaps in the trees, he viewed the road and checked left and right. A car zoomed by, and he waited until the taillights dimmed. The road was clear. Rain slashed down. His pulse hammered. *Now.*

He raced across the street and kept running until he slipped into the embrace of the trees and entered the United States. Walking quickly, his boots silent on the sodden remains of last autumn's leaves, he heard only the pounding of rain. He found the deer path and followed it deeper, avoiding breaking brush and watching where he placed his feet.

Not too far away, he heard something move. *A patrol? In this weather?*

This close to the border, even if they hadn't seen him cross from Canada, they'd take him in. And they'd open his backpack. Depending on what was in the cylinders, he could go to jail for a long time. He froze and waited.

Two yellow eyes blinked at him and then disappeared. Coywolf. Not a threat, except to deer. He let out his breath in relief and sped up, wanting to put distance between himself and the border.

Two miles into Vermont, he turned west, followed a dirt road to where a bulldozer had carved a turn-around and where a black 4-Runner was parked.

Jean Claude rapped on the roof, and the driver's door cracked. The interior lit up, and the man he knew only as Charlie unfurled an umbrella through the door and stepped out under its shelter.

"Nasty night." Charlie angled the umbrella to protect the car's leather interior. His right hand rested in the pocket of his raincoat.

"Necessary for business." Jean Claude offered the backpack.

Charlie's gloved hand emerged from his pocket to accept the backpack, which he placed on the driver's seat. He picked up a briefcase. "Did you open it?" Charlie's voice was nonchalant.

"I checked that everything was okay."

"You didn't see what was inside?"

"Steel containers. Couple small bottles of something—maybe perfume."

"You're not curious?"

"No. Why would I care? I'm a businessman."

"I respect a man of business." Charlie handed over the remainder of the ten thousand dollar payment.

Despite the rain, Jean Claude opened the case. Water flooded inside. He angled the lid down and thumbed through the stacked bills. Enough for his boat.

"Ever watch 'The Godfather'?" Charlie asked.

"Yeah, sure."

"One of my favorite movies. Hey, does your wife like perfume? This is French, very expensive."

It seemed odd to be smuggling French perfume. Usually it was something a little more sinister, but Jean Claude never asked what or why. "Don't all women like French perfume?"

"You can take one for her if you like. As a gift from me—and the whole organization. The small ones are samples. We will be making more with what's inside the containers."

This seemed odd. Why smuggle perfume across the border if he were just going to take it back? On the other hand, he didn't want to offend Charlie by refusing a gift.

"*Merci.* That would be kind. She would like that."

Charlie unzipped the backpack, unwrapped one of the blue bottles, and handed it to Jean Claude. Then he closed the pack, moved it to the floor in front of the passenger's seat, slid into the car, and started the engine. Then he rolled down the window. "You should smell it. Quite unusual."

Jean Claude opened the bottle as Charlie drove away. He gave a sniff. It did not smell like perfume. It didn't smell like much at all.

That was his last thought before the convulsions started.

* * * * *

The first Vermont state trooper who found the body unfortunately established the cause of death for the known smuggler by touching the body with an ungloved hand to take a pulse. His partner, who had taken a call at the car, was more fortunate. He was radioing it in when he saw his partner collapse and begin to convulse, and he was smart enough to keep his distance. He called in federal authorities who raced to the scene and rushed his partner, still alive but critical, to isolation in a hospital. It would take laboratory analysis to establish that both had been exposed to Novichok, a nerve agent that had been designed in the former Soviet Union. As far as the intelligence community knew—the only source of Novichok was in Russia.

Within hours, officials from the FBI as well as CIA were on the scene.

A few hours more, and the dead man was identified as a regular smuggler for a Russian gang, headed by Vladimir Rzaev—an oligarch and confidant of the Russian President, Yuri Bykovsky.

It was unknown whether more Novichok had been smuggled into the country and where it might be. Or why was the Rzaev gang smuggling nerve poison into the United States?

The news was kept quiet—because the resulting panic could be a disaster.

All intelligence agencies went on full alert. A frantic call was put through to Russia, but the Russian President denied any knowledge of nerve agent in the United States.

The was only one course of action: find the current members of Rzaev's gang in the United States. Not an easy task. The gang had managed to operate in secret for years. That they knew the smuggler worked for Rzaev was due to his personal carelessness in telling his wife the business he was in.

However, there was one person who might know something about Rzaev or his operations in the United States. Every other known associate of Rzaev was dead or had slipped out of the country. That one person, Dmitri Lemonsky, was in federal prison—and had been put there by his childhood best friend, Kolya Petrov.

5

SUNDAY MORNING, CUMBERLAND PRISON, MARYLAND

DMITRI ANDRIOVICH LEMONSKY UNWRAPPED his ice cream sandwich. It was difficult with his hands cuffed to the table, but he'd bought it from the commissary just before he'd learned that a government official wanted to talk to him. He liked ice cream, but he was also making a statement. He'd spent his own money on fucking ice cream, and he was damn well going to eat it.

He was in control. In shackles, in shabby prison uniform, but he was in control. Not some government flunky.

The waiting official was short, balding, overweight, and dressed in a cheap suit. *Not FBI.* They were better dressers.

The room matched the prison: gray walls, no window, steel door, a smell of men, urine, and mold, an odor so persistent that Dmitri barely noticed it anymore. Here was where he'd met his attorney, who'd given him the news about his appeal, but at least, then, he hadn't been cuffed to the table.

It would've been a sign of respect to leave his hands free. After all, what could he do? There were guards right outside the door. But the handcuffs were the government's statement. Or maybe just a statement from this man—who'd badly miscalculated.

"Stephen Kowolsky." The man held up a State Department Identification.

Polish. Dmitri squinted across the table to better see the ID. The picture matched. The fact that he was pretending to work for State confirmed Dmitri's guess. *CIA, not FBI.*

21

"So Dmitri Lemonsky. Convicted of racketeering—and a suspect in multiple murders. Sentenced to twenty-five years, another fifteen to go." Kowolsky spoke in Russian, with a hint of a Moscow accent.

Dmitri bent his head to take a bite of the ice cream sandwich. It was chalky, a mediocre imitation of what ice cream should be. Still, it was all that was available.

"You ran the North American operation for Vladimir Rzaev before you were arrested." Kowolsky continued. "Rzaev's got people in New York, L.A., and Washington D.C., doesn't he?"

"The ice cream here is not very good, but it is at least ice cream." Dmitri spoke in English.

"Who reported to you on the East Coast?" Kowolsky switched languages.

"Problem is the only ice cream in this prison is vanilla sandwich shit. Sometimes chocolate. Boring. I like different flavors."

Kowolsky crossed his arms. He looked amused. "You can keep up the charade. Or you can do yourself some good. Give me the names of Rzaev's network in the United States and his location in Russia, and something to your advantage can be worked out."

Dmitri took another bite of his sandwich. "I am a wrongly convicted businessman. I have nothing to say."

Kowolsky snorted. "Yeah, right."

"You know Ben & Jerry's? Great ice cream. All kinds of good things in Ben & Jerry's." Dmitri finished eating before speaking again. "They don't carry it here. Shame."

"Cooperate, and you'll be out in five years."

"You have a tissue?" Dmitri showed the palms of his hands. The ice cream had left a sticky residue.

Kowolsky fished out a yellowish handkerchief. Dmitri had won this one. Dmitri slowly wiped each hand and dropped the handkerchief on the table.

"Give me names and locations, and ten years off your sentence. Once we verify."

"*Yob tvoyu mat.*" It was one of the most common of Russian insults, involving sex and mothers. "I don't talk to CIA."

"State Department."

"I also do not talk to liars."

22

Kowolsky tapped the table. "You got another fifteen years. You think this place is bad? I can get you sent to max or put in solitary. You want to play tough with me?"

"Five years more is too much time."

Dmitri liked playing poker—especially when he had a full house.

"You got a stark choice here—fifteen hard years or five easy years."

"You think fifteen years here is hard? Even in max? In *vorovsky mir*, prison is a badge of honor. You ever been to a Russian prison? In Siberia, where you sometimes work in twenty below? Where you eat moldy bread and rotten potatoes? That is hard time. Make your max seem like Hilton hotel. In a Russian prison, it's not good to snitch—not for ice cream, not for ten fucking years off your sentence. You know what a Russian *mafiya* boss like Rzaev would do to a snitch?"

"At least you admit knowing Rzaev. Progress."

"Every Russian knows Rzaev."

"Have it your way. You're an innocent little lamb, wrongfully convicted. You're not the only one getting this offer, you know. The first person to cooperate gets the deal."

This was funny. There was no one else. Dmitri knew it, and he knew Kowolsky knew it. "OK, so good luck. Nice meeting you."

"But on the other hand, Rzaev will never know it was you."

"You think? You think he does not have sources of information in your government? You think Rzaev can't get to me here?"

"We can protect you."

"You doing comedy now? The only way to protect me in prison is solitary confinement—and even in solitary, he could get to me. You come here and you try to scare me, like I am a little girl, with threats of hard time if I don't cooperate, and you offer me five years solitary as a reward? Not a strong negotiating position."

Kowolsky shrugged, accepting Dmitri's refusal, although Dmitri knew it was only for the moment. There would be another round.

"There's a chance we can work something else out that's more appealing if you give us what we need."

"You have a cigarette?"

Kowolsky offered Dmitri a Marlboro. Kowolsky had to know that smoking was banned for federal prisoners. It didn't stop smoking; it just meant buying black market. Dmitri held the cigarette in cuffed hands and leaned forward to take a drag as Kowolsky touched a match to the tip.

"I'm representing the United States here. I'm willing to work with you, but you have to play ball."

Dmitri exhaled smoke. Not a good habit, but the odds of him living to an old age were slim. "I do not know you, and I do not play ball, as you say, with people I do not know. Tell you what, Mr. CIA, you bring me someone I trust, and we can talk."

Kowolsky considered him, his eyes dark with suspicion. "You have someone in mind?"

Dmitri leaned forward and took another drag. "Bring Kolya Petrov next time. I trust him." He watched the suspicion grow.

"Why? Petrov put you here."

"You don't like Kolya? Is that because he is Russian? Or because he is a Jew?"

The round face froze. "Neither. That's crap. I don't have a problem with Petrov, and you should. Anyway, it's not possible—he quit the government, and he's not interested in coming back."

"We go way back, Kolya and me. He put me here because he has honor. So maybe I am angry, but I know he will not lie to me. You, I do not know, and I do not trust people I do not know. So, Mr. CIA man," Dmitri remembered Kowolsky's name but chose not to use it, "I would ask Kolya to come back to work if I were you."

Dmitri stubbed the cigarette out on the table and signaled the guard. "Bring your best offer next time, not five years in solitary shit. And Ben & Jerry's. I like Cherry Garcia, and I hear good things about Americone Dream."

6

SUNDAY MID-DAY, SILVER SPRING, MARYLAND

BRIGHT LIGHT AND THE scent of May roses enveloped the living room of the expanded ranch home in this well-to-do suburb, where a brunch birthday party for the eighty-six year-old aunt was in full swing, or as in full swing as things ever got in this family. Former intelligence operative Kolya Petrov leaned against a wall on the far side of the room, on the edge of the circle of couches and chairs where family members communed together.

His fiancée, Alex, was laughing at her aunt's retelling of a story. He didn't want to interrupt her enjoyment, but the pressure was building. The only alcohol on display amidst the offerings of grilled chicken, olives, pickles, rolls, salads, and pastries was a single bottle of kosher wine. Not what he needed. He slipped out and headed for the kitchen at the back of the house.

Normally immaculate, the kitchen bore evidence of a family party. Dishes filled the sink; packaging littered the counters. He checked cabinets and then sorted through the freezer. Three different kinds of bagels. A kosher pound cake, and two boxes of kosher cookies—just in case the sugar on display in the other room ran out, he supposed. He found vodka behind a box of Popsicles and located some glasses in the cupboard over the dishwasher.

For a second, he contemplated whether vodka fit into the category of milk or meat under kosher laws and whether he was choosing an inappropriate glass. Orthodox Jews keep two sets of dishes—to avoid a dairy item ever even touching the same plate as a meat item, the really

25

orthodox have two sinks and two refrigerators. While he was proud of his Jewish heritage, he wasn't religious, and his knowledge of kosher rules was a bit sketchy. His mother who'd died when he was nine had not been religious—and anyway, he'd been born in the last gasps of the Soviet Union. Practicing Judaism wasn't even legal until he was about four years old. His cousin, Rifka, who'd adopted him when he was fourteen, had kept only a few rules—no bacon and no ham in the house—and no bread at Passover—and he didn't even follow those looser rules. Alex's family, though, were strict on the kosher laws, and even if he didn't believe, he didn't want to offend. Not that he cared about offending Aaron, Alex's asshole brother, but he did like the rest of the family, even though he sometimes found being with them to be trying. In any case, they were Alex's family. For her sake, he'd put up with worse.

Deciding the choice didn't matter, he selected a glass and poured a shot. He downed it Russian style, in one gulp and felt a trickle of warmth spread down his throat. The world took on a softer glow. *Better. But not good enough.*

Not enough to get rid of the images in his mind.

"Is it that bad being with my family?" Alex's voice murmured behind him. "Or is your leg hurting?"

He turned and leaned back against the granite counter to ease the leg that was aching but was not the reason he was drinking. He should have brought a crutch to the party. Too much time standing, and he shouldn't have pushed his morning run up to three miles—which was still less than he'd run daily eight months earlier, before his knee and leg had been smashed with a golf club. Now he was paying for it.

But seeing her was compensation. To him, she was always beautiful, long dark wavy hair, oval face, and dark intelligent eyes.

She looked concerned.

"My leg's fine." He knew that she knew he was lying, just as he knew that she knew why he was drinking.

"Come out and pretend to be sociable. Half an hour more, then we leave. Promise. I'll make it up to you later." She leaned in to kiss him. She tasted of grapes and strawberries.

The promise compensated for much. "Offer accepted. After another shot." He still needed to get through the party.

"Fine. One more."

"Perhaps two." He knew what she wanted to say, so he saved her the trouble. "I won't get drunk."

"I know. You get close sometimes."

"Close. But not over."

"It's a family party. Close is too close."

"Another shot. At most two. Then I'll join you."

"Fine." Her tone held a tinge of disapproval but not enough to worry him.

She disappeared. Kolya poured another shot. Listening to the rise and fall of the voices in the other room, he drank and felt the further softening of the edges. *Another drink?* Or would he get too close to the unacceptable?

There were lines he tried not to cross, in drinking and in his relationship. But he didn't fit in—and the family party in Aaron's upscale home underscored that fact. They were nice people, who talked about their jobs and their families and Judaism. He had no living family except for Alex; he disliked his new job but couldn't talk about his former job; and he was agnostic. Politics was risky. Literature? While he was currently reading a Jewish philosopher, Martin Buber's seminal work, *I and Thou*, on the relationship between individuals and the world around them, he doubted that any of Alex's family would be interested in a discussion of the distinction between "I and thou" and "I and it" that formed the thesis of the book. Then there was the fact that he couldn't answer when Aunt Shelly asked him about Russia or his years in the *dyetskii* dom— the Russian boys' home he'd lived in between his mother's death and Rifka adopting him. Too grim. Maybe he could talk about Rifka, who'd occasionally attended a reform temple. But it felt disrespectful to her memory to use her to score points.

If there had been a piano, at least it would have been something to do. And playing jazz banished the demons as effectively as vodka.

He poured. As he lifted the drink, he glimpsed a shadow in the back yard. Maybe a neighbor chasing a dog. Maybe a kid. Maybe any number of things. *Never trust the innocent explanation.*

He peered out the kitchen window. Nothing obvious. Then he focused on a framed mirror engraved with images of rabbits and squirrels, inserted in a rose trellis at the edge of the patio. The height of bad taste, but now—useful.

In its reflection, he saw a figure in a Grinch mask, carrying an assault rifle with a suppressor, flattened against the house near the back door. Grinch glanced at a watch, which could only mean one thing. *More of them, probably in the front, coordinating.*

Kolya was unarmed. *Why had he fucking agreed to leave his gun in the car?* But he'd understood—guns didn't belong at this family party—any more than he did. But now, he was vulnerable. Worse, he couldn't protect Alex and her family.

Kolya set his glass down—hands trembling —*adrenaline, not nerves*— and grabbed a Shun chef knife from a wooden knife block.

The kitchen door opened inward. An invader would have to do a 180 to check behind the door—which might give him just enough time. Not a sure thing, but Kolya didn't have many options. He slid into position behind the door.

7

SUNDAY MID-DAY, SILVER SPRING, MARYLAND

AS SHE SAT ON the white couch, Alex Feinstein sipped a glass of too-sweet kosher wine and tried not to worry. Kolya felt uncomfortable at family gatherings, and she couldn't blame him. She loved her brother, her aunts and uncles, her parents, but sometimes they were a little too intrusive and often more than a little boring, repeating the same stories—the cousins who stole from a dying mother, the uncle who deserted his pregnant wife.

Still, it wasn't Kolya drinking out of boredom and physical discomfort that worried her, but that he was drinking because despite his denials, he was continuing to struggle with PTSD. He'd seemed better, but then, he was a good actor, which had been an asset when he worked in the world of intelligence. It was less so in personal relationships.

And where was he? He'd said one more drink—then he'd rejoin the party. It shouldn't take this long.

Lost in her concern for Kolya, she was barely paying attention to Aunt Shelly's description of her last surgery. Instead, her gaze wandered around the room and then to the large picture window framed with heavy linen curtains.

Something moving on the front lawn caught her attention. She'd hadn't seen anything distinct, just a glimpse of movement.

Kolya wouldn't just duck out, would he?

Probably not.

Maybe. He's such a goddamn introvert.

It wouldn't hurt to check.

She was putting down her glass, with an apologetic murmur of *I'll be back* in the middle of Aunt Shelly's detailed description of the handsome young surgeon who'd operated on her—when the front door slammed against the wall, and two men wearing character masks and carrying semi-automatic rifles stormed inside. A second crash sounded from the kitchen.

Aunt Shelly let out a piercing scream. Aaron, next to the buffet table, stacking a plate with brownies and cookies, froze.

Alex's first instinct was to reach for her Coach bag, but she stopped herself. Like Kolya, she had locked her gun in the car. She could do nothing.

A man in a Bart Simpson mask swung his semi-automatic at Aunt Shelly. "Shut up!"

Aunt Shelly fell back against the chair, hands clasped over her mouth, eyes large and terrified.

* * * * *

Kolya heard the commotion in the living room, as the front door and the kitchen door slammed open simultaneously, and the man in the Grinch mask strode inside. *Alex. Alex was in there.* She was smart and capable—he never would have survived Romania without her—but she had no gun, and even if she'd been armed, the intruders had weapons and surprise on their side. And although Alex knew how to handle a gun, she was a lawyer, not an operative, not fully trained to deal with this sort of thing.

He was.

But before he could help Alex or her family, he had to take care of the man in the mask.

Through the crack between the kitchen door and the wall, Kolya watched the man in the mask survey the room. He was about six foot two, just a touch taller than Kolya, and muscular. His size didn't worry Kolya as much as the assault weapon, an HK-91. A very good weapon. A weapon he would not want fired in his direction.

The question was whether Kolya could get to the intruder before he could shoot. Which meant getting to Grinch before he knew Kolya was in the room.

If the man were intelligent, he would do a 360-degree spin to check the room.

But he didn't turn.

"In." Grinch shouted the words.

Standard American accent. Nothing unusual. Not a voice that Kolya recognized.

Kolya slipped around the door, knife ready. Then he re-evaluated. He was pretty sure that the man was wearing body armor under his shirt.

That meant he had to cut the man's throat, and he had to do it fast. But the mask extended below the collar, which meant cutting his throat would require pulling the mask up. Then the knife across the throat.

Two motions meant an extra second or so.

Kolya could still make the kill with the knife, but in that fraction of a second that pulling up the mask would take, the man could fight back. Or could alert the intruders in the living room. The kill needed to be quick, and it needed to be silent.

New plan.

Kolya lunged. Before the intruder even realized the danger, Kolya grasped the man's chin with his left hand, and the back of his head with his right, letting the knife drop. Then he twisted fast and hard. The neck snapped.

He caught the body, lowered it to the floor, and removed the mask. He didn't recognize the face. Clean shaven, short brown hair. Then he turned to the HK-91. Ammunition—7.62 NATO rounds. Military grade. Was the intruder current military—ex-military?

Later.

In the here and now, he needed to focus on what was important. He checked for body armor under the long sleeve back shirt, and he had been right. The man wore a lightweight military grade vest. That meant the others would also be wearing vests.

His leg and knee had ached earlier with the stress of standing—now pain was rising, no longer dull, but sharp, stabbing; he must have twisted his knee in his lunge. Then he pushed the pain out of his mind, picked up the gun, brought it to his shoulder, approached the door to the living room, and listened.

* * * * *

"On the floor. Sit. Hands on your heads. You," a man in a Mickey Mouse mask, motioned to Aaron, who still clutched the plate of cookies, "now." Then he raised his voice. "He in the kitchen?"

Alex listened, throat so dry she couldn't swallow. What had happened in the kitchen? Had Kolya been surprised? Was he injured, dead?

"No." A man's voice shouted from the kitchen.

"Hold position."

This can't be happening. Not here. Then she forced herself to stay calm. If Kolya'd been hurt or captured, there would have been noise. A gun shot. Something. He wouldn't go down without a fight. But there'd been nothing. He was okay. She didn't know where he was, but he was okay.

Maybe he'd made to the car, got his gun.

Maybe he was hiding, waiting for the right moment.

Mickey turned back to the family frozen in terror. "Did you hear me? On the floor. Now."

As Alex helped Aunt Shelly down, her aunt's billowing sleeve covered her hand. Using the sleeve for cover, Alex slipped her hand into her jacket pocket, tapped one character, and hit *send*. Then she sat on the carpet and placed her hands on her head.

Bart moved near the dessert table, where he had a clear view of the room, and covered the family with his weapon.

Mickey pointed at Aaron, who sat between Moishe, his twelve-year-old son, and Alex's sixty-three-year-old mother. "You." As he walked toward Aaron, Mickey fished a phone from his pocket. He thrust the digital face at Aaron. "You know this man?"

Aaron's mouth thinned in a grim, stubborn line.

Mickey glanced at Moishe. "Answer, or I shoot the kid."

Aaron blanched. "My sister's fiancé." His voice was barely audible.

"Where's your sister?"

Aaron didn't speak, but his eyes moved.

In two steps, Mickey Mouse man moved to Alex and showed her a picture of Kolya, blond and rangy, a carefree look about him she hadn't seen in a long time. "This your fiancé?"

"Yes." Never lie about unimportant information interrogators already have.

"We don't want to hurt you. We just want Petrov. Where is he?"

"Not here." *Lie about the important things.*

"Bullshit." Mickey leaned closer, reeking of tobacco. "You wouldn't come without your fiancé to a family party. Where is he?"

"Alex is right. He left." Aunt Shelly lifted her chin. "Fifteen minutes ago. He went out to get more beer. He'll be back. Half an hour."

Later, Aunt Shelly would get a hug for that lie. If they survived.

* * * * *

Kolya could hear but not see into the living room. They wanted him—*only* him. It didn't mean that the others wouldn't be killed, but the attackers would want to keep things calm for now. It bought him time.

He had no idea who they were or why they were after him. He no longer had access to classified intelligence, so they couldn't want information. But a long list of people wanted him dead. After ten years in the game: to be expected. He'd worry about that later. Right now, he needed to end the threat to fifteen people without any of them getting hurt.

He felt the vibration of a text. *Alex?*... yes, alerting him that two had come through the front door.

He was a good marksman, but the vests meant head shots, which required good aim and better luck. Two assailants made difficult shooting even more complicated. He didn't know their positions, which made rushing the room risky—even if he could move quickly enough. Odds were against his being able to shoot both men before either got off a shot. That the invaders carried HK-91s made it even more dangerous. One round could tear through several people.

He studied the body of the man he'd just killed. Black long sleeve shirt over the body armor and jeans. Height was off by an inch, and the man was stockier, but not significantly. Close enough.

* * * * *

"How many bedrooms?" Mickey pointed down the hall and directed his question at Aaron.

Aaron licked dry lips. "Four."

"Bart, watch them." He raised his voice. "Grinch, watch the back door." Then to Alex: "I'm going to search the house. If he's not here, we'll wait. If he's not back in half an hour, I shoot your family. One by one. The old lady with the red hair first."

8

SUNDAY MID-DAY, SILVER SPRING, MARYLAND

A NOISE IN THE kitchen? Alex wasn't sure. Something scraping on the floor, maybe. *Was it Kolya?* Bart, his gun and his attention focused on the group on the floor, didn't react. Mickey was out of sight.

Moishe mumbled familiar words in Hebrew, a prayer that Alex had memorized as a child raised in a Conservative Jewish household but that she hadn't said for years. *Shema Yisroeal.* When facing death, Jews had repeated the words of the Shema for over two thousand years. In the gas chambers, Jews had chanted the ancient words.

Echoing whispers all around her. *Shema Yisroeal.*

Hear O' Israel. The Lord is God. The Lord is One.

Alex quietly said the prayer with them. She wasn't sure that she believed, but it couldn't hurt. And the familiar words were comforting.

"We should rush him," Aunt Shelly whispered. "He can't kill us all."

Aunt Shelly, who couldn't get up from the floor without help, wanted to rush a gunman?

"No, Aunt Shelly. Just stay still." Alex didn't bother to whisper, and Bart pointed his gun at her.

"Shut up. All of you. Shut the fuck up."

Noise from the kitchen again. This time she was sure. A thud, then one more. Bart's head turned briefly, but he didn't move. Instead, he shouted. "Grinch, report!"

The noise intensified, sounds of breaking glass, and then silence.

Alex could hardly breathe. She said a silent prayer for Kolya.

A figure wearing a black shirt, jeans, and a green Grinch mask,

35

rounded into the living room, gun in position, voice a hoarse whisper. "In the kitchen. Petrov was hiding—tried to choke me. Thought he'd crushed my neck, but I got him."

"Dead?"

"Knocked out. Let's grab him and go." He coughed, voice barely audible.

Bart didn't move, and the gun didn't waver. "Mickey's in the back."

"Get him." Grinch was inching forward and was a few feet inside the living room. "We've got Petrov." The hoarse voice was impossible to identity, but the build was familiar. Tall. Thin. A favoring of the right leg. She could breathe again.

Bart's weapon still pointed at her and her family, finger inside the trigger guard, and he'd kill some of them even if he went down. "My orders were to stay here. Why are you out here? What if someone else comes—" What started as a simple question hardened into suspicion.

Bart swung the muzzle of his gun toward the man in the Grinch mask who raised his gun and shot a second before Bart.

As the suppressed gunshots reverberated, the bullet caught Bart in the middle of the mask, exited his head, and hit the wall. Blood and plaster dust sprayed. Bart's gunshot shattered the vase on the fireplace mantel.

Aunt Shelly screamed again, but Alex clapped a hand over her mouth. "Quiet. It's Kolya."

"We need to get out!" Aaron stood, his voice high with anger and terror.

"Get down." Kolya ripped off the mask. "There could be more of them waiting outside." He glanced at Bart's assault rifle and then at Alex.

Alex scrambled across the floor and picked it up. The make was unfamiliar, but she'd shot assault rifles before. She checked it hurriedly. "I'll get his phone, too."

"Good. Hurry."

She steeled herself to touch the dead man, found a burner phone in a pants pocket, and tossed it to Kolya. He caught it, took out a second phone, and glanced from one to the other. He leaned momentarily against the sofa, as if in pain, and then straightened.

"On the floor, as low as possible, away from the windows. Alex, stop anyone but me coming through the doors."

"You're not going after him!"

"He's still a threat."

And he'd want to know who the man was—what he wanted.

"I'll come with you—back you up."

"No. Stay here." He nodded towards her parents.

She understood. Someone had to protect her parents, her brother, the aunts, the cousins, and if Kolya was going after the man in the Mickey mask—that left her.

But who would protect Kolya?

Then she noticed a streak of blood running down the back of Kolya's left hand. "You're shot."

"Just grazed."

"Let me see."

But he was already moving at a limping run out of the room. "No time. Call the police in fifteen minutes."

Alex raised the unfamiliar gun into position against her shoulder. "Just don't do anything stupid, goddamn it."

9

SUNDAY MID-DAY, SILVER SPRING, MARYLAND

SENSES ON HIGH ALERT, Kolya listened and moved carefully, the carpet muffling his footsteps. The pain from the wound to his arm competed with the pain in his leg, but he couldn't let either distract him.

Later. He'd tend to both later. Right now, adrenaline had kicked in enough to keep him going.

He unscrewed the suppressor on the HK-91 and silently set it down, making the HK more maneuverable. Beige walls reflected the fading light. Seven doorways visible, four bedrooms, three baths, some doors open, others partially closed.

Mickey would have heard everything: the firing of the rounds, the shattering of the vase, and Aunt's Shelly's cut-off scream. If it had been Kolya's operation, he would have checked on his team. That neither phone had rung nor had Mickey made an appearance since shots were fired indicated that either he had decamped through a window—or he was waiting for Kolya to come for him.

Kolya could just retreat to the living room to protect the family and call the police. But Mickey might get away through a window in the time it would take the police to arrive. And once the police arrived, Kolya would lose any chance ask his own questions.

So he had to search seven rooms. Seven doorways, any one of which could hide a gunman.

A flash of cold enveloped him as the vivid memory of a different gunfight took hold. Counting rounds. Gunmen closing in. He felt the hot pain of the bullet plowing into his leg. Watched his captors put a bullet through the head of his fellow agent.

Concentrate. He focused on the feel of the gun in his hands, on the light on the walls, the sound of his own breathing… and was at Aaron's house again and in the present.

The closest door, to the guest bathroom, was ajar. His shirt damp with sweat and blood, the gun against his shoulder, his back against the wall, Kolya halted. Through the door gap, he could see the bathroom sparkled. Striped white and pink towels, purple floor tile, maroon toilet and bathtub. No sign of Mickey. He nudged the door wider with his foot.

Still nothing.

Were the cabinets big enough for Mickey to hide in? Could he be behind the shower curtain?

Kolya'd have to go inside to be sure. He'd have to search every possible hiding place in every bathroom and bedroom: closets, under beds, behind doors. Every time he entered a room, he'd be at risk. Seven fucking rooms.

Maybe try something different.

He pulled out one of the two burners, the one he had removed from Grinch's body. He hit the first number from Grinch's phone and heard the tones—down the hall, but not too far. A jaunty melody that didn't fit the situation. The sound emanated from the second bedroom, on the right. He cautiously slid past the first bathroom and then the first bedroom, flattened against the wall, and checked behind him.

The jaunty melody played, for another minute and then stopped. Perhaps Mickey was already gone—abandoning the phone. Perhaps Mickey was deciding whether to pick up. Perhaps…

Kolya called again.

The same annoying melody jangled out from the second bedroom.

Had Mickey left and abandoned the phone?

But this time someone answered. "Bob's pizza. Today's special—bacon and mushroom."

Kolya heard the voice both on the phone and from the second bedroom. He had held the phone away from his ear to be sure.

"Sorry, bacon's not kosher."

"Keeping kosher Petrov? I thought you weren't religious."

"And you heard that where?" Kolya aimed the HK-91, clutching the gun with his right hand, his left hand on the phone, and edged closer to the bedroom.

"Oh, around. Both of my guys dead?"

"There's that possibility." Another step. Second step. Quietly.

"Well, fuck. They said you were good."

"Who are they?" He inched forward until he was just to the right of the half open bedroom door. Only an edge of the bed was visible. Mickey had to be on the far side of the room. Or behind the chest of drawers.

"My employers."

"Identify them, and we can work something out."

"Like you'll let me go?"

"Not exactly." Kolya couldn't let a killer go. But cooperation won points and a shorter time in prison.

He watched for movement. If he could locate Mickey before going in, his chances would be better. Mickey, defending the space, was in the stronger position to come out alive.

"Not interested. It's bad business anyway. Employers don't like to be identified. You're in the hall, aren't you?"

"What do you think?" Kolya could hear the voice without the phone. Near the window or behind the chest of drawers. Definitely not behind the door.

"So you're going to kill me, or I'm going to kill you."

"If you insist. I don't suppose you'd care to surrender."

"Nope. You can, though."

"Not planning on it."

"Didn't think so. But I'm glad we had this little chat. Because I wanted to tell you that my employers also said you have a hot fiancée. They're right."

The blood rushed to his head, anger competing with fear even though he knew Mickey was goading him to do something stupid.

He dropped the phone, both hands on the gun now.

"You might want to reconsider surrendering, because someone's going to come back for you." The voice was fainter. "Me or someone else. And if I have to come back, next time I'll kill that hot fiancée…."

Before Mickey finished the sentence, Kolya kicked the door. It slammed against the wall. The HK-91 braced against his shoulder, he stepped into an empty room, a phone and mask on a table near the wide-open window. Kolya's pace quickened to a limping run, and he reached the window. A man tore across the front lawn to a black Mercedes parked across the street, reached it, and yanked open the driver's door.

Kolya aimed and fired. Mickey ducked inside behind the steering wheel. The bullet buried itself in a tree. And the door of a brick colonial opened on the other side of the street, directly in the line of fire. A gray-haired woman peered out.

Kolya aimed at Mickey's head inside the car, but if he missed, he could hit the woman. He lowered the gun and vaulted out of the window. When he tried to run, his leg buckled. As he stumbled, the engine roared to life, and the Mercedes pulled away from the curb.

He forced his leg to move, made it to the middle of the street and caught the plate number before the Mercedes turned right and disappeared. He muttered his favorite Russian curse. *Yob tvoyu mat.* Up and down the street, neighbors opened their doors at the noise and then retreated. They were afraid of him, not the fleeing gunman. After all, he was the one with the weapon.

As Kolya limped back to the house, the pain rising both from his leg and arm, he heard the wail of approaching police cars. He took out his phone and tapped in a number that he hadn't called for a long time—and had vowed never to call again—the number for the highly secretive intelligence agency known by its agents as the ECA.

10

SUNDAY MID-DAY, SILVER SPRING, MARYLAND

THE MEMORY SURFACED BRIEFLY before he managed to push it back.

Eight months earlier—*only eight months*—he'd traveled to New York City for what he thought was a low-risk operation—a field test of the ECA's computer security system and to search for supporters of Mihai Cuza, a Romanian neo-Fascist. He had anticipated an easy week, to be followed by Alex arriving the following Friday night to celebrate. After a ten-year friendship dating back to their time together in law school—ten years that he'd loved her but kept his feelings to himself—and then a more recent intense romantic involvement, they were engaged. He'd planned a wonderful weekend listening to live jazz and shopping for her diamond ring.

Instead, he was ambushed, wounded, captured, and flown to Romania. Imprisoned by the man he'd been hunting, Kolya endured days of torture—beaten, whipped, burned, starved—rather than give his abductors access to the ECA's computer system. Only when Alex was also kidnapped and her life threatened did he give in, soon afterward realizing that Margaret Bradford, the head of the ECA, had leaked information setting him up—and later Alex—to induce Cuza into downloading a Trojan horse that would give the ECA's technical department access to Cuza's computer. Bradford had done so, knowing that he'd be tortured and that he and Alex would then be killed in a particularly brutal fashion.

He sometimes wondered why he'd been selected to be sacrificed. There had only been two other Jews in the agency, and he was the only Russian Jewish immigrant. During the interview for the job years

42

earlier, Bradford had questioned him about any conflict he might feel in choosing between American and Israeli interests. It had struck him as odd, maybe anti-Semitic, but he had let it go at the time. Still, was that why he was chosen? And was that why the President had ordered that he not be rescued? Or was it just politics as usual?

His captors' hatred for him for being Jewish had been open and violent. But was it any better to be selected to be sacrificed because of a quiet and unspoken bias?

Or was he being paranoid, as Jonathan, one of his closest friends, had told him before it had all unfolded?

That he hadn't died was due to Jonathan and a group of his fellow agents defying orders to mount a rescue and to Alex's stubborn refusal to take a chance at escape without him.

After returning to the United States, he spent weeks in a hospital. Once out, he resigned.

With Alex's help, he found a job with a mid-sized law firm, returning to a career he'd previously rejected. He had graduated from law school with honors a decade earlier but had applied to the FBI after three months in a large New York law firm and from there had been recruited into a new ultra-secret intelligence organization. He disliked the practice of law: the intellectual analysis interested him, but so much of law was reading documents and dealing with bullshit from clients. He'd liked his career as an agent. He'd liked that he'd not only used his brain, but that he'd been in the field, not stuck behind a desk. And he'd liked to think he was doing important work for the country that he loved for rescuing him from abuse and neglect and for opening opportunities that he would never have had in Russia. Still, being with Alex was compensation for all the shortcomings of being a lawyer. And at least, Alex was safe.

Until today. Until half an hour ago.

* * * * *

On the other end of the line, a familiar voice. In calm tones, he identified himself, described what had happened, and explained what he needed. Then he ended the call and returned the phone to his pocket.

He stepped through the front door to the rising cacophony of the relatives and placed the HK-91 on the floor just as flashing blue lights lit the room from the first police car to arrive.

* * * * *

The chaos of officialdom followed the chaos of the invasion. Police officers outside held back curious neighbors; police inside cordoned off the sections around the corpses. Techs took photos of body positions and blood spatters. The HK-91s were tagged for evidence and removed. The medical examiner certified death. ENTs bagged the bodies and wheeled them out.

Family members huddled together in front of the fireplace, at the far end of the room except for Kolya, Aaron, and Alex. Kolya sat on a chair near the center of the room while a furious Aaron cleaned his injured left arm. A brother-in-law who was a doctor came in handy at times.

Except Aaron wasn't technically a brother-in-law yet.

Alex, behind Kolya, rested her hand on his good shoulder. Her touch reassured, but it also reminded him of his failure. Because he couldn't run fast enough—or shoot accurately enough—the man who had threatened her and her family had escaped.

Two detectives took charge. A woman, short red hair, khaki pants, white shirt, badge and gun on belt, spoke to uniformed officers while a man with thinning brown hair in a wrinkled blue suit questioned Kolya. He inspected Kolya's credit cards, driver's license, and firearm license. He paused at Kolya's identification card as an employee of a non-existent division of the IRS, which had been Kolya's cover for ten years.

"Nikolai Ivanovich Petrov." The detective read, his tone polite and casual. "But everyone calls you Kolya. So, the IRS, huh. Still work there?"

Kolya wasn't fooled by the friendly tone. He'd just killed two people. He would be of interest to the police, even if the killings were justified. Nevertheless, he obeyed the stricture never to identity his former employer.

"No. I'm a private attorney now."

"For how long?"

"Eight months." Kolya winced at Aaron's thorough, if not gentle, ministrations.

The detective tilted his head to look at the arm. "Nasty. Are you sure you don't want to go to the hospital?"

"It looks worse than it is. I'm fine."

"Don't you think he should be checked out?" He questioned Aaron.

"This isn't brain surgery. He doesn't even need stitches." Aaron projected hostility not at the detective, but at Kolya. He applied antibiotic cream and taped gauze into place. "You were limping. Let me take a look at your knee."

"It just needs ice and rest."

"Stop playing the hero. Alex, tell your *fiancé* to roll up his pants leg."

Even though Aaron could be an asshole, Kolya couldn't blame him for the anger. Aaron's entire family had just been held hostage and the only reason they'd had been at risk was his presence.

Alex's fingers tightened on his shoulder. "He's a good doctor, Kolya. Let him take a look."

Kolya rolled up his pants leg, revealing a swollen knee. Aaron moved to a footstool and began his examination.

The detective pointed to a scar on the side of his leg above the knee. "You were shot?"

"Yes."

"What happened?"

Aaron chose that moment to rotate the knee, and Kolya avoided the question with a yip. "Aaron, a little gentler, please."

"How were you shot?" The detective repeated.

It didn't have to be the truth, just a reasonable answer. "I was mugged."

"An unlucky guy, aren't you? Why were these men after you?"

"Maybe my former job for the IRS. Perhaps they were unhappy about their taxes."

"How does a former IRS employee come to be so good at killing people?"

"YouTube."

"You think this is funny?"

"No."

"Try it again. Are you ex-military?"

"No."

Aaron began winding an elastic bandage around Kolya's knee, and the pressure helped the pain. Even if pissed, Aaron took medicine seriously. Kolya liked that. It gave him a new perspective on Aaron.

"Looks like it hurts." The detective dripped sympathy. "Your knee was injured before, too, wasn't it? Maybe the time you were shot?"

"Maybe."

"How'd you hurt it tonight?"

"I think I twisted it, but I wasn't paying attention."

"So not military. You just happen to know how to snap a man's neck. You also can hit a man in the middle of the forehead. Twice. Pretty cool about it, too. Why were these men after you?" The detective's questioning didn't bode well. Kolya didn't want to spend the night in a jail cell—waiting for a phone call that should come—sooner or later.

"No idea." Mostly true. It had to do with his former employment, but exactly who was behind the attack and why they wanted him remained a mystery. He glanced down at his leg, as Aaron twisted off the bandage.

"Done." Aaron pinned the end. "Until you see your orthopedist, stay off it as much as possible. Ice."

"Thank you." Kolya rolled down his pants leg.

But Aaron didn't acknowledge the thanks. He left Kolya and Alex to the detective and re-entered the circle of the family.

When she returned from outside bearing two evidence bags containing guns, the red-haired detective spoke quietly to the second detective. The questioning detective was unimpressed. "Go through it with a dog." She walked off.

"We have permits for the guns, both of us," Alex said.

"Yes, I know. But why do lawyers need guns?"

"Some people are very litigious," Kolya said.

"And some people are full of shit. We'll continue this conversation at the station."

"Why?" Alex leapt in again.

"I need answers. We ran some preliminary information on him, and nothing comes up. Not even a parking ticket. I don't buy it. I'm running his prints and DNA, and blood tests for drugs."

"Are you arresting him?" Alex went into full lawyer mode.

"He just killed two people."

"Justified."

"Maybe. He also nearly shot a neighbor. If nothing else, I could charge him with reckless discharge of a firearm. But there's more here. I think this is some kind of gang war over drugs."

"Based on what evidence?"

Kolya let her argue. She was better at it than he was.

"I got two dead people. I got a bullet in a tree across the street. He's got an old bullet wound. And he's lying to me. If he was an IRS agent, I'm the tooth fairy."

"None of that is evidence of a gang war. None of it would stand up in court. Having a scar from being shot before is evidence of nothing except of the fact that he was shot at some point."

"Maybe. Maybe he got shot in a mugging. But I got enough for an arrest, and I'll see what I can find. He's a Russian who's good at killing. We had a lot of problems with Russian gangs recently. Or he could be a Russian sleeper agent. How long you been in this country?" He turned to Kolya.

"Since I was fourteen. I'm an American citizen."

"Which is why you get the benefit of the American judicial system, which is more than you'd get in Russia. And where are the phones?"

"The what?" Kolya asked, his face an innocent mask.

"Neither of the dead guys had a phone. Not a burner, nothing. Don't you think that's kinda unusual?"

"Maybe the third guy drove off with them."

"And maybe someone took them—because the phones would have information. Where these guys'd been. Who they'd been talking to."

Which was why Kolya wanted the phones.

"You can search me," Kolya said.

"And me," Alex said. "And my purse."

Neither of them glanced at Aunt Shelly.

"I intend to search every inch—at the station. I'm arresting you for the careless discharge of a firearm in a residential area."

"It's not necessary," Kolya said. "I'm willing to come in."

"Yeah, it's necessary. I'm putting you in cuffs. You've already demonstrated how good you are at killing people with your bare hands."

"He's injured," Alex protested.

"He's received treatment, and we arrest injured people all the time. You know your rights, don't you, you being a lawyer and all?"

"Yes, I know my rights."

"Good." He took a pair of handcuffs off his belt. "Let's do this nice and easy. Stand and put your hands behind your back."

Kolya felt Alex's gaze on him. She knew how he'd feel about having his hands restrained, and he forced himself to speak calmly. "Okay."

He stood, his weight on his good leg, and put his hands behind him. When the cuffs closed on his wrists, he took a long breath to fight down the panic. It was an arrest, not a kidnapping. He wasn't going to be tortured. He'd be out soon.

Family voices rose in protest. He could distinguish Aunt Shelly's tones as the loudest.

The detective gripped his right arm. "Can you walk to the car or do you need assistance? You know, with your bad knee." His voice oozed fake concern.

But the red-haired detective returned, shaking her head at her partner, and handed him a phone.

Kolya exhaled in relief. The call had come through.

The detective had a succinct and unhappy conversation. He said, "But he's Russian" four times, and then finally, "yes, sir." He hung up with a "Goddamn it," and handed the phone back to the red-haired detective. Then he stepped behind Kolya and unlocked the cuffs.

"Apparently, this is a matter of national security. You could've told me."

"No, actually, I couldn't." Kolya refrained from the classic rub of wrists. It would have been a sign of weakness. Then he turned to the red-haired detective. "Our guns, please."

She removed the guns from the evidence bags and set them on the coffee table.

The detective in the wrinkled blue suit turned to Aaron. "This is a crime scene, and our technical people will be collecting evidence for a few hours. Maybe you should make other arrangements for the night." The detectives exited through the shattered front door, leaving uniformed officers and the technicians. Offers of accommodation were extended by various aunts and uncles, and Aaron's wife and son disappeared to pack.

Alex rounded on Kolya. "You called them."

"Would you have preferred I go to jail?" He checked his HK-40 and tucked it into his belt. Alex's gun went into her purse.

"No. Of course not. I just don't trust them."

"I don't either—but sometimes, they're necessary. Can we go home now?"

Aunt Shelly looked worried. "Do you think that we're safe in our own homes?"

Kolya doubted Mickey and company would go after extended family members if he wasn't with them. He wasn't sure how the attackers had found Aaron's home, possibly by tracking Alex's car, but it was highly unlikely they'd have the addresses of the other relatives. "I think so." He looked at Aaron. "But staying away from here for a few days until you can get a good security system wouldn't be a bad idea. I'll get you the name of someone."

Aaron glowered at Kolya. "This is your fault."

"Shut up Aaron," Alex's mother weighed in.

But Kolya understood. "Yes, and I'm sorry. I promise to find whoever was behind this and stop them." There were murmurs of concern from the family, but it was the best he could offer.

Alex hugged her aunts and uncles, her parents, her cousins, and her nephews. Kolya submitted to a series of hugs and collected the three phones that Aunt Shelly had hidden in her pocket. He declined Alex's offer of her shoulder for support—concerned that it would hurt her more than it would help him—and limped to her Volvo. When they got home, he'd pull out the crutches for a few days.

His priority now was protecting her while hunting down whoever had ordered the attack. He owed it to her to do so quickly. He owed it to her family.

11

SUNDAY MID-DAY, NEIMAN MARCUS, BOSTON

SUSAN RILEY, A FORTY-SIX-YEAR old high school history teacher with two children, a nine year-old daughter and a seven-year-old son, didn't shop at Neiman Marcus all that often, although her lawyer husband's salary was enough that she could afford to shop at a high-end department store. Still, she was pragmatic and overspending was against her general character. She would sometimes get the designer dress on sale for a special occasion, but generally she preferred to spend money on vacations and to put savings towards the children's college education—which kept getting more expensive by the day. However, when it came to gifts, especially for her hard to please mother-in-law, Susan would swallow her principles and spend the money. If she didn't, she'd hear about it for weeks.

Her mother-in-law's seventieth birthday was the reason she was spending a precious Sunday afternoon in the store, instead of grading papers or supervising her children's homework. But her husband had taken on homework duty, packing her off with a terse, "For God's sake, get her something nice from both of us."

The blue crystal bottle, sitting on the counter in the midst of a sampling of various luxury perfumes, was unusual and lovely, but unlabeled. Susan was drawn to the color and the shape. But if it wasn't a designer brand, if it wasn't obscenely expensive, her mother-in-law wouldn't be impressed, no matter how lovely the bottle. But maybe the lack of a label was because of its expense.

She tried to catch the salesclerk's eye, but the clerk was busy with a customer on the far side of the perfume booth. Instead, she picked the blue bottle up, and removed the stopper.

When she fell, Susan dropped the bottle. It shattered on the floor. The first person to rush to Susan's aid, as she convulsed, also died, as did the sales clerk. Store security had the presence of mind to cordon off the area, but not before thirty other people in the vicinity were affected and required hospitalization.

Media reports stated that a gas leak had caused a fatal level of carbon monoxide to be released.

NUMBER ONE LINE, NEW YORK

No one saw who left the blue bottle on a seat on the Number One train, the Broadway subway line, in Manhattan. No one knew how long it had been there. Most people who rode the subways in New York were trained to keep their eyes on their phone—or at the very least—not to look around at other riders, because catching the eye of the wrong person could trigger an unpleasant incident. Fortunately, it was a Sunday, so the train was far from full. It was also fortunate that in New York, people tend to be generally suspicious of items left on the subway. No one handled the blue bottle, and no one sat next to it.

The best guess was that whoever left it had gotten on at Penn Station and off at Times Square. Because the passengers began to feel sick around 59th street, and by 72nd street, several people had passed out.

At 92nd Street, the train was stopped and met by a team in hazmat gear. All the passengers in the car with the blue bottle were transported to the hospital, several people in critical condition.

After the train was evacuated, the team found the blue bottle. While not completely open, the stopper on the bottle was slightly loose, allowing enough fumes to escape to sicken but not kill. The subway car was retired for deep cleaning.

News media were informed that a toxic cleaning material had been used by mistake.

SUNDAY AFTERNOON, FOGGY BOTTOM, WASHINGTON, D.C.

There was no sign over the door. The building could have been an apartment complex or business offices on F Street near 20th Street. Just a black façade and a larger than usual satellite dish on the roof. Nothing indicated that it was the office of the ECA, an elite intelligence agency that reported directly to the president and was charged with covert anti-terrorism missions, both domestic and international.

Margaret Bradford, the powerful director of the ECA, waved her guest, a man with thinning gray hair and a gray goatee, to the upholstered chair opposite her desk.

It was rare that Ben Smithson, CIA director, came to her for assistance. She'd headed ECA since its birth fifteen years earlier, and she'd had to fight off his constant battle to bring her agency under CIA control. That he had deigned to come to her office instead of summoning her meant things were bad.

"How bad?" she asked without preamble.

"Three dead in Boston. Thirty hospitalized. Five critical in New York but thankfully no deaths."

"Cameras?"

"Reviewing still, but no clear images of whoever left the bottles. This is now the top national security priority, and Dmitri Lemonsky is still our best bet."

"But your man's approach this morning was unsuccessful, I take it."

"Lemonsky refused to negotiate without Kolya Petrov present. That's why I'm here."

"Petrov doesn't work for me anymore."

"I'm aware."

"You may not be aware that I've reviewed reports from his therapist. There is concern over whether he is in any kind of shape to come back, even if he were willing, which I doubt he would be. He's still very angry."

"But you're not asking him to return to field work—just to speak to a former friend. You can do it, Margaret. I have great respect for your abilities."

Bullshit. But urgent or not, she was still going to do what she had to do. "I understand you've put Stephen Kowolsky in charge of this operation. He and Petrov don't exactly get along."

"They're both professionals, and both will handle themselves professionally. Or I'll get involved."

"Petrov will be hard enough to get on board. It will be harder if the CIA is in charge."

He sighed. "What do you want?"

"That the ECA take charge of any operation involving Petrov."

"You're not serious."

"Deadly serious. No major decisions will be made without consulting you, but anyone working on this from my agency, including Mr. Petrov, will take orders from me."

He hesitated but then nodded. "Agreed. But you need to get him today. Soon as possible."

"Of course." She didn't need a lecture from Smithson.

He followed her to the door. She swung the door open, the polite host dismissing the guest who'd stayed too long. He paused and turned back. His glance wandered the room, lingering on the *Vanity Fair* prints and the view of K Street. "By the way, is Kolya Petrov any relation to Stanislav Petrov, the Russian who prevented global nuclear war in 1983?"

"No. Petrov is one of the more common Russian surnames."

"But not a Jewish Russian name."

"His grandfather on his father's side wasn't Jewish."

"I guess that explains it." Smithson rested his hand on her door and turned to look around the room. "Nice office you've got here, Marge. First time I've seen it. A bit small, but nice." He smiled at her and left.

12

SUNDAY EVENING, CHEVY CHASE, MARYLAND

JONATHAN EGAN WAS GRILLING hot dogs and steak kebabs, and he liked the smell of the sizzling meat. His grill was a six-burner job, and along with the hot dogs and the steak kebabs, corn on the cob roasted in its husk, and spiced potatoes steamed in aluminum foil.

It was what fathers did in the summer, fire up the grill in a show of domesticity. Hot dogs for the kids. Steak kebabs for the adults. It was what he used to do, beginning with Memorial Day and going through Labor Day. Before the divorce. Before he'd screwed everything up by, well, screwing another woman.

The grilling was a stereotype, but still, he'd enjoyed himself, all the more so since Jonathan's father, the Senator, had never grilled hot dogs; he'd employed people to do such mundane tasks. Jonathan tried not to copy his father's example in much. Although living in a house in the expensive area of Chevy Chase on the trust fund established by his grandfather wasn't exactly an act of rebellion. His job, which his father hated, on the other hand, was. His salary wouldn't even pay the taxes on the house.

His son, Dylan, age nine, seated at the picnic table, played a game on his phone, unimpressed by Jonathan's display of domestic skills. Tousled reddish brown hair, Dylan looked like a younger version of his mother. He didn't look up as Jonathan handed him a plate with a perfectly roasted hot dog, doused with the Dylan-appropriate amounts of catsup and mustard, corn and potatoes.

One hour before his ex-wife took his son away.

"Phone down."

Unenthused, Dylan laid the phone on the table next to his plate and started on his hot dog.

"Interested in a Washington Nationals game next Saturday?" Jonathan sat down, next to Dylan, with his own plate. Nearby, the electronic bug catcher buzzed as another victim hit the wires.

"Sure." A show of genuine interest. Encouraging. Then it faded. "But's it's okay if you cancel. I know your job… the IRS… and all that."

They ate their hot dogs in silence.

Dylan didn't know Jonathan's real job, as an intelligence agent. He just knew that Jonathan frequently missed promised outings. As much as Jonathan wanted to reassure Dylan that he'd make it this time, he couldn't. He never knew.

His ringing phone underscored that fact. He checked the number. It was his boss, Margaret Bradford. He ignored it and the call went to voice mail. A minute later and the tones chimed again.

"You gonna answer that?" Dylan started on his potatoes.

It was Margaret again. Jonathan walked a few feet away from his son before answering.

She didn't bother with pleasantries.

"I need you to talk to Kolya Petrov. Immediately."

"You have his phone number." As did Jonathan. He and Kolya remained friends, although they saw each other with much less frequency than when they were working together, and there was a slight tension between them—perhaps from Jonathan continuing to work for the agency that had set Kolya up to be captured and tortured. "You should know—he's not completely recovered—and he still harbors homicidal thoughts towards you."

"I am aware of both, but we need his assistance for an emergency. And he'll listen to you."

Jonathan's eyebrows rose. "What's the emergency?"

She told him.

Five minutes later, he was in his Acura NXC driving his son to his ex-wife's house.

13

SUNDAY EVENING, GEORGETOWN, WASHINGTON D.C.

KOLYA STRETCHED OUT ON the couch, ice bag on the knee doing little to alleviate the throbbing, while Alex rustled in the kitchen. Normally, he prepared dinner. Not tonight. Tonight, she was making chicken in a spicy sauce. He hoped she wouldn't burn it. He loved her deeply and completely, but she was a terrible cook.

It had only been a few hours since the attack. After dinner, they'd discuss whether it was safe to remain in D.C. He knew she wouldn't want to leave her law practice—but while she was capable with a gun, she would be vulnerable. They both were. Unless he could find who had paid the attackers first.

But he no longer had access to the type of information that would allow him to do so.

He lay facing the front door, his HK .40 on the coffee table within easy reach, and on the floor, a Mossberg 500 Tactical Tri-Rail Forend shotgun with an extended magazine. The alarm system was set. They'd pushed a bookcase against the steel back door. Ground floor windows were barred. The only entrance was the front door, and he had a clear shot from the couch. He would have liked a drink—not a drink, a whole bottle—but he had never drunk during a mission—and he was again on duty, protecting both of them from unknown assailants. Ellis Marsalis and sons played *Twelve's It* on the turntable, while he tried to read Martin Buber, but the day's events coupled with a poor night's sleep had caught up with him, and he was tired. He closed his eyes and dozed.

The doorbell brought him back to full consciousness. He picked up his phone, checked the security image, and then reached for the crutches on the floor. "It's Jonathan. I'll get it."

Alex was already out of the kitchen. "I'm there. Stay off your leg." She crossed the room to the small entranceway and unlocked the door.

"Hey, Alex. Kolya around?" Jonathan's voice was friendly and warm.

Kolya traded his gun on the coffee table for the remote and turned down the elegant sound of the Marsalis family ensemble.

It had been a month since they'd last met at a bar for a few drinks. Jonathan looked the same as he'd looked for the ten years they'd worked together—immaculate brown hair, designer jeans and polo shirt.

Kolya repositioned his leg on the coffee table and replaced the ice bag. "Would you like a beer? Or join us for dinner?"

"Nah. Thanks. Already ate. Had Dylan over for a barbecue." Jonathan took in the ice pack and the crutches on the floor. "Hell, you hurt your leg again? What happened?" He seated himself in an armchair across from Kolya. Alex remained standing.

"I twisted my knee taking down gunmen who attacked Alex's family. To get to me."

"Jesus. What the fuck. Today?"

"Few hours ago. I called in for a get out of jail free card. You didn't hear?"

"I heard you called in, but no details. Any idea who or why?"

Kolya shook his head. "None. I had a chat with one of the gunmen before he got away. Claimed he was hired. No clue as to the employer. I have a partial on the car plate and three burners, but I no longer have access to the kind of data that would allow me to do an in-depth search. The police are fucking useless."

"Especially when you don't give them the partial plate number or the phones."

"There's that."

"Both of you okay otherwise?" He looked at the gun on the coffee table and the shotgun on the floor. "Sorry. Stupid question."

"Yes, it is a stupid question. Kolya is going to play the tough guy as usual, but he is most definitely not okay. He hasn't been okay since Romania." Alex caught Kolya's gaze. "Okay, fine, I'll go check on dinner. And, yes, the chicken's probably charring. But just in case Jonathan's here for anything other than a friendly visit—which I doubt given the timing—remember that the ECA nearly killed both of us."

"It's not something I'm likely to forget."

"And that's the issue, isn't it?" She turned to Jonathan. "I know you're a friend. Today brought a lot of it back." She headed for the kitchen.

Jonathan waited until Alex was out of sight and earshot. "You should've called me. I can get into the office database to see if we can track down these people."

"Not exactly legal. I wouldn't want to get you in trouble."

There was a slight undercurrent of tension, maybe because Kolya suspected that Jonathan was there on ECA business. Jonathan had risked his life and his career to save both him and Alex, and Kolya was grateful. He owed Jonathan a debt he could never repay. Still, Jonathan had continued to work for the agency that had betrayed him. On the rational level, Kolya understood. Jonathan liked the job, which was why he did it despite being a trust fund brat. Kolya had also liked the job until Bradford had lied to him and sent him out to be strung up and tortured. On the other hand, he wouldn't have continued at the ECA if Jonathan had been the one betrayed.

It was nothing he'd ever said to Jonathan. Nothing he would ever say. He still considered Jonathan to be his closest friend. Nevertheless, he wasn't past the anger at what had happened to him. Maybe it wasn't fair to direct any part of that anger at the friend who had rescued him, but this wasn't about being fair. Or rational.

Maybe that was why they didn't meet up that often. Maybe that was why he hadn't called Jonathan to ask for his help finding Mickey and company.

"I'll get on it first thing tomorrow," Jonathan said. "And sorry that it happened. As if you needed more fucking trauma."

"I'm okay. Except for the knee."

"Yeah, sure you are. Just so you know—if you ever need a sounding board—someone besides Alex—I'm here for you." Jonathan grinned. "Not that I expect you to ever take me up on it. But if you need a drinking buddy...."

"Thanks. I'll keep the drinking in mind for the future. Right now, seeing what you can find out on the attackers is good enough." And another debt to Jonathan.

"No problem."

But if Jonathan hadn't known about the attack, why had he just dropped in? Not something he normally did. Kolya knew there were few coincidences in his business. His former business. "So are you going to tell me why you dropped by?"

"It's a little awkward, given everything, but I'm here to ask you for a favor."

"Are you asking—or is Bradford?"

"Both. Sorry, yeah, I know. But hear me out. Did you catch the news today? About a gas leak in a department store in Boston—and then toxic fumes from a cleaning product on a subway in Manhattan?"

"I saw the headlines when I checked the news, but I didn't read the stories. Not a gas leak or a cleaning product?"

"No. Although the fumes were toxic enough. It was Novichok."

"*Yob tvoyu mat.*" Kolya knew exactly how dangerous the nerve poison was—and that only one country manufactured Novichok. "Are you sure?"

"Pretty sure. Tests haven't come back on Boston or New York, but in both cases, a blue crystal bottle held the toxin, and a blue crystal bottle containing Novichok was found near the body of a smuggler in Northern Vermont. That was kept completely under wraps."

"How much is in the country?"

"No idea how much, where it might be, or the next possible targets. Apparently, the terrorists are in Boston or New York—maybe both. Although maybe they're moving on to other cities. Very scary."

"Agreed. Did the FBI identify the smuggler?"

"A freelancer from the Eastern townships of Quebec Province who made runs for Rzaev's gang."

"Rzaev? Vladimir Rzaev?"

Jonathan nodded.

Kolya's mind flashed to Second Avenue in Manhattan. Dmitri Lemonsky in a two thousand dollar suit. *I can make you rich, my friend. Have you heard of Volodya Rzaev?* And an older memory—of himself as a child—of Dmitri approaching him at the *dyetskii dom*—the orphanage where he'd been placed after his mother's death and before his adoption by an American cousin. *I'll teach you how to fight.* "I assume President Lewis has contacted Yuri Bykovsky and expressed an appropriate level of indignation. And Bykovsky denied any involvement or knowledge."

"Bingo. Bykovsky may be involved, although Rzaev doesn't clear all his ventures with Bykovsky—and it's also possible that Rzaev is smuggling Novichok for terrorists. He's done it before. Bykovsky doesn't seem to give a shit as long as Rzaev gives him a healthy cut of his profits."

"Yes, I know. Also possible, though, that Bykovsky is planning to kill some of his enemies in this country. Who is on his kill list?"

"A few dissidents and some former FSB officers who defected. They've gone into protective custody until we find answers."

"Maria Andropov and her daughter?"

"They've been moved to a safe house."

"Does Bykovsky know who smuggled them out of the country?"

"Our source inside the FSB says not. Fyodor—remember him?"

"He can only report what he actually knows. Assassination in a foreign country would be handled by the SVR or GRU."

If Maria Andropov and her daughter were targets, Kolya very well could be on the list.

Could this have any connection to the events of the past day or so? But the invasion at Aaron's home was not Bykovsky's style. Nerve poison would have been on the handle of Alex's door—or someone would have jabbed Kolya with the tip of an umbrella. Whoever had hired the thugs to come after him was someone else. Probably.

"And the favor?"

"There's only one person who could give us immediate information on Rzaev's network in the United States."

"You can't be thinking of Dmitri."

"Yeah, I am."

"Dmitri would just as soon kill me as talk to me. Someone else would be preferable."

"Someone else tried. Steve Kowolsky. Dmitri refused to cooperate without you present."

"When did Kowolsky talk to him?"

"This morning."

"This morning?"Then shortly thereafter Kolya and Alex were attacked. Another coincidence? "Shit. How closely is Dmitri monitored?"

"Very closely. And constantly." The implication of the question hit Jonathan. "All of his phone calls, attorney meetings, are recorded. Not likely he was behind the attack."

Kolya rolled his eyes. "And no one in prison ever has a cell phone illegally or communicates with the outside through corrupt guards."

"Okay. Maybe a chance. But, off the top of my head, I could probably list a dozen people who'd like to kill you. Starting with our friend from Romania."

Kolya didn't flinch at the mention of the man who still made regular appearances in his nightmares. "Yes, he's on my list too."

"I'm going to track down who attacked you. If it was Dmitri, we'll know. In the meantime—we still need to locate Rzaev's network and figure out who smuggled in the Novichok and why. Which means we need Dmitri's cooperation."

"I don't know what game Dmitri is playing—but he's not going to cooperate because I ask him."

"No, he'll cooperate because we offer him a deal—and he trusts you not to fuck him over."

"I already did."

Jonathan shrugged. "Still. He thinks you have honor. Which you do. So, if you say the deal is real, he'll believe it." There was a long silence, finally broken by Jonathan. "I'll help you find whoever was behind the attack, no matter what you decide, but as a personal favor...."

"Stop it. I don't want people dying of nerve poison any more than you do. Still, we were just attacked. Alex may be competent with a gun, but I don't want her alone. She'll need additional protection if I'm going to be out of the house."

Jonathan took out his phone. Two minutes later, he glanced over at Kolya. "Tehila Melaku can be here in twenty minutes."

Kolya knew and respected her. Tehila, a half-Ethiopian and half-Ashkenazi Jew, was a former Mossad agent. The ECA had recruited her after she fell in love with an American history professor and wanted to marry her, which would not have been possible in Israel. "You want to go now?"

"Now. Or at least after you eat something. You okay to go?" Jonathan nodded at Kolya's leg.

"If you drive, and I don't have to scale walls."

"No physical exertion required." He pocketed his phone. "But you get to tell Alex. She might shoot me."

14

SUNDAY NIGHT, CUMBERLAND, MARYLAND

WITH THE HELP OF a half moon, Kolya could make out the dim shapes of newly planted fields and deep woods that lined both sides of the road. Lights glimmered in isolated houses, but ahead of the car, a harsh glow lit the horizon. When they drew closer, Kolya saw what it was. With floodlights illuminating red brick buildings on the far side of a barbed wired fence, the prison despoiled the tranquility of the silent countryside.

Kolya and Jonathan pulled into the prison parking just outside the illuminated barbed wire and stashed their guns in the car. Carrying a small cooler, CIA officer Steve Kowolsky waited near the gate with the assistant warden.

"Thanks for doing this, Kolya." Kowolsky's voice was friendly but insincere. It was also the first time he'd used Kolya's given name. He extended a hand.

"No problem." Kolya shifted his weight on the crutches to accept the gesture. He could be just as insincere as Kowolsky.

"Just so we're clear, this is my show."

"The ECA is in charge at this point." Jonathan's voice was equally friendly.

Kowolsky's face momentarily lost the smile. "I don't even know why you're here, Egan."

"Chauffeur and bodyguard," Kolya said. "Don't be a dick, Steve."

"Fine. Whatever."

* * * * *

Dmitri, a few lines around the mouth, but intelligent green eyes in a round boyish face, hadn't changed much in ten years. Kolya still saw the boy who'd once been his best friend in the man shackled to the table in the oppressive concrete room.

Kolya took a seat directly opposite him and rested the crutches against the wall, Jonathan to his left, Kowolsky to his right.

"*Privyet.*" Dmitri offered the Russian greeting between friends. Then in English. "Long time, Nikolai Ivanovich. What happened to your leg?"

"Twisted my knee. Nothing serious." Kolya watched for a sign that Dmitri knew how Kolya had been injured. He saw nothing to justify suspicion—and nothing to dispel suspicion. "By any chance, did you send men to attack me?"

Dmitri's unwavering gaze met Kolya's. "If I sent men to attack you, you would be dead. I do not fucking fool around. But no, I did not. I was angry, very angry ten years ago, but I have had a long time to cool down. Now I have an opportunity to get out of this shithole, and I trust you. Not him." He nodded at Kowolsky. "But you fuck me over again, that will be different. I will have you killed Russian way. Understand?"

"Yes." The Russian way would be to rip his stomach open and yank out his intestines, leaving them to writhe outside his body while he died.

Kowolsky shoved a container of Ben & Jerry's Cherry Garcia and a plastic spoon across the table to Dmitri. "Showing good faith here. You asked for Petrov and Ben & Jerry's."

"And I asked for your best offer." The ice cream was within reach of Dmitri's shackled hands, but he ignored it.

"Yeah and I have. Twelve years off your sentence. So just three short years until you're free. It's a damn good offer, Lemonsky."

Dmitri turned to Kolya and asked in Russian. "This asshole in charge?"

Kolya answered in the same language. "He thinks he is."

Dmitri nodded towards Kowolsky. "He speaks Russian. Does Egan?"

"Some. Not fluently. Does it matter?"

"I wanted the chance to talk to you without them listening. We were friends. Brothers. Have you forgotten when I taught you to fight? So that when that bastard wanted to shove his dick up your ass, you broke his nose?"

"No, I haven't forgotten. But I'd prefer not to talk about it here."

He didn't look at Jonathan or Kowolsky. If Kolya'd never told Jonathan, his closest friend, the details about what had happened to him as a child, he certainly would prefer not to discuss it in front of Kowolsky, who was anything but a friend.

Dmitri's voice brought him back to the present. "It's funny. I think you got the better deal. You got as good at fighting as me, better maybe, but I never got any good at playing piano. You still play Bill Evans? Or moved to more modern shit?"

"I keep up with new musicians but still mostly jazz. And I will always play Bill Evans." Kolya switched to English. "Did you want me here to discuss music?"

"No, I ask for you to—how you say—reconnect." Dmitri also spoke in English. "I also know you will not bullshit me. Does this asshole think I will cooperate for three years in prison and a pint of ice cream?"

Kowolsky broke in. "It's a damn good deal—and you'd be smart to take it."

"I told you bring your best deal." Dmitri swung to look at him in disdain. "If this is it, you are wasting my time." The Cherry Garcia had started to melt; droplets of ice cream oozed onto the table.

Kowolsky slammed a hand on the table. "You're damn lucky to be offered this. I already told you the alternative."

"They turn lights on here at 5 a.m. If we are just going to redo the last conversation, then I prefer to go to bed."

"You'll stay here until I say differently." Kowolsky shot a glance at Kolya and Jonathan.

Dmitri shrugged. "Okay." The puddle of cream on the table was growing.

"Fine. We can sit here all night, until you pee on yourself." Kowolsky growled. "Or you can cooperate. I'm done playing games."

Dmitri looked at Kolya. "Remember—carrots?"

He did. Dmitri and Kolya, along with several other boys, had stolen carrots from the kitchen intended for the next day's soup, but only Dmitri was caught. Three days of starvation and beatings—but Dmitri never gave up any of the other boys.

"Enough, Steve. Dmitri isn't going to give in because you threaten him." Kolya turned to Jonathan. "It's time."

Jonathan nodded. "This is our best offer. If the information is good, you can walk out of here."

"Goddamnit, Egan," Kowolsky gritted his teeth. "My show. I told you."

"ECA operation," Jonathan responded. "Bradford okayed it with the President."

"No deal until I confirm." Kowolsky pulled out his phone and walked to a corner, where he huddled and muttered.

"Kolya?" Dmitri raised eyebrows. "This real or more bullshit?"

"Real."

Kowolsky returned to the table—composed but grim. "Yeah. The fucking offer is real."

Dmitri pulled the ice cream over. "Okay, then. I can give you a list of people who worked for Rzaev when I ran the North American operation. But here is the problem. Most of them are dead. Or in prison. Couple guys retired to Florida and California. Rzaev will have new people running the Northeast since you sent me here. You want to find his people in my territory, you need to talk to Rzaev directly." He dug out a spoonful of Cherry Garcia and ate it with obvious enjoyment.

"Where is Rzaev?" Kowolsky tried to retake control of the interrogation.

"No idea. I have not had contact with him or heard anything about him in years." Dmitri licked the spoon. "When I worked for him, he had five or six houses. He has probably different houses now. I can get the addresses from my contact in St. Petersburg, but he will only deal with me face to face. That way he is sure who I am and that no one is pointing a gun at me. Same with Rzaev. So I will have to go to Russia to find him. Then we can talk to Rzaev together." He held up a spoonful. "Kolya, want some? This is good shit."

Kolya shook his head.

Dmitri shrugged and downed the spoonful.

"Out of the question," Kowolsky retorted. "You can get in touch with your contact online or on the phone."

"You think Rzaev's people will give addresses in an e-mail? And even if they did, you think Rzaev will talk to you, Mr. CIA man? Even if you speak Russian? Do you think he will not know you are American when you show up on his doorstep? Your Russian is not bad—but an idiot would know you are American." He paused to eat more Cherry Garcia. They waited while he slowly consumed the rest of the pint. After reaching the bottom, he scraped the cardboard and with a sign of contentment and dropped the spoon into the container.

"Even if you take Kolya here, who is Russian—if Rzaev thinks you work for the CIA or another spy agency, he will gut you and leave you on the side of road. Maybe, you can contact the FSB and go in to talk to him, but you would not be here if you could call the FSB."

"All we need from you is a good address," Kowolsky said.

"No. You need me. Because I will not be walking out of prison if American agents wind up gutted on the side of road."

Jonathan glanced at Kolya, who shrugged. Dmitri was right. Kolya'd spent enough time working undercover to know that going for Rzaev without someone like Dmitri getting them in would be suicidal. "Your call, Jonathan."

Jonathan turned back to Dmitri. "How would you get us in?"

"I will tell Rzaev that you are businessmen who want something smuggled into the US. We first go to the guy I know in St. Petersburg, who will know how to find Rzaev. What you do then, will be up to you, but you better think of a clever story."

"He'll know you were in prison," Kowolsky objected. "He won't trust you."

"It's a badge of honor. In the *vorovsky mir*—Thieves World—a man doesn't gain stature until he's served in prison," Kolya said. "Rzaev won't know how Dmitri got out of prison. You'll just need a good story for that as well."

"It could work," Jonathan said. "Kowolsky speaks fluent Russian. We have several agents fluent in Russian as well."

"This is a CIA operation," Kowolsky grunted.

"ECA operation." Jonathan focused on Dmitri. "What guarantee do we have that you won't betray us to Rzaev?"

"Your government took ten million dollars of my money when they arrested me. I want it back. But you can hold it until everyone returns safe. Then I will buy a place in Florida. On the Intercoastal maybe—in Boca or Palm Beach."

"Absolutely not!" Kowolsky said. "The American government isn't giving you ten million."

"It's my money."

"From illegal activities."

"No one proved the money dirty. I had legit businesses. Real estate. Import/export. Your forfeiture laws are very unfair."

"What do you think?" Jonathan asked Kolya quietly.

"It would be a hedge against his betraying you." Kolya didn't bother to lower his voice. "Dmitri does like Florida. He also likes money."

"There you are. If I betray you, I will lose my money and cannot return to the U.S. More than that, I can never leave Russia—and it is damn cold in Russia."

"Christ, Egan, you can't be considering this," Kowolsky said.

"Not my call. My boss will decide. All I know is that finding Rzaev was important enough for us to drag up here in the middle of the damn night."

Dmitri picked up the spoon again, apparently spotting a speck of Cherry Garcia that he'd missed. He captured the drop and then licked the spoon again. "Meantime, I will write down names of everyone from my network. And June is beautiful in Russia. Kolya, we will be together in St. Petersburg for the White Nights celebrations. Brings back memories."

"Not me. I'm not going."

Dmitri dropped the spoon back into the container. "Then this is all for nothing. I will not go either."

"Are you shitting me?" Kowolsky said. "You're going to give up freedom and ten million dollars if Petrov doesn't go?"

"I trust him to not kill me when we are done. It is what Russian intelligence would do. Get the information. Kill me. Save ten million dollars. Kolya is—how you say—straight shooter. He will not kill me so your government can keep my money. He will not let any American agent kill me either. Kolya does not go, the deal is off."

Kolya reached for his crutches, the visible symbol of why he no longer worked for the ECA. He pushed his chair back from the table and rose, leaning heavily on the support. "Your game, Jonathan. I'm done. I'll meet you outside."

15

SUNDAY NIGHT, CUMBERLAND, MARYLAND

ONE OF THE GUARDS offered Kolya a chair in the prison corridor while he waited for Jonathan. He rested the crutches against the wall, stretched out his leg, and took out his phone to read *The New York Times*. But there was no signal, so he returned the phone to his pocket and stared down the gray corridor, thinking about what it would feel like to be locked inside these walls—bleak days stretching into bleak years.

And remembering.

The *dyskeii dom*—the boys' home. Constructed in the 1920s—the early Soviet era—in the Southern suburbs of St. Petersburg, near the Moskovskiy Prospeckt, the building that served as a school and a home for orphaned boys was a testament to the concrete architecture and poor construction that characterized that era, and its exterior served as a perfect metaphor for the grimness inside.

He didn't remember every detail of the five years he'd spent there: it had been what—over twenty years since he'd left—but some things stood out. That first horrible day when devastated by the loss of the mother he'd adored, the social worker had walked him into the *dom* where everything was gray and everything was cold. He remembered clutching a suitcase that contained clothes, books, and his favorite sheet music. Then she'd left him with a pat on the shoulder. He'd been nine years old.

One of the teachers took his suitcase, and he never saw the contents again. Instead, he was issued gray oversized pants and a shirt, and told that he was a spoiled bourgeois brat by a different teacher who in the mid 1990s still bitterly mourned the downfall of the Communist party in Russia. The same teacher had stood him in front of the class and announced that his mother had been a famous Jewish pianist before she'd been banned from the concert stage for anti-social activities.

That night, two boys cornered him in the bathroom and beat him up for being a "fucking Jew." He'd fought back, but he'd never been in a fight before, and they were bigger than him. He'd lost badly.

The next few days had been more of the same. At best, the teachers ignored him. At night or at meals, the same two boys targeted him. He did locate the school's piano in the auditorium where he'd sneak off to play jazz.

A few days after his arrival, Yelseyev, the head of the school, had called him into his office. Kolya had hoped he might intervene with the teachers or the bullies. Instead, Yelseyev shoved his hand down Kolya's pants. Someone knocking on the door gave Kolya the chance to escape before being raped.

He'd hidden in the school's auditorium under the piano for hours, missing classes and missing meals. He didn't care. He made his plans—he'd wait until night then he'd run away. He'd had nowhere to go but even living on the street had to be better. Then, in the late afternoon, huddled in a space under the stage, he'd heard footsteps.

The footsteps neared the piano.

"I heard you playing the other day." It was a boy's voice.

Kolya didn't move.

"That was American music, wasn't it? It was cool." Long silence while he waited for an answer that didn't come. "I know why Yelseyev called you into his office."

Kolya didn't want anyone to think that Yelseyev had succeeded. "I got away."

"He'll get you eventually." The voice was right above him.

"Not if I run away."

"You ever live on the streets?" The round face framed by shaggy brown hair of a boy Kolya'd seen in passing, peered around the edge of the piano. "This is bad, but the street is worse. You have to be good at stealing if you want to survive. That or you have to let a lot of dirty old men fuck you. I'm Dmitri by the way." The face was smiling, friendly.

It was the first friendly face he'd seen in days. Kolya crawled out from under the piano.

"Does everyone know about Yelseyev?"

Dmitri shoved hands in his pocket and nodded his head. "Everyone knows. He likes soft boys. Like you. And you're blond and skinny. He likes that too."

Dmitri pressed a key down on the piano. The sound was tinny. "What was the song you were playing the other day?"

"Maybe 'Autumn Leaves'?" Kolya leaned over and played the melody with his right hand. The piano was slightly out of tune, not so badly that it was painful to hear it. He thought of the piano that he'd learned to play on almost as soon as he learned to walk, and then with a flash of pain of his mother, sitting beside him.

"Can you teach me how to play?" Dmitri walked his fingers up the keyboard.

"I can teach you, but it takes a long time to play well."

"If you teach me how to play even a little, I'll teach you how to fight. Yelseyev doesn't fuck the kids who fight back. You fight back, and he'll leave you alone. And I'll help you with those little shits Boris and Pyotr. I never liked either of them. So you're a Jew?"

"Yes." Kolya, who'd begun to relax, tensed.

"That means you don't believe in Jesus?"

"No." Kolya wasn't sure that he believed in God, but he did know he didn't believe in Jesus.

"I don't either. Bunch of bullshit." He surveyed Kolya. "I don't know what the big deal is about Jews. I've only ever met one other Jew. He was fucking my mother, but that's what they all did. The Jewish guy was nice to me, though. He paid for me to have martial arts lessons for a while. You seem okay. Do we have a deal?"

Kolya considered the offer. What did he have to lose? If he learned how to fight, he could protect himself. And he desperately wanted not to feel alone.

"Okay." He extended his hand.

"Great." Dmitri grasped his hand and then with a smooth move, knocked Kolya's legs out from under him. Kolya fell to the floor. Hard.

His rear end stung with the weight of the fall, but worse than the minor sting was the realization that he'd been suckered. That he had started to trust someone... that he thought he might have a friend... and he had just been a fool.

Kolya pushed himself up and swung at Dmitri. Dmitri stepped aside and repeated the motion. Kolya hit the ground a second time.

"Lesson one. Never completely trust anyone." Dmitri stooped and extended his hand to help Kolya up. Kolya hesitated. Then he accepted the offered hand and yanked Dmitri to the ground. Then Kolya stood up and brushed himself off.

"*Yob tvoyu mat.*"

Fuck your mother.

It was a particularly nasty Russian curse that Kolya had only used once or twice in his previous life—but that life was as dead as his mother.

Dmitri laughed and got to his feet.

"Good start. You learn fast. Now let me show you how I knocked you down."

Kolya narrowed his eyes. "You just told me not to trust you."

"I told you to not completely trust me. You can mostly trust me. And I will mostly trust you." Dmitri grinned and that sealed the deal. "Start with staying balanced. Everything comes from that. After that, knowing the best places to hit—nose, knees, balls, throat—and how to hit."

Dmitri ran with a small gang of boys at the school. After Dmitri befriended Kolya, his gang did as well. Boris and Pyotr tried bullying him a few more times, but once they lost a few fights with Kolya and his new friends, they found someone else to torment. And when Yelseyev again cornered Kolya, Kolya slammed his palm against Yelseyev's nose, breaking it. He'd been beaten and starved as punishment, but Yelseyev never tried to rape him again.

Looking down the prison corridor reminded Kolya of what he might have become had he never left Russia. Without Dmitri, he might not have survived the *dyskeii dom.* His friendship with Dmitri had started as transactional, both of them offering something of value to the other, but eventually evolving to something akin to brotherhood. Not for the first time, he regretted the path that Dmitri had chosen—if Dmitri had even had a choice. The choices for most of the boys who aged out of the school were the army or one of the gangs. Or the streets.

Or death.

But thanks to his cousin and his adopted country, Kolya had again lived in a caring home, where his interests in literature and music were indulged. He'd lost his cousin when she died of breast cancer in his

71

mid-twenties, but he had been able to go to college, to law school—and then to become an intelligence operative. He'd had choices that Dmitri never had. He still did. As he waited for Jonathan and his ride back to Georgetown, he contemplated the choices he now faced. And he knew, despite his residual anger and mental and physical injuries from eight months earlier, he couldn't make a choice that would leave people to die.

16

MONDAY EARLY MORNING, GEORGETOWN, WASHINGTON D.C.

TEHILA MELAKU, RESPLENDENT IN a red embroidered blouse that accented her dark skin, sat on the couch, the shotgun against her shoulder aimed at the door—and Kolya.

He closed the door and reset the alarm code.

Tehila returned the shotgun to her lap and picked up her phone. "Alex went upstairs an hour ago."

He thanked her and maneuvered up the stairs to the dark bedroom. One a.m., and he was exhausted. His gun went into a holster nailed behind the headboard, his crutches against the wall. He undressed, slid under the covers, and settled his arm around her waist. She wrapped her arms around him. She was soft and warm and smelled of lavender.

"I'm sorry I woke you." He kissed her.

"I couldn't sleep. So tell me."

"There are pleasanter things to do than talk." He stroked her breast, starting on the soft outside and circling toward the nipple. "Since you're awake."

He'd have to tell her. Tonight or tomorrow. He'd just prefer it to be tomorrow. He'd had an hour nap in the car—which had given him a little energy. And this would be the last opportunity to make love until he returned. If he returned. Grim thought—but a possibility. He was going to Russia. Yuri Bykovsky might or might not have identified Kolya as the agent responsible for exfiltrating Maria, but if he were caught, Kolya could still count on the full Lubyanka treatment—torture followed by a bullet in the back of his head. Then there was the question of whether

73

Dmitri had in fact let go of the past, which Kolya didn't completely trust either.

Maybe he really was crazy. None of which he could say to Alex.

She captured his hand, brought it up to her lips and kissed his palm. "What are you avoiding telling me, love?"

He sighed. "Can't it wait until the morning?" He saw her expression and gave in. Not in the morning. Now. "I'm leaving tomorrow—for a few days."

"What's going on?"

"You know I can't tell you, but it's important. Unfortunately, I'm the only one who can do this."

"There's always someone else."

"Not this time."

"You're on crutches. You barely sleep. You're in no shape to go on a mission."

"The crutches are temporary. I'm just using them to give my knee a rest for a day or so. And as far as being in shape, I did just save your family from home invaders."

"That incident only lasted a few minutes, and you had a surge of adrenaline. Can you sustain that level of concentration for days? While, as I assume, you're playing the usual high stakes spy games? You still have flashbacks. Constant nightmares."

He had the same concerns, and he didn't have an answer. But did it matter? He was going because Dmitri would only work with him. "If I didn't think I could do this, I wouldn't go. And I wouldn't go if it wasn't necessary. Please trust me."

She was visibly fighting back tears. "I trust you. I'm just afraid for you."

"I'm not going to die."

"You can't promise that."

"True. I can promise to be careful." It would have to do. "But I'm also asking you to leave town in the morning. Washington's not safe right now, even with Tehila as bodyguard." He watched her reaction and then slipped in the argument most likely to persuade her. "If I know you're safe, it'll be easier for me to focus—and stay safe myself. The house in Vermont perhaps?" He thought about the dangers of being in D.C.— the unknown assailant who'd already tried once. Then there were the terrorists and the Novichok. They had come across the Vermont border, but they had moved on from there, attacking with the nerve agent in Boston and New York. Washington could be next.

She had half ownership of a vacation house in Stowe with one of her cousins. They had stayed there frequently, for skiing and for summer getaways. Vermont would be safer.

"If I can be found here, I can be found in Vermont."

"Not as easily. The house is in your cousin's name. Leave your phone here and use a burner. Don't check in with your office. Use cash instead of credit cards—or Tehila can use her card."

"I have cases, Kolya. You're not the only one with people depending on you."

"You have partners. And you can get a continuance on anything pressing. You can download your briefs and work on them, even if you can't be in contact. It'll be less than a week. Just think of it as a vacation. Mountains in the spring—and maple syrup."

"With a bodyguard."

"She's good company—I've worked with her. You'll like her wife by the way."

"It has nothing to do with liking Tehila or her wife. My job is important, too."

"Please, Alex. The only thing that really scares me about accepting this assignment is the risk to you."

"Fine, damn it. I'll go. I don't want to be used against you, and I don't want you distracted with worrying about me."

"I'll be okay." He pulled her close, and she nestled against his chest. "Try to sleep." But she raised her head and kissed him long and deep. Then there were no more words. Afterward, she slept, curled against him. But sleep eluded him. He lay in the dark, images from the past twenty-four hours alternating in his mind with images from Romania and his childhood.

17

MONDAY MORNING, LANGLEY, VIRGINIA

BEN SMITHSON'S OFFICE WAS institutionally cold, as befitted the Director of the CIA. Large white desk. Large white filing cabinet. No personal pictures. No comfortable couch. No wall decorations except a yellowed copy of the Declaration of Independence and framed letters of commendation from three presidents. The closest to any warmth: a bookshelf filled with well-worn leather-bound volumes of world history, biography, and literature situated behind the desk. Kowolsky assumed it was deliberate—that the décor was intended to discourage lingerers.

Kowolsky seated himself in a metal chair facing Smithson, who occupied the only comfortable chair. Kowolsky knew the stakes—but knowing the stakes and liking how the game was played were two different things. "I don't like that Petrov and Lemonsky are going to Russia without me."

Smithson stroked his goatee as if he were actually considering Kowolsky's objections. "Yes, I'd prefer if it were you going and not Petrov; I'd prefer if the CIA and not the ECA were in charge. But I'm a realist. I deal with situations that I've got. So we'll monitor the situation and all information from here."

"I could go over covertly."

"And do what? If you got close enough to see what they're doing, Petrov would spot you. Or Egan—he'll be there as back-up. That could negatively impact locating Rzaev."

"Still, I don't trust Petrov. Even if he wasn't dirty before, he wouldn't be the first agent to turn after a mission went south. And his pal Dmitri won't work with anyone else. Kinda suspicious. By the way, did you know that Petrov was sexually abused in that Russian school where he was a kid? That twists people."

Smithson gestured towards the door. The meeting was over. "Unless you uncover evidence against him, leave Petrov alone so he can do his job."

"And if I uncover evidence?"

"Then bring it to me."

MONDAY MID-DAY, FOGGY BOTTOM, WASHINGTON, D.C.

It was one of the smaller conference rooms at the ECA, seating at most eight people, but it had a view of the sidewalk on F Street three floors below. Kolya balanced on crutches in front of the darkened window and watched pedestrians hurrying along the sidewalk under the cover of umbrellas. The slight drizzle had turned into a downpour.

"Lunch," a familiar voice announced behind him. "Hey, Kolya, great to see you."

He turned. Teo Lorenzo, fluent in Russian and maybe fifteen other languages at the tender age of twenty-one, as fresh faced, eager—and annoying—as the first time Kolya had met him, placed a tray filled with sandwiches in the middle of the conference table. Elizabeth Owen, dark hair and eyes, elegant in black pants and a blue shirt, whom he'd briefly dated three years earlier before reconnecting with Alex, followed Teo into the room. She rolled her eyes at Teo's enthusiasm but refrained from any snide remarks. In the past, she'd called him the boy wonder, but the two of them had reached a tacit détente. The two of them had joined with Jonathan and two other ECA agents to rescue Kolya and Alex eight months earlier.

Elizabeth poured herself a cup of coffee from the side table and sat down opposite Teo. Jonathan positioned himself in the seat at the head of the table. Kolya maneuvered to a chair between Jonathan and Teo. He checked the tray of sandwiches and found a tuna salad. Boring, but otherwise unobjectionable.

Jonathan ran through the history, starting with the Novichok, the dead smuggler, and the meeting with Dmitri.

"Kowolsky must be pissed." Elizabeth selected a ham and cheese.

"One hopes." Kolya took a bite of his tuna sandwich. Soggy. Bad choice after all.

"Maybe. Still, not a good person to have as an enemy." She removed the bread from her sandwich and ate the cheese and then the ham with her fingers.

Kowolsky was not Kolya's concern. "I'm more worried about Rzaev and Bykovsky than about Kowolsky." He took another bite of the sandwich and then dropped it onto a paper plate.

"It's irrelevant, anyway. The decision was made between the higher ups."

Between Lewis, Smithson, and Bradford, no doubt.

Kolya had arrived at the office, obtained an identification card, spoken to several colleagues, and made his way to the conference room without even a glimpse of Margaret Bradford. That unpleasantness was yet to come.

He felt on edge, more nervous than he'd ever been before a mission. It wasn't the mission; it was being in the building. He'd only been back once since Romania.

Jonathan handed out passports and Russian visas. "Our contact inside the FSB got us the visas. Normally it takes several weeks. Kolya, he'll meet up with you, and update you on any developments. Usual place, usual precautions."

Kolya opened the passport to examine his photograph and an unfamiliar name. "Michael Harding? How solid is this?"

"We didn't have time to build a good legend with social media, etc., so we found a guy in Chicago about your age, and borrowed his identity. He's on Twitter, not on Facebook, and no pictures online. We have something similar for Dmitri, but given that he still has a strong Russian accent, he's a naturalized Russian American living in Miami. The official story is that you and Dmitri are there to look into buying investment property. You have a different story for Rzaev and company. Background sheets for both. If anyone looks deeply, the covers won't stand up. But you're not doing deep cover—and for the short term, it should be secure."

"Unless I'm arrested by the FSB."

"Try not to be."

"I always do."

Jonathan held up a small device about the size and shape of a postal stamp from a pocket. "A GPS device. We've got them small enough to tape to a hornet. This could be taped to your arm with a Band-Aid over it. So we can track you if necessary."

Kolya shook his head. "It would set off an alarm if Rzaev has the appropriate sensors, and I would assume he does. He'll know that I'm not what I'm pretending to be and kill me."

"You sure?"

"Yes, I'm sure."

"Okay, but I'll keep it with me in case you change your mind."

"And our cover?" Teo opened his passport.

"St. Petersburg's White Nights celebration attracts huge numbers of tourists. It's a family trip. You're my younger brother."

Elizabeth flipped open her passport. "And I'm your wife?"

"It's what we could come up on short notice."

"It'll be fun. I can humiliate you in public. And, by the way, you get to sleep on the floor."

"I figured."

There was a vibe between them that Kolya tried to decipher. Had they slept together? Jonathan had never said anything—and Kolya decided it wasn't his business. As long as their personal entanglement didn't endanger him. "Moving on—Dmitri is not to know that you're there. Final question. Any progress on identifying the people behind the attack on Alex's family?"

Jonathan nodded. "So far we've got IDs on the two dead guys. They were ex-military, as you guessed, and I have a couple researchers tracking down every known associate. Mark Leslie is running down any data from the phones. It'll be a couple days before we have any answers. Probably after we get back from Russia. Alex is leaving town, isn't she?"

"She and Tehila are leaving today."

"She'll be safe, then. Tehila's excellent, and Alex is no pushover herself. Don't worry. We'll get the bastards, even if it takes some time."

"Not too much time, I hope. Alex will want to get back to work." Kolya caught Teo's gaze on him. He raised his eyebrows. "What now?"

"You sure you're okay to do this, Kolya? You're on crutches again."

"They're a temporary aid. I'm transitioning to a knee brace before the flight. Unfortunately, I am the only one who can do this."

"But what…" Teo hesitated. Elizabeth shot a hard look across the table, but he kept going. "But what about, you know, any psychological issues from… from… you know, the stress, and all that…."

He hated the look of concern. He hated even more that he had the same question, that he could feel the shakiness. "From being held prisoner and tortured, you mean? I've been through therapy, and I'm fucking fine, Teo."

A lie, but what else could he say.

"Of course, you're fine. And this time, you won't be alone," Jonathan said.

It was easy for Jonathan to say. Yes, Kolya trusted the three of them. But he'd still be alone. Even if the team was nearby, he'd face Rzaev with only Dmitri at his side. By the time the team even knew he was in trouble, he could be dead.

It had always been like this. Going undercover had always meant that he was alone. The job hadn't changed—but he had.

The next stop was going to be difficult. He had to report to Bradford before leaving the building. He had no idea why she'd required him to speak to her.

"Do you want me to go with you to see Margaret?"

"Thanks, but no." Kolya pulled himself up on the crutches. The cozy relationship between Bradford and Jonathan would do nothing but anger him more. "You don't need to protect her from me."

* * * * *

Margaret Bradford's office had changed little. The *Vanity Fair* prints on the walls were different, but she had always rotated through her collection of 19th century writers. Today, it was Twain, Ibsen, Browning, Tennyson, and Tolstoy—the only Russian writer that she owned. Sunlight poured through the large glass windows.

The last time he'd been in this office—he'd been given the assignment that was intended to lead to his being taken prisoner. To being tortured. To Alex being kidnapped to pressure him.

Margaret Bradford sat at the same oak desk with the same crystal vase filled with the flowers of the day. Same silver framed picture of her granddaughter on the desk, although no one ever thought of her as a grandmother or grandmotherly. She looked as he remembered. A few more wrinkles around the hard eyes, a bit more sagging around the thin mouth, but the silver hair cut in the same short no-nonsense style, a designer blue suit that he didn't recognize. She'd apparently been reading a report of some kind, which she closed as he entered.

"Mr. Petrov." She gestured towards an armchair. "Please sit."

Mr. Petrov. It had always been Mr. Petrov, just as Jonathan had always been Jonathan. The easy explanation was class: Jonathan was old money and so was she. There were less pleasant possible explanations as well.

He seated himself and leaned the crutches against the chair. Then he waited for her to speak.

"I was just skimming a report your therapist sent me. She is concerned that you may not be fit yet for field work. So I wanted to ask you directly—what is your opinion?"

He said nothing. As a former intelligence agent, he could only see therapists connected to the ECA who had a high enough security clearance to hear operational details, but Margaret receiving details of any confidences he may have disclosed felt like a betrayal.

"I am genuinely concerned, Mr. Petrov."

"Are you, Mrs. Bradford?"

"Yes, I am. I know you harbor resentment for what happened to you, and I am truly sorry that you suffered and are still suffering."

"Resentment?" The word didn't come close. The non-apology—that she was sorry he'd suffered while showing not the slightest tinge of remorse for her own responsibility for his ordeal—would have been funny if he weren't still so angry.

"Not the best word, is it? But I still need to know that you can perform."

"If I didn't think I was capable of carrying out this mission, I wouldn't have agreed. My next stop is medical for a knee injection and a brace. It should be adequate."

"I was asking about your mental state."

"It also should be adequate. But whatever state I'm in doesn't matter, does it? You'd have me go anyway."

"It does matter. But you're correct. I am ignoring medical advice in allowing you to go."

"Then why require this meeting?"

"I wanted to confirm personally that you're not quite as bad off as the therapist reports. That despite your PTSD and your anger, you have sufficient self-control to be in the field. That you handled the emergency yesterday is strong evidence that you are coping better than your therapist may think." She allowed herself a small smile. "You haven't tried to kill me yet. I regard that as an additional positive. I also wanted to thank you, not on my behalf, but on behalf of the people of this country, for your service and for your sacrifice both in this instance—and for what happened in Romania. I hope you know that you did save thousands, maybe tens of thousands of lives, even if it came at a terrible cost to you. And, again, I am sorry for your pain, but what I did was necessary."

That she was still justifying what she had done to him was infuriating. But he swallowed his rage. With the help of the crutches, he rose. "You should have asked me to volunteer. I might have agreed."

"But you might not have."

"Also possible." But he probably would have. If he had volunteered, he would still have been hurt, but Alex wouldn't have been in danger and a fellow agent wouldn't have died unnecessarily in the ambush that she had set in motion. He would have known the plan and had a measure of control. Still, because Bradford didn't see him as a person, but as a means to achieve an objective, she hadn't asked. That the deception had saved lives didn't make what had happened to him any more acceptable. "Is there anything else?"

"I…." She stopped herself. "Not at this time."

Without another word, he left her office.

18

MONDAY AFTERNOON, STOWE, VERMONT

CHARLIE FRYE, NOT HIS birth name but a name chosen to sound more American, lay on the couch, thumbing through channels on the television and drinking single malt Scotch. He thought of the smuggler he'd killed near the Canadian border. Jean Claude had been useful over the years, but he should have known that no one retired in this business. Still, he'd kind of liked the bastard. Charlie felt something that was close to but not quite regret. Still it was part of the job, and Charlie was very good at his job.

He felt nothing for the three people dead and the others hospitalized in Boston and New York. Killing people he didn't know meant even less than killing someone who'd worked for him.

The initial plan had been to call in a warning to local authorities in the two cities and let them find the bottles, instead of letting civilians come into contact with the nerve poison. But it was so much more effective if a few people died. The American government would be frantic to find the Novichok, and they'd be hunting in major East Coast cities, not in a small resort town in Vermont.

It had been a busy Saturday, driving from Vermont to Boston to New York and back. He'd changed his appearance and his clothes after each stop, leaving the discarded outfits and wigs in bags in restrooms. He'd been careful to avoid cameras, but even if a camera had caught him leaving the bottles, he would be difficult to identify.

And getting rid of the clothes, the gloves, and the shoes after leaving each bottle lessened the chances of any accidental exposure to the Novichok.

What was left, the two containers with the different chemicals that would need to be mixed to become the deadly nerve agent, were resting in a closet in the basement in the backpack that Jean-Claude had carried across the border.

He turned his thoughts to his current circumstances. There was a view of the nearby mountains, but views didn't matter much to him. It was on the cold side for early June, but he could stand it. For now. The temperature was one of the reasons he wouldn't want to stay in Vermont long term, even if the country of his birth was cold as shit.

When it was all over, he'd head to an island somewhere in the Caribbean or the South Pacific. He preferred warmth and beaches to the chill and mountains. Maybe get a boat. A big boat. Big and powerful. He liked fast boats, the surge of power as he cut through waves. Women also liked boats, and Charlie liked good looking women. They liked him back—why not? He was in his mid-twenties, athletic, and good looking. Once he had money, he could have any woman he wanted.

A soccer game caught his attention, and he paused in his channel surfing long enough to watch the English goalie deflect the ball. Then the phone chimed.

"She's leaving the house, and she's got a woman friend with her."

"And him?"

"Left before her with a suitcase."

"You know what to do. Don't screw it up." Charlie clicked off. Then he put the phone on the coffee table, poured himself more scotch, and turned up the television. The soccer started to bore him, Spain and England, and he didn't really care. He switched channels and found an old movie—*The Godfather*. He'd seen it a million times, but it never got old.

PART III

19

MONDAY AFTERNOON, MOSCOW, RUSSIA

THE PRESIDENT'S OFFICE DEEP inside the Kremlin was designed to impress: The eagle crest on the wall, directly behind his seat; the long dark wood desk, and at a right angle to the desk, the credenza lined with white phones that connected directly to leaders of countries around the globe. The flag of the Russian Federation and the President's flag flanked the desk with Yuri Bykovsky seated on a gold-lined chair between the two banners. It reminded Tomas Grigorovich Orlov, Direcktor of the *Federal'naya Sluzhba Bezopasnosti*, which had inherited the power of the KGB, of the old czars. Too bad the title of czar had been abandoned. It would have fit his brother-in-law.

Today, though, Tomas barely noticed the décor. Yuri was angry. That never boded well.

"A few minutes ago, I spoke with the American President, Thomas Lewis," Yuri spoke each word with exquisite disdain. "He actually accused Vladimir Rzaev of smuggling a poison into the United States. I told him that Rzaev was a legitimate businessman, not a mafiya head."

Tomas nodded. He knew that the description of Rzaev was a lie—as no doubt, the President of United States had known. *Still, play along.*

"Shall I talk to Rzaev—straighten things out?" Tomas could have offered to send some lower levels FSB agents over, but Rzaev's wealth and his close connection to Yuri warranted a more delicate approach. Still, if Rzaev was smuggling Novichok into the United States, Tomas as head of Russia's internal spy agency should know. Novichok was supposed to be controlled by the State. Where had Rzaev gotten hold of it, and why was he smuggling it into the United States? If it was released in an American city—there could be sanctions—or worse, if enough Americans died. After all, fewer than 3000 Americans had died in 9-11—and that had started two wars. Then there was the worry over who had provided Rzaev with Novichok—and whether it could be used in Russia.

"It's just another American trick to make Russia look bad." Yuri slapped the table. "I've had enough of America's dirty tricks. Americans are thieves, and they're criminals. They're harboring the woman who stole billions from Russia, from me—at the instigation of their spies—and they've refused to return a penny. Instead they come up with lies against one of Russia's finest citizens."

Tomas cleared his throat. "I would be very discrete in my questions, but we should know. If there's any chance that Rzaev did this—he has to be working for or with someone. We should know who. And where he got the nerve agent."

Yuri was starting to look irritated. "Whatever Rzaev is doing is his business."

"Do you know where he is?"

"I haven't spoken to him for months. It's not been necessary, since he's been sending his monthly payments. He could be in Moscow or in St. Petersburg—or in London or Miami."

"Do you have a phone number for him? Or a list of where he could possibly be in Russia?"

Rzaev changed properties almost as often as he changed phones. Tomas tried to keep track of everything in Rzaev's name—but it was difficult. Rzaev also had property in fake names or in the names of his subordinates.

"I can get in touch with him if I need to, but I don't. And you don't need to either. I'm concerned with the Americans, not with Rzaev. And did you ever find out Maria Andropov's address in the United States? Or that of her daughter?"

"Unfortunately, no. It's a big country, and U.S. Marshalls are very good at their jobs. Has the SVR or the GRU found anything?" The SVR was the equivalent of the CIA, and the GRU was military intelligence. Both targeted other countries, while the FSB was the internal security apparatus, but functions sometimes overlapped.

"If anyone had found them, I wouldn't be asking you. Keep looking." Yuri waved a dismissive hand. "Thank you for dropping by, Tomas Grigorovich. Tell Lyudmila that I'll call her soon."

Whatever Tomas decided to do or not do with respect to Rzaev and the question of Novichok in the United States—he wouldn't risk openly defying Yuri. He stood, bowed his head respectfully, and left the room.

* * * * *

"He's kind of an idiot," Yuri's assistant entered the room after the door closed behind Tomas. "But he seems to treat your sister well."

"That matters. Along with the fact that he does what I want him to do," Yuri said. "Even if he is an idiot."

Why his sister had married a fat little bureaucrat like Tomas, Yuri had no idea. But she had, and now he was family. Whether he liked Tomas or not, Yuri believed in family. He liked doing things for his sister. He truly cared about his sister's children and enjoyed their visits to his country home. And while Tomas might be an idiot, he was not ambitious, which was a plus. Tomas was not likely to try to take over the Presidency.

But Yuri didn't completely trust anyone.

Maria Andropov had taught him a lesson, although her disappearance was intensely frustrating.

If he couldn't find either of them—he would still have his revenge. Against the United States. Against the traitorous spy who'd helped her escape.

MONDAY EVENING, MOSCOW, RUSSIA

Tomas surveyed the delicacies laid out on the linen tablecloth in the formal dining room—a room so big his entire first apartment could have fit inside—and beamed at the wife he adored seated next to him. Lyudmila had cooked Tomas's favorites, stuffed dumplings, and beef with sour cream and noodles. They were her favorites, too, and part of the reason neither of them was particularly slim. The children were in bed, each in his/her own bedroom. Only a Russian would appreciate what a luxury it was to have a four-bedroom apartment with a formal dining room in the heart of Moscow.

For a few hours every evening, Tomas enjoyed the benefits of the position he had neither wanted nor deserved. He lived in an apartment that in other times could have housed five or six families, and he could give the family that he loved anything they wanted. That had to count for something.

Lyudmila filled him in on the children as he ate. Emma, nine years old, had won a prize in her English class. The two boys, Alexander, seven, and Zahar, six, had both been praised by their teachers. As a reward, the boys wanted a new video game.

"I told them no. They have enough. Emma, on the other hand, wants a cat. I told her maybe."

He didn't particularly want a cat, but he'd leave that up to Lyudmila.

As he reached for a second helping of dumplings, he saw her untouched plate.

He patted her hand. "What's wrong?"

"I'm worried."

"You have nothing to worry about."

"I do. And you do too."

"Have you spoken to Yuri?"

"This morning. He said that you need to remember why you're in this position—and he asked if the children and I wanted to visit his new summer house in July."

"Nothing bad about that."

"He didn't invite you."

"I have a job. He expects me to be doing it." Seeing her expression, he decided to add something more comforting. "Or it was just an oversight—I'm probably included in the invite to you and the children."

"I know Yuri. He doesn't respect you, Tomas. He thinks you're a fat idiot."

"Well, I am a bit overweight."

"It's not funny. I know what Yuri's capable of. You have to be very careful to do exactly what he wants."

"I'm doing what he wants. He asked me to ensure the safety of the Russian federation—and to protect him. That's what I'm doing."

She silently picked at the dumplings on her plate. "You're not doing anything he told you not to do?"

Technically, he wasn't. Yes, he was going to look into the question of Rzaev and Novichok, and yes, Yuri had said that whatever Rzaev was doing was his business. But Yuri hadn't explicitly forbidden investigation. And Yuri had told Tomas on more than one occasion to watch for terrorists. If somehow or for some reason, terrorists used Novichok in Russia—wouldn't Tomas also be blamed? He also had a concern that if there were a large-scale attack in the United States—it could have dire consequences for Russia. What would President Lewis do—impose sanctions, retaliate in some fashion? If any of that happened, Yuri would want a scapegoat. The head of the FSB who had allowed it to happen could serve that purpose. Even if, and Tomas was smart enough to admit the possibility, even if Yuri himself had ordered or sanctioned what Rzaev was doing.

So—Tomas was caught. Any way he went, he could be in trouble. His only choice was to just do his job the best he could. The danger from some crazy person releasing a deadly nerve poison either in the United States or Russia seemed to be the bigger threat at the moment.

"You're not answering," Lyudmila pushed.

"I'm thinking."

She reached for him across the table. "Don't think, Tomas. It's not a valued commodity. Just do whatever Yuri wants."

"Even if it could hurt him?"

"Even if it could. He's dangerous."

"He's your brother. He wouldn't hurt you. Or me." Yuri wouldn't hurt his own sister or her children. Probably wouldn't hurt Tomas either. Probably.

"He killed my kitten when I was six. He smashed it. Then threatened to kill me too if I told our parents."

"I know. You've told me this story several times." That Yuri was mean and a little crazy wasn't exactly news. It just meant he had to be careful. Tomas wasn't stupid even if he'd only become head of the FSB because Yuri wanted someone under his control. It was a delicate balance—find out what Rzaev was up to without angering Yuri. To do so he needed information, which was why he was meeting with an informer who worked with Rzaev. It was the type of meeting that the head of the FSB should have delegated to someone else—if there were anyone else that he trusted enough to send. He'd told Lyudmila that he was going out, not where he was going.

Tomas leaned over and kissed her cheek. "Now can we eat this excellent meal you've prepared? And maybe we will get a cat for Emma."

20

MONDAY NIGHT, MOSCOW, RUSSIA

A THREE-PRONGED CANDELABRA LIT the Borodin, the posh Moscow restaurant named for the composer and specializing in Russian and Chinese dumplings. Tomas clutched his briefcase filled with American dollars, waited for his eyes to adjust, and pushed down his doubts. He had to do this.

He swung his gaze around the room and found his appointment.

Overweight, double chins, bald, Gavrill Alkaev sat with his back to the wall, a clear view of the room and the entrance, close to a corridor leading to the bathroom, the kitchen and a back door. Wine and dumplings were delivered by a blonde waitress in a red and gold dress as Tomas reached the table.

"*Dobry vercher*, Tomas. Have some dumplings." Gavrill indicated the plate and then helped himself with his fingers. "Best in Moscow."

Tomas seated himself. "I've already eaten, and I don't have a lot of time. What do you have for me?"

Gavrill licked a finger. "First, what do you have for me? Information is a commodity."

Tomas placed the briefcase on the table and shoved it across the table.

Gavrill finished a dumpling filled with potato and leeks, wiped his hands on a napkin, and snapped open the case. "I said a million in American dollars. This is maybe fifty thousand."

"It's what I could get together quickly."

"It's not enough."

"The rest will come in installments. Information first."

Gavrill drank some of the wine. "Do you know what Rzaev would do if he found out that I was talking to you?"

"I have a pretty good idea. Which is why I gave you enough to get out of the country. You have my word that I will pay you the rest."

Gavrill filled his wine glass again. "So here's what I'll do. I'll tell you something to whet your appetite. I'll tell you the rest when you pay up."

Tomas didn't change expression. "Fine."

"Rzaev smuggled something very dangerous into the United States."

"I already knew that. He smuggled Novichok across the Canadian border. The Americans also know."

Gavrill raised a finger. "There is much that you don't know."

"Which is why I'm here. And why I'm paying you. Where did Rzaev get the Novichok? Is he working with terrorists?"

"What neither you nor the Americans know is that there's enough Novichok to kill thousands, if dispersed in crowded areas. The Americans, by the way, are sending spies to St. Petersburg to find out about the Novichok."

This was big news. Yuri couldn't object to his hunting down American spies.

"Where? When?"

"You should ask Fyodor Mikailovich Dyakov who is an FSB officer, I believe. He spies for the Americans."

"How do you know this?"

Gavrill shrugged. "You have sources. Rzaev has sources. And that's all I'm saying until you come up with all the money." He started to reach for another dumpling, and then he froze. Tomas turned in his seat. Three large men had entered the restaurant and were surveying the patrons. He swiveled back to ask Gavrill who they were, but Gavrill had already acted.

For a man of his girth, Gavrill could move quickly. He pushed past a startled waiter, knocking a tray of dumplings, and broke into a run. Tomas pushed his chair back and stood.

The three men ignored Tomas and chased Gavrill.

Tomas followed them. He drew a gun from his pocket, but he was a poor shot. And the three men intent on Gavrill probably could shoot accurately. If he opened fire, they'd shoot back.

Lyudmila and the children. He needed to stay alive for them.

So why was he following? What could he do?

It didn't matter that he could do nothing. He couldn't stop himself.

Patrons screamed and dishes crashed as the men shoved their way through the restaurant. Gavrill slammed through the double doors into the cavernous kitchen with the men close on his heels.

Tomas forced himself to run, but he was out of shape and much too slow. Ahead of him, gunfire exploded, and glass shattered. He pushed through to the kitchen, where the cooking staff cowered behind a steel counter, the floor littered with shattered white china, crystal glasses, and bits of dumplings.

"Where?" He panted.

A woman, black eyes shining in terror, pointed towards a half open screen door to an alley.

Tomas ran through the kitchen, shoes crunching on the debris, and through the door.

The three men had vanished. Gavrill lay on the ground in a pool of blood. Tomas groped for his phone and dialed for an ambulance.

The ambulance would be too late. Gavrill was still breathing but he was split open from his navel to just below the ribcage, his intestines pulled outside his body.

The briefcase was gone.

As Tomas knelt next to him, Gavrill's eyes fluttered open. He grabbed at the front of Tomas's shirt. Then he died.

21

MONDAY AFTERNOON, I-95, DELAWARE

ALEX DROVE NORTH ON the interstate out of D.C., doing a comfortable five miles above the speed limit. Tehila rode shotgun—literally. A large duffel bag containing the Mossberg and several other weapons rested on the floor, out of sight but within reach. Her presence should have been reassuring. It wasn't.

Damn the whole business.

Annoyed as she was at a forced vacation from her law practice, worried though she was about her own personal safety from the attackers, it was nothing compared to how afraid Alex was for Kolya. She knew what could happen. She'd seen him chained to a floor, barely alive after days of torture. She'd pushed the image away while he'd been working as an attorney, even though she knew he hated the job. He was bored, but he was safe. No longer. He could be in agony somewhere, and she wouldn't know. They would tell her if he died, but they wouldn't tell her how he died—or what had happened to him before he died.

I'm not going to die.

As if he could promise he'd be safe.

Alex increased her speed to pass a truck.

"Not too fast, Alex. If we're stopped, the state police might ask about the guns, and it could be awkward." Tehila pulled down the passenger visor mirror as if checking her makeup. But she wasn't. She shifted in her seat, and Alex saw her check the driver side mirror.

"What?"

"The same car has been behind us since Georgetown."

Alex hadn't seen Tehila looking earlier.

"Which car?"

"Black Mercedes. Three or four cars back. Don't change speed."

"Shit. Are you sure?"

"I'm sure it's been behind us. I'm not sure it's following. Let's find out. Take the next exit. I could use a coffee anyway."

A sign advertised a Starbucks and a Burger King at the next exit.

Alex put on her right blinker and changed lanes. She looked in the mirror. Three cars back, a black Mercedes changed lanes, but it was far enough back that she couldn't see a license plate. Then she signaled again and moved onto the exit lane, slowing her speed. She was at the bottom of the ramp when she again caught sight of the Mercedes trailing behind. Almost too slow.

"Starbucks." Tehila pointed. "Turn right."

She turned. The Mercedes let her get a few hundred feet ahead before it turned as well.

The green two-tailed mermaid on the Starbucks logo on the left side of the street beckoned with a promise of caffeine. Next door, Burger King welcomed travelers to red meat, carbohydrates, and fat. Alex waited for a Toyota Highlander to pass, and then pulled across the lane into the nearly empty Starbucks parking lot.

Alex checked her mirrors. No Mercedes. "Where?"

"He drove past us to the Burger King." Tehila nodded towards the parking lot next door. She leaned over, unzipped the duffel bag at her feet, and pulled out an assault style gun.

Tehila saw Alex's expression. "Galil SAR. Israeli make. How is your high-speed driving?"

"I know some techniques." She'd had some courses in defensive driving and weapons during the short period she'd worked as legal counsel to the ECA. Kolya had reinforced the training. "What's next?"

"Coffee from the drive-thru. A latte for me, triple shots of espresso. Then we'll see." Tehila calmly placed the Galil SAR in the crevice between the door and her seat, her body blocking it from sight, pulled out her phone, and tapped it. She glanced over at Alex. "It's a special app—from the office."

Alex steered around the building, ordered, and picked up the coffees from a friendly teenager who smiled at both of them. Alex smiled back, hoping Tehila's gun was sufficiently hidden, and set the coffee in the drink holders. Then she drove past the building to a parking spot. She caught a glimpse of the Mercedes in the Burger King parking lot next door.

"Why the coffee?" Alex's stomach was tightening. She ignored her steamed latte in the cup holder near her. She was already on edge.

Tehila picked up her cup, removed the lid, and drank off half the contents. "I didn't sleep much last night. Caffeine helps. And lattes taste good." She replaced the lid, returned the cup securely to its holder, and retrieved the Galil.

"You know, we could just shoot out the tires of that car. Right now."

"Are you serious?"

"Not completely. But it'd solve the problem, wouldn't it?"

"Yes, but it wouldn't be discreet. There are cameras. We'd have police on us before we went ten miles."

"Yes, the ECA motto. Be discreet." Be discreet and betray your agents.

"Always. This will be better. No cameras. Are you ready?"

"It doesn't matter if I am or not."

Tehila reached over and patted her hand. "We'll be fine." She glanced over at the Mercedes, then she slung the Galil on her shoulder and climbed over the space between the seats to the back, situating herself directly behind Alex. "Just follow my directions. Out of the parking lot, turn right."

The entrance to the interstate was to the left. "Fast or slow?"

"Slow out of the parking lot. Then I'll direct you. Okay?"

"Okay," Alex lied.

"Then go."

She gripped the steering wheel. Her hands felt sweaty, and her heart raced. She drove through the parking lot and turned right onto the street. Traffic was light; one car ahead of her going maybe fifty. The road they were on veered away from the interstate. She passed a gas station, a convenience store, and then they were in the country. Trees and open fields. She heard the faint sounds of the highway reverberating to her left.

"Slow," Tehila said.

Keeping the car at thirty, Alex checked the rear-view mirror. A green pick-up truck tailgated her, the driver gesturing and flashing his lights.

He honked and the truck swung into the left lane, speeding past. The driver, a young man in a baseball cap, lowered the window and shouted an obscenity. Alex waved back. A friendly wave.

"Always assholes on the road. Concentrate." Tehila's voice was directly behind her. "We're almost there. Right turn in half a mile. A quarter mile."

Alex calmed her breathing. She could see the green street sign ahead.

"Five hundred feet. Two hundred. One hundred. Now. Turn slowly, proceed a hundred yards, then floor it."

Alex took the turn. With the Mercedes momentarily out of sight, she cruised a hundred yards and then shoved the gas petal down. The Volvo roared forward.

"Are they following?"

Tehila voice in her ear again. "Just made the turn, and now they're speeding up. Good. That they're chasing us means that they are not innocent and that they're going to try to force things. Maybe push us off the road."

"It's good?"

"If there were a second car to call in, they wouldn't risk chasing us. And perhaps there's some overconfidence about dealing with two women. Turn in five hundred feet. Four hundred. Three hundred. Two hundred. Now!"

Alex tapped the brake, slowing enough to control the car for the turn. Her tires screeched in protest, and she remembered Kolya's instructions on not over correcting with the steering. The Mercedes would be following in a few minutes. Maybe a few seconds. She made a wide turn onto a two-lane road. The open fields on either side of the road fresh smelled of newly turned earth. She increased her speed again.

The road was empty except for a propane truck rumbling in the other direction.

"The truck needs to get off the road before our next move. Keep going." Tehila bent forward and whispered new instructions.

She pressed the gas petal and checked her mirrors. The Mercedes was coming, but it was still half a mile behind. The truck was at the corner, its turn signal flashing red. "The truck's turning."

"A little farther," Tehila said.

The steering wheel vibrated with the speed. She glanced at the speedometer. 120 mph. She glanced in the mirror. The truck's front end had disappeared around the turn. The Mercedes was gaining. "Now?"

"Now."

Nothing in the on-coming lane. Only the Mercedes behind her.

She slammed on the brakes, pulled on the handbrake, and hand over hand, turned the wheel to the left. She fought for control of the car, swinging the car 180 degrees. She released the handbrake.

And stopped.

A breeze chilled the back of her neck from the lowered rear window. She watched the Mercedes hurtling towards them. She could now see only one form in the car—the driver.

The Mercedes was slowing, the driver leaning sideways towards the passenger seat as if reaching for a gun.

Out of the corner of her eye, she saw the barrel of the Galil SAR extend from the back window and heard the deafening explosion of gunfire. The windshield on the Mercedes shattered. The Mercedes shuddered to a stop. The driver ducked under the dashboard.

Tehila changed her aim. The front tires on the Mercedes exploded.

"GO!" Tehila ordered.

Alex hit the gas, and they sped past the Mercedes. Tehila, leaning out the window, fired one last burst behind them—blowing the rear tires as well. Alex turned left at the end of the street, slowed down to the legal limit, and took the entrance ramp back onto I-95.

* * * * *

The driver of the Mercedes, unhurt except for a few facial cuts from the shards of windshield glass, jogged back to the Burger King in less than thirty minutes, where he ordered a Whopper and a chocolate milk shake. He carried his food outside to a bench where he sat alone and ate the burger between slurps of the shake, calming down as he ate. Then he took out his cell phone and texted. *Heading north.*

22

TUESDAY MORNING, FRANKFURT, GERMANY

KOLYA, IN THE WINDOW seat, listened to a jazz version of Stravinsky's Rite of Spring by the Bad Plus, that he had downloaded onto the burner phone that he would be carrying, as the plane's landing gear groaned into position. He liked it—the discordant tones were Stravinsky, but it was an innovative take on the piece.

He leaned his head against the glass to watch first rays of the sun touch the city of Frankfurt spread out beneath the plane. It would be a quick stop over then on to St. Petersburg.

Next to him, Dmitri stirred. "I have never been to Germany. You?"

"Just in passing." Kolya turned off the music.

"You never worked here? I thought all spies came to Germany."

"It's not the Cold War anymore."

"Maybe not, but America does still hate Russia."

"Were you under the impression that Russia is no longer a bad actor in the world?"

"Every country acts badly. It is how they hold power."

"But some are worse than others. Much worse. Russia is on top of the much worse list."

"Maybe. Still, how do you work with people who dislike you for who you are? That CIA agent at the prison for example."

"We had a work issue. He doesn't like Egan either."

"I watched him when we all talked together. I am good at judging people. Usually. He might not like Egan, but he despises you. Tell me that is not because you are Russian and a Jew."

"Perhaps. But I work with people I trust."

"Do you? How did you hurt your knee?"

"Skiing."

"Bullshit. You got hurt on the job. That is why you quit, isn't it?"

"Okay, yes. I quit after I was injured on the job."

"It had to be more than just an injury to make you quit."

"It was sufficient."

"If you say so. But do not tell me not to lie to you when you are lying to me."

"Enough." Kolya turned the music on again.

TUESDAY NOON, THE KREMLIN, MOSCOW

Yuri was in a good mood. He'd called the lunch meeting at the last minute, and there were only three of them, Tomas, Yuri and Yuri's current mistress, Galina, in attendance. They ate in Yuri's private dining room, a room that almost shimmered from the crystal chandelier overhead, the crystal glasses and gold plates on the table. Tomas sat on the long side of the twenty-foot oak table. Galina sat on Yuri's lap. Servants offered trays of sturgeon caviar and Kamchatka crab, fried in a sweet dough, herring in beetroot and pickles—while Yuri hand fed Galina delicacies and made jokes.

Tomas distrusted Yuri's good moods even more than he feared Yuri's anger. Under other circumstances, he would have appreciated the quality of the food, but waiting to hear why he'd been summoned and watching what could only be described as foreplay between Yuri and his mistress made Tomas more than usually uncomfortable.

They finished the main course, shashlik—meat kabobs, made from pheasant—and with a smack on her rear, Yuri sent Galina out of the room.

"Did you enjoy lunch?" Yuri wiped his hands and mouth on a silk napkin. "I have important information to give you, as my head of the FSB." He raised a hand, summoning the head server, signaling for the desert, honey cake, and coffee.

Tomas sipped his coffee, waiting.

Yuri took a large bite of cake. "Rzaev did not smuggle nerve agent into the United States. It's all a lie. You can relax."

Tomas nibbled a corner of his cake. He was full from the indulgent lunch, but it was hard to pass up on the cream and honey combination. "Why would the American President call you and be upset about Novichok in the United States if it was just a hoax?"

Yuri finished chewing, swallowed, and then slammed his hand on the table. His good mood had disappeared. "Are you doubting me?"

"No. It just seems odd."

"The Americans are always trying to make Russia look bad. To make ME look bad."

Tomas could almost hear Lyudmila's voice. *He's very dangerous. Do whatever he wants.* He raised another forkful of the cake, feeling the heat of Yuri's gaze on him, chewed, swallowed, and forced himself to smile. "Of course. The damn Americans. Never taking responsibility."

Yuri's face relaxed a little. "Exactly. Always blaming Russia. Or in this case, a perfectly innocent businessman like Rzaev."

Did Yuri actually believe this? Tomas wasn't sure. But Tomas knew better. Rzaev might have legitimate business interests, but he was not an innocent businessman. Tomas knew from Gavrill Alkaev that Rzaev had not only smuggled Novichok into the United States, but had smuggled enough to kill thousands. And Gavrill Alkaev had paid with his life for giving Tomas that meager bit of information.

Tomas ate another bite of his cake. It was suddenly dry and tasting like paper.

He thought about the other information that Gavrill had revealed and decided to share. "On another subject, I have learned that American spies are arriving today in St. Petersburg. I am planning to fly up this afternoon to oversee an operation to intercept and arrest them."

"Source?" Yuri asked.

"I had an informer who unfortunately died last night."

"Too bad," Yuri said. "But I like your thinking. Find out what the spies are up to. That's what I pay you to do."

And if the spies led him to Rzaev and the Novichok? Tomas remained concerned that he could be blamed if Rzaev had indeed smuggled Novichok into America. He would follow the information to where it led.

Best though, not to indicate what he was thinking. "This cake is wonderful. Is there any extra for me to take to Lyudmila and the children?"

"Of course." Yuri beamed and waved a hand. The head server reappeared, and Yuri ordered slices of cake to be boxed for Tomas's family.

TUESDAY AFTERNOON, LUBYANKA, MOSCOW

At his desk in the Lubyanka, Tomas felt the weight of the history of the building. Here in his office with the large desk and the leather chairs, the thick carpet, the bookshelves and his desk decorated with pictures of his wife and children, orders had originated to round up and execute men and women for nothing more than the vague suspicion of disloyalty. In the courtyard below, so many "enemies of the state" had met their fate—a bullet in the back of the head.

And now *he* was in charge.

Natalia, his secretary, tapped and then opened the door. Young and attractive, but wearing too much eye make-up and perpetually low-cut blouses, Natalia had come with the office. Despite his appointment as Director, Tomas had no authority to replace her. Yuri had made that quite clear. It had to do with seniority, Yuri had said.

Early on, she'd offered herself for extra-curricular evening work, but Tomas had no interest in any woman besides his wife. Even if he had, he knew better. Natalia was undoubtedly a graduate of the sparrow school of seduction.

He also suspected her placement in his office was not only to spy on him, but a test—whether he was stupid enough to fall for the oldest espionage trick in the book.

But she was very good. She appeared to be nothing more than the most loyal of secretaries. "Fyodor Mikhailovich has arrived from St. Petersburg and is waiting outside."

"Please."

Natalia ushered in a man wearing glasses who looked more than slightly nervous and whose lined face made him appear older than his actual age. She announced his name again, and he stood in front of Tomas's desk, shifting his weight uneasily.

"Please sit, Fyodor Mikhailovich. You're in time for tea. Natalia, for both of us, please."

Fyodor sat, took off his glasses, and cleaned them with a handkerchief. Natalie returned and set the tray with glasses, a gleaming white tea pot, cloth napkins, two silver spoons, and a jar of strawberry jam on his desk, bending over, her blouse falling open to the bra. She checked whether he'd noticed.

She didn't give up easily, but Tomas wasn't tempted.

"Thank you, Natalia." Tomas poured steaming tea into his heavy glass and stirred a spoonful of jam into the tea as she stalked out. Fyodor followed his lead. Tomas sipped his tea and waited until Fyodor raised his own glass to his lips. "How long have you been giving information to the Americans?"

Fyodor's hand shook, and he spilled tea and jam onto his shirt.

"Napkin." Tomas pointed to the tray. "That must have burned."

Fyodor mopped his shirt and took the moment to compose himself. "I don't know what you're talking about."

Tomas folded his hands on top of the desk and waited until Fyodor replaced his napkin. All he had against Fyodor was the word of a known criminal. He'd gone through the files and been unable to verify one way or another. The only one who could verify the information was the suspect himself. But wasn't the information already verified by Fyodor's demeanor?

Maybe not. This was the Lubyanka, after all. How many innocent people had died here? But then no one was truly innocent, were they— as Stalin had once said? Stalin, the monster.

Tomas didn't like the idea of following in Stalin's footsteps. Nevertheless, he had a job to do.

"I haven't told the President of your treason," Tomas said. "Yet. But if you insist on denying the truth, I will have to inform him—and he won't be as understanding as I am."

Fyodor set the glass on the desk. "You wouldn't have vodka, would you?"

Tomas pulled a bottle out of his bottom right desk drawer and handed it across the desk. Fyodor poured two fingers worth into the tea and drained the glass. He poured another half a glass and drank that as well.

"Let's start again," Tomas said. "How long have you worked for the Americans?"

The vodka had had an effect. Fyodor's face was flushed instead of pale, and he had the determined look of a man who thought he was going to die. "Five years."

Five years was before Tomas's tenure as FSB director. Yuri would have been president for four years before that time. Had Fyodor betrayed Russia out of some sense of idealism or for money?

The reason didn't matter. Nor did the sympathy that Tomas was feeling for Fyodor. All that mattered was that Fyodor had information that would be useful.

"Who is your contact?"

Fyodor shrugged. "I don't have any one contact. We communicate through dead drops and burner phones—occasionally we set up an in-person hand-off."

Tomas suspected that it wasn't the full truth, but whether it was or not didn't really matter. He poured Fyodor another drink and then poured vodka into his own tea.

"Has anyone been in touch lately?" Tomas drank his tea and watched Fyodor—who hesitated. Then he added a different question. "Your wife's a teacher, isn't she?"

He saw true terror in Fyodor's face. "She didn't know what I was doing."

"I'm glad to hear that. I'd hate to have to bring her here." Then he repeated, "When are the American spies arriving and what information are they after?"

Fyodor reached for the bottle. "They wanted to know why Rzaev smuggled Novichok into the United States, whether President Bykovsky had ordered it, and whether I knew Rzaev's location."

"Are you going to meet with them?"

Fyodor drank again and didn't answer.

"Do I have to bring your wife here?"

Fyodor set the glass on the desk. "I am supposed to meet an agent this evening in St. Petersburg. I have a flight in two hours."

"And that agent is?"

"I don't know his name. All I know is that he's a former Russian national working for the ECA."

"Do you know where he's staying or what name he's traveling under?"

Fyodor shook his head. "There's a set meeting place and a set time. Otherwise, I know nothing of his plans."

There were hundreds of thousands of visitors in St. Petersburg this time of year. Thousands of Americans among them. A spy could easily blend in.

Fyodor poured and drank again.

"Okay, so we are going to fly to St. Petersburg together. You will not alert this spy or anyone else that you have been compromised. If all goes well, I will forget that you have betrayed your country and your service."

23

TUESDAY LATE AFTERNOON, NEVSKII PROSPECKT, ST. PETERSBURG, RUSSIA

BRIGHT SUNLIGHT STILL FLOODED the Nevskii Prospeckt. This city of bridges and canals had been the capital of Russia under the czars, and the recently restored museums and palaces reflected that past glory. The crowds of White Night revelers were just starting to emerge from homes and hotels where they had slept off the traditional late-night overindulgence. People came from around the world to this yearly festival of nights of unending sunlight with music, fireworks, food, and other appetite indulgences, and even though most activities occurred at night, people wandered the city throughout the day.

Kolya and Dmitri proceeded slowly down the Prospeckt. Dmitri paused every few steps to look in store windows, to point out sights, or to smile at attractive women. The slow pace was fine with Kolya. The knee brace helped, the injection had helped, but the pain was there, an unwanted companion, like the PTSD. He also wore his gun under a sweater and jacket, his HK .40 that he'd managed to smuggle into the country inside specially constructed fake cans of shaving cream and a hair dryer, and a knife strapped to his leg. It was risky smuggling the gun into Russia, but given that he was meeting with a mafiya boss, he didn't want to go unarmed. The knife would only be good for close personal defense, but he liked the extra insurance.

The last time he had walked the Prospeckt during the White Nights, the city had still been shabby, with decaying facades and few tourists. In the 19th century, St. Petersburg had been compared to Venice, but with

World War II and Soviet policies, the city had deteriorated. He'd still loved it. He'd especially loved the White Nights. But then, he'd been nine years old.

Still, a beautiful city then and now restored to its full glory, the city shone during the White Nights. Someday he'd like to visit when he wasn't on a job. Someday when there wasn't a dangerous autocrat running the country. He pictured walking the Prospeckt with Alex on an endless bright evening in June, as he had with his mother on a long-ago June—and then he banished the thought.

He caught a glimpse of Jonathan and Elizabeth across the street, strolling arm in arm. No one looking at them would think they were anything but a loving couple on vacation. No sight of Teo. Had Teo developed such good tradecraft that Kolya couldn't spot him?

"You know, it is easy to get laid during White Nights." Dmitri stopped to admire a dark-haired woman who caught his gaze and smiled back. He spoke in Russian, even though their passports were American. There were American and British tourists there for the festival, but using English could still draw unwanted attention. "I have already seen some prospects. And they are looking at you as much as at me."

"We're here on business." Even if Kolya were interested in anyone besides Alex, which he wasn't, having sex would be a good way to get killed or compromise an operation. "Not for sex."

"Easy for you to say. You were not in prison for ten years, jacking off to pictures in magazines." Dmitri smiled at another passing woman.

"A few days, and then you'll be in Florida. I'm sure you'll find plenty of women who would be interested in a man with ten million dollars and a house on the Intercoastal."

"I am not looking for a relationship—just a good fuck. Or maybe a dozen good fucks. I first got laid during the White Nights, when I was sixteen. Did I ever tell you?"

"No. But then I was in New York, and we'd lost touch."

"Not completely. You sent me some letters."

"You didn't reply. I'd call that out of touch."

Dmitri shrugged. "I did not read them. I was pissed you got to go to America, and I had to stay in that shithole. I asked you not to leave."

"And I asked my cousin if she could bring you to America. She couldn't manage it."

"You never told me that."

"I did. In the letters that you didn't read."

The scorching sun was directly overhead. Too warm for St. Petersburg in early June. Global warming was reaching here as well.

Dmitri turned his face to the sun. "Good just to be outside, no? I kept one letter, even if I never read it. That's how I had your cousin's address when I got to New York. You should text your woman, by the way. Tell her you arrived safely."

"I'm not involved with anyone." Dmitri'd already tried to draw Kolya into a discussion of his personal life—but Kolya wasn't biting. Even if he had regrets for their lost friendship, he knew better than to reveal his greatest vulnerability.

"I know you. You are the kind of man who would always be involved with someone. Remember when we met up for drinks—right after I arrived in New York. You were in love with some woman who had a boyfriend—and you were trying to decide whether to tell her what you felt. What was her name?"

Alex. How could he have been so stupid, even ten years ago, to mention her name to Dmitri? But that was before he realized what Dmitri was doing—before he knew that Dmitri's gang was killing people in Little Odessa in Brooklyn. Before he'd found his cousin Rifka sobbing over a friend who'd been caught in the crossfire. It was also years before Kolya and Alex became romantically involved.

The perils of youth and vodka.

"I'm not sure; it was a long time ago. There have been a lot of women since then. I'd like to sit for a few minutes." Kolya spotted a bench next to the Russian Library and headed for it, Dmitri trailing. He leaned back on the bench, relishing the warmth of the sunlight, stretched his injured leg, and winched as the knee straightened. Dmitri sat down next to him.

"Knee?" Dmitri asked.

"Just tired." He glanced across the street, searching for Elizabeth and Jonathan, hoping that they wouldn't be visible. Dmitri wouldn't know Elizabeth, but he knew Jonathan. Fortunately, they were out of sight.

"Bullshit. You are in pain. You need to trust me and stop lying."

"I trust you. But not completely."

Dmitri laughed. "I don't trust you completely either. So we are back to the beginning."

"Not really. Too much has happened, and we've both changed."

"You have changed more than I have."

"Perhaps."

"No perhaps about it. You were on the same path I was on. We would have both gone to work for Rzaev. Maybe you would have been in charge of North America and not me. Instead here we are. Anyway, where are we walking now? We have to see Ivan Minsky after midnight. Maybe you should rest that leg."

Kolya was bringing Dmitri to the meeting with Fyodor to keep an eye on him, but Dmitri had no need to know in advance. While he was trusting his own life to Dmitri's questionable loyalties, Kolya was not going to increase the risk to Fyodor by informing Dmitri in advance even though Kolya wasn't sure that Fyodor had worthwhile information.

Still, information was a weapon, and he didn't like the idea of walking blind into a meeting with Rzaev. On the chance that Fyodor had learned something of value, Kolya would give it a try.

"We're meeting a friend."

"This friend have a name?"

"Most people do."

"We are playing games then."

"It's what I do." Or what he used to do.

"This is stupid, Kolya. We will get to Volodya through Ivan and talking to an unknown "friend" will get you nothing. Except maybe caught by people who will kill both of us."

"Volodya might be working with Yuri." Kolya used the first name of the Russian president and well as the first name of the oligarch. "That's important to know. For many reasons."

Dmitri raised his hands in a gesture indicated frustration. "Okay. What it is the Americans say—dig your own grave. Only it will be a grave for two."

"Maybe." Kolya checked his watch and reluctantly pushed off the bench. He glanced around again. Still no sign of Jonathan, Elizabeth or Teo. "But hopefully not."

* * * * *

The Anichkov *most*, which stretched across the Fontanka River, was a famous tourist destination, with statues of rearing horses on the four pillars of each end. The bridge, with museums and palaces on either side of the river, was well trafficked and in many ways, a good location for spies to meet.

It was the preset meeting spot between Fyodor and the Americans. A perfect place to meet and to set a trap.

Fyodor waited for the American spy in the middle of the bridge. FSB officers stationed on either side of the bridge were under instructions to let the spy speak to Fyodor—and only afterwards, take him into custody.

Tomas had ten people, five on each side of the bridge, who could move in quickly once the spy appeared. Tomas had decided to keep the numbers down, to avoid detection and because these ten were loyal to him. While Yuri had okayed capturing an American spy, Yuri might not be happy if that capture led to information about Rzaev. Tomas still didn't know why Yuri was protecting someone who had, according to Yuri, smuggled a deadly poison into the United States without Yuri's knowledge. But, by finding out the truth, Tomas was protecting himself from being blamed as well as protecting innocent people. Best to only have people whom Tomas knew he could count on.

Unfortunately, he had no idea what the man looked like, let alone his name. He hadn't found any pictures, and Fyodor had been vague in his description. On the tall side, medium weight—whatever that meant, nondescript features. Nothing to really go on, and even if there was, a good spy can easily change his appearance.

Of course, there was the possibility that Fyodor was lying and that the cap he was wearing to signal all clear would signal just the opposite. Still, Tomas had watchers and cameras on everyone who even came near Fyodor. Hopefully, the American would be caught, even if Fyodor tried to warn him off.

But given that an American spy might recognize the FSB Director, Tomas decided to wait a little farther off. At a café a block from the bridge, he ordered coffee and pastries, and checked that his people were ready and waiting.

24

TUESDAY NOON, STOWE, VERMONT

TEHILA ROOTED THROUGH THE refrigerator and the cupboard, having nixed the idea of picking up take-out. She also nixed Uber Eats or any other delivery service, if they even had delivery in Stowe. Although she found it a little excessive, Alex understood—Tehila was protecting her, and that meant keeping out of sight. If there'd been a team, someone could have gone out for egg rolls—or pizza—or anything besides canned tuna and canned salmon. The lack of a team meant scrounging through cans and frozen food that she or her cousins had stocked on previous visits.

But pathetic food options were the least of her concerns. She hated just sitting around—she loved her work, and here she was—forced to remain incommunicado. It made her uneasy—even though things were under control in her dual life as a law firm partner and as founder of a non-profit working on innocence projects. She had a continuance for two appearances that week in court, and her partners were picking up the slack even if they grumbled about it. Her innocence non-profit had volunteer attorneys handling any urgent matters. And she could do some work—she was writing an appellate criminal brief for the non-profit and a summary judgment motion for her practice. Still, she missed being in the middle of the action, the day-to-day interaction with her colleagues, the ability to pick up the phone to call clients or witnesses.

She also had no idea how long she had to remain hidden. Until Kolya returned—or the ECA located the people who'd attacked her family. Whichever came first.

113

Then there was Kolya. The never ceasing worrying over him.

Alex checked her phone. It was a burner, but he had the number. He could have texted. He hadn't.

"You know he's on a job." Having volunteered to make lunch, Tehila mixed mayo and jalapenos into canned tuna, tasted it, and then for good measure, stirred in cumin, turmeric, and coriander. "And it's just not always possible to stay in touch, frustrating though it may be. My wife hates it, too."

"I know." It was part of the bargain when she'd made the very conscious decision to move from being friends with Kolya to being lovers. She had always accepted his profession, trusting that he would come back safe. She no longer did.

He wasn't dead. They would have told her.

Maybe.

"He'll be okay." Tehila tasted the mixture and stirred in red pepper.

"It wasn't true last time."

"That was different. He'd been set up. This time, he's not. And he's got a good team. Why is it so cold in here?" The room was about sixty-five degrees. Tehila wore a long-sleeve shirt and had pulled on her leather jacket for good measure. The Galil rested on the floor within easy reach, and she wore a Glock on her hip.

"It's Vermont. June isn't exactly balmy. There might be a can of soup if you'd like something hot." Alex hated to cook, but microwaving soup was something she couldn't screw up. In the cupboard she found a can of clam chowder that she'd bought for a ski trip two winters ago. Not kosher. She found tomato soup for Tehila.

She turned, can of soup in hand, and saw Tehila had abandoned the tuna salad and had picked up the Galil.

"Get down, Alex."

Alex obeyed, falling to the floor and pulling her own gun from her pocket. Tehila flattened against the wall and took out her phone, glancing alternatively checking the windows and her phone.

On her knees and elbows, gun in hand, Alex crawled to a spot out of view of the windows. She cautiously stood, back to the wall. "What did you see?" She refused to be helpless. If necessary, she could defend herself. "Sensor alert?"

Kolya had placed sensors around the property a year earlier, and

Tehila had downloaded the app to check them.

"No. A glint through the trees. Light reflecting off something metal or glass. Someone, not on your property, on the trail behind the house."

Sterling Forest ran past the back of the property, and hikers frequented the trail.

Tehila tapped her phone and then showed Alex a picture of a man. "Do you know him?"

A twenty-something guy in typical Vermont gear, flannel shirts, jeans, was carrying a camera with a long lens and taking pictures—apparently of the house.

"I've never seen him. You put a camera on the trail?"

"Yes, several. And several on the road up to the house. I was a little concerned that someone could get close without my knowing it. The sensors that Kolya put up are good, but only when someone is actually on the property—which wouldn't give me much time to react."

"You think this guy could be a threat?"

"I'm not sure. That's why I'm watching."

Tehila continued to watch both the area of the trail and her phone for another twenty minutes, at which point, she replaced the rifle on the floor and slipped the phone into a pocket. "He's gone. I think it's okay for now." She returned to the tuna salad, stirred, tasted, and nodded. Then she toasted rye bread and made two sandwiches. "Let's have lunch."

Alex pocketed her gun, accepted a plate, and followed Tehila to the kitchen table. Tehila laid her phone next to her plate, before pronouncing the blessing: *Baruch atah, Adonai Eloheinu, Melech haolam, haMotzi lechem min haaretz.* Alex knew the prayer but hadn't said it since Hebrew school. She didn't believe in a God that heard prayers or answered them. But the prayer linked her to her childhood, and to hundreds of years of her people's history—and since Romania, she'd become more interested in connecting to that history. Not enough of a reason for her to become religious, but enough that she found hearing the Hebrew to be comforting.

What she also found odd was that Tehila, a deadly operative, seemed to have a different view—either of God or the rituals.

"Do you really believe there's a God that hears your prayers?" Alex asked in between bites of her sandwich. "And isn't it difficult to be an observant Jew on this job?"

"I believe that HaShem left operating instructions, which may or may not be a bit obscure, but day to day things are pretty much up to us. I do what I can when I can. I'm not orthodox. There are times I cheat on the dietary rules and times I violate Shabbat—or some of the other rules. I figure HaShem will forgive lapses on my part, since it's for a greater good. And I don't find it difficult. I find it restorative. Like meditation."

"Killing people?"

"I only kill bad people. Have you ever read the Bible? The ancient Israelites killed people right and left."

"Which is one of the reasons I'm not religious."

"We're not Quakers."

"And being gay?"

"I don't belong to a congregation that would find it problematic."

Tehila's phone buzzed and she picked it up. Alex tensed, but Tehila glanced at it and put it back on the table.

"It's not about Kolya?"

"No. And it wouldn't be either. Anything about Kolya is *need to know*. I don't need to know, and you don't either."

Alex narrowed her eyes. "Au contraire. I'd say I have very much a need to know what's going on with Kolya—given that the ECA fucked him over last time."

She didn't get a rise out of Tehila. "You and Kolya will both need to clean up your language if you have kids. Alex, if I had any information about Kolya, I'd share it with you. But both of us are out of the loop." Tehila swallowed her bite of tuna sandwich. "The text was from Mark Leslie. I sent him the pictures of the man on the trail."

"And?"

"Nothing." Tehila took another bite. "At least nothing so far. Mark will dive a little deeper. It may be nothing more than a guy who took a fancy to your house."

"So you think it's safe?"

"I'm reserving judgment. But I think we're okay to eat lunch."

25

TUESDAY EVENING, ST. PETERSBURG, RUSSIA

KOLYA SAW NOTHING OF his back-up team for the next ten minutes, as he and Dmitri continued their walk to the Anichkov bridge. He assumed they were ahead, checking the area around the meet. If Fyodor had been compromised, he'd be under surveillance—and there would be FSB agents nearby waiting.

He was deliberately walking slower, not because his leg hurt, which it did, but to spot anyone who might be trailing them. Or waiting for them.

More people strolled the Prospeckt as the afternoon turned to evening. Kolya paused in front of a sidewalk café to read the menu, watching for anyone stopping or turning away. Nothing.

Next to him, Dmitri also read the menu. "I would not mind something to eat. We have time?"

Kolya was always up for coffee. "We do." The Anichkov bridge was a block away, and they had close to an hour before the scheduled rendezvous. Never be early. Or late.

He surveyed the café tables. Two couples enjoyed dinner. A family with three young children very loudly shared desserts. In the corner, a middle-aged man, plump, dark haired, phone on the table in front of him, sat with his back to them, a glass of tea and a platter of desserts in front of him.

Dmitri was waiting. "So?"

"Why not?"

They were waved to a table with a full view of passersby. Since they didn't have enough time for a full meal, they ordered dessert and coffee.

"So your cousin…." Dmitri spoke with a mouth full of cream and cake. "Did she tell you why she couldn't bring me over?"

"Not in detail." Kolya finished his slice of sharkotka, apple cake with powdered sugar, and picked up his coffee cup. "She indicated that there were visa issues and money obstacles in bringing over a non-relative. I know you thought all Americans were rich, but she wasn't."

"She had enough to get you."

"She didn't have much left afterward." Kolya remembered his cousin's constant worrying about bills, her nagging at his leaving lights on or eating too much. It wasn't until after she died and he went through her papers that he realized she'd spent all of her savings to bring him over from Russia. "But if you'd bothered to read my letters, you'd know she'd invited you to live with us if you could make it to the States after you turned eighteen."

Dmitri finished the napoleon and wiped his hands. "I'm sorry I didn't read them. But even if I had, it would not have mattered. I ran away from the *dom* at fifteen and signed with Rzaev. By eighteen, I was already rising in the organization. And I liked it. The money. The power. It was addictive shit. Better than Ben & Jerry's."

"Is it still?"

"Addictive? No. I went, how you say, cold turkey. One thing in prison—you learn what is important. Freedom is pretty fucking nice." Dmitri drank more tea and leaned back in his chair, nodding at a young woman with black hair, a short skirt, and a good figure. "Are you sure you do not want to take a few hours to get laid?"

"We get back to the States alive—and you're free to fuck whoever. But not here. Not now." Kolya picked up his coffee and drank.

* * * * *

Jonathan bought Elizabeth an ice cream cone, and they continued arm in arm onto the Anichkov bridge. She nibbled on his ear. "Did you notice the ice cream vendor?" She breathed the words heavily.

The bite had been unusually hard.

"Damn, darling. I'd like to keep my ear. And yes, I did. Walk to the other side?"

She squeezed his arm. "Of course, darling." Then she nipped his ear again. "Your brother is meeting us there?"

He restrained a small yip and pulled her in for a kiss. She let him.

Crossing the bridge, Jonathan spotted Fyodor, whom he'd met twice before. Fyodor was leaning against a rail, tossing bread to the ducks in the river below. And he was wearing a baseball cap. Blue cap, but the color didn't matter.

It was the fact that he was wearing a cap.

"Fuck." Jonathan's curse word was under his breath.

Elizabeth pulled his head down to hers, the woman in love. "Don't slow down."

Fyodor didn't seem to notice them.

On the far side of the bridge, Teo, hands in pockets, walked towards them. "Hey, guys. Isn't this place great?" Then in an undertone, "They're doing electrical work right next to the entrance to the bridge."

"Huh," Jonathan said. "And right in the middle of White Nights."

* * * * *

Tomas checked his phone. Twenty minutes. He tried to stay calm. If he caught a spy, it wouldn't just be a coup for him. He might learn the truth about the Novichok, whether it was a hoax by the American government or whether there was a real concern. He would at the very least learn what the Americans hoped to do in Russia.

He sent encrypted messages to his people. *Ready?*

The answers came back. *Ready.*

They were in place. Fyodor was in place. Any time now.

* * * * *

Kolya paid for the coffee and deserts, and the two of them left the café. His stomach was tightening in anticipation. He'd seen nothing out of the ordinary, had he? As they left the café, Kolya glanced once again at the patrons enjoying a late afternoon snack. Two couples had left, and three more couples had taken tables. The family was long gone.

Only the middle-aged man remained, his pastry plate now empty, drinking tea and tapping on his phone. A long time to be sitting there.

But it didn't necessarily mean anything. He could just be waiting for someone… or something.

Kolya had only seen the back of the man's head. Maneuvering to get a better view would be obvious. The last thing he wanted to do was draw attention to himself.

But the man's continued presence troubled him.

He had always trusted his instincts, but was he paranoid now? Seeing dangers that didn't exist—because his perception of danger had shifted? *Maybe.* He'd re-evaluate when they got to the bridge.

* * * * *

Close to the entrance to the Anichkov bridge, where tourists marveled at the bronze statues of rearing horses, a cart partly obscured the view of the luxurious Beloselsky-Belozersky Palace across the river. An older woman scooped cones of *morozhenoe*, a sweet Russian ice cream.

"One minute." Dmitri paused.

"You just had dessert."

"Ever eat prison food? I am making up for lost time."

Kolya glanced at his watch. Ten minutes. Don't be early. Don't be late. "Fine."

Dmitri bought a waffle cone filled with strawberry *morozhenoe*. He took a lick with obvious enjoyment. "Come on, Kolya. After twenty years, why not? Live a little."

On June nights, in that brief period of happiness as a child, he'd sometimes shared a chocolate cone with his mother. He fished into his pocket and pulled out ten rubles. "Small. Chocolate."

He watched as the woman scooped the ice cream. The hands were smooth. Her fingers bore the faint impression of several rings, and a round area on her wrist was lighter than the surrounding the skin on her hand. She owned jewelry that she wasn't wearing. Her eyes, as she handed him the *morozhenoe*, were bright, inquisitive, and intelligent. Neither the eyes nor the hands were what he would expect from an older Russian woman selling ice cream.

Yob tvoyu mat.

He tasted the ice cream, as overwhelmingly sweet as he remembered. He walked away from the ice cream seller and leaned on an iron rail that gave him a view of the bridge and the river, still hesitating over whether he should proceed. If Fyodor was in the middle of the bridge as agreed, he wouldn't be visible from either bank.

Dmitri leaned on the rail on next to him. "What is going on?"

"I'm not sure."

"I am trying to keep us alive, and you are going to get us killed."

"I'm trying not to."

"Nothing that you could get from this meeting will help. And it is dangerous."

"I could say the same about being with you."

Dmitri snorted. "If you believed that, you would still be in Washington."

"Eat your fucking ice cream."

From this position, he could see people entering or exiting the bridge. The suspicious ice cream seller continued to scoop cones of *morozhenoe*. She was watching people with more intensity than would be warranted, given her job.

If she were an FSB agent, there would be others around. He looked for anyone who seemed, like him, to be lingering.

But it was White Nights, and there were people everywhere. Tourists taking selfies next to statues of men holding rearing horses. Couples entangled with each other. He remembered the man in the café, finished with his plate, but lingering as if waiting for something.

Any of them could be FSB.

He glanced at his watch. If he was going to make the meeting with Fyodor, he had to go—now. Was it worth the risk? He made his decision, took another bite of ice cream, and then tossed the remainder into the river.

Then he heard a voice behind him.

"*Izvinite*, do you have a light?"

Spoken in perfect Russian, but with an American accent. Kolya turned and looked into Teo's face. Teo held out a cigarette. It was one of the more classic moves for a spy to communicate with another spy. Kolya had used it himself many times. And that made Kolya uneasy. They were close enough that the suspicious ice cream vendor might be able to see.

But making a big deal of it would also be suspicious.

Dmitri, a few feet away, still eating his *morozhenoe,* gazed down at the river. If he'd heard or seen Teo, he made no sign. But then he'd never met Teo, either.

"*Da.*" Kolya pulled out a matchbook from his jacket pocket and handed it to Teo, hoping that Teo wouldn't cough or choke, a sure giveaway.

"*Spacibo,*" Teo struck a match and inhaled.

"Aborting," Kolya said softly.

"What I was going to say." Then Teo turned and walked back in the direction of the hotel and away from the bridge.

Kolya glanced at the Anichkov bridge one last time, and saw Jonathan and Elizabeth entwined in an embrace.

The ECA would try to help Fyodor, but right now, Kolya had to get away. Before the ice cream vendor or anyone else marked him as suspicious.

He tapped Dmitri's shoulder. "I've had enough sight-seeing today. I'd like to get some sleep if we're going to hit the clubs tonight."

Dmitri turned around, glanced from Kolya towards Teo's figure disappearing in the crowd, then back to Kolya. "What I said earlier."

"And you were right."

"I usually am. At least about Russia. Besides, I do not want to miss the jazz. My friend Ivan always puts on a good show."

But they would be going in blind, without any information that Fyodor might have provided as to Bykovsky's involvement or Rzaev's contacts. Well, better going in blind than arrested by the FSB.

They pushed off from the rail. As they passed the ice cream vendor, Kolya felt the burning of her gaze on him. But she did nothing, and they retraced their steps down the Prospeckt. The hotel wouldn't be safe, nothing in Russia was safe, but it would be safer than the vicinity of the bridge.

* * * * *

The meeting had been set for eight-thirty, or so Fyodor had said. By eight-forty-five, Tomas knew that the spy was not coming. He waited another half hour just to be sure, but at nine-fifteen, he walked the block to the bridge. In the middle, Fyodor Dyakov in a blue baseball cap leaned against the green rail and threw bread scraps to a frantic gathering of ducks in the water below.

"I didn't see him." Fyodor's voice quavered. "I don't know why he didn't show."

Tomas looked around at his assembled team. Had one of them slipped up? Had the spy noticed something out of the ordinary? Had Fyodor, despite his words and obvious fear, signaled danger?

No way to know.

Tomas wasn't angry, just frustrated. Once again, he'd screwed up—this time allowing an American agent to slip by. And he still had no idea what was going on with Rzaev and the Novichok.

His own failure, and whose fault it was, wasn't important.

He had to come up with another way to get to Rzaev, and to find the American agents. "You have until midnight to get me a list of every contact Vladimir Rzaev has in this city. And I want to see the video from every camera around the bridge." Maybe the spy had been caught on camera. Maybe not. But it wouldn't hurt to look.

26

TUESDAY NIGHT, BELMONT GRAND HOTEL, ST. PETERSBURG, RUSSIA

KOLYA HUNG BY HIS wrists from a chain fastened to the ceiling in a small room, dimly lit by a barred window, grey walls streaked with blood. His blood. *It's a dream.* Or was it? Had he ever left the cell? Was it his life after Romania that was a dream? He tugged at chains that felt real, and the panic began to rise.

"So you're not ready to cooperate?" Mihai Cuza, dressed in riding clothes—jodhpurs, high boots, and Kolya's leather jacket—sat in a chair in front of him. Fear shot through Kolya, as Cuza raised a hand. A stocky man with dark blond hair smiled and showed Kolya a cigar. Cuza sipped coffee as Kolya's jeans were pulled down and the cigar pressed against his genitals. He screamed and retched. Then Alex was there, a gun against her head.

He woke, tears streaming down his face. It had been a nightmare, just another nightmare.

In his sessions with his therapist, she had told him that he needed to allow himself to re-experience the ordeal.

"I re-experience it every night," he'd responded.

She'd shaken her head. "Having nightmares isn't the same. You need to allow yourself to feel the emotions that you repressed while you were being tortured—all the rage, all the fear—because to survive a horrific situation, you had to shut down."

"I felt everything."

She'd smiled. "I was talking about emotional feelings, not physical pain. You told me that you got through it by thinking about music. Now that you know it's safe, you need to experience the emotions that were too dangerous to feel at the time. We could talk it through here—in a safe space."

"I'd prefer not."

A long silence.

"Perhaps we could work on some grounding techniques."

"Fine."

"Okay. But think about what I said. The grounding techniques will help with the disassociation, but if you want to really deal with the symptoms of PTSD, you will have to consciously acknowledge the past and your feelings. Either here. Or somewhere you feel safe."

He hadn't yet followed her suggestion, and he didn't know if he would. He could, however, practice the techniques to bring himself into the present.

He took several deep breaths, turned on a lamp, and looked around the room. Bedside table, with his phone on top. He shifted his gaze to the wall. Painting of the Church of the Savior of Spilled Blood—one of the more beautiful landmarks of the city. He listened to traffic outside the hotel, and took a physical inventory, feeling the ache in his leg, the silk of the sheets, the plush feel of the pillows and bed. He was in St. Petersburg, not Romania. He was in control.

Light with the soft quality of an early summer's evening streamed in through the window. They were staying in the Presidential suite in the Belmont Grand Hotel. The bathrooms were marble, the décor white and gold. The mics and cameras, which he knew were there, were out of sight.

Calmer, he picked up his phone.

The plan was to head out at one a.m. to locate Ivan Minsky at the Platonov jazz club near the river. According to Dmitri, Minsky showed up late at the club to play a set with his band.

After returning from the bridge, they'd gone to sleep in separate bedrooms, Dmitri in a bedroom directly across from Kolya.

Little after midnight. It would be three p.m. in Vermont. He tapped a short message: *I'm okay. Love you and miss you.*

Within seconds, a reply. *Okay here too. Love you back.*

Alex, who could argue for hours on obscure legal points, knew the drill. Say nothing of consequence in email or text. Just say the essential. One of the rules she'd accepted when they'd started dating.

That she'd replied told him everything. She was safe—and that was what mattered. Finish the job, and he could go home to her.

He settled on his side, but he wasn't relaxed enough to sleep. He mentally ran through his repertoire of jazz standards, chose the Ellis Marsalis tune, *Twelve's It*, and pictured his hands on the keyboard. Within minutes, he dozed off and then jerked awake at the sound of a door shutting.

"*Dermo.*"

He struggled into jeans, sweater, jacket and shoes, strapped on weapons, and grabbed his phone. Dmitri's bedroom door was open. No Dmitri. Through the open door to the attached bathroom, he saw a pile of towels. No Dmitri.

He had started to relax, not fully trusting Dmitri, but trusting him enough to go to sleep in separate rooms. How could he have been so stupid?

Maybe he really wasn't up to the job anymore.

He'd fucking worry about it later.

Kolya grabbed a room key and headed out the door. The hallway was empty, the elevator grinding down towards the first floor. Even if he'd had a fully functional leg, he'd never make it down the stairs in time. He hit the elevator button and pulled out his phone.

"Dmitri snuck out. Where are you?"

"Across the street," Jonathan said. "He just came out of the hotel. Teo's with me. Elizabeth's behind him."

"Stay with him."

"We're on it."

Kolya rode the elevator down and continued through the gilded lobby. From *Mikalovskaya* Street, he limped the half block to Nevskii Prospeckt. The White Nights celebration was in full swing. Throngs of people, German, English, French, Russian, crowded the Prospeckt; music poured from bars, and street musicians played on corners, the clash of different styles and music creating a cacophony of guitars, pianos, violins, accordions. The scent of grilling meat wafted from street vendors. A group of young women, all blonde, all carrying cups of what looked to be vodka-laced fruit drinks, giggled together and blocked his view. No sight of Dmitri in either direction.

"He met someone, and they're heading down *Kazanskaya*," Jonathan reported.

Away from the bright lights and the night long party—towards Sennaya, the poor district of St. Petersburg that had been the scene of the most famous murder in Russian literary history.

"Any sight of a shadow?"

"Not from my vantage point."

He ignored the pain in his leg, increasing his speed to catch up. Fewer people. A heavily made-up woman thrust herself into his path. "Hey, handsome." Russian, middle-aged, but wearing it well. Professional. But why working a back street, not the Prospeckt?

"Not interested." He pushed past her, tensing for the possibility of an attack. Sometimes prostitutes were just that, and sometimes they were decoys for a robbery.

But she let him pass without incident.

He caught up with Jonathan, Elizabeth, and Teo near *Sennaya Ploshchad*. The riotous crowds were blocks away but could have been a continent away. He noted the address with irony. Near this spot, a fictional pawnbroker in Dostoevsky's *Crime and Punishment* had been bloodily murdered by the intellectual Raskolnikov to prove the theory that extraordinary men had the right to commit crimes—a theory that had not worked out well for Raskolnikov.

Jonathan tilted his head towards a shabby apartment building across *Sandovaya*. "They went in there. A light went on in a window on the fourth floor, right side, two minutes after they entered. It could be a trap."

"A reasonable possibility."

"We'll go in with you," Teo said.

"No."

Jonathan nodded. "Kolya's right. We don't want Dmitri to know we're here. Kolya needs to play this out, even if there's a risk."

"I'll leave my phone on." It was something, but not much. If it were a trap, he'd be dead before they got to him. Still, he'd traveled to St. Petersburg to locate Novichok in the United States. To protect the people of the United States. If keeping himself safe defeated that purpose, he should have stayed home. "You'll know. One way or the other." He slid his gun from his holster and held it at his side. "If all goes well, I'll head to the Platonov Club after this."

"We'll be there ahead of you," Jonathan said.

"Assuming you make it out alive," Elizabeth added.

He crossed the street and tried the front door of the building. Unlocked. He slid it open. The hallway stank of cabbage and rotting fish. Narrow, steep stairs were lit by a single bulb. Something crunched underfoot as he started up the stairs. A dead mouse. Then he moved upward. Two steps. Stop. Listen. Two more. Stop.

Passing the second landing, he heard a baby faintly cry from one of two apartments. Only other sound: his footsteps and his breathing. He eased past the third landing. Two steps. Stop. Listen.

He halted on the fourth and top landing. Four apartments. Only one door had light shining in the crack between the floor and the door. He could hear men talking inside—and whimpers of distress.

He gripped his gun, raised it to firing position, and touched the door. It cracked open, not just unlocked, but unlatched. A blast of stale air hit his face. With his foot, he pushed the door all the way open and advanced into a shabby living room.

Dmitri, leg over the arm of a tattered green wing chair, looked comfortable and relaxed. A taller man, brown hair tied back into a ponytail, wearing black leather boots and a matching jacket, lounged on a sofa that might once have been white.

A wizened old man, hands tied behind him, a belt around his chest and through the back of a kitchen chair, wept loudly.

"*Privyet*, Kolya." Dmitri waved a hand at a second wing chair. "What took you so long?"

27

WEDNESDAY EARLY MORNING, SENNAYA PLOSHCHAD, ST. PETERSBURG, RUSSIA

"YOU REMEMBER ARKADY?" DMITRI asked. The man with the ponytail smiled, and Kolya saw an echo of the boy who had also been a friend at the *dyskeii dom*. He did not holster his gun, but he nodded.

"How the fuck are you, Kolya?" Arkady had been the joker of the three, always playing pranks. He'd paid for it too. "You look good. What the hell has it been, twenty years?"

"More or less." Kolya didn't lower the gun. "You breaking into people's homes these days?"

"Not normally. I drive cabs. Sell shit online. But I stayed in touch with Dima, and this was a special request."

"My gift to you," Dmitri said.

"A gift?"

"Yes, gift. I knew you would not agree, but I also knew you would follow." Then he gestured at the weeping old man. "You remember Yelseyev? This is my gift. For what he tried to do to you—and did to so many kids."

Now Kolya recognized the withered face of the man who'd beat him, molested him, and would have raped him, but for Dmitri.

"And what do you expect me to do with this gift?"

"Whatever you want. Start by cutting off something?"

"His dick, maybe," Arkady reached into his boot for a double-edged knife. "Or burn it off."

Kolya had a sudden flash of memory—of a cigar burned into his

129

genitals. His hands started to shake. He forced himself to focus on sensory details: the shabby couch, a red and gold threadbare rug, a musty smell mingled with the odor of cooking cabbage. Then he was back in the present. The shaking eased. He switched to English, which Yelseyev and Arkady wouldn't understand. "This is not why we are in Russia. We have business that doesn't involve torture and murder."

"I understand. We will go see Ivan after this." Dmitri switched back to Russian. "Why not have fun with our friend here first? He deserves it."

"Torture is not my idea of fun, whether he deserves it or not."

"Thank you." Yelseyev wept. "Thank you."

"Shut up." He looked at the figure with revulsion. Pink skin shone through the wispy white hair. The features contorted with fear.

"You could just shoot him." Dmitri leaned back in the chair, relaxed, as if he were discussing a movie. "Think of the little boys you would be saving. Don't tell me you are not tempted."

"Please. Please." The old man sniffled as tears continued to stream. "It's a disease. I couldn't help myself."

"And we can't help ourselves, either, *govnyuk*," Arkady toyed with the knife.

And Kolya was in truth tempted. It wasn't as if Yelseyev didn't deserve it, for all the suffering he had inflicted on defenseless children. It wasn't as if Kolya had never killed anyone.

But for all his talk of exacting revenge on those who had set him up eight months earlier, he didn't kill in cold blood. He wasn't an assassin. He only killed those who posed an immediate threat to his life or to the lives of others—which Yelseyev did not.

In any event, killing a civilian in Russia would be a serious mistake. He would have the *Politsiya Sankt Peterburga* after him for a murder that did nothing to forward the mission. It would also give Dmitri power over him—which was probably the reason for this expedition, for all of Dmitri's talk of bonding and brotherhood. Power and control.

But there remained the question of what to do about Yelseyev.

"Does he still work with children?" Kolya holstered his gun, slipped his hand into his pocket, and turned off the phone. The team had heard enough.

"I don't know. Do you, *govnyuk*?" Arkady directed the question to the old man.

Yelseyev shook his head violently. Dmitri waved a hand toward an ancient desktop computer. "Kolya, I bet you can find what he has been up to."

To check the computer would mean turning his back on Dmitri and Arkady. But if they'd wanted to kill him, they'd had plenty of opportunity.

He seated himself in front of the computer and turned it on. "Password?"

Yelseyev blubbered.

"*Yob tvoyu mat*! Password!" Yelseyev stuttered out a series of letters and numbers. Kolya typed them in.

He checked the history. Yelseyev had been talking to twelve-year-old boys, posing as a sixteen-year-old on VK, Russia's largest social media. Kolya checked e-mail. Then he swung around in his chair. "Not just a pedophile, but a liar. You work part time at a school. Still."

Yelseyev's terror was almost palpable. "Please. I will resign. I needed money. What else could I do?"

Ironic. Russia was so homophobic that gay men holding hands risked prison or worse, and yet this man had been allowed to molest children for over twenty years.

Kolya returned to the computer. First, an e-mail to the school. Posing as Yelseyev, he explained that he felt an irresistible urge to have sex with children and resigned. Then he posted a similar notice on Yelseyev's VK account, giving Yelseyev's true age, and did the same in the chat room where he'd been talking to young boys. Finally, he sent an e-mail to the police as Yelseyev confessing to sex with young boys, dating back twenty years. He rose and limped across the room. "The police are coming. We're done here."

"You're letting him go?" Arkady uncoiled from the couch, knife in hand. Kolya grasped Arkady's wrist and twisted. The knife clattered to the floor.

Arkady raised fists. "This shithead doesn't deserve to live."

Kolya stepped back. Even with his bad leg, Kolya knew he could end this quickly—and not pleasantly for his former friend—without resorting to a weapon. "I don't want to hurt you, Arkady. Let it go. No one will let him near children again."

Arkady's face turned red.

Dmitri rose from the armchair. "He's right, Arkady. Let's go."

"*Dermo.*" Arkady gestured at Yelseyev. "He'll tell the police."

"Tell them what? That men he abused as children revealed his secrets? He's not worth going to prison."

"Fine. Okay. I don't like it, but okay."

Kolya found a towel in the kitchen and wiped down all the hard surfaces he had touched. Arkady stooped and retrieved his knife. They left Yelseyev blubbering, tied to the chair. Last out of the apartment, Kolya shut the door using his shirt and followed the others. Outside, no sign of the ECA team.

Arkady slapped Dmitri on the back and headed to the right. Kolya and Dmitri watched him turn a corner. Then Kolya nodded toward the Bridge of Four Lions. "We have a long walk to the Platonov Club. Let's go."

"You have gone soft, Kolya." Dmitri shook his head in disapproval. "Like the boy I first knew, not the man I now know. Not what I expected."

* * * * *

The old man continued to weep. Alone in his apartment, he knew that the police would arrive soon. But at least, he hadn't been murdered or mutilated.

Footsteps in the hall. Maybe if he paid the police enough, they'd just go away. They had before, when he'd been caught stupidly approaching a boy in Mikhailovsky Gardens.

The door swung open. But it wasn't the police.

A hand over his mouth stopped the scream as the knife sliced into his stomach and then upwards.

28

THE HEADQUARTERS OF THE FSB in St. Petersburg was a large rectangular building known as the Big House. It had been KGB headquarters, and like many buildings of the Soviet era, the architecture was plain, box-like—intimidating in its simplicity and in stark contrast to the decorative facades so well-known and loved in the rest of the city. In his position as Direcktor, Tomas had visited it several times, and disliked it on general principle: the building had the air of a mausoleum.

Tomas sat at a desk in one of the offices reserved for visiting officials, a picture of Yuri decorating one wall, the rest of the walls bare, again doubting what he was doing and wishing he were home. If he were, he'd be working out of the office that Lyudmila had decorated and painted. At home, there were bookshelves, a cushioned desk chair, and an oak desk. And a framed painting by each of the children. His daughter had painted a purple cat. The oldest boy, a tree by a river. Simple clear strokes. The youngest boy: a painting of a vaguely horse-shaped creature with four legs with white and black spots. Here, he sat at a borrowed bare desk with desktop computer, under the uncomfortable watch of Yuri's photograph.

It couldn't be helped. He was doing this for them.

He scrolled through videos and images of people around the Anichkov bridge, and his team, scattered through the building, was doing the same. So, far it had been an exercise in futility. Fyodor had claimed not to recognize anyone. Tomas had seen no one who looked particularly suspicious in the videos. Of course, he wasn't a trained spy. Before being elevated to this uncomfortable position, he'd been in border security.

He was in over his head.

A soft tap on the door. Karine, who had posed as an ice cream vendor at the bridge, stuck her head in. He motioned her inside. She came in, carrying a laptop.

"First, I have the name of an associate of Vladimir Rzaev. Ivan Minsky. Word is that he's Rzaev's top lieutenant here in St. Petersburg. He owns one of the clubs in town."

Tomas waved her to a chair. "Do you have a name for the club?"

"Platonov."

"Good." Tomas felt less like a fool. "And what else?"

"I went over the images multiple times. There are about four people who interest me." She showed him half a dozen images of men who had approached the bridge but not crossed it.

Tomas had already seen them all, but this time, he paid closer attention. He went through all of the videos twice, then settled on one image—that of a man offering a pack of matches to another man.

"Can you enlarge the faces on this one?"

Karine did.

He studied the image. Something was vaguely familiar about the blond man offering the pack of matches.

"This one. I think I've seen him somewhere."

She looked at the picture. "He bought ice cream from me. He and a friend. Didn't notice anything."

Still, it was something. "Send a still of his face around to the hotels. Find out who he is." It might not be the right man, but it wouldn't hurt. "Send the others around as well. And get Fyodor in here."

* * * * *

"We should have waited for Kolya," Teo said.

They sat at a table in the shadows, on the far side of a large room, decorated with photos of American jazz icons, crowded with people speaking English, German, Swedish, French, and some languages that Jonathan couldn't identify. Drinks flowed freely, and a few people swayed together on the small dance floor. The group on stage was blaring "Take the A Train," which Jonathan recognized because Kolya had insisted on playing jazz on so many of their joint operations.

"He wasn't in danger. He wouldn't have turned off his phone if he'd been worried. And we don't want Dmitri to know we're here." Jonathan toyed with his beer. It was outrageously priced, but they had to drink something to fit in. Beer was the safest bet.

Elizabeth didn't even pretend to drink her beer. "I'm with the kid, Jonathan. This is Petrov's first mission since Romania. His judgment and reflexes may not be what they were." She glanced over at Teo. "Don't let it go to your head."

"We're to stay below the radar," Jonathan said. "Unless absolutely necessary, we're not to intervene."

"We disobeyed orders to rescue him last year." Teo shot a sideways glance at Elizabeth. "And if Elizabeth agrees with me, it means I'm right."

"Yes, we did disobey orders before. And I'll do it again if Kolya's in danger. He wasn't. Your Russian is much better than mine—and you agreed that he didn't need our help."

"So where the hell is he?" Elizabeth asked. "It's been an hour."

"He'll be here."

"You don't think Kolya'd actually kill that old guy, do you?" Teo asked. "From what I heard, the old man's a pedophile, but still...."

"No. Not Kolya's style. And it would be stupid. Also not Kolya's style to do something stupid."

Elizabeth picked up a French fry, dipped it into ketchup, and ate it delicately. "His style may have changed, Jonathan."

"Nevertheless."

"You should have snuck that GPS tracker into his pocket."

"He said no for a reason, and I wouldn't do that to him." It was too much like a betrayal, and Kolya already had trust issues.

"Okay, yeah, but still… where the hell is he?"

Jonathan looked at his watch. An hour and ten minutes. "We wait another half an hour then we'll double back and check on him."

* * * * *

Tomas was dozing in his chair when Karine returned to his office. She rapped on the door, and he started awake.

135

"The man at the bridge?"

Fyodor had not definitively confirmed that the picture was that of the spy. He'd said, maybe, claiming both that the image wasn't distinct and anyway it had been a long time. Fyodor could be lying or not, but the blond man remained high on Tomas's suspect list.

"Nothing yet, but Minsky should be at the club tonight. White Nights."

Tomas rubbed the sleep from his eyes. "OK, get our people together."

29

WEDNESDAY EARLY MORNING, ST. PETERSBURG, RUSSIA

KOLYA LET DMITRI LEAD. They were not heading towards the Neva River but back towards the Prospeckt. "We're not going to the Platonov Club." It wasn't a question. He was also not surprised.

"No. Ivan will not be at the Platonov. Trust me."

"You keep making it difficult to so do."

"Tell me you're not pleased that you stopped Yelseyev from molesting children."

"Perhaps I am, but I'm not particularly pleased that you forced me into it. Or that you lied to me about the Platonov Club." But the sideshow with Yelseyev hadn't really been a betrayal. And, he had to admit, there was a level of satisfaction in getting some small revenge against the bastard.

Dmitri stopped and felt in his pockets. "Okay, I misled you a little. Platonov Club has good jazz, and Ivan does own it. That was not a lie. It is just not where he hangs out."

"And you didn't mention this before—why?"

"Maybe I don't trust you completely either." Dmitri found the pack and extracted a cigarette. He struck a match and inhaled smoke. "So be honest with me—admit that you have friends shadowing us."

They stood face to face under a streetlight. They were still a few blocks from White Night festivities, but the sound of voices and music drifted over them.

"I didn't lie to you. I just omitted a few details."

"Are you going to tell me the details now?"

"No." Kolya wasn't about to identify the team. It wasn't information that Dmitri needed, and it would put the team at greater risk if he were caught by the FSB.

Dmitri took another drag on the cigarette, then he dropped it on the ground and stepped on it. "If you want to talk to Ivan, better not have a spy convention. If you want to contact your friends after we leave Ivan, fine. But I don't want them following us. It's my life, too, on the line. That young man at the bridge—he was very obvious. If Ivan suspects that we are spies...."

"I know."

"So you know. Good. Now, before I take you to Ivan, turn off your phone so your friends cannot track you and show up at Ivan's."

The request was a surprise. Kolya narrowed his eyes. "I'm not fucking turning it off."

"Then I'm not fucking moving."

They stared, an impasse.

"If I wanted to kill you," Dmitri said softly, "you would be dead. Like I fucking told you two days ago. I could have killed you tonight when you were sleeping."

"Maybe. And maybe you enjoy playing me first."

"If I was luring you into a trap, would having your phone on save you?"

Kolya let the question hang in the air, even though he had already come to the same conclusion. Then he finally spoke. "No."

"Then turn it off so your friends don't rush into Ivan's and fuck everything up." Dmitri shoved his hands into his jacket. "You are armed. You can kill me if I screw you over. Can we fucking come to an agreement and do this thing, so we can get back to the United States?"

"Fine." It was a risk, but then the entire mission was risky. Kolya reached into his pocket, took out his phone, sent a text, and turned it off.

* * * * *

Elizabeth tapped her watch. "It's been another half hour."

Jonathan took out his phone. A message: *Minsky not at Platonov. Going to meet him. Contact you later.* Nothing more. He sent a text back. *Where?* No response. He sent a second text. *Are you in trouble?* Nothing.

He tried to call. Kolya's phone was off. "Let's go."

"Finally." Teo drained his beer. "We going back to the old man's place?"

Elizabeth shrugged. "As good a place as any."

Jonathan agreed. Afterwards, they'd walk downtown St. Petersburg in a grid pattern. Sooner or later, hopefully they would find Kolya.

A minute after they stepped outside, five cars roared up to the front of the Platonov club, and the three of them stepped into a doorway to watch.

Twelve people piled out of the cars and raced into the club, followed by a stout middle-aged man.

"*Politsiya Sankt Peterburga?*" Teo asked under his breath.

"No." Elizabeth jerked her head towards the last man entering the club. "Do you recognize him, Jonathan?"

"Tomas Orlov."

"Who?" Teo asked.

"Head of the FSB and Yuri Bykovsky's brother-in-law," Elizabeth said. "From what I understand, he was put in the job so Bykovsky would have someone he could control."

"I've heard that too," Jonathan said. "Although word from Fyodor is that he's smarter and more capable than people think. I'd say his presence here confirms that."

"Shit. Is he after Kolya?"

"Or us." Elizabeth took Jonathan's arm. "Time to get our butts out of here and find Kolya before the FSB does."

They headed down the street, blending in with the drunks and celebrants, and steered towards the apartment building where they'd last seen Kolya. Jonathan just hoped they weren't too late.

30

ON A SMALL STREET closed to traffic, Cyrillic letters on a battered sign over the open door spelled Vinyl. Dmitri tried to remember when he'd last been there. More than ten years ago. He'd visited the club on his last trip home to Russia and then returned to the United States and an arrest warrant.

A short line of Russian jazz enthusiasts waited near the door. A grittier club than Platonov and without the big names in Russian jazz like Sergey Manukian, Russia's most popular jazz vocalist, Vinyl attracted few tourists. Vinyl specialized in new musicians and the occasional student from the St. Petersburg Institution of Culture. Then there was Ivan's house band—reliable if not particularly outstanding. And Ivan's name did not appear on any official records as the owner of the club, which made it, for his purposes, a safer hangout than Platonov.

Dmitri recognized the bouncer blocking the door. Same guy as the last time—stocky build, six feet tall, no neck—but hair flecked with gray now. He pushed his way to the front of the line, Kolya behind him, despite the murmured protests of those already waiting for admission.

The bouncer glared at the protestors, who fell silent. Then he turned small angry eyes onto Dmitri. "You fucking think you can cut ahead?"

"Fucking good to see you, too, Efim." Dmitri handed him a passport with $500 in hundred dollar bills tucked inside. The bouncer opened the passport and pocketed the money. "Dmitri Andriovich, you son-of-a-bitch." The tone turned friendly. "I didn't recognize you. Long time."

"Very long time. Ivan inside?"

"Where the hell else would he be?" The bouncer waved Kolya and Dmitri inside. "Band is on break."

The club was packed. The crowd was young. Some were students, drawn by the music and the attraction for the outlaw. Some probably worked for Ivan. Minor unaffiliated criminals knew it as a safe place to hang out.

Despite the recent Russian ban on cigarettes inside public accommodations, the air was foggy with smoke. Ivan would have paid off any officials inclined to enforce the law.

They halted next to the bar and ordered vodka, as if there were anything else to order.

With the band on break, a mellow sax from an album emanated through loudspeakers. Dmitri had listened to a lot of jazz in prison, and he appreciated the quality of the piece that was playing. Life was funny. He liked jazz, and he owed everything he knew about jazz to Kolya and to prison.

"Do you know this?" The tune was familiar, but he didn't recognize the album.

"Charles Lloyd. *Bess, You Is My Woman Now*. From a 2013 album, *Hagar's Song*. You see Ivan?" Kolya drank off a shot.

Dmitri downed his own glass and let the warmth spread through him. He'd missed this—the music, the drinking. And the women. With the interest of a connoisseur, he scanned the room for attractive women. It was a bit of an exercise in frustration; he knew Kolya was right about getting laid in the middle of a job, even if he enjoyed annoying Kolya by repeatedly suggesting a sexual frolic and detour.

He signaled the bartender, who poured again. Dmitri surveyed the room, this time for Ivan's signature black fedora. He found it and, under it, Ivan's broad face, at a table near the stage with four other guys, all of them in black.

"Come on, I'll introduce you."

Ivan Minsky and his four companions shared a bottle of vodka and played poker. Seven card stud. Two down. Four up, the last about to be dealt. Ivan had a pair of fives showing. Across from Ivan, a thin man displayed a pair of kings. The other three men had shit showing. Dmitri looked at the stack of bills. Couple hundred dollars—small change. Then he surveyed the four men. He knew the thin guy; he'd played piano in Ivan's band the last time Dmitri had been there. Not bad, not great, but not bad. The others were new. They all had guns, tucked into belts. And they didn't bother to hide their weapons. Why would they? Police were paid off, and the crowd loved it. Part of the mystique of the club. Gangster musicians.

"I'm playing poker, Dmitri Andriovich, you shit." Ivan didn't look up.

"*Yob tvoyu mat.* That's how you greet friends you haven't seen for years?" But he waited. Ivan dealt the last card, face down. Three men folded.

The thin man turned over his cards. Three kings. Ivan turned over his cards. Full house. Threes and fives.

Ivan raked in the bills and stacked them. Then he turned his attention back to Dmitri. "Where you been for the last what the fuck is it—five years?"

"Ten years. Prison."

"Here?"

"America."

Ivan grunted approval. A prison sentence was like losing your virginity. "Does Volodya know you're back?"

"Don't know where he is. I thought you might tell me."

"That's up to Volodya. Who the fuck are you?" He looked at Kolya.

"Michael Harding." He hoped the name would withstand scrutiny. "I have a business proposition for Rzaev." Kolya spoke fluent Russian, but the years in America were evident in his accent.

"I am not fucking talking to Russian speaking American." Ivan turned to the other four men. "You ready to play some music?"

"He is also a jazz pianist." Dmitri liked the idea of making Kolya play jazz. Bringing them both back full circle, so to speak. "Better than your guy." Kolya shot Dmitri a dark look. Dmitri ignored it.

"How you know he's better?"

"I heard your guy ten years ago. Has he improved? Besides, if your guy were any good, he would not be here playing with you."

The four bodyguards tensed. Had he gone too far? But Ivan laughed. "And if your friend were any good, he wouldn't be here trying to make a deal with Rzaev."

"Maybe you should hear him play. If you think you can keep up with him."

Ivan gave Kolya an assessing look. "Is he shitting me or do you actually play?"

"I do actually play. I'll let you judge whether I'm any good."

"Okay, then. Mr. American jazz pianist. You take over on piano, and then we talk after. If you play good. You don't, maybe I will shoot you."

31

WEDNESDAY EARLY MORNING, ST. PETERSBURG, RUSSIA

KOLYA SEATED HIMSELF ON the bench in front of the Yamaha piano and glanced back at Ivan's table. Dmitri raised the bottle of vodka in salute. *Bastard is enjoying the hell out of this.* But Kolya found himself as much amused as annoyed that Dmitri had used Kolya's passion for jazz to defuse the situation.

He turned to the keyboard and played an arpeggio. Not bad. The piano was in tune, and the notes rang clear. The saxophonist blew a tentative note. The bass player did a quick tuning. The guitarist strummed a C7 chord. Ivan seated behind the drums, tapped a rhythm on the cymbals. The crowd quieted.

"So, Mr. American jazz pianist. Show me what you can do." Ivan Minsky's wide face glowed with perspiration and menace. "Take Five?"

Kolya rested his hands on the keys and glanced at the other musicians. "E flat minor?"

"E flat minor," the saxophonist agreed.

It was the original key played by Dave Brubeck's quartet, more challenging than transposed versions. Ivan began with a soft drum beat. Kolya followed with chords, and the sax swung into the main theme. They followed Brubeck's music until the individual solos. The bassist led off, followed by the sax, Ivan, and then Kolya. The audience applauded loudly at the end of each solo. Kolya caught Dmitri's wave of the bottle.

Ivan grinned approval. "Call it."

"Ellington, *Satin Doll*."

Satin Doll got a good reception.

144

"You do any vocals, Mr. American jazz pianist?" Ivan asked.

Kolya did not. But Ivan did. He crooned in English through *Moonlight in Vermont*. Then he nodded back at Kolya. "Choose a song. We'll follow."

He swung into *Waltz for Debbie*, in the major key of A.

"*Horosho*," Ivan followed on drums; the sax and the bass joined. The original did not have any sax, but jazz was jazz. Kolya moved into G major and then down to F, losing himself in the music.

They continued to play American jazz: *Mood Indigo, Someday My Prince Will Come, A Night in Tunisia, Ain't Misbehaving*. Close to three a.m., a waitress brought rounds of vodka. Kolya wanted to pass, but it would be interpreted as weakness.

"Want to try something different? Maybe something Russian?" Kolya asked.

"You lead, we'll follow."

Kolya swung into Nikolai Kapustin's Opus 41 blend of jazz and classical, one of the few jazz pieces that his mother had taught him, aware that a classical pianist who shared his name had been a major promoter of Kapustin's work. The crowd knew the piece and applauded. The saxophonist picked up and then the bass. Ivan tapped out a rhythm.

Kolya lost himself in the heat of the music and the vodka. Kapustin had never considered himself anything other than a classical pianist, but his music reflected the influence of Oscar Peterson, Art Tatum, and George Gershwin. Kolya played it as written and then swept into an improvisation.

The room hushed as they played without stop for half an hour—and at the end, the crowd stood and cheered. Seated at Ivan's table with half the bottle of vodka gone, Dmitri gave a thumbs up.

Ivan stood and bowed to the audience. One by one, each of the musicians stood and bowed—except for Kolya, who waved an acknowledgment from the piano bench.

Ivan leaned into the mike and announced the end of the set. The room again buzzed with conversation.

"That was fucking not bad at all," Ivan moped his brow. "Not fucking bad at all, Mr. American pianist. Now, you and that shithead, Dmitri Andriovich, follow me."

32

TUESDAY EVENING, STOWE, VERMONT

THE MAN WHO HAD labeled himself Mickey for the raid in Silver Spring, and who had adopted it as a working name, sprawled in a large leather chair while studying the photos on the screen. Mickey was somewhere in his forties, with a thick body build, although more muscle than fat, with thinning black hair and the look of perpetual annoyance. Even if he was on the old side, Mickey was a highly competent killer, which was all that mattered to Charlie. "Yeah, it's her. And that's the bitch who shot out my tires." He closed the laptop and handed it back to Charlie.

It was what Charlie needed confirmed. He'd seen pictures of Alexandria Feinstein on the Internet, but Mickey had seen her in person. "You're sure?"

"Yeah, I'm sure."

"Good."

"So." Mickey blew out a breath. "We're close."

Being close just made Charlie nervous. Things could still go very wrong—and they had a lot to do before they had the money in hand. Enough money to live like a king for the rest of his life.

Kidnapping Alexandria Feinstein and killing her bodyguard were next on the to-do list.

They'd already gone over the plan several times. The cabin Mickey'd rented to hold Feinstein for the short term was even more remote than Charlie's rented ski house. "Get there around two. They should both be asleep. Rip and Tom here yet?"

Mickey nodded. "They got in this afternoon."

"Don't fuck up." But if something went wrong, they'd deal with it.

* * * * *

Alex finished a draft of an appellate brief for her nonprofit. It wasn't due for a week, so she didn't need to break security to send it. She saved, shut the laptop, and then wandered out to the screened in porch where Tehila nursed a cup of tea and read messages on her mobile, Galil rifle on the wicker couch next to her. Tehila clicked off her phone as Alex approached.

"Nothing about Kolya." Tehila sipped the tea.

"I figured." Alex sat on a cushioned chair. "But it's okay. I heard from him." The text had been brief, but at least he'd been alive and in a position to send a message. He'd never communicated much while out on assignment, and she'd never let it bother her. Before. Before she had to leave her practice and go into hiding. Before she'd seen him chained to a wall.

"Good. Now you can relax and enjoy the evening."

"More or less. It's beautiful here, isn't it?" From this angle, she could see open fields and beyond them, a range of mountains. "Peaceful."

"Do you ever go camping here?"

"Not big on camping. Although about a year ago, I was on a back-to-nature kick—and I talked Kolya into taking a camping trip to the Adirondacks. We were eaten alive by bugs. He kept saying cheery things like it was much worse in Afghanistan and to think about the natural beauty instead of the mosquitoes."

Tehila laughed. "That sounds like Kolya. What happened?"

"I told him it was our goddamn vacation, not an ECA mission, and there was no reason to suck it up. He agreed that it wasn't much fun and he'd been just trying to put on a good face for my benefit. We decamped to a very nice inn nearby that had a piano bar."

"Personally, I love camping—if not mosquitos. There are ways to deal with bugs." Tehila's voice was relaxed but nothing was relaxed about her posture. "You should give it another try. Camping is very spiritual."

33

WEDNESDAY EARLY MORNING, ST. PETERSBURG, RUSSIA

THEY COULDN'T GET NEAR the apartment building. There were police officers surrounding the building, police cars and an ambulance blocking the street. A small crowd of neighbors had gathered on the sidewalks, held back by yellow tape.

"What the hell?" Teo's voice registered shock.

"Someone's dead." Elizabeth's voice was matter of fact. "You don't have this many cops and this much fuss without a body."

"Shit! Kolya?"

"Well it would explain why he didn't show."

"Jesus, Elizabeth, you say that so casually." Teo was scanning the faces in the crowd.

Elizabeth shrugged. "Just realistic."

Teo elbowed his way into the crowd while Jonathan and Elizabeth hung back. Jonathan watched him speak to a woman in a headscarf, and then Teo returned.

"Apparently, the old man had his stomach slit open." He shoved his hands into his jacket pocket. "According to the woman I was talking to. The neighborhood was buzzing with the news that he molested children. Someone put it up on the Internet. She had a few extra comments about him deserving it."

Whether he deserved to be killed or not was beside the point.

"Kolya wouldn't have killed him." Jonathan spoke with certainty.

"He turned off his phone while he was in the apartment," Elizabeth said.

"He's very private. He wouldn't want us hearing the details of what happened to him when he was a child. He doesn't kill people for the thrill of it, either."

"That's one explanation," Elizabeth said. "And the other explanation is that he didn't want us to know what he was doing. And don't tell me it's not his style. Petrov may not enjoy killing, but he is very good at it when necessary. Maybe he decided this was necessary. Anyway, if it wasn't him, where is he?"

"Why don't you try reserving judgment until we find him? And we should get out of here. Head to Kolya's hotel. Maybe they're there." Although, why would Kolya go back to the hotel? It made no sense.

"Fine. But I'm calling to let Bradford know what's going on."

"Why not just wait until we find him?" Teo asked.

"I don't like doing this either, Teo." Elizabeth took out her phone. "But if the mission goes south, and we haven't kept Bradford in the loop, we're screwed."

"Okay. Call her, but don't accuse Kolya of murder without any proof." Jonathan felt coldness in the pit of his stomach. The friend he'd partnered with for ten years would not execute an old man in cold blood, even if the old man was a pedophile. Yes, he knew that Kolya still suffered from the aftereffects of torture and imprisonment, but that didn't mean that Kolya'd kill like this. But would he really know if Kolya had changed so fundamentally?

He shook off the thought. Kolya deserved better from his friends than suspicion.

* * * * *

Kolya and Dmitri followed Ivan up dark stairs to a room so bright it almost glittered: a marble-and-crystal bar against the wall, white couches facing a glass coffee table, marble floors, white walls. White armchairs faced the only dark objects in the room, a walnut desk and a leather executive chair.

"You have a gun?" Ivan asked Kolya. He nodded. "Give it to me. Also your phone and your passport. Then let my men search you." Ivan seated himself behind the desk.

Kolya slid over his HK .40, phone, the knife from the sheath on his leg, and extended his arms. The thin pianist conducted a thorough body search, fingers probing Kolya's waistband, hands patting intimate areas.

Dmitri held up his hands, and the saxophonist conducted a similarly thorough search. The saxophonist signaled no weapons—also no phone. Dmitri had not been trusted enough to be given a phone, something that now could raise suspicion.

But Dmitri could handle it—or so Kolya hoped.

"No phone?" Ivan asked Dmitri.

Dmitri shrugged. "Pickpocket."

Ivan chuckled. "Petty criminals ruin this city. I'm surprised you let him get away with it. Back in the day, any man trying to take your phone would have his guts spilled."

"Not a man. A woman. Very attractive woman. I guess she thought she deserved it for fucking me. But a good fuck is worth a phone, no?"

Ivan laughed out loud. His men laughed as well. Still laughing, Ivan Minsky motioned Kolya and Dmitri to the white chairs opposite his own. "You are correct, Dmitri Andriovich. A good fuck is worth a phone." Ivan examined Kolya's gun. "Did you get this in Russia?"

"No."

"Nice. Someday, you can tell me how you got it past airport security. Sit and put your hands where I can see them. You, too, Dmitri Andriovich."

Kolya obliged, laying his hands lightly on the arms of the white chair. Dmitri also complied. The three musicians arranged themselves a few feet behind the chairs. Kolya didn't look to check, but he knew guns were trained on him. He felt his hands trembling. *Deep breaths. Calm.* He could do this.

"So you play good, Mr. American jazz musician. You play professionally?" Ivan checked his iPhone and tapped keys.

"I jam in clubs sometimes. Nothing formal."

"You should play more. You made me, what is the phrase, step up my game. And I like that you played a Russian piece. Under other circumstances, I would tell you to come back another night." Then he picked up Kolya's gun, ejected the magazine, checked that it was loaded, clicked it back into place, and aimed the HK at Kolya. "Now tell me why I shouldn't blow your brains out for sending the FSB to my club."

The change in tone was sudden and chilling. Kolya tried to still his hands. *Calm. Stay calm.* "There's no FSB here."

"Not at Vinyl. But they showed up at Platonov." Ivan aimed the HK at the middle of Kolya's forehead. "Why does the FSB show up at one of my clubs at the same time as you?"

"I used to work in intelligence." Kolya's hands felt clammy. Sweat dampened the back of his shirt. Worse, the stirring of a flashback. A memory of the last time he was held at gunpoint. The face of the man who had tortured him flashed into his mind. He gripped the arms of his chair, felt the texture of the material, and reminded himself where he was. He was in Russia, not Romania. He'd handled situations like this before—and he could handle this one. The moment passed. Then, he spoke. "I operated in Russia a few times. Someone must have spotted me, and it's known that I like jazz. I doubt the FSB knew I was looking for you. Otherwise, why aren't they here?"

"My ownership of this club is not public knowledge. So, you used to work in intelligence? Once a spy, always a spy."

"Not when your service fucks you over." Kolya told a variation of the truth, with the anger that he genuinely felt. "Eight months ago, I was injured on the job when my agency didn't back me up. And then I resigned."

"And your name?" Ivan picked up the passport. "If your real name is Michael Harding, then I'm Tom Hanks. This is not a Russian name."

Kolya shrugged. "I changed my name. Americans are a little prejudiced against Russians. Dima knew me from years ago, and he vouches for me."

"He does. But then, who vouches for that shit?"

"Rzaev perhaps? Ask him." Dmitri weighed in. "Volodya is always interested in new ways to make money."

"Already done. I sent him a message and asked if he wanted me to kill you."

"And?"

"And I am to ask you what business you want to discuss?"

"I want to make people well." Kolya leaned back in his chair, a nonchalant pose to combat the tension in his body. "And to get rich."

"What does that mean?"

"I have contacts in Quebec, Canada, that will allow me to obtain rare and expensive medicines cheaply, but I need to move the product across the border. Rzaev's North American network would be perfect for the job. So call him and ask him if he wishes to meet with us. Otherwise shoot us or let us go. It's late, and I'm tired." Kolya said the words casually. His stomach tightened, but his mind remained in the present. Good. He didn't need another fucking flashback.

Ivan stared at him and then laughed. Behind him, Kolya could hear the echoing laughter of the musicians. Ivan, still chuckling, lowered the gun. "You're okay, Mr. American jazz pianist. Rzaev told me to send you if I thought you were okay. Especially since you're with this shithead, Dmitri Andriovich." He scribbled on a piece of paper and held it out. "He's at his dacha in Peredelkino. You be there tomorrow evening—seven. And, by the way, if the FSB shows up, he'll kill you. I'll send a couple guys to your hotel, get your stuff. Then you can drive to Peredelkino. I am loaning you a car—leave it with Rzaev."

"Drive? Why not fly?"

"If the FSB is looking for you, the airport will be watched. Better you drive."

If he refused the offer of a car, he would be insulting Ivan. "Thank you."

"Now let us go back downstairs and play some tunes."

It was almost five in the morning. Kolya loved jazz but even love has its limits—and he'd have preferred catching a few hours sleep, especially right before a twelve-hour drive. He also didn't like Ivan's men going through his things, as he knew they would, even though he had nothing compromising in his luggage. But he wasn't being presented with options.

"Fine. My weapons, passport, and phone please."

Ivan handed him the passport. "You can have your weapons when you leave. But I'm keeping the phone. Buy a new phone in Moscow."

"I may have business calls."

"Everyone spends too much time on their phones these days. Not enough face-to-face." Ivan signaled his men. "And my men will follow you until you are out of St. Petersburg. This way, I am sure you are not calling anyone for at least a few hours. Just in case. Or I could just shoot you now."

"Fine. Keep the phone." Somewhere on the road to Moscow, he'd find a phone, and the opportunity to make an unobserved call.

34

WEDNESDAY MORNING, MOSCOW, RUSSIA

YURI BYKOVSKY WAS UP at five in the morning. It was early, but he couldn't stay in bed. Galina lay on her side snoring and drooling onto the pillow. He thought of waking her for a quick screw, but he was too on edge at the moment. Things were coming to a head. Besides, she was starting to bore him—and that took some of the fun out of it. That was one of the things that had annoyed him most about Maria's treachery. She had never bored him.

He pulled on his white satin and gold embroidered robe and headed to his office, where he checked the news and messages on his computer. He texted a reprimand to his personal chef for providing the same dessert two days in a row. It had been good, but even so, he liked variety.

He liked to keep his staff on edge, too. If they thought he was a pushover, they would take advantage.

At five-thirty, his assistant arrived, slightly disheveled, but alert. Well, his assistant should know that he was expected to keep pace with Yuri, even if Yuri's ability to operate on little sleep was beyond that of most people.

"Nothing. No news." His assistant stifled a yawn and ran a hand through his hair. "No news on your idiot brother-in-law. He's chasing spies in St. Petersburg but hasn't caught anyone yet."

"I didn't think he would."

"No, but he does seem to be trying."

"Good enough." If Tomas did as he was supposed to do, all would be well. "And get my sister on the phone."

"Now?"

"Now."

The assistant took out his phone and dialed.

ST. PETERSBURG, RUSSIA

Bottles and empty cups littered the almost-empty street. A bearded man, wrapped in a wool coat, slept in a door frame. A small crew of elderly women was already at work cleaning up the debris. Tomas, accompanied by the reluctant Fyodor and his team from the bridge, tried not to show his sadness as he picked his way down the street and past the evidence of wild drinking. Alcohol had been the ruin of so many Russian men— and yet here the city of St. Petersburg glorified alcohol in the yearly bacchanal that was the White Nights.

That Tomas knew about Ivan Minsky's second club, Vinyl, was due not to any of the staff or the musicians from the Platonov Club, whom he'd detained for hours and questioned, but from a hotel clerk who not only recognized the blond man as a guest traveling with an American passport but knew that Ivan Minsky often played jazz at a small, little-known club. The blond man had not been in his room. Minky's club was the logical next step.

The Vinyl Club's fluorescent sign over the door was dark, the front door unattended. Tomas held up a hand and listened. Music was playing. It sounded like notes were being missed, and the rhythm less than smooth. Were the musicians drunk?

He hoped so.

His officers fell into position, and Tomas nodded at the first in line. "Go."

They surged inside, the Vitaz-SNs, the version of the Kalashnikov used by the Russian police, held in position, and he followed.

Ten patrons, scattered at tables throughout the bar, and a band of five musicians on the stage, froze. The bartender raised his hands. Two waitresses clung to trays of drinks.

"Everyone stay seated. Keep your hands in clear view," Tomas announced.

The five musicians on the stage glared. The pianist, whose gun was prominent in his waistband, moved his hand from the keyboard. The officer nearest Tomas pointed his weapon and shouted a warning.

A man in a black fedora behind the drums said something, and the pianist returned his hand to the keyboard.

"Ivan Minsky? Please join me for a chat." Tomas pointed to an empty table.

* * * * *

"Where is the American?" Tomas sat opposite Ivan Minsky. The bartender had brought coffee, and then he, the waitresses, and Ivan's band of musician-bodyguards had been herded into a hallway. Five men with guns remained to secure the room. One stood directly behind Ivan, gun pointed at Ivan's head. The remaining patrons had fled into the bright morning.

"Who?" Ivan raised his hands in a question.

"Russian-American spy. I think he went by the name of Michael Harding. Keep your hands on the table."

"I don't know what you're talking about." Ivan placed his hands as directed.

"Are you saying he wasn't here last night?"

"My club is popular. Lots of people come here who I don't remember."

An officer returned from the hallway where the musician-bodyguards were being held. "The American was a guest pianist."

Ivan shrugged. "I have a lot of guest musicians."

Tomas reached for the pot of coffee in the middle of the table and poured another cup. "Are you aware he is an American spy?"

"All I knew was he wanted to play piano. He was pretty good, too."

"He was a spy. What else did he want?"

Ivan shook his head. "I have no idea what you're talking about."

Tomas put the coffee cup down and nodded at the officer standing behind Ivan who pressed the muzzle of his gun against the back of Ivan's right hand.

"You won't be playing drums for a few weeks if my officer pulls the trigger. One last time. Where is the spy?"

"I don't know where he is, you shit."

The shot passed through Ivan's hand and buried itself in the table. He screamed, and blood pooled around his fingers.

Tomas swallowed his revulsion and asked the question again.

"Go fuck yourself."

Tomas glanced up at the officer. "The other hand." The gun muzzle moved from the shattered right hand to the left.

"Okay. Okay. He is on his way to meet Vladimir Rzaev at his dacha outside Moscow." Ivan's voice came strained through gritted teeth. "In Peredelkino."

"Address?"

"In my phone."

"Where's your phone?"

"In my pocket, where the fuck do you think it is, you fucking motherfucker?"

The man standing behind Ivan reached inside the left shirt pocket and retrieved an iPhone. He placed it on the table in front of Ivan. Then he shifted his gun to aim at the back of Ivan's head.

"The address, please," Tomas said.

With his good hand, Ivan tapped in his code and then shoved the phone across the table. The blood continued to pulse out of the shattered hand.

Tomas copied the address from the phone into his own and pulled a handkerchief out of his pocket. He passed the phone and the handkerchief to Ivan. Ivan wrapped the handkerchief around the hand.

"Do you know this man's real name?"

Ivan's face was shiny with sweat, but his eyes remained defiant. "No idea."

"Or why he wants to see Rzaev?"

"Same fucking answer."

"Two last questions—these you'll know. When did the spies leave here—and how are they getting to Peredelkino?"

"Two hours ago. By car. Fuck your mother sideways on a horse." Ivan muttered the words, but his tone was defeated.

"Manners." The officer behind Ivan pressed his gun against Ivan's skull. Ivan froze.

Tomas raised a hand. "Stop." The officer looked questioningly. "I have what I need. This is not necessary. Let's go." He spoke in a low tone to Ivan. "If you say anything to Rzaev, either he will kill you—or I will. Do you understand?"

"Perfectly."

Tomas wanted to catch the American spies—and that led to Rzaev. Maybe he'd find out about the Novichok that Rzaev had smuggled into the United States as well. Yuri couldn't complain that Tomas was violating orders—since Yuri had approved tracking down American secret agents.

He didn't like what he'd just done to get this information, but it had been necessary. Killing Ivan was not.

35

MICKEY PARKED THE VAN at the beginning of the driveway. Two a.m. They'd walk the half-mile to the house. The dirt road leading to the house had only a few driveways, houses hidden behind bushes and trees. No neighbors within sight to call the police about men in black carrying assault weapons. Even if there had been neighbors, clouds covered the half moon, and the only light visible shone from the small flashlights that they carried. All in all, a perfect set up.

Mickey's adrenaline surged in anticipation of action. He liked the feeling, which was why he'd loved the military—and why he'd joined up with Charlie after he had been dishonorably discharged from the army after an incident in Afghanistan. He might be a little older, but he still craved the action.

There was the money, as well.

But compared to the raid in Silver Spring, this should be a piece of cake. Okay, yeah, Feinstein's bodyguard had shot out his tires, but it had only taken a few minutes for Petrov to take down both his men. He had barely gotten away from that bastard.

He doubted the woman bodyguard was anywhere near as dangerous. Still, he was playing it safe. He and his men all wore Kevlar vests and helmets. The protection wasn't absolute—they could still be hit in the face. But most people aimed for the center mass, and he assumed the bodyguard would do so as well, buying them just enough time to kill her.

Alexandria Feinstein—she'd meekly submitted when they'd raided her brother's house. She wouldn't be a problem.

And they had night on their side. The dark house evidenced that both women were asleep—or at least not watching for possible home invaders. He glanced at his men, Rip and Tom, buddies from Afghanistan. Rip, short and thin, could outfight men a foot taller than him, and Tom, good looking, with a misleading affable affect, was a deadly killer. Both of them were much more competent than the two men he'd hired to hit the house in Silver Spring. And both of them had worked as part of Charlie's network for the past three years.

They halted a hundred feet from the house—a sprawling two-story colonial that Mickey estimated cost around a million—and turned off the flashlights. Rip went left, Tom right, and then they returned.

"No lights anywhere," Rip said.

"Don't see any cars, but the garage is locked, and no windows." Tom said. "We could go in that way."

"Negative. Good odds that there's an alarm."

The best option would be to send his men up to the second floor and through a bedroom window. Even if there were a security system, it was unlikely that the system would cover the windows on the upper levels.

And, if an alarm went off when they exited the house, by the time the Stowe police arrived, they'd be long gone. Just in case the women inside woke, evaded Rip and Tom, and tried to escape, either by car or on foot, he'd stay on the ground to block their exit and provide cover.

Tom gave a thumbs up, and they headed for the side of the house.

Mickey stationed himself about ten feet from the front porch where he had a direct line of fire to the front door and the garage. He checked his phone.

In position. Text from Rip.

He texted back. *Go.*

The moon emerged from the clouds as Rip shot a grappling hook up to the roof that caught onto the chimney. He slung his weapon around his back and went first, pulling himself up on the line, with Tom close on his heels. From his position and with the help of the moonlight, Mickey watched their progress.

Rip reached the second floor. Mickey saw him peer inside the window. Rip cut a small circle in the glass, reached in, and unfastened the lock. He pushed the window up two feet and slithered inside. Tom followed.

Mickey adopted a shooting stance, feet spread wide, gun leveled and aimed at the front door. He took deep slow breaths and waited. Five minutes. Ten minutes. No sound. No frantic exit from the house by the two women. No shots.

Then Rip and Tom emerged from the front door without Feinstein.

"The house is empty," Rip said. "No sign of the women. No suitcases. We looked in the garage, too. No car."

Tom nodded. "Looks like they left town. Do you know where they could have gone?"

"No fucking idea." They'd counted on Feinstein being at her family's vacation house, and they had no idea where else she might be. There was not time nor manpower to track them down. Mickey took out his phone and dialed. He spoke briefly to Charlie and then clicked off. Then Mickey turned to Rip and Tom.

"Okay, aborting mission. Tom, you head back to Boston and wait for additional orders. Rip, you're going to stay with me."

****

Hidden in the trees, Alex Feinstein held the Galil firmly against her shoulder, following the shapes of the men walking down the driveway. If she had to shoot, it would be tricky. They probably had on body armor, which meant hitting them in the neck or the head. And there were three of them. While she was competent at shooting, she wasn't confident she could shoot three men before they returned fire. That was apart from the fact that she didn't like the idea of killing anyone, even kidnappers, if it wasn't necessary.

But she was providing cover for Tehila, who was planting a GPS tracking device on the black Subaru at the end of the driveway. If the men saw Tehila, then Alex would shoot. Only then—and only to protect Tehila.

But it wasn't necessary.

She watched, gun ready, as the men swung the doors open, into the car, and then roared down the dirt road.

Tehila slid out of the shadows. "Done."

Alex relaxed, lowering the gun. "What now?"

"We climb back up to the camp and catch an hour or two of sleep, and then early tomorrow, we leave the area."

"We're not going to follow?"

"Not necessary. The GPS device will lead us—or someone else—to these guys—whenever. And I'm asking the office if someone else can follow up. My job is to protect you, not to track down idiots. Besides, I'm tired."

The campsite was in a small clearing, half a mile up the mountain and far enough off the usual trail as not to be easily spotted—unless you already knew it was there. Alex's car was concealed behind trees nearby.

At least the location had good cell reception—which was how they knew that the men were approaching the house. Alex and Tehila had made it down the mountain just as the two men began their climb up the side of the house.

"How are you enjoying camping?" Tehila asked.

"Still hate it." Alex handed the gun back to Tehila. Alex was competent with a gun. Tehila was an expert. "But it's better than being kidnapped or killed."

And it was the second time that someone had tried to kidnap her. Second time in less than a year—to use her against Kolya, no doubt. She didn't even want to think how he'd react.

"Don't text Kolya." Tehila had an uncanny ability to know what she was thinking. "It'll distract him—and that could be dangerous for him and for the mission."

As if she didn't know.

36

IT WAS A SMALL meeting. The President, Ben Smithson, CIA director, and Margaret Bradford, ECA director were in the Oval Office, the President in an armchair, Margaret seated on a couch with Smithson on a second couch directly across from her. Margaret preferred small meetings, although she would have preferred this to be smaller by one. That Smithson was in on the meeting was annoying. This was her operation now, and Smithson and the CIA had nothing to do with it.

Still, she knew better than to say so out loud.

President Lewis shifted his gaze from one to the other. "Glad to see that the two of you have put aside your differences for this matter."

"Locating the Novichok and determining who's behind it is more important than our personal rivalries, eh Margaret?"

"Of course," she murmured.

Lewis was looking grim. "It doesn't take much Novichok to kill. If Bykovsky commits a terrorist attack on American soil—I'll have to respond. This is very serious. What are you hearing from your team?"

She thought about the communication from Elizabeth Owen and the fact that Petrov was missing and possibly had committed murder. That he might have killed a man who'd abused him as a child didn't bother her morally, but it did concern her. The therapist had warned about Petrov's mental state. If Petrov was out of control, he was a danger to the mission. The mission was what mattered.

She'd given the back-up team twelve hours to locate Petrov—and then they were to pull out. Under other circumstances, she might not have been so generous. But these things were complicated, and Petrov was operating undercover, on enemy territory, communicating with dangerous men. There very well could be an innocent explanation for his silence. As long as the job was getting done. If Petrov failed, there could be serious loss of life—and a serious international incident.

She remembered her last conversation with Petrov—when he indicated that he might have volunteered to allow himself to be captured—if she'd asked. Should she have trusted him? She still thought she'd done the right thing then—but this time—she'd give him the benefit of the doubt—for ten hours more.

"There's been initial contact and my people are following up on it." It was vague enough that it was probably true.

"And Petrov's not," Lewis hesitated on the words, "not having any issues being back in the field. I understand he's still not fully recovered."

"No issues that I've heard." Also true, technically.

"And his fiancee?" Smithson asked.

"Out of town, under the protection of a very competent ECA agent."

"Good." Smithson nodded. "We don't want someone using Petrov's fiancée to get to him."

He met her eyes—knowing that she was the one to use Alex Feinstein against him on Petrov's last mission. *Well, fuck you, Ben.*

"As soon as Petrov or the team has anything concrete to report, I'll inform you."

She was taking a chance here. Something could have happened to Petrov—the FSB could have picked him up, or Dmitri could have betrayed him. And while it wasn't good for the mission—or for Petrov—for him to have been caught or killed, it wouldn't create political fallout for her or the ECA.

It would be a whole different question if it turned out that Petrov was off the reservation. But if necessary, she'd deal with the situation—and neither Smithson nor Lewis had any need to know everything.

Besides, Petrov was the best shot to find whoever had smuggled Novichok into the United States.

A little more time for him to get back in touch. She owed him that much.

WEDNESDAY NOON, ST. PETERSBURG, RUSSIA

Jonathan checked his watch. Margaret had given them twelve hours to find Kolya. There'd been no sign of Kolya or Dmitri at the hotel, but there had been quite a few FSB agents lingering on the premises.

They returned to their own hotel and packed. Orders were for them to get on a plane out of the country once the time was up. Kolya could have been killed or captured, and while Jonathan trusted Kolya not to give them up, security would be tightened, and they could be trapped.

For now, they were holed up in the room that Jonathan and Elizabeth were sharing. Elizabeth sat at a table, reading. Teo paced, cracking fingers nervously.

Jonathan continued to text and call, and there continued to be no answer.

A few more hours—and they were out.

Come on, Kolya. Call.

37

WEDNESDAY NOON, M11 FROM ST. PETERSBURG TO MOSCOW

ST. PETERSBURG TO MOSCOW is 430 miles of neglected roadway. Parts of a new roadway had been completed, but most of the route required taking the old M11, a twelve-hour drive, barring snowstorms or accidents, which could increase travel time to twenty-four hours or longer.

It was Dmitri's turn to drive. Kolya had slept past Novgorod—where he could have bought a phone—and now they were into the countryside. The world outside the car was one of ghosts—of what Russia had been, what Russia could be, and, at least in this part of Russia, what it was not. They passed deserted villages and dilapidated buildings against a flat, sometimes lush natural landscape. Ghost towns. Yet, this stretch of Russia held no personal ghosts: as a child, he had never been outside St. Petersburg until his flight to New York.

So he napped off and on. But the naps turned to nightmares, his Romanian nightmare mingled with images of the dead, some of whom he had killed. He startled awake to a car full of cigarette smoke.

He pulled his seat up and coughed. "Please put it out."

Dmitri rolled down the window and tossed the butt. "You've become very American."

"Because I like my lungs?"

"Neither of us is likely to live long enough to worry about cancer."

"I thought you were going to retire to Florida." Kolya straightened in his seat, regretting the lack of sleep. "And after this, I'm out. Lawyers live a long time." A long unpleasant time.

Dmitri made a snorting noise.

Kolya watched out the window. A few more hours to the outskirts of Moscow, traffic allowing. He needed a phone. They'd pass Voldai soon—a renovated town with restaurants and shops. Maybe he could buy a phone there.

He thought about Alex, missing her and wishing he could call. But at least she was safe in Vermont, and Tehila would keep her that way.

"Are you awake?" Dmitri asked.

"Pretty much."

"Tell me you did not enjoy being in St. Petersburg."

"I didn't enjoy being in St. Petersburg."

"It's a beautiful city. Okay, there are lots of bad memories. But some are good. We should have gone to your old apartment in St. Petersburg. Remember when we snuck out to see it?"

"Yes."

* * * * *

Twenty- five years earlier, a few months after his first fighting lesson, and a month after he'd broken Yelseyev's nose, Kolya had woken up before dawn, dressed quietly, and slipped out of the dormitory where he slept with a dozen other boys.

Dmitri had followed.

They crept down the stairs, freezing at every noise. There was supposed to be a teacher on night duty, but often they slept—and no one complained.

"Yelseyev's going to beat us bloody," Dmitri whispered.

"You don't have to come."

"Sure I do. What kind of friend would let you go alone? Besides, I want to see where you used to live."

Kolya and his mother had lived in five rooms on Moskovskaya Avenue. An apartment of that size had been a rarity in those times of communal apartments, but his mother had had the remnants of money and status as a concert pianist from the time before she'd married the wrong man.

It wasn't that far from the *dom* to the apartment building in a residential section of St. Petersburg.

The building had been simple in the Soviet style of the time and in contrast to the ornate palaces and museums in the center of the city. Kolya gazed up at the windows on the third floor where he'd once lived. Someone was moving inside. He pictured his mother's morning routine—fixing him tea with jam, bread and jelly, and afterward, she would sit next to him at the piano until it was time to leave for school. But it was no longer his home. Whoever was inside was a stranger. The piano was probably gone, too, although maybe not. Pianos were valuable.

"Big building," Dmitri said. "Were you rich?"

"I didn't think I was, but maybe. It was wonderful. Especially my mother." Kolya felt tears stinging his eyes. He swiped them away with a sleeve.

"I'd like to see your old apartment. Want to see if they'll let us in?" Dmitri started for the door.

"No, stop. No point. It'll all be different. All our things will be gone. My mother won't be there." Kolya gazed for another minute and then turned away. "I just wanted to see the building. Because sometimes I think it was just a dream. My previous life, I mean."

"Maybe the *dom* isn't real." Dmitri lightly punched Kolya in the arm. "Maybe you're just having a nightmare now. Maybe you just made me up."

"Well, you are a nightmare." Kolya gave a light punch back. "Let's get back before Yelseyev realizes we're gone."

But Yelseyev was waiting when they returned.

* * * * *

"I couldn't sit for a week after that beating," Dmitri said.

"I know. I couldn't either. Still, there's no point to revisiting it all."

"Do you think we can leave the past behind?"

"No. But we can't cling to it either."

"There is some truth in that. My mother was a whore—*pizdorvanka*—who treated me like shit." They were speaking in English, but Dmitri resorted to the Russian insult. "She didn't die. She just left. But *suka*—bitch that she was, I loved her. Thought she was the most beautiful woman in the world. Then she was gone, and I hated her and loved her. I thought about her for years."

"We talked about trying to find her, but you decided against it."

167

"Did you ever find out anything more about your father?"

"No." Kolya's father, Ivan Denisovich Petrov, had been a journalist who'd been sent to prison for articles that the KGB, in the dying days of the Soviet Union, had found offensive. He had died and been buried there soon after Kolya's birth. In his teenage years, he had read some of his father's articles but never felt the urge to track down an unmarked grave. His father had been an honorable man who had died opposing repression. That had been enough. "You?"

"I would have needed DNA testing of every drunk my mother ever slept with, and there were just too many. So, about my mother—I tracked her down a few years before I came to America. She was living with some bastard and still selling herself. She had lost most of her teeth and her looks, and she didn't know me until I told her who I was. Then she made up excuses why she left. But it didn't matter."

"Why look for her if it didn't matter?"

"That's the fucking thing about the past. You want to leave it, but it doesn't want to leave you. Love and hate both hold you back. You only get rid of the past if you face the past. I thought I might kill her or maybe we would have a big emotional reunion, and I would forgive her. But when I saw her, she was pathetic. There could be no reconciliation: there wasn't enough left of her to love, but there wasn't enough left to hate, either. The mother I loved and hated had disappeared and left an old hag. I walked away, and then I told friends to give her the drugs she wanted. Free. I heard she died from an overdose. It didn't matter to me when I heard."

Kolya struggled to keep his eyes open.

"Go back to sleep." Dmitri swerved the car around an eighteen-wheeler. The trucker made an obscene gesture. Dmitri rolled down his window and shouted, "*Yob tvoyu mat.*" Then he increased his speed.

"I can take over driving."

Dmitri laughed. "I like driving. And it is more likely we'll die in a car crash because you are tired, than because I yell at some fucking asshole. Sleep."

Kolya eased the seat back. It was fortunately a German-made BMW and not a Russian car. He settled in again and closed his eyes.

38

WEDNESDAY AFTERNOON, VALDAI, RUSSIA

THE FIVE GOLDEN DOMES of the 17th century Iversky Monastery dominated the landscape of the city of Valdai and reflected in the lake that surrounded the city. During the Soviet era, the monastery had housed tuberculosis patients, but it had since been restored to full glory and become a tourist destination because of the lake, the forest, and the proximity to the summer home of the previous president of the Russian Republic.

They found a small café within the shadow of the monastery. The cafe also offered souvenirs—of the type found in every tourist destination around the world. Snow globes containing images of the monastery. Coffee cups with the name of the town in Cyrillic. Key chains.

No phones.

They took a table near the back of the café. A young woman, dark hair pulled back, blue jeans and a black shirt, hurried over. She was attractive—the job and the burdens of a life on the financial edge not yet showing in her face or figure—but the early signs were there—a strain around the eyes, a weariness around her mouth.

Dmitri smiled up at her. "What is good here?"

"Everything is good, but especially the pancakes." She had a no-nonsense tone.

"Then I'll have the pancakes." Dmitri winked at her. "And coffee. Your name is what, beautiful?"

"We only sell food here." She scribbled the order on a small pad of paper. There were places in Russia where that wasn't true.

"I wasn't looking to *buy* anything but food. But a man dreams of love."

"You can dream of whatever you want. But what you get is what is on the menu." She turned her attention to Kolya. "And you?"

Kolya ordered coffee and sausage. She wrote it down and walked away.

Dmitri leaned over the table. "I think she likes me."

"I know you've been out of circulation, but women these days don't actually like that shit."

"Russian women aren't so politically correct. Besides it's fun to annoy you."

"I figured. But maybe you should consider other ways to amuse yourself. Take up chess. Learn Chinese. Practice piano."

"Too much work. Besides, if there was a piano around, it would not be me playing it." He pushed back his chair. "I need to piss. You?"

"After we eat."

Dmitri headed down the hall towards the bathroom, and the young woman returned with two cups of coffee. "Where is your friend?" She didn't sound eager to see him.

"Bathroom. I'm sorry if he offended you."

She set the coffee down. "If I offended easily, I would work somewhere else."

Kolya reached for sugar. "Understand. Still, I'm sorry. By the way, do you know where I can buy a phone in town?"

"No. I bought mine on the Internet. You're going to Moscow? Buy one there."

He would, but he also needed a phone now. "Could I pay you to borrow your phone?"

"How much?"

He did a calculation and offered what he considered generous. "Twenty dollars American."

"A hundred."

It was an extortion level price for a phone call, but he had the money and he'd been out of touch for too long. "Okay, but I'll need the phone for at least five minutes. Now, before my friend comes back."

Dmitri had had opportunities to run, sabotage the mission, or kill Kolya, and he had refrained. Kolya was beginning to trust him. But still, he didn't want Dmitri to overhear a conversation with Jonathan. Dmitri didn't need to know the names or locations of ECA agents in Russia—and the less he knew, the less he could say if they were arrested.

She offered her phone. "Money first."

He peeled a hundred dollars off a roll and laid it on the table.

She scooped up the bills. "Keep it as long as you want. Just give it back before you leave."

She walked off, and he tapped in the number for Jonathan's burner. Three rings, and Jonathan answered. "Yeah?"

"It's me. I borrowed a phone."

"Thank God. Are you okay?"

"Fine."

"Good. Now where the hell are you and what is going on? We've been going nuts."

"Sorry. Things got a little out of hand." He summarized the events of the previous night and recited Rzaev's address in Peredelkino.

"You could have called."

"I texted you."

"You were fucking vague."

"Sorry again. I planned to contact you after we left the club, but Minsky kept my phone. There hasn't been an opportunity before this."

A pause. "What happened in the apartment with Yelseyev?"

"You heard what happened."

"Not after you turned off your phone." There was something strange in Jonathan's voice.

"I posted online that he was a pedophile, called the police, and left."

"But he was alive when you left?"

"Of course, he was alive." Kolya suddenly felt cold. "Why?"

"When you didn't show up at the Platonov Club, we doubled back. The police had the whole place cordoned off. Someone had slit Yelseyev's stomach open."

"*Yob tvoyu mat.* The son-of-a bitch."

"Dmitri?"

"No, he was with me. Arkady. Arkady had a knife. I watched him leave, but then we left." Kolya cursed again to himself. Stupid. Fucking stupid. He should have known Arkady might do something of the sort. Did Jonathan think him capable of this kind of a murder? "I wouldn't have killed the old bastard. I don't kill people for the hell of it. And I'm not stupid."

"I know, and I believe you. You weren't wearing gloves, were you?"

"No, but I wiped down anything I touched."

Jonathan sighed. "Still. If anyone spotted you coming or leaving, you'd be a prime suspect."

"I know." Kolya's voice rose—and then he lowered it again. "I know. This is not good."

"At least you're out of St. Petersburg, and as long as you're not stopped by the authorities, no one will connect the dots. But you should know—when we couldn't find you, Elizabeth called Bradford to fill her in. She gave us twelve hours to find you, and then she was pulling us out."

"Fuck Bradford. How close did I cut it?"

"You still had time." Jonathan switched back to business. "Okay, so we'll take a plane to Moscow and be in Peredelkino before you."

"Stay out of sight. Rzaev will kill us if he suspects anything out of the ordinary."

"Of course. Unless you need us. Just be careful, will you? Anything happens to you, Alex will kill *me*."

"There's that possibility." Kolya spotted Dmitri who paused to exchange a few words with the waitress. Her body language flashed open hostility. "After I buy a phone, I'll text you the number." Dmitri grinned in his direction.

39

TWO HOURS SLEEP ON the private plane to Moscow, and now back in his office in the Lubyanka, Tomas was enveloped by the adrenaline that continued to surge. It was like being on drugs. He liked it, hated it—and it would come with a crash. The crash might not just be the physical letdown—it could be the crash of a personal disaster. For the hundredth time, he regretted leaving his job overseeing border security and accepting the job of FSB *Direktor*. But it wasn't as if he'd had a choice. Yuri Bykovsky had made that quite clear.

Tomas hadn't wanted the job. He'd been forced to take it. And yet he felt himself morphing into someone he'd never intended to become. He could still hear Ivan Minsky scream when the bullet shattered his hand. But he had to find the spies and uncover whether Rzaev had smuggled Novichok into the United States—and who he had smuggled it for.

Then again, who was he fooling? Who was he anyway? He was just the brother-in-law. The patsy.

He picked up the phone and called Lyudmila to tell her he was back in Moscow.

"Yuri called me. He just wanted me to say... to remind you... what you owe him."

"I'll never forget, dear. I have some work to do before I come home. I will see you late tonight."

He remembered one of his first dates with Lyudmila. They'd walked through Gorky Park in the springtime. From the top of the Ferris wheel, they saw the city laid out beneath them. He could almost feel the fresh breeze moving through his hair. Then the most beautiful girl in the world kissed him. Two weeks later, he'd met her parents and her brother—who at the time was an officer in the FSB, moving up through the ranks. Even back then, Yuri had made him nervous, with crude stories of sex and violence. But he'd seemed to care about his family, so Tomas overlooked it.

After Tomas married Lyudmila, Yuri helped Tomas get a position with the FSB border security. It had been low level—little chance of advancement, but it had been safe.

It took ten years more for Yuri to become head of the FSB—and the close confidant of the President. Another three years: the President suffered a heart attack—and put Yuri in as his replacement. Two of the old guard challenged Yuri's right to the highest office in Russia. Both had died mysteriously within weeks of Yuri's ascension. Then there was the plot by the last *Direktor* of the FSB—which led to Tomas's ascension.

In the beginning, it wasn't terrible. Tomas had listened to Yuri's jokes and stories, complemented Yuri on his accomplishments and on the attractiveness of the succession of young women he paraded on his arm, and had thanked him for his leadership. It was uncomfortable, but it worked. Tomas had pushed papers and left the running of the agency to those who knew what they were doing.

Now Tomas was doing something that wasn't exactly what Yuri had told him to do—even though he had approved catching American spies. He had not approved heading to Rzaev's compound—even though that was where the spies were headed.

Was he being stupid?

Probably.

He still wanted to know the truth. To protect his country. To protect his family. The only way to do that was to follow his current course.

Lemonsky and Petrov should arrive in Peredelkino in the late afternoon. Tomas opened his computer and scrolled through the names of the FSB officers inside the building, looking for officers loyal to him. Then he picked his crew. Twenty men, three women.

40

THE DACHA, THE COUNTRY retreat where city-dwelling Russians escaped urban grime and grew vegetables, had changed in the years since the dissolution of the Soviet Union. Once small modest cottages, many dachas were now elaborate mansions for the newly wealthy. Peredelkino had shared in this fate, perhaps even more so, since it was within the city limits of Moscow.

Jonathan, Elizabeth, and Teo reached Peredelkino hours ahead of Kolya and Dmitri. They drove by high stone walls that hid Rzaev's compound and three men in suits guarding an iron gate across the driveway. Through the bars, Jonathan caught a glimpse of a stretch of lawn and an imposing brick mansion. The guards, eyes covered in dark sunglasses, turned their heads to watch their car. Jonathan continued past without changing speed, glancing in the rearview mirror as he reached a junction in the road.

He turned onto a two-lane road. Rzaev's compound was somewhere on the left side. But he couldn't see the mansion or the walls surrounding it, the view eclipsed by a small forest of pine trees.

"Between the guards and the walls—if Kolya has a problem—how'll we get in to help?" Teo asked.

"Beats me. We just need to stay close by—and then we'll figure it out if we have to. Which way to Pasternak's house?"

Peredelkino had once been a writer's retreat: the summer home of Boris Pasternak, author of Dr. Zhivago, built in the shape of a ship, had been preserved as a museum. They toured the museum before retreating to the restaurant *Dyeti Solntsa*, near the church and the graveyard, both tourist magnets. They seated themselves at an outside table and flipped through a menu of Russian specialties, which Jonathan could read with difficulty, before choosing coffees and pastries that were the specialty of the house.

Jonathan checked his phone. Kolya'd bought a burner when he hit the outskirts of Moscow and had texted the number, but there were no further messages. Nothing from Margaret. Before leaving St. Petersburg, Jonathan had informed her that Kolya was back in touch and that the mission was on track.

Now they just had to wait.

Teo had already eaten a *coulibiac*, a pastry filled with sturgeon, mushrooms, eggs, onions, and dill. Now he was working on a slice of Kiev cake with a napoleon waiting in the wings.

"You're going to get fat if you keep eating like that." Elizabeth toyed with a simple croissant and drank coffee.

"No, I won't. Fast metabolism. Runs in the family. What are we doing next?"

"We kill time and try not to look obvious." Jonathan polished off a meat pie.

Elizabeth snorted. "So far, this whole thing has been one screw up after another. This is a tiny town. How are we going to look inconspicuous?"

"There are tourists," Teo said.

"Americans? We're not in St. Petersburg anymore."

Jonathan shrugged. "Maybe. We just have to avoid any of Rzaev's men...."

"The FSB. The police," Elizabeth cut in.

"Yeah, all of them—but be available if Kolya needs us."

"On the small chance that we could even get to him in time." Elizabeth crossed her arms. "Don't give me that look, Jonathan. You know as well as I do that if things go south, he's dead."

"Maybe. Stop being such a pessimist, Elizabeth."

"It's who I am."

"Well, it's fucked up." Teo took a large bite of the Kiev cake.

"Spying 101. Everything's always fucked up." Jonathan hoped it wasn't true this time.

41

THE CAR STOPPED IN front of three men guarding the closed iron gate to the high walled compound. It would be hard to get in—and harder to get out. Kolya pushed down his uneasiness. The legend was good; the team was nearby—and he had done this kind of work for ten years.

But he'd been a lawyer for the past eight months. And he hadn't had PTSD during those ten years.

Stop it.

A tall man in a well-cut suit and sunglasses, with thinning dark hair slicked straight back, tapped on the driver's window.

Dmitri rolled the window down. "Good to see you, Boris, motherfucker."

"You, too, Dmitri, you shit. The old man's going to be happy to see you." The sunglasses turned in Kolya's direction. "Michael Harding?"

"Obviously."

The man gave a nod. The other men stepped aside, and one punched a code into the electric opener. The gate swung wide. Dmitri drove through the gate, up a hundred foot circular driveway, past trimmed grass and flower beds, and parked in front of a red brick mansion.

Kolya estimated the wall that encircled the property to be about twelve feet high. Three armed men at the gate. Six more patrolled the grounds. If things went bad, he'd be trapped. He felt his heart pounding.

"You okay?" Dmitri asked.

"Fine."

They exited the car and climbed marble steps. Kolya's leg, which had the benefit of resting for the drive, only made minor protests. At the door, a stocky older man in butler garb who could have been in a BBC production—except for the not quite concealed gun in a shoulder holster—conducted a polite but thorough search, confiscating Kolya's gun and knife.

They followed him through the passageway, light wood floors gleaming with polish, to the kitchen—and then exited the house into a pristine garden that stretched all the way to the wall, ending in beds of red, orange and yellow flowers. In the center of the garden, a small gazebo, and in rows stretching from the gazebo to the flower display, beds of newly planted herbs and vegetables.

An older man with a neatly cut gray beard, wisps of long white hair showing under a battered straw hat, knelt on a mat in the grass next to freshly turned earth. He patted dirt around a small plant.

The butler nodded towards the gardener. "He's expecting you."

The man leaned back on his haunches. Kolya recognized the face that bore an odd resemblance to the man on KFC buckets. Vladimir Rzaev. Volodya to his friends. His smile was that of a kindly grandfather.

"A beautiful evening for planting." He pointed at the tray of seedlings. "Cucumbers and tomatoes. Dill." The butler stepped forward and helped Rzaev to his feet. "Do you know anything about plants?" The question was directed at Kolya.

Kolya shook his head. "Except for what goes in a salad, no."

"You have been out of Russia too long, young man. Even musicians in Russia know the value of working the earth. And you, Dima?"

"You know I am allergic to real work, Volodya."

"I am aware." Rzaev embraced Dmitri. "Good to see you, Dima. It has been too long."

"It has." Dmitri's voice held genuine warmth. "My replacement did not let things go to shit?"

"Do you think I would let things go to shit? But he was less amusing than you." The old man looked at Kolya with keen blue eyes. "And you are Dima's friend?"

"Since we were boys," Kolya said.

Rzaev oozed warmth and charm. If Kolya hadn't known better, he might have bought the act. But he was also an actor in this charade.

"In the *dyskeii dom*." Rzaev nodded. "Michael Harding is not your real name, is it? I remember Dima talking about his friend in America, and that was not the name he used. If I recall correctly, his friend was called Kolya."

Kolya inclined his head. "I prefer not to use my Russian name, except with very close friends. Too many in the intelligence world would recognize it."

"As long as Dima knows you—and how to find you if I need to kill you, you can call yourself Santa Claus for all I care. A cousin in America adopted you, correct?"

"Yes."

"But poor Dima had to stay in that place until he signed up with me—then you put him in jail."

"But I also got him out."

"So I understand." Rzaev turned to Dmitri. "Why did he put you in and why did he get you out? And why are you working with him?"

Kolya tensed. How much loyalty did Dmitri feel towards Rzaev—who'd sponsored him and put him in a position of power? Had Dmitri really moved past his anger for the betrayal of their brotherhood?

Dmitri glanced sideways at Kolya, just the trace of a smile—as if he knew what Kolya was thinking. "He believed it was his duty to the country that had adopted him. When it became clear that his loyalty had been misplaced, he got me out through various legal maneuvers. He's also a lawyer. I was angry—at first. But I kicked the shit out of him, and I felt better. And now, we are friends again. I trust him."

"But we are not talking friendship here, we are talking money. So I ask you again, do you trust him to make you money?"

"Of course. He is smart about money. Even if he made a stupid decision about working for the United States government for a while."

Rzaev turned to Kolya. "So you are disloyal to America?"

"Not exactly. I am just making money. Like you. Are you disloyal to Russia?"

Rzaev laughed. "Not in any way that counts. Let us go sit."

Inside the gazebo, they sat on wrought-iron chairs with comfortable cushions, around a glass table near a sideboard, painted white, topped with crystal glasses and vases of flowers. From his chair, Kolya had a good view of the garden. Bees hummed around white flowers on the tall bushes that decorated the garden wall. "The flowers are lovely."

"Nadiya, my wife, she planted them. The raspberries, too. They're coming in well this year."

Dmitri turned to Kolya. "You would have liked her. A graceful and charming woman."

"Thank you for your kind words," Rzaev said. "I didn't deserve such a woman, but I didn't argue with her for choosing me."

"I'm sorry I didn't get to say goodbye. She's gone, now, a year?"

"Eighteen months. Eighteen months and two weeks." He placed his hat on an extra chair. "Sometimes I'll be out here, planting, and I'll see a shadow—and for a second, I think it's her. Then I look up—and it's not."

"Fucking breast cancer," Dmitri said.

"Fucking breast cancer. It kills too many Russian women. American, too. Now let us have refreshments and talk of something else. It's hot out here, isn't it? Moscow didn't use to be this hot in June."

"Global fucking warming," Dmitri said.

"Global fucking warming," Rzaev agreed. "Pavel, vodka. And you, Mr. Harding," his voice held mockery, "please take out your phone. I know Dima does not have a phone. And, yes, you were scanned walking through my house."

Kolya laid the phone on the table, grateful that he had not taken up Jonathan's offer of the GPS tracker.

Pavel picked up the phone, checked that it was neither recording nor transmitting, and set it in front of Rzaev. Then, from the sideboard, Pavel retrieved a large engraved case in the shape of a Fabergé egg. Inside the case was a bottle of vodka with four crystal glasses. He filled the glasses with vodka and distributed them.

"Imperial Collection." Rzaev took a sip and put the glass down. "Tell me what you think."

Kolya drank off the shot. It was possibly the best vodka he'd ever tasted. "Very nice, but it should be for what it costs."

"Ah, you know the price." Rzaev sipped his glass and set it down.

"I do and am suitably impressed, which was the point, wasn't it? Because," Kolya let his gaze fall on Rzaev's nearly full glass, "Russians do not sip vodka. You either don't care for it, or you are not allowed to drink anymore."

"I'm on medication for my heart, and my doctor gives me orders. He's a shit, but he knows what he's doing. Still, I taste it now and then and don't tell him." He raised the crystal glass, and light emanating through the crystal broke into a cascade of colors. "I buy the best—because I can. Which gets to the question of money—and exactly how you propose to make us both money. You want to smuggle in drugs?"

"Well, yes, but not the kind you're thinking of. Prescription medicine. Very expensive prescription medicine. Take for example, Acthar—used for a type of rare infant spasms and for multiple sclerosis. A vial sells for $40,000 in the U.S. but sells for $33 in Canada. Insurance might pick up some of the cost, or may refuse to pay altogether. Given how cheap the purchase price in Canada, I can significantly undercut the cost and still make a huge profit. There are twenty or thirty drugs that are on this level of expense in the United States but relatively cheap in Canada."

"How would this work?"

"I have signed up procurement officers in Canada to sell me various expensive drugs. I am also purchasing drugs from various Canadian pharmacists who, for something under the table, will fill the prescriptions. Then once the drugs are across the border, my company that purports to be a discounter of orphan drugs has signed up American hospitals, doctors, and insurance companies to distribute. I am also buying a small amount of the drugs in the United States, so it would not be easily discovered that the bulk of the drugs I am selling come from Canada. I am also looking into bringing in non-FDA approved drugs that are used to fight cancer in other countries, but that's down the road."

He'd rehearsed the pitch until he almost believed in its truth. Now it was on the table. Either Rzaev would buy it, or not. If not, he and Dmitri were both dead.

Silence. Rzaev looked out at the garden, at the white flowers and the raspberry bushes. "The United States does have very good hospitals and doctors, but it is too expensive for a lot of people. I wanted Nadiya to go to UCLA. There was this clinical trial... but she wouldn't go. She was tired. Nadiya would like that I help sick people. But I am a businessman, not a philanthropist. How much do you think this is worth?"

Kolya turned the crystal glass in his hands. The butler stepped forward to offer him another drink, but he shook his head. "The estimate is that Americans spend $385 billion a year on prescription drugs. If we could get even a small part of that market, it would be incredibly lucrative, especially since the profit margin would be so high." He could feel the sweat on his shirt inside the suit, beads of sweat on his forehead. He could blame it on the warmth of the evening if Rzaev noticed.

"What can I do for you?"

"What I do not have is a way to move the drugs from Canada into the United States. It is illegal to import Canadian drugs for use in the United States. I know that Dmitri worked with you ten years ago setting up a smuggling network. I assume you still have people in place."

"Of course. New people who law enforcement wouldn't know and Dima wouldn't know, though Dima did not turn on his own. Which is why he is still my son—and still alive." Rzaev took another small sip of the vodka. "I also assume that American intelligence would no longer care if I slit your stomach open and pulled out your intestines." Rzaev smiled as if it were a joke. "Not that I'm thinking of doing that. Let's go back to talk about money. What do you think, Dima? Can he do this?"

Dmitri reached across the table for the crystal decanter. "He can. We can." Dmitri poured himself another shot of the vodka. Pavel, the butler, frowned at him but said nothing.

Rzaev handed the butler his vodka glass. "*Lemonad.*" Pavel poured the contents into the grass, a casual discard of such expensive vodka, and refilled the glass with lemonade from a silver pitcher. "What is your percentage?"

"Dmitri gets twenty percent. I am offering you twenty-five percent," Kolya said.

The percentage was lower than what Kolya knew would be acceptable. But someone in his position would start low.

"Who do you think you are dealing with?" Rzaev pulled a handkerchief from his pocket and mopped his face. "You come into my house, you say nice things about my garden and my wife. You want to help sick people, and you think you can buy me cheap, like a whore? Sixty percent."

"All you are doing is providing the transportation." He couldn't give in too easily. "I've arranged the deals. I set up the company. I'm taking huge risks."

"Then carry the drugs yourself."

"There are other people who could do this—for a lot less money."

"Who?" Rzaev held out his glass for more lemonade. Pavel poured. Rzaev drank.

"We can find someone."

"Go ahead. But you will lose much of your products. The others are incompetent."

"He has the best people and the best network," Dmitri turned to Kolya, face flushed from the vodka. "Everyone knows that."

"Maybe," Kolya said. "And maybe I'll take a chance."

Rzaev's face changed. The affable gardening grandfather disappeared, and in his place was the hardened criminal that Kolya knew was the reality. "Look behind you, *Michael Harding*."

Kolya didn't move. Turning to look would demonstrate weakness. He could see enough reflected in the windows of the house, a dim image of several men, maybe twenty yards behind.

"Fuck you and the horse you ride. You came to me, asshole. Now we'll do business on terms that I like, or you can stay here in my garden, permanently. Human bodies make good fertilizer. The terms are sixty percent."

Don't show fear. A flash from Romania, chained to the wall, men standing over him, the terror of helplessness. He mentally repeated calming words in his mind. This was not Romania. Romania was in the past, and the past did not dictate what was going to happen. He was in control here. He could do this. This was just a show by Rzaev.

The image dissipated, and the terror ebbed.

Don't give him everything he wants. Act in character—and the character he was playing would not give in easily.

"Thirty-five percent. You want to kill me, that's your choice. But threatening me to up your percentage is a poor negotiating tactic. If I were that afraid to die, I'd be in another business."

"I like him." Rzaev turned to Dmitri. "Cool under pressure. I see why you were friends." Then Rzaev smiled. The friendly grandfather was back. "Pavel, give him some lemonade. And me too."

Pavel approached with the lemonade pitcher.

Kolya held up a hand, declining.

Rzaev drank and set his glass down. "Fifty."

"Forty."

"Let's split the difference. Forty-five."

"Of the profits."

"Of course, after expenses are paid. Although I will want verification that expenses are genuine."

"I would expect nothing else." Kolya held out his hand. "Agreed. And you will arrange for me to meet with your smuggler in the United States."

"Good but first—what is it your Reagan said—trust but verify. After I finish this very excellent lemonade, you will give me the website of your discount company for me to check out. If everything looks good, I will arrange for you to meet the current head of my North American operation. If it does not check out, my men will kill both of you, and I will finish planting. My seedlings are waiting, and summer is short here, as you know."

42

TOMAS ARRIVED IN THE village with eight cars and a van for the drone and its operator and to transport prisoners if the spies were there—or if Rzaev's men resisted. He preferred taking prisoners to killing anyone, although he knew that tonight's raid was dangerous. Rzaev's compound was guarded by at least a dozen armed men. He was banking on Rzaev not wanting to get into a shootout. Still, he'd be prepared if it did happen. The situation was serious enough—the questions he needed answered were important enough—that it was worth the risk.

The other cars and the van circled the town, scouting for anything unusual. He didn't know if there could be other American spies in town—although Minsky had only mentioned the two. Still a quick check of public spots for anything suspicious—either American spies or Rzaev's men—would be wise prior to descending on Rzaev's compound. He didn't want to have either more spies or gangsters showing up behind his people when they engaged Rzaev's guards.

They parked near the town center, and ten officers exited the cars. After they returned, Tomas would make his move.

* * * * *

From the table in *Dyeti Solntsa*, where the three of them continued to nurse coffees and the restaurant staff cheerfully ignored their presence, Jonathan had a view of the colorful church where Pasternak's burial service had been held. Three men in dark suits crossed the graveyard

185

towards them. They did not look like lovers of literature. Jonathan fished in his pocket, pulled out a roll of bills and tossed a handful on the table.

The restaurant had a back entrance for discreet departures—the town's new and prominent mafiya residents liked back doors. Jonathan led the way through the kitchen. On the wall, white jackets for the staff hung on hooks. Jonathan motioned, and each of them each slipped one on. From a nearby countertop, Jonathan pocketed a pack of Camels.

Then they slipped outside.

Two men approached the back door. Jonathan gave Teo and Elizabeth cigarettes, stuck one between his own lips, struck a match, and inhaled.

The men glanced at them. Jonathan gave a nod and exhaled smoke. Elizabeth smiled and tapped ashes onto the ground. The men continued into the restaurant.

"Police?" Teo asked in an undertone.

"FSB more likely," Elizabeth answered. "They have that look."

They dropped cigarettes, peeled off the jackets and headed for the car, half a block away. It would be tricky getting near enough to Rzaev's compound to assist Kolya without running into either Rzaev's men or the newcomers. Find a place to park closer to Rzaev's but not too close.

Meanwhile, Kolya would have no idea that men who appeared to be police or FSB were searching the town.

Jonathan pulled out his phone and hesitated. Would texting Kolya endanger him?

"It's a risk." Elizabeth read his thoughts. "But you have to alert him."

Teo nodded agreement. Jonathan tapped out the message.

43

WEDNESDAY NIGHT, PEREDELKINO, RUSSIA

"STILL FIVE MEN BEHIND you." Dmitri said.

Small solar lights interspersed among the flowers and around the gazebo glowed dimly as day changed to twilight. Moscow was further south than St. Petersburg, so there was an actual night during June. Harder to see Rzaev's men positioned some ten yards away, but Kolya wasn't about to turn to look.

He checked his watch. Late. Despite everything, there had been a level of exhilaration from pulling off the deception, or maybe just from the surge of adrenaline. Still, the surge could only last so long. Now, waiting, adrenaline ebbing, he felt his exhaustion. How long since he'd slept more than a few hours?

Kolya watched Dmitri pour himself more of the Imperial vodka. Dmitri held up the bottle and looked inquiringly towards Kolya. Kolya wanted another drink. Hell, he wanted the whole damn bottle—but he knew better. He shook his head.

"Do you know them?" Kolya indicated the men standing behind them.

"No. Muscle gets killed off and replaced from time to time. Anyway, it would not matter if I did. On Rzaev's orders, they would kill their mothers. If Rzaev comes back unhappy...." Dmitri drank and poured again. He still appeared sober but was pushing it. "Will Rzaev come back unhappy?"

"I hope not." Kolya hoped that the website created by Mark Leslie in the ECA technical department held up to scrutiny. ECA staff were answering any calls in his pretend company. It should work. If no one screwed up—or screwed him over. The plan had been put in place quickly, and anything put together quickly sometimes fell apart.

Ironic that once Rzaev pulled up the fake website, the technical department would use a Trojan horse to obtain data from Rzaev's computer.

Two tasks: locate the Novichok and determine who had paid Rzaev to smuggle it. Both of those questions might be answered with what the technical department at the ECA could retrieve through Rzaev's computer—unless Rzaev employed multiple computers, and the pertinent information was not on whatever he was using to check Kolya's story.

Dmitri glanced again over Kolya's shoulder. "They are still watching." Was Dmitri also nervous? Kolya wasn't sure. Dmitri held his glass of Imperial vodka up in the dimming light. Then he downed it.

"Maybe you should slow down. This is not the place or time to get drunk."

"What the hell. I am just out of prison, and we might die." Dmitri reached for the bottle.

Kolya placed the bottle out of Dmitri's reach. "Enough."

"You are kind of boring these days, my friend." Dmitri settled back in his chair. "If we don't die, you will have to go out drinking with me to make up for this."

"Fine." Would it be strange to go out drinking with Dmitri? Maybe. Kolya had to admit that he still liked Dmitri and would probably enjoy having the occasional drink with him. He imagined introducing Dmitri to Alex—that could be amusing. If Dmitri stepped out of line, he wouldn't know what hit him.

Still, he wasn't yet to the point of trusting Dmitri enough to tell him about Alex. After the mission was over—maybe.

He checked his watch again. Another ten minutes had passed. It was growing darker. A firefly ignited close to him, and a half a dozen flashed in answer.

Then a flood of light into the garden as a door opened from the house.

Whatever would happen would happen. Kolya watched Rzaev and Pavel exit the door from the house to the garden. He was too far away to see Rzaev's expression in the dusk, but the men behind him hadn't moved or fired. It was probably a good sign.

"It's okay," Dmitri said. "If he were unhappy, Rzaev would just send Pavel."

Rzaev returned to his chair. Pavel took up his position near the side table. "So, okay, everything checked out. As you know, because you are not dead." Rzaev motioned to Pavel. "Give him his weapons and his phone. We are business partners now."

Pavel, without a change in expression, put the HK, the knife, and the phone on the table in front of Kolya.

Rzaev tapped on an iPhone. "I use an app. Encryption is not perfect but does the job. I have already messaged Charlie."

"Not a Russian?"

"As Russian as you." Rzaev handed Kolya the phone.

The message was brief. *Irish pub. Main Street, Newport, Vermont, 6 p.m. Friday.*

Newport, Vermont? Kolya felt a chill. Alex was in Stowe, a little over an hour from Newport, but close enough to worry him even though the location of the meeting had to do with the proximity of the border and nothing to do with Alex.

Probably.

Was there a connection between this matter and the failed attacks on him and Alex?

He did admire the strategy. Hiding in a small state known for vacations and maple syrup instead of the larger, more populated cities on the East Coast was clever. Especially since the entire United States intelligence apparatus would be searching the larger cities for whomever had left the blue crystal bottles of nerve poison.

Rzaev was waiting. Whoever Charlie might be, he was also waiting. Friday was two days away. It would be enough time to set up a back-up team. Maybe he wouldn't even need to go to Vermont.

It would be enough time to get Alex out of the state.

He tapped his agreement back to Charlie. New text. *Photos of you and Lemonsky. Anyone else shows up, it's off.*

OK. You?

No. You don't need to know what I look like. After I confirm that it's just the two of you, I'll approach.

Kolya snapped two pictures, sent them, and handed the phone back to Rzaev. He'd hoped to be done after Russia, but this meant he and Dmitri had to at least make the meeting. Even if there were teams backing him up. They wouldn't know what Charlie looked like—and he might not even be in the pub until after Kolya and Dmitri entered.

Just two days more.

"Good." Rzaev switched off the phone. "What is that noise?"

The noise was the buzzing of a phone on vibrate. Kolya's phone. The only person who knew the new number was Jonathan. If Jonathan was texting him, it had to be urgent.

"Who would be texting you?"

"Most likely, my people in the town. You didn't think I'd be stupid enough not to have back-up nearby, did you?"

Kolya pulled out his phone. The message was brief. *Men searching town. Police or FSB.*

44

WEDNESDAY NIGHT, PEREDELKINO, RUSSIA

TOMAS, IN THE MERCEDES van, was second in the entourage. A black Mercedes SUV in front. Three more cars behind the van. The line of cars halted around the corner from the gate to Rzaev's compound. Either side of the street was lined with trees, and neither houses nor people were visible. They waited while the drone was launched, and then for the report from the drone operator.

"Three men sitting talking in the gazebo. Five men with guns watching the three of them."

"Other men?"

"One, two, maybe four on the grounds. Three at the gate. Maybe more in the house."

"Any of them Rzaev?"

"I can't see faces. Wait." He changed angles and flew the drone lower. "A man in the gazebo looks like Rzaev."

Tomas could feel the tension from the three men in the van with him. He gave the order. "Go." The SUV in front gunned its engine and rounded the corner, his van close on its bumper, the rest of the cars following. They screeched up to the barred gate, the SUV and the van pulled in the driveway, the other cars in a line behind them on the street.

Rzaev's three guards aimed assault weapons at the cars. Tomas reached for his door, but Boris, in the driver's seat, grabbed his arm. "Stop. The Director should not expose himself to danger."

Well, he was doing that anyway. But he stayed inside the van.

Instead, Masha, one of the three women in the group, tall, slender,

191

and tough, stepped outside the SUV directly ahead. She showed her identification. "We're here to speak to Rzaev."

Instead, they opened fire, and a round struck her in the middle of the chest, knocking her to the ground, her vest hopefully protecting her life. Then all hell broke loose.

* * * * *

Kolya heard the rumble of cars followed by gunfire. He swiveled in his seat, but the house obscured his view. The guards in the garden raced towards the front gate.

He showed Rzaev the message on his phone. *Men searching the town. Police or FSB.* "Do you have a back way out?"

"I am not afraid of the FSB."

"Given my former employment, it would be awkward for me to be found here."

Rzaev calmly sipped lemonade. "You can go over the garden wall, if you wish. There's woods on the other side—and you should be able to get away."

Twenty yards away, on the other side of the beets and the tomatoes, and red and yellow lilies, there was a space between a tangle of purple roses where the wall would be easy to assess. Then he'd just have to scale a twelve- foot stone wall, with a leg that still collapsed from to time and good odds that FSB agents would be waiting on the other side.

Another message from Jonathan.

"Drone."

He could hear the faint buzz. More gunfire from the front of the compound. A man screamed. His mind flashed back to another gunfight, but it was easier this time to suppress the memory. He turned to Rzaev.

"Your men may hold them temporarily, but they'll get in. I have a bad leg, and getting over the wall wouldn't be the easiest for me right now. You must have another way out, and you should leave too."

Rzaev shook his head. "I'll be fine. I have connections."

"Your connections will not be useful if you're shot."

Dmitri leaned forward. "I agree. And do not give me any shit about climbing walls. I know you have an exit. You always do."

A fusillade of gunfire followed Dmitri's words.

Rzaev drained his glass, carefully placed it on the table, and rose. "All right, Dima. Let us go back into the house."

* * * * *

There was just enough light to make out shapes. Jonathan, Elizabeth, and Teo had watched the beginning of the assault on Rzaev's compound from the shelter of trees. Jonathan hated being out of the action, but that was his role. Support only. Watch. And text Kolya.

On *Dovzhenzo*, the street where Rzaev had his compound, they'd positioned themselves in the woods a few yards down from the gate, where they could see but not be seen. The car was parked another mile or so away. Less convenient for a get-away, but also less obvious. They hadn't expected a raid on Rzaev's compound—but it was happening.

Five minutes in, and the sides seemed to be equally matched: the FSB officers hid behind their cars and fired. Returning flashes of fire from Rzaev's men. Maybe two FSB down, maybe one of Rzaev's thugs.

"We can't do anything here," Elizabeth murmured. "Let's get back to the car."

Teo shifted uncomfortably. "We can't just leave."

"We're not leaving the area," Jonathan said. "But Elizabeth is right. If Kolya makes it out, we need to be at or near the car—so we can pick him up and get out of town."

45

WEDNESDAY NIGHT, PEREDELKINO, RUSSIA

PAVEL LED THE WAY into Rzaev's kitchen. An older woman with a headscarf and an apron, interrupted in the process of making dumplings, cowered in a corner from the noise of the battle. The gunfire, which had been pounding incessantly, stopped. Then Kolya heard the slam of metal against metal—the sound that a heavy vehicle ramming an iron gate might make.

Pavel flung open the door to the cellar. Kolya hated basements, but he hurried down the steep steps to a large wine cellar, Dmitri behind him.

The cellar smelled of damp. Concrete walls were lined with wooden racks filled with French wine. Pavel punched a code into a panel on the wall. A wine rack swung wide and revealed a metal door, and behind it, a concrete tunnel five feet high, three feet wide—dimly illuminated by bare light bulbs.

Kolya peered down the length of the tunnel and couldn't see an exit.

"Where does it come out?"

"The woods. The door is well camouflaged. I do not often share the secrets of my escape route. After you."

If there were FSB waiting when they emerged, Kolya would be the first one out—and the first one shot or captured. But it wasn't as if he had other options.

His six-foot frame was tall for the tunnel's ceiling. He stooped and entered, followed by Dmitri, Rzaev, and Pavel. The door swung closed.

* * * * *

Tomas followed three burly men into the house where the cook denied knowing Vladimir Rzaev. He seated himself at the kitchen table as men searched the house.

Five of his people dead. How could this have happened? How could he have been so stupid? He hated the idea that he was responsible for people's deaths. Why had he tried to go after Rzaev? Was arresting spies or finding out about the Novichok really worth it?

Maybe. If he'd found information that could stave off an attack in the United States or in Russia. Maybe if he'd detained two American spies. But he had done neither.

He was going to have to face Yuri and explain what had happened, and he might not survive that meeting.

He had to improve his odds. Only way to do so: find Rzaev and the Americans. Persuade Rzaev to tell who had paid for the Novichok smuggling. Arrest the spies. He was so absorbed in his thoughts that he almost missed the smashing of glass and shouts from the basement.

"Hidden locked door in the wine cellar. Maybe a tunnel."

Tunnel? Then the words penetrated his consciousness. He raced to the basement door and down the steps. "Break it down."

46

WEDNESDAY NIGHT, PEREDELKINO, RUSSIA

ROUGH CEMENT WALLS WERE covered in water stains, and the air smelled of mold. Bare bulbs illuminated a swarm of gnats, and spider webs stretched across crevices. With the door closed behind them, there was silence except for the sound of their footsteps on the concrete and the buzzing of insects. Kolya swatted a mosquito away from his face. Two minutes into the tunnel, the lights flicked off. As unpleasant as it had been lit, the tunnel was worse in the total dark. Kolya slowed, and Dmitri bumped into him.

"Did you pay your electric bill, Volodya?" Dmitri's voice sounded next to his ear.

"Obviously, they made it into the basement and cut off the lights." Rzaev's voice was calm. "They will be coming as soon as they manage to open the door."

Or they'd be waiting on the other end of the tunnel. Maybe both.

Kolya felt in his pocket and found his phone. He turned the phone flashlight on and held it up. In the dim illumination, he could see a few feet ahead. Then he increased his speed despite the ache in his bad leg from the damp and the effort. "How far?"

"Not far." Rzaev's voice.

Kolya gritted his teeth and they continued at something between a fast walk and a run. *Twenty yards? Fifty yards?* Hard to tell distances in a tunnel. Kolya glanced over his shoulder at the dark behind him. He could barely see Dmitri's face. Rzaev and Pavel a little farther behind were just dark shapes. Behind them, just blackness.

Before Romania, when he used to run five miles every day, this would have been a breeze. Not anymore. The knee throbbed, and the leg muscles were cramping. He paused, hand against the damp concrete to steady himself, and pushed on, but at a walk not a run.

"Do you need help?" Dmitri's voice again, at his right shoulder.

"I'm fine."

They must have passed under the wall surrounding the compound—and they would be somewhere under the neighboring woods. Once they exited the tunnel, they'd need to get out of Peredelkino quickly. The car that he'd driven from St. Petersburg was parked in Rzaev's compound. But he would have transportation, assuming Jonathan and the team hadn't been caught themselves.

He checked for service on his phone. None. No texting Jonathan.

He heard faint sounds from behind. Loud and persistent thumping, following by the slam of metal on metal. Maybe an ax?

"Hurry." Dmitri was close to his shoulder.

He picked up the pace again. The pain surged. *Fucking knee. Fucking leg. Fucking tunnel.* The damn tunnel just kept going.

Another thirty yards, and the lights flicked on again. He felt momentary relief at the sight of a metal ladder, the top disappearing into a round circle on the ceiling, but he also knew what the lights meant. The pursuers were coming. He heard far-off voices echoing against the cement walls and floors.

He reached the ladder and craned his neck to look up. It was maybe twenty feet to the top where a metal plate barred the exit.

In the tunnel behind them, the sounds of pursuit grew louder.

"You first, Michael Harding." Rzaev glanced behind him, down the tunnel. "Pavel. Go back. Take out the lights here and then shoot the first man who comes through. That will make them think twice about proceeding in the dark."

It would also block the narrow passageway and give them time.

Kolya grasped the metal rungs and began to climb. Light bulbs popped below as Pavel smashed them with the butt of his gun. By the time he reached the top, Kolya was again in total darkness. He heard Dmitri behind, and he knew Rzaev was climbing behind Dmitri.

Kolya felt for the handle on the metal plate the sealed the opening. He found it, twisted, and then pushed upward. The plate didn't move. He set his shoulder against the plate and heaved. Nothing. He climbed up two rungs and put his back against the plate, balanced on his good left leg, and pushed. Nothing. He pushed harder and started to lose his balance. He grabbed the top of the ladder again to steady himself.

"It's a little heavy." Rzaev's voice came from below on the ladder. "I had the plate buried. Only a foot or so of dirt."

"A foot or *so?*"

"Maybe two. A young man like you should have no problem with the weight. Pavel can move it."

But Pavel had gone down the tunnel to shoot FSB agents.

"Move over." Dmitri climbed up, and Kolya shifted his position. There was just enough space for the two of them. "Together."

They balanced together on the rungs, backs against the metal plate. Kolya braced himself. "Now."

They shoved. The plate shifted. A crack opened, and clumps of earth sifted down on their faces. Kolya blinked dirt from his eyes.

"Again."

Backs and shoulders strained. The plate moved an inch, then another inch, and then, with a final effort from both of them, flew open. Dirt showered down on their heads and their shoulders.

"Wait." Kolya pulled his gun and cautiously peered over the edge. Not yet shrouded in full darkness, the forest stood silent. Gun in hand, Kolya clambered out onto his stomach. Dmitri pulled himself out onto the ground next to him.

Kolya pushed himself up with his left leg taking most of his weight, grasping onto a tree. The knee brace was not doing anything.

The faint sound of gunshots echoed up the tunnel.

Dmitri stooped to offer Rzaev a hand. Rzaev, expression annoyed, batted the hand away and climbed out.

Kolya typed a message to Jonathan. The response was immediate. *Through the woods. Gogolya.*

Then Pavel emerged, tucking a gun into a shoulder holster.

Kolya checked the map on his phone. It showed their location—middle of the woods—and it showed *ul.* Gogolya—the street where Jonathan would be waiting—to be due east.

Then he heard the sound of mechanical humming and the whirl of wings and he remembered. *Drone. Somewhere above him. Where?* He craned his neck and scanned for it. But between the heavy foliage and twilight of the Moscow evening, the drone was invisible.

The drone meant the FSB would be here quickly—and not in the mood to take prisoners—not after the confrontation at the gate or the shootings in the tunnel. The drone also meant they would be unable to get away. Wherever they went, it would follow.

Unless it was taken out. To do that, he needed to see it. He moved his position, gun raised, searching. He thought he caught a glimpse of movement overhead but lost it before he could fire.

"What?" Dmitri craned his neck to look up as well. "What are you looking for?"

If the drone moved, he might spot it.

"Drone. Go." He nodded in what he hoped was the right direction. "*Ulitza Gogolya.* My people are parked there." It would be only minutes until the FSB arrived. They'd come through the tunnel or through the woods, but they'd come.

"And you?"

"The drone will follow you—and if it moves, maybe I can see to take it out. Go. We don't have much time."

Dmitri hesitated.

"Go! I'll catch up."

Dmitri nodded, and the three disappeared into the trees. Kolya watched and listened. The drone hummed overhead, following. He caught a glimpse of something metal just above a leafy branch. He aimed and fired.

47

WEDNESDAY NIGHT, PEREDELKINO, RUSSIA

JONATHAN SAT IN THE driver's seat, Teo on his phone, beside him, Elizabeth in the back seat. They were parked on a darkened tree-lined street where dachas were tucked out of sight and residents tucked in bed. His phone vibrated—*exit through tunnel in woods Four of us.* Four? That would be Dmitri and Kolya—Rzaev, and someone in his organization. Maintaining Kolya's cover meant helping Rzaev, as distasteful as that might be. How long would it take them to arrive? He glanced at his watch for the tenth time. It wasn't quite time to worry. Not quite.

A distant shot reverberated. He turned to look. The street was empty.

"Could've been Kolya. Shooting or being shot." Teo looked up from his phone.

"Give him ten minutes, and then we leave," Elizabeth said.

"No. We're going to wait."

"How long?" Elizabeth asked.

Jonathan looked at his watch. "Until we stop waiting."

"The FSB is going to start looking around the neighborhood. Americans in a rented car on a side street—that's not going to be suspicious?"

"Maybe." A few minutes more should tell either way. Jonathan checked the street again and exhaled in relief. Three shapes jogged towards them. He opened the door and stepped out.

Dmitri Lemonsky, hair and face covered in dirt, led an older man in work clothes, and a stocky menacing man in a formal suit. Jonathan recognized the older man as Vladimir Rzaev.

"Where's Michael?" Jonathan asked.

"He told us to leave. Drone. He was going to try to take it down so," Dmitri said.

"He can't run right now."

"I know. *I fucking know.*" Dmitri's voice rose.

"We should leave," Rzaev said. "They will catch him. It will do no good if they catch us too."

"I will go back for him." Then Dmitri turned to Rzaev. "This is Jonathan. He and the others work for Michael." At least Dmitri was maintaining cover.

"I'm going back for him. Get in the damn car," Jonathan said.

Elizabeth got out of the back seat. Rzaev followed by the third man squeezed inside. Dmitri followed. Teo stepped out and spoke to Jonathan over the roof.

"I'm coming, too."

"You're not." He tossed keys. "Both of you stay here. Give me twenty minutes, then go. Watch out for the big guy in the meantime. He looks like trouble."

Jonathan ran.

* * * * *

His shot in the dark hit home. After the drone crashed to the ground, Kolya took a running step on his right leg. The knee buckled, and he went down. He broke the fall with his hands, keeping hold of his gun.

Behind him, men searched the woods. Kolya could hear them crashing through underbrush from the direction of the house. They'd be coming up the tunnel any minute, too. He stayed low and crawled forward, using elbows and his good leg, until he reached the shelter of a clump of trees and pulled himself up. He leaned against a tree trunk and calmed his breathing. Where his leg had throbbed earlier, the pain was now like a living thing. When he tried to put weight on his right leg, his knee buckled. He caught himself before he went down.

If he kept the knee straight, maybe he could maneuver. He straightened the leg, kept it rigid, and hobbled a step forward. *Progress.* He took another awkward step and didn't fall. *Good.* It hurt, but he was moving. But too slowly. He not only had to make the edge of the woods, he had to make it down a side street. Maybe half a mile. Without getting caught or shot. With the search on and his slow speed, he might as well try to make it to Novosibirsk, Siberia.

He cursed himself again for agreeing to this mission. What had he been thinking? Alex had been right. The thought led him to another. He had to reach Alex and get her to leave Vermont. Then he imagined how she'd feel if he were captured or killed. He'd told her he'd be careful.

Stop thinking about Alex.

He focused his attention on the terrain. Another fall could be disastrous, and the forest was nothing but an obstacle course. Underbrush, fallen tree limbs. *Pay attention.* One step, two steps, ten steps. He braced himself against another tree. The pain hadn't diminished, but he was getting the knack of this gait. He started off again, a little faster, not fast enough, but better. Ten yards. Twenty.

Behind him, the beam of a flashlight moved in his direction. He slid behind a tree and waited, gun ready.

But the man with the flashlight missed him.

He waited twenty seconds and then pushed his awkward limping gait forward. Zigzagging from tree to tree offered him a little cover from the searchers and short breaks.

How long since he'd come out of the tunnel? *Five minutes? Maybe ten.* The longer he took, the worse his chances of getting away.

Logically, the pursuers should block the surrounding streets. If there were enough of them. There might not be—yet. But if they blocked the streets, he wouldn't be the only one caught. Jonathan, Teo, Elizabeth and the others could be trapped in a dragnet. If he could make it to the car— before the searchers caught up, before more back-up arrived to block roads, he had a chance. They all had a chance.

For that, he needed speed, which he didn't have, and luck, which he couldn't count on.

But luck stayed with him as he avoided beams from flashlights, and the men searching the woods. He paused again and listened to the crashing of underbrush. They were behind but not too close. No second drone. No dogs.

He had almost reached the edge of the woods when his luck ran out. The silhouette of a man advanced straight towards him. No hesitation. One person—a dark shape, only twenty yards away.

One man would be easy to take down. He felt a momentary twinge at killing an unknown man only doing his job. Still, he didn't have a choice, not unless he wanted to be taken prisoner.

Kolya wrapped both hands around his gun, aimed at the gun center mass of the approaching form, took a steadying breath, ready, felt for the trigger... and stopped to reevaluate. The shape looked familiar. In the dark, it was hard to be certain, but better to risk capture than to kill a friend. The silhouette paused. It was too dark to see features. Then he heard the urgent whisper that confirmed his guess.

"Kolya?"

He lowered his weapon and hobbled forward. "I almost shot you, Jonathan."

"How's the leg?"

"Bad."

Jonathan offered a shoulder. Kolya accepted. "Let's get out of here."

48

WEDNESDAY NIGHT, PEREDELKINO, RUSSIA

"WE SHOULD GO. YOUR friend did not make it." Pavel made the pronouncement in Russian.

In the back seat: Rzaev leaned against the door, Pavel was crammed in the middle, and Dmitri was jammed against Pavel. At least Pavel showered frequently. Dmitri had shared close spaces with thugs who didn't shower, and it was less than pleasant.

The young guy and the woman whose names Dmitri didn't know waited outside the car.

"Get the woman or the kid to drive, or kill them and get the car key," Pavel was still going.

Dmitri had never particularly liked Pavel, even if he was Rzaev's man. Pavel was a psychotic killer when he wasn't playing butler. It was generally good not to alienate psychotic killers—but Dmitri hadn't become head of Rzaev's North American organization by worrying about alienating tough guys.

"We're not fucking going anywhere yet. We're going to wait."

"You're more loyal to this American than to your *vor v zakonye.*"

"I am loyal to my *vor v zakonye.* Volodya knows my loyalty. But this is business. Without my friend, everything falls apart. And just to be precise—he is Russian, Pavel. Not American."

"Whatever he used to be, he is American now. Michael Harding, the American."

"Shut up, Pavel. And we can wait," Rzaev said. "For now. Money is what matters—and for that, we need Dmitri's friend."

"OK, but when you tell me, I shoot the Americans and take the car."

"You know they might be able to hear you," Dmitri said.

"Why I'm speaking Russian. You think these Americans speak Russian?"

"Maybe. Who knows?"

"If up to me, I would give it only ten minutes more," Pavel said.

Longer than ten minutes probably did mean that Kolya and Egan were captured or dead. Rzaev would make the final call, of course, and he was quite capable of getting impatient. But Dmitri couldn't let Pavel shoot the Americans standing outside the car. Neither the ECA nor the CIA would believe that it hadn't been Dmitri's fault. Everything Dmitri'd been working to accomplish for the past ten years would be lost.

He felt in his pocket for a knife that he'd bought from a street vendor in St. Petersburg. If necessary, a quick stab to Pavel's heart would do the job.

* * * * *

With Jonathan to lean on, Kolya limped faster, and the sounds of the searchers grew dim. They stayed under the cover of the trees until they reached *ulitza Lermontova*—the street dividing the large woods behind Rzaev's house. More woods offered shelter on the other side of the street. They just had to cross safely.

From the edge of the woods, the view was limited. From what they could see, no cars lingering, no men staking out positions.

"Think you can run?"

"No. But don't let that stop you."

Jonathan half dragged Kolya in a dash across the street. A moment after they entered the trees on the far side of the street, two cars with flashing lights sped towards them—and then past.

"We're not out of the woods yet," Jonathan said.

"Amusing, Jonathan. How much farther?"

"Five minutes, normally. Longer, given your leg. Take a minute. Messaging the team."

Kolya leaned against a tree and waited while Jonathan tapped on his phone. The adrenaline was ebbing—and he was exhausted. Not far, though, and then he could rest until the flight to Vermont.

Jonathan returned the phone to his pocket, and Kolya roused himself for another push.

* * * * *

When they reached the car, Teo and Elizabeth waited, guns in hand. In an undertone, Teo relayed the conversation they'd overheard. Kolya listened with interest—Dmitri had stood up to Pavel on his behalf. Elizabeth, Teo and Jonathan slid into the front of the car, Kolya squeezed in back, next to Dmitri. "No run-ins with curious neighbors on your way here?"

"You forget life in Russia, *moi droog*. Neighbors are interested in staying alive not in checking out men with guns. I am glad you made it okay."

Jonathan put the car into gear and pulled out.

It was a straight shot from *Gogolya* to *Gorkoga* and then north. Kolya was surprised at the lack of roadblocks. It was at least half an hour since they'd emerged from the tunnel. Long enough for the FSB to muster enough manpower to block the roads. Why hadn't they?

Jonathan observed speed limits until he hit the M1 where cars zoomed with reckless disregard for laws. Jonathan increased speed, weaving in and out of traffic. From the M1, he took the MKAD, which circled Moscow, to the M9, and headed for the city.

"How did they know we were there?" Dmitri asked Kolya.

"I have no idea. Would Ivan Minsky know?"

"Ivan Minsky is no longer answering anyone's questions," Rzaev said. "He answered the wrong person's questions, which is why we had this trouble tonight."

"How do you know this?" Kolya asked.

Rzaev shrugged. "I know it."

"When did you know it?"

"I knew before you arrived."

"You said nothing."

"There was nothing to say. I called someone on my payroll and asked him to take care of it. I thought he had. Then I took care of Ivan."

"Too bad," Dmitri said. "I liked his club."

"Yes, but business is business, and he disclosed something to someone he should not have."

So Rzaev had had Ivan Minsky killed. Kolya wasn't surprised, but the news was unsettling. Kolya generally disapproved of cold-blooded murder, but he wasn't going to grieve for Minsky. Minsky was a mafiya boss who had probably killed or ordered the killing of dozens of people. Of greater concern: Rzaev had known of a leak—and yet had gone ahead with the meeting? Puzzling. Why would someone like Rzaev take the risk?

And who was on his payroll?

He watched the road as Jonathan maneuvered through light traffic and turned off the M9 and onto Moscow city streets. Moscow was perilous—filled with cameras, with informers, and secret police. He'd be on a next flight the next day, and it couldn't be fast enough. Russia remained a dark place—personally and professionally.

He also didn't like that he had to go to Vermont and meet up with the smuggler—but after that, he was done. He could return to his life as a lawyer.

Boxes of documents. Memos to partners. Late nights writing briefs over obscure legal points that would give one side leverage in working out a financial settlement. Moving money from one corporation to another. Nothing that he could believe in or feel proud of doing.

Alex's practice—at least she took cases that meant something. She represented injured people. She had saved innocents from being executed. He could work with Alex. No, not a good idea. Better to keep private and work life separate.

"I liked that house," Rzaev finally spoke again. "Where Nadiya had planted flowers."

"I'm sorry about your house," Kolya said.

"You are sorry. I lose my house, and you are sorry. Still, it was the fucking FSB and not your fault." Rzaev peered out the window. He pointed to where a Metro sign shone underneath a streetlight. "Stop the car, please." He spoke in English. "Thank you for the ride. I appreciate that you got us all away, but do not fuck up our business. That I will not forgive."

49

TOMAS'S FOOTSTEPS ECHOED AS he walked down the empty corridor. He'd undertaken the evening's operation to answer questions about Rzaev smuggling Novichok out of Russian and into the United States—and to catch two American spies. He had failed spectacularly. No sign of Rzaev. No sign of the Americans.

He plodded the two corridors to his own office. Once inside, he locked the heavy oak door behind him and flipped on the light. It was so familiar and yet somehow not. For the first time, he realized that he was as much a prisoner as the unfortunate souls locked below in the Lubyanka. The thick carpet, the bookshelves, even the pictures of his family on his desk were just the elaborate decorations of a cell.

He gazed at a picture of Lyudmila and the children on the beach from their last vacation on the Black Sea. They looked so happy.

He'd put them all in danger, and every attempt he'd made to fix things had just made it worse. Yuri was more than capable of killing them all, if he were angry enough, and he would be angry. Tomas had nothing. He should have set up roadblocks, but he had been worried about using too many state resources on this wild goose chase.

Nothing. He had nothing. Unless he could locate either the Americans or Rzaev. He typed messages and sent images of Rzaev and the blond man from the bridge.

He was prepared to wait all night for reports to come in, but he felt it before he heard anything. A slight tingle on the back of his neck. A tightening in his stomach. Then the softness of a footstep down the corridor, faint and not very close.

He normally didn't carry a weapon—he didn't like them. And that hadn't changed with his receiving the bogus honor of his current position. He wasn't any kind of fighter. But tonight had been different. He had carried a weapon, uneasy though he was with it.

Now, he drew the gun from his pocket as the sound of footsteps grew more distinct. One person's footsteps.

He wrapped trembling hands around the gun and aimed it at the door as the footsteps stopped outside.

Cock the gun. He pulled the slide, and a bullet rose into the chamber.

Then a soft knocking on the door.

"Tomas?" It was the voice of Yuri's assistant. "Are you in there?"

He didn't answer.

"Tomas, Yuri wants to see you in his office. Now."

"What are you doing here at this hour?"

"What are you?"

Tomas didn't answer. He braced his elbows on the desk to still the trembling of the hands holding the pistol.

"Call him. I'll wait. He's expecting you."

Tomas dialed with one hand, still holding the gun. Yuri's secretary answered. She spoke three words, and he hung up.

"Tomas?" Yuri's assistant was right outside the door.

"Coming."

He opened a drawer, placed the gun inside, and locked it. The gun wasn't going to help him.

50

THURSDAY EARLY MORNING, KOMSOMOLSKAYA SQUARE, MOSCOW

"I'VE HAD WORD FROM Margaret. Technical downloaded data showing that Rzaev had a meeting with known jihadists from Yemen." Jonathan lit a cigar and offered one to Kolya. Kolya shook his head. The cigars were an occasional indulgence for Jonathan—and also an excuse to be outside at a little after midnight since nothing of importance should be discussed inside a Russian hotel. Elizabeth and Teo were babysitting Dmitri.

Jonathan and Kolya occupied a bench near the fountain in Komsomolskaya Square, famous for its proximity to three train stations and for the blend of Tsarist and Stalinist architecture surrounding it. During the day, the square was packed. Now, after midnight, the area was empty—except for the occasional pedestrian—if they were indeed simply pedestrians.

Kolya looked bad, but Jonathan pushed down concern. They were almost done. They'd be flying out of Russia in the morning, and in three days, the whole operation would wrap up.

"Do we know what was discussed with the jihadists?" Kolya asked.

"Apparently, they arranged to meet Rzaev two months ago to discuss a business matter and request that his organization carry something for them. No details on what or where."

"He uses encrypted apps for most communications."

"Well, figures. But still, pretty much confirms that terrorists were in communication with him—and that they wanted to use his smuggling network. It strongly suggests that they were responsible for the Novichok.

It's the right time frame."

"I wouldn't dismiss Yuri Bykovsky as a suspect just yet." Kolya shifted his position as if trying to find a way to get comfortable.

"If Bykovsky were working with Rzaev, would the FSB have conducted the raid tonight? And do you think Rzaev anticipated our using malware against him?"

Kolya raised his hands in the I-don't-know gesture. "Rzaev said he knew that Ivan Minsky had given information on our meeting to someone in the FSB. Yet Rzaev went ahead and met us."

"What do you think it means?"

"I don't know. But I find it unsettling. Rzaev is not the type to take unnecessary risks."

"Maybe he has someone from the FSB in his pocket."

"Undoubtedly. Still, never trust anything we get too easily."

"You think that was easy?"

"Relatively speaking."

"There you go, overthinking again." Jonathan tapped ashes from his cigar onto the ground. A man and woman, arm-in-arm, strolled by.

Kolya watched the couple disappear and then continued his thought. "Maybe we are being misled. Russians can be clever bastards."

"You're a cynical son-of-a-bitch."

"Part of my charm. Doesn't mean I'm not right."

"That too." Jonathan watched a woman hurrying along the sidewalk, head covered in a scarf. But she didn't linger.

Kolya took a minute to absorb this information, but he clearly understood the implications. "Question: do you still have that GPS tracker you offered me back in Washington?"

"In my wallet. Why?"

"In case something happens in Vermont. At the meeting. Or on the way to the meeting. Now that the meeting with Rzaev is over, having the tracker on me is no longer a risk."

"Are you worried about Dmitri?" Jonathan blew a smoke ring, tapped the cigar, and then pulled out his wallet.

"So far—he's more than held up his side of the bargain. Still, something doesn't feel right."

"You mean something other than trying to induce you to murder Yelseyev and his lying about where Minsky would be playing jazz?"

He placed the postage-size tracker in Kolya's hand. Kolya nodded and slipped it into his pocket.

"Yes, something besides those. Although I do have paranoid tendencies. As you've said on previous occasions."

Jonathan blew out another smoke ring. "I was a jerk to say that. You weren't paranoid about being singled out. You were right."

"Thank you for that." There was a long pause as if Kolya were considering an additional response. But whatever he was thinking, he kept it to himself. "We should move from here."

By Moscow rules, they had stayed too long in the same place. Time to walk—if Kolya's leg wasn't in such bad shape.

Jonathan stood, stretched, and checked for possible watchers. That he saw no one meant little. Watchers could be concealed in doorways or behind statues or could be listening from inside of one of the buildings that lined the square.

Kolya pushed himself up and grimaced. It was painful just to watch him put weight on his leg.

"I guess the shot didn't do it for the knee." Jonathan matched Kolya's slow pace.

"Not strong enough for the indignities I've inflicted on it over the past twenty-four hours or so."

They headed in the direction of the Kazansky railway station. The largest and busiest in the city, the station was still open. In the daytime, people would be streaming in and out. Now, just a trickle.

They steered towards the main entrance into the station. Jonathan smoked his cigar. Kolya explained the distinct features of the architecture of the train station, built between 1913 and 1940. "Signs of the Zodiac," Kolya pointed to the gold-rimmed clock on the façade. "Very famous. No smoking inside, by the way."

Jonathan dropped the remains of his cigar into the gutter. They climbed the few steps, Kolya using the handrail for support. Inside, wrought iron chandeliers hung from an arched ceiling and lit walls painted in a soft pastel green. A few travelers sat on benches or wandered through the massive space.

Jonathan and Kolya proceeded in the direction of the trains.

"So, if you have a bad feeling about Dmitri, maybe I should follow you back to Vermont."

"The bad feeling isn't necessarily about Dmitri. I just have this feeling that I missed something. It may have nothing to do with him, and I hope it doesn't. He's been very helpful. In any event, isn't there a team on the ground to grab Charlie when he meets with us?"

"Yeah. ECA agents, FBI agents, CIA agents. Spooks doubled the population of the town, if not the state. It'll be a hell of a party. That's not going to help you if things go bad before they move in."

"I don't see how your following us to Vermont would be of any more help to me than the team on the ground."

"Why the GPS chip then?"

"If I should be taken—or killed—I would prefer to be found sooner rather than later. After Romania that is something of a concern."

"Understandable. Still, I'd feel better if it were me and the gang backing you."

"Someone needs to confirm whether the information about jihadists in Rzaev's computer is legitimate—and that Bykovsky's isn't responsible. The only other American agents in Moscow are CIA, and I don't trust them to approach one of our assets. Fyodor is the best bet." Kolya paused at a kiosk and steadied himself. "Assuming he's still alive and not in a prison cell. You'll need a team to distract watchers and get a message to him. Afterwards, he may need to be exfiltrated—which will also be difficult. Whatever happened at the bridge in St. Petersburg, he's been a reliable asset up to now."

"Okay. If you're sure you'll be okay."

"I'm not sure of anything of the kind. But I am reasonably sure that Bradford would agree with me on what you should be doing. I suggest you check with her."

"So you no longer want to break her neck?"

"I didn't say that. I'm just acknowledging her position as director of the agency."

51

WEDNESDAY EVENING, BURLINGTON, VERMONT

TEHILA USED HER VISA to rent a room in a Hilton in Burlington, an hour from Stowe. Alex had insisted on staying close, and Tehila had agreed that the last place anyone would look for them—would be Vermont. And, they kept an eye on the GPS tracker that Tehila had planted on the Subaru. Given that they would have an early warning if the would-be kidnappers arrived in Burlington, Tehila had decided that the risk was acceptable.

Whatever was going on—the men who had attacked her family to get to Kolya and the men who'd tried to kidnap her—the epicenter was in Vermont. Alex didn't know where Kolya was, but she had a feeling he'd wind up here sooner or later. And in case the ECA fucked him over again, she'd be near.

Tehila had finally agreed that it was reasonably safe to order food into the room, and an Uber Eats driver had left a box containing crepes and salad outside the door.

"Have they sent anyone to check out our wannabe kidnappers?" Alex cut a sliver of her crepe, filled with scallops, cream, and mushrooms. Delicious. And not kosher. Scallops, one of Alex's favorite foods, were on the forbidden list.

Alex could feel Tehila's disapproval, but the agent kept silent.

"No." Tehila's dinner was vegetarian, mushrooms, leeks, cheddar cheese. "From what I understand, every available agent has been put on alert—and there's no one to send at the moment."

"On alert for what?" Alex sipped her ginger tea and feigned innocence. It didn't work.

"You know I can't tell you."

"And the man who was taking pictures from the trail?"

"Mark hasn't had time to do more in depth search."

"Because of whatever everyone is on high alert for?"

"More or less."

The conversation was interrupted by the muffled tones of "Landslide," the old Fleetwood Mac tune. Alex liked the tune—her mother had played it all the time when she was young. She pulled her phone out of her purse and checked the number. Unknown. She clicked it on.

"I hope it's you."

"I hope so too. If it's not, please inform me." Kolya sounded tired, but he was alive. And obviously not a prisoner somewhere.

She laughed, both at his response and in sheer relief. "I've been worried, love. You're okay?"

"Basically, yes. Not quite done yet, though. A couple days more. Are you still in Stowe?"

Obviously no one had informed Kolya about the attempted kidnapping. Not the time to do so, either. "No, we're in Burlington."

There was a long moment of silence. "Why did you leave Stowe? Did something happen?"

Alex glanced over at Tehila. If Kolya could keep a secret, so could Alex. "No, nothing happened. I got bored."

"You're under protection, Alex. By definition, it's boring."

Normally, he wouldn't have accepted such a lame answer. The fact that he had reinforced that he was tired or not operating at full capacity.

"We're safe, staying out of sight. And Tehila is very good."

"I know she is. And I'm sorry, I don't have much time to talk. You need to leave Vermont all together."

"You're the one who insisted I come here." What did he know?

"I did, but I've re-evaluated. I no longer think it's safe."

"Why?"

"I can't say. Just trust me."

But all he was doing was reaffirming what she already knew—that whatever had happened in Silver Spring and in Stowe was connected to Kolya and his work.

"You know I trust you." That didn't mean she would do what he said. "When will you be home?"

"If all goes well, Saturday night."

And if it didn't go well, he could be dead. "You think Georgetown is safe? After all this?"

"I wasn't suggesting you return home until I do. Maybe New Jersey? Or Long Island? Just not Vermont. You should leave immediately, by the way."

"So you said."

"Alex."

"What?"

"I wouldn't be asking you to leave if it wasn't serious."

"I know that. I'm taking it under advisement."

He said a few choice curse words in Russian. "Don't do anything stupid, goddamnit."

"Do my best. And don't you do anything stupid, either."

"Do my best as well." There was a sigh. "Please do this. I'm asking because I love you."

"I love you too." And the phone went dead. Alex looked over at Tehila. "We're staying in Vermont." If something involving Kolya was going down in Vermont, she wanted to be close by. She didn't trust the ECA to put Kolya's life as the top priority.

52

MARGARET BRADFORD NODDED TO Ben Smithson as they entered the oval office. Ben nodded in return. Things were moving that mattered more than their dislike of each other.

President Lewis sat on one of the white chairs in front of the fireplace in the room that had been the seat of American power since Howard Taft first occupied the space in 1909.

Lewis was alone. No chief of staff. No retinue of generals or the secretary of state. Just the three of them. Margaret seated herself on the white sofa. Smithson selected another white high-backed chair.

"Petrov and Lemonsky will be flying back tomorrow morning." She smiled at Smithson in her gracious lady manner and turned her attention to the President. "They have a meeting set up with the smuggler in a popular local spot, but he's not going to identify himself until he has a visual on the two of them. There will be teams stationed close by. If all goes well, we'll have the smuggler in custody and then we can locate the Novichok."

Lewis steepled his fingers. "Good. So, the second question. Is Yuri Bykovsky responsible—as I assumed?"

"Right now, we're proceeding on the theory that Islamic terrorists were responsible," Smithson said. "Given the download of data that Margaret passed on to me."

Lewis frowned. "Margaret, any word from your team on the ground?"

"My people in Russia have questions about the reliability of the information."

"On what basis?"

"That it was too easy. Petrov believes we should have secondary confirmation before accepting the data as true."

Smithson cleared his throat. "I hate to say this, but Kowolsky is concerned about Petrov's loyalties and whether Petrov and Lemonsky are working with Rzaev."

Margaret turned to glare at him.

"Well, Lemonsky was in charge of Rzaev's North American enterprise before being shut down, and Petrov does have cause to resent the United States."

"And if he were, would he tell us that he's worried that the data on Rzaev computer might be fake? It just doesn't make sense."

"If he's turned, he could be throwing up a smoke screen. How better to throw off suspicion than to do exactly what he's doing? And just to throw another question into this mess—if Petrov wanted revenge for what happened to him, couldn't he be working with terrorists but wanting to focus on attention on Bykovsky?"

"Evidence of any of that, Ben?" Lewis tapped his fingers.

"Not at this point, but why would the FSB go after Rzaev if he were doing Bykovsky's bidding? Petrov and Lemonsky were childhood buddies, weren't they? We should be aware of the possibilities."

"You're just casting aspersions on a man on a dangerous mission who still isn't fully recovered from serious injuries?" Margaret kept her tone even. No reason to mention that her betrayal of him was the reason he had the serious injuries, since everyone already knew. And that the President and Smithson had ordered her to abandon Petrov to die in a particularly painful way. Maybe Petrov did have reason for revenge. But she didn't believe it. "If Petrov was working with Rzaev and terrorists, he could have arranged for Rzaev to give us false data, blaming Bykovsky, instead of pointing towards terrorists."

"I don't have all the answers, but Petrov did go on a frolic and detour to murder some old man while he was in St. Petersburg."

Damn. How did Smithson find out?

"Do you have proof he murdered anyone?"

"There's a report the Moscow CIA station chief received...."

But Lewis interrupted. "Stop this. I don't care who Petrov kills in Russia except if it impacts his mission. He can kill his own grandmother for all I give a damn. I asked you here because there's a deadly nerve agent loose in the United States. I want it found, and I want to know who's ordered this, so I can hold them responsible. I'm not interested in refereeing another squabble between the two of you."

"At this point, we seem to be on track for answers to both. If the meeting is real, we'll have the Novichok—and at this point, it appears to have been smuggled in on behalf of Islamic terrorists." Smithson's voice was smooth.

"Our the team in Russia will try to contact our asset in the FSB." Margaret shot a glance at Ben. "To see if we can confirm that Bykovsky isn't involved."

Lewis checked his watch and rose. "The Secretary of State is waiting. Both of you, get whatever information you can as fast as you can. If Bykovsky is responsible for a nerve agent attack on American soil, I will have to consider possible counters."

And that worried her. "Be careful with Bykovsky. He's an egomaniac and not that stable. We don't want to go from the possibility of fatalities from a nerve agent to all-out war with Russia by threatening a crazy man."

53

THURSDAY EARLY MORNING, THE KREMLIN, MOSCOW

YURI SAT ON HIS gilded chair in the office of the President. It just been a few days since, in this very room, from that chair, he'd told Tomas that the Novichok was an American hoax. Since then, everything had changed for Tomas—and nothing had changed.

An empty armchair was positioned next to his. Tomas wondered about it.

Yuri cleared his throat and raised an imperial finger at Tomas. "Do you know what time it is?"

Tomas didn't look at his watch. "Late."

"Very late. You should be at home with your wife and children." Yuri kept his gaze on Tomas. "So I ask you, why are you out getting FSB officers killed instead of sleeping next to my sister?"

Tomas considered answers and decided on the simplest. "I wanted to know whether Rzaev smuggled Novichok for terrorists and whether terrorists would use it either in the United States or in Russia. And I was trying to intercept two American spies here in Russia."

Yuri sighed heavily. It was the sigh of an exasperated and annoyed adult speaking to a child guilty of stealing a cookie. "Do you think I put you in as Director of the FSB because of your intelligence? Or your investigative skills? Or your proven administrative capacity?"

"Not really."

"Good. Because I didn't. I put you in because you are my sister's husband—and so I wouldn't have to worry about being stabbed in the back."

Tomas nodded.

"Because you're a fucking idiot."

Tomas nodded again. He understood that he was an idiot to think he could have pulled it off. He understood that he hadn't uncovered anything—and he understood that he would be lucky if he were allowed to go home to his family.

Yuri reclined in his chair and put his feet up on the desk. "But even with family, I'm concerned when someone starts to think he's smarter than me. That changes the game. When they become arrogant, that's a problem. Do you think *I'm* an idiot?"

"No. Of course not." Tomas shifted in his seat.

He nodded at one of the guards who swung the door open. Two men strode into the room, Rzaev, followed by a stocky man in a formal suit.

"Greeting, Volodya," Yuri waved towards the third chair, and Tomas now understood. "I understand you've had a difficult night."

"One could say that." Rzaev sat. The second man positioned himself behind Rzaev's chair.

Yuri turned to Tomas. "Did you think that Rzaev would do something as dangerous as smuggling Novichok into the United States without my agreement?"

Stunned, Tomas could no longer contain himself. "Why?"

"The Americans are going to pay for what they did to me. They took ten billion dollars from me, and now they're going to give it back. And I'm going to get more than money from them. I wanted Maria and her daughter, but none of my so-called crack intelligence officers can find them. But the Americans did this to me, and America is going to be sorry."

"If you do anything against Americans, the American government will come after Russia," Tomas said. "Sanctions will be the least of it."

"Which is why the Americans have been led to think that Islamic terrorists are responsible, not me."

"You told me to go after the American spies. Did you also want me to attack Rzaev last night?" Tomas still couldn't quite believe what he was hearing.

"No. You weren't supposed to take it that far. I didn't expect you to locate Rzaev. I did want you to chase the Americans a little, so they would think that they were doing something I didn't want, but I didn't think you could actually make a serious effort to catch them. I was mistaken. Also, Ivan Minsky should have kept his fat mouth shut. Which is why Rzaev shut it for him."

Tomas shifted his glaze from Yuri to Rzaev and then back again.

"Are you going to shoot him later—or would you like my man to do it now?" Rzaev spoke for the second time since he'd arrived.

Yuri spoke to Rzaev with grave respect. "I appreciate your anger, but we're putting on a magic act, using smoke and mirrors to get the Americans to believe what we want them to believe. So far it seems to be working. And despite his killing a few of your people, his attack on your compound was a good thing. The spies will not think that you and I are working together. If they should learn that the director of the FSB was shot, they might start wondering exactly what is going on. We need to maintain the illusion—so that the Americans are not just hunting for the Novichok, they are looking elsewhere to assign blame. American presidents tend to become testy when Americans die. Anyway, he's my sister's husband. My sister is fond of him."

"Americans dying?" Tomas asked.

Yuri waved a hand. "Not your concern. Tomas, you are going to go back to doing exactly what I tell you to do. No more trying to think on your own. You may be an idiot, but you're my idiot. Understand?"

There was only one way to answer and leave the room alive. "Understood."

"Go home, now. No more adventures. Stay away from Americans." Yuri made a shooing motion with his hand. "The adults have business to discuss."

54

THURSDAY EARLY MORNING, MOSCOW, RUSSIA

AFTER SHUTTING THE DOOR to his apartment, Tomas plodded to the kitchen and flipped on the light. Lyudmila, alone at the table, gazed at him with red-rimmed eyes. He sat next to her and took her hand. "You should be in bed."

"How could I sleep?"

"Yuri called you?"

"He said that you were an idiot and lucky to be coming home to me. Whatever you're doing, it's not worth your life or the lives of your children. If you think Yuri wouldn't kill us if he was angry enough, you don't know him."

"I know him pretty well. Go to bed, my love."

"And you?"

"I need to relax."

"I'll make you hot milk and honey."

"Just go to bed. Please. I don't want anything."

"Talk to me, Tomas."

He leaned over, kissed her cheek, then rose and headed for his office. He skimmed the volumes on his bookshelf and chose Gogol's short stories. Reading might calm him. But he doubted it. In the past, sharing with Lyudmila had helped.

This time he couldn't share with her.

Tomas couldn't tell her about the FSB agents lying dead in front of Rzaev's compound in Peredelkino. He couldn't tell her what he'd done to Ivan Minsky or that as a result of his torturing information from the man, Minsky had been murdered, or how he'd forced Fyodor to work for him. Any one act, resting on his conscience, would have been enough to keep him up for hours—and he couldn't share his dirty secrets with the wife he loved. He wouldn't want to sink in her eyes.

But there wasn't just his own guilt to keep him awake. He now knew that Yuri had used Rzaev to smuggle Novichok into the United States in some sort of twisty revenge plot.

American presidents get testy when Americans die. He'd been shut down when he'd asked what it meant, but the refrain kept repeating. Was the plan to kill Americans with a Russian nerve agent? Where? In a subway system? At a baseball stadium?

Tomas would put nothing past Yuri.

The terror attacks of 9-11 had sparked two wars. How much motivation would a nerve agent attack on American soil be?

The best scenario, if that happened, was that the Americans blamed Islamic terrorists. The best scenario would still result in a lot of dead Americans.

That was the best scenario.

The best.

The worst scenario was that the Americans uncovered the truth. That they realized that the President of the Russian Federation had attacked America. Because that's what it was. An attack. The result could be anything from severe sanctions—to outright war. War with the United States.

Was that even a real possibility? Even if Yuri was a psychopath, Thomas Lewis, the American President wasn't. He wouldn't escalate things to the point of a world war.

But would Yuri?

One thing Yuri could do—blame someone else. Someone high up enough that the Americans might accept the story. Maybe the guy who'd chased and nearly caught the American spies.

He'd be the fall guy, wouldn't he, the person blamed for deaths in America? Because Yuri had no loyalty to anyone but himself.

Tomas stared unseeing at the pages of his book. Maybe the Americans wouldn't find out. But he couldn't count on that—the United States had a very good intelligence network. Sooner or later, they'd figure it out.

Maybe not. Maybe Yuri could pull it off.

Is that what he was reduced to—hoping that if Yuri poisoned Americans—no one would find out who was responsible?

He'd know. He'd have to live with himself. Every day, he'd look at his children and know that people had died in the United States because he'd done nothing. Quite apart from his fear of taking the fall if the Americans found out.

But what could he do? Warn the Americans? If the Americans knew the truth—if Lewis called Yuri's bluff and warned him of the consequences—maybe Yuri would call it all off. If Tomas warned them— if he could even find a way past the watchers that he knew were always there —maybe this could all be stopped before anyone else died.

Or maybe not—because Yuri was a lunatic.

Meanwhile Tomas's reward would be his own death and the death of his entire family.

It was stupid to speculate. There was no way to get in touch with the Americans, even if he wanted to risk his life and his family. He would never make it into the American embassy. And his phone, personal, landline, everything, was being monitored. He was as trapped as the Americans who would die.

PART IV

55

THURSDAY MORNING, STOWE, VERMONT

IN THE CUSTOM SPRINTER, purchased a week earlier, Charlie drove to various hardware stores in Morristown and in Montpelier, buying supplies. Mickey rode shotgun and checked the list as Charlie piled each item in the back of the van.

Charlie put the van into gear and pulled out. "You and Rip dropped the Toyota?"

"Later. Don't want it to sit too long. Someone might notice. Still pissed that those fucking bitches got away."

"It'll work without Feinstein. Like we talked about."

"You think *he'll* be okay that she got away?"

Mickey never mentioned the name of the man from whom Charlie was taking his orders, although he knew it. It was a sign of respect. Also of fear.

Charlie was nonchalant. "Eventually, she'll head back home. She has a business and family in the area. If he wants us to, we can still find her. After that—I'm heading for the islands. I already have a place picked out. Things are going to be hot here for a while. If you're smart, you'll do the same."

"You sure that we're okay?"

"Don't worry about it. We're still on track."

THURSDAY MORNING, MOSCOW, RUSSIA

Approaching a blown agent was risky. Doing so without surveillance ahead of time, especially in Moscow, was more than risky. It was reckless. And stupid.

Fyodor lived on a quiet street with old, pre-Revolutionary buildings that resembled brownstones in New York, small trees and flowers lining the sidewalk and only a narrow lane for traffic. He left his building at the same time every morning and walked the same route to the Metro. Jonathan knew this from previous trips to Russia. The routine made it easier for a quick pass off of information. This time, however, Jonathan assumed that Fyodor would be followed. Jonathan assumed that fact for several reasons including the FSB personnel around the Anichkov bridge, and the FSB raid on Platonov.

But before they made an approach, they had to know exactly what they were facing. After Kolya and Dmitri left for the airport, the team executed a dry run.

Elizabeth walked past Fyodor's building at 6:25 a.m., a few minutes before he exited. A black car was parked just opposite the door to his building. As she passed, she noted two people inside the car.

She strode past Jonathan on the corner. He started towards the Metro, not too fast. Not too slow. He descended into the Metro, spotted Fyodor when he arrived on the platform, and stepped into a separate car, where he was packed in with and jostled by morning commuters.

Fyodor got off at his usual stop. Jonathan saw no one suspicious follow behind him, although he assumed that the black car would be waiting outside the stop. Teo would be buying pastries at Fyodor's usual breakfast spot.

Jonathan rode to the next stop and then exited. He climbed the stairs and waited until Teo, with Elizabeth in back, pulled up.

"All good," Teo said. "They didn't follow him into the shop."

"Just the one car. Two watchers." Elizabeth stifled a yawn. "So we're good to go tomorrow morning?"

"Good to go," Jonathan agreed.

"Any word from Petrov?"

"His plane takes off in half an hour."

"I bet he's happy to be getting the hell out of Russia," Teo said. "Has he been in contact?"

"I don't expect to hear anything." Jonathan felt in his pocket for his phone. It didn't hurt to check. But the pocket that had held his phone was empty. "Fuck. Goddamn fuck."

Elizabeth turned cool eyes on him. "What?"

"Phone is gone. The Metro." He had been packed tightly in the train and a pickpocket had seized the opportunity. What a fucking amateur move.

"Are you kidding me, Jonathan? You lost your phone? Did you also lose the nuclear codes?"

He tried to calm down. "It's an annoyance, not a security breach. It's a burner that can't be traced back to me. It's locked, and any communications on it were either encrypted or self-destroying. I'll pick up a new burner before we approach Fyodor tomorrow."

"Kolya can't reach you, though, and he won't know you don't have a phone," Teo said.

"Kolya's not anywhere we could help, even if he needed it." Jonathan thought about the conversation he'd had with Kolya hours earlier. There was something worrying Kolya, which concerned Jonathan. Kolya's instincts tended to be on target. At least he had a GPS tracker on him. "Anyway, he'll have multiple teams on the ground to back him up. The serious risk is to us—here in Moscow."

THURSDAY NOON, OVER THE ATLANTIC

On the flight from Moscow to Newark, Kolya dozed lightly. Whatever had bothered him when he had been talking to Jonathan stirred just below consciousness. Then he woke. He stared out at the clouds. Something was wrong. What was it? He glanced over at Dmitri, who was sleeping in the seat next to him.

He had not admitted it to Jonathan or to Dmitri, but he had enjoyed the mission, as painful, nerve-wracking, and exhausting as it had been. He liked being in the field, testing his wits against an adversary. And being with Dmitri in St. Petersburg and Moscow had reawakened memories, not all of which had been bad.

They had been brothers. For five years, Kolya would have put his life on the line for Dmitri. When Dmitri had arrived in the United States twelve years earlier, Kolya had thought they could renew the bond they'd had as kids—until he realized what Dmitri was doing and how many people were getting killed by Dmitri and his gang.

He'd broken their friendship by putting Dmitri in prison. But now, was it possible to go back? On this trip, Dmitri had deceived Rzaev to protect Kolya and the mission, and Kolya had begun to trust him again.

Or was he was being overly sentimental? Was he off his game after eight months out? Because something was trying to surface. Something he should have noticed. Something wrong.

What?

He ran the entire operation through his mind—from the arrival in St. Petersburg to Yelseyev's apartment to the Minsky's club to the drive to Moscow and the encounter with Rzaev.

Something about that meeting with Rzaev bothered him, and he didn't know what.

Kolya revisited the entire encounter. The initial greeting, the discussion of his "proposal", Rzaev's agreement—and the escape through the tunnel. All along the way, Dmitri had been reliable, more than reliable.

Or was he?

Wait. When they first arrived at Rzaev's compound.

They had talked about the garden. Rzaev was proud of the vegetables he was planting. Rzaev's wife had planted the flowers, but she had died of breast cancer eighteen months earlier.

I'm sorry I didn't get to say goodbye. She's gone, now, a year?

Dmitri had known that Rzaev's wife had died—not only that she'd died, but that it had been at least a year.

Fucking breast cancer.

Dmitri had been in prison at the time a year earlier. So how did he know not only when she died but what had killed her—when he had told Kolya at the prison that he hadn't had any contact with Rzaev or members of his gang.

Had he lied? Had he taken Kolya on a tour of Russia—when he knew all along how to contact Rzaev?

If that was true, that meant that Dmitri was in on whatever Rzaev was doing.

Did it?

Couldn't there be an innocent explanation? Maybe Dmitri at the prison had seen an obituary in a Russian newspaper. Maybe someone in the prison had known Rzaev. Or one of Ivan Minsky's people had told Dmitri about Rzaev's wife. It was possible.

But not likely.

Kolya felt stupid, and he felt betrayed. But what to do about it?

His goal was still to find the Novichok—and to use whatever means he had to do so. If Dmitri were indeed in on the plot, then he would know where the Novichok had been hidden—and why.

Contact the ECA, tell them his suspicions, and take Dmitri into custody.

But if Kolya did so, Dmitri would tell them nothing. There was no threat or promise that would get Dmitri to talk.

Remember, carrots?

Even as a ten year old, Dmitri had refused to give up his friends. He was now a member of the mafiya, and he had kept to the code in prison. He'd informed on no one, even though before trial, he'd had offers of more lenient treatment if he cooperated. Even if Kolya didn't have moral qualms about torture, which he did, it would be ineffectual against Dmitri. And whatever had been planned with the Novichok would go forward.

Play it out.

If Dmitri had just wanted to kill him, he'd be dead. Dmitri had something else planned.

What?

He had no idea.

Stirring of panic. He pushed the thoughts away, gripped the chair, and counted. Deep breaths. The panic slowly dissipated.

It wasn't Romania. This time he knew that he could be walking into a trap. This time his own agency wasn't orchestrating it—to the contrary, they'd be able to find him through the GPS tracker that he had placed underneath a Band-Aid on his upper arm.

He stood and pushed past the sleeping Dmitri, headed for the bathroom at the back of the plane, and locked himself inside. He tapped out a message to Jonathan on an encrypted app.

Dmitri may be in on plot. Playing along. Track me, wearing GPS.

He trusted Jonathan, even though Jonathan was still in Russia. He didn't know that he could trust Bradford or any of the ECA teams. He'd let Jonathan make that call. Meanwhile, he had to keep from alerting Dmitri that he was suspicious. Whatever game Dmitri might have set up had to be played out.

He thought about Alex.

What mattered was that she was safe. And that she knew he loved her. He'd told her so in his last phone call. While he would like to hear her voice again, he wouldn't contact her. It would worry her—and she might put herself in danger in an effort to help him.

He closed his eyes and pictured her lying in bed next to him. The hardest thing about risking his life was knowing that if he died, he would never see her or touch her again. Still, if he died, he wouldn't feel the emptiness. She would. He hated the idea of causing her pain, but there were people who could die from a nerve agent if he didn't take the risk— and maybe, just maybe, he could prevent it.

He knew what she'd say, too, if she knew. *It's not all on you. Don't be fucking crazy. You don't always have to be the one. You still have PTSD.*

But there was no one else. And he was managing the PTSD, more or less.

Maybe he *was* crazy. Because anything could happen. He would not be in control. His PTSD could flare at any time.

If he was right.

He hoped he was wrong.

He didn't think he was.

56

THURSDAY NIGHT, BURLINGTON, VERMONT

DURING THE STOPOVER IN Newark, they ate at a steak house with décor that celebrated the high points of New Jersey: the shore, Princeton, the Pinelands. None of which Kolya thought really captured the essence of the state: expensive suburbs alternating with decaying cities. Kolya sipped a light ale. Fuzzy with exhaustion, he felt the weight of the perpetual motion, the changes in time, and the constant tension, all of which he'd previously managed with little effort. But he was calm. He could function well enough. What would happen, would happen.

Dmitri, on the other hand, was upbeat as he lined up four shots of vodka. "You should drink real stuff, Kolya, not that weak piss. Meeting in Vermont is not until tomorrow. Relax."

"I'm relaxed." Besides, he was downing Advil to reduce the swelling in his knee, and anything stronger than beer was inadvisable.

"You're like an old man. No sex. No alcohol." Dmitri raised his third shot. "*Za zadarovnya*. When I buy my house in Florida, you have to come visit. You can wade in the waves and sun yourself with all the other old people."

"Not this old man." Kolya had to smile at the description of himself. "I'm not fond of sand."

"Okay, then. Come for friendship, not for the beaches. We can drive to Miami. Great jazz clubs, although more in the Cuban flavor."

Maybe he was wrong. He hoped he was wrong. "I like Cuban jazz. I will consider it."

The flight departed two hours late due to weather somewhere in the Midwest.

235

When they touched down in Vermont, it was almost ten. The overweight security guard waved them to what passed as a main terminal. Kolya hobbled through halls painted a welcoming yellow, past the two souvenir shops in the terminal, shuttered and closed. The entire airport could have fit in the baggage area of Newark.

"This is it?" Dmitri looked around. "The biggest airport in Vermont?"

"It's a small state."

"Do you think we will see Bernie Sanders?"

"One never knows. One can hope."

Dmitri grinned. "You've returned to your Soviet roots and become a communist, my friend?"

"Democratic socialist. I like Denmark and Sweden."

At the luggage carousel, tired passengers circled the luggage belt. Dmitri waited while Kolya rested, his leg propped sideways on a bench. The bell rang, the belt shuddered into motion, and passengers wrestled ribboned suitcases to the ground. Dmitri grabbed both of their bags, and Kolya pushed off the bench.

They stopped at a men's room opposite the luggage carousel. Kolya carried his bag into a stall, Dmitri entered a different stall.

Kolya used the toilet and then retrieved what appeared to be a can of shaving cream, a soda can, and a hair dryer from his luggage to quickly assemble the gun parts that had been concealed inside the seemingly innocuous objects. He slipped his HK .40 into his waistband and then stepped out before Dmitri.

At the car rental desk opposite the baggage carousel, a bored young man with a mop of black hair checked the reservation and proffered a key.

A short walk to the garage where the rental cars were stored took Kolya, limping stiff legged, ten minutes. Kolya offered Dmitri the key to a red Subaru Outback, Vermont's state car. "Since you enjoy driving."

"I drank four vodkas in Newark and one while flying here. You drank beer at dinner and nothing since. Who do you think is safer to drive? Besides, I want to see Vermont."

"It's night."

Dmitri shrugged. "Then I will look at the stars. And watch for moose."

They loaded their luggage into the trunk and slid into the car. Kolya pushed his seat back so he could drive with minimal pressure on his knee, punched the address of the Newport inn where they had a reservation into the car's GPS, started the engine, and wove out of the parking lot onto a dark and empty street. When he merged north on I-89, traffic picked up marginally. One set of taillights ahead of him. A car in the far lane passed at a highly illegal speed.

Dmitri found a classical station. Violins enveloped the car. "Nice. You know this piece?"

"Mahler's fourth." Kolya enjoyed classical, if not quite as much as jazz. If it had been Jonathan, it would have been country. On something so important to Kolya—music—his taste aligned more with Dmitri than with the friend to whom he owed his life.

Life was odd.

Once he exited from the highway onto a country road, the traffic diminished further. Occasional headlights from the opposite direction lit trees and dark fields—and beyond them, low mountains.

Adrenaline coursed through his body. *Listen to the music.* But it was hard—suspecting what he suspected. Maybe he was wrong. He hoped he was wrong.

They circled a roundabout—passed a sign for Jeffersonville—and continued in the dark. One car passed. Then another. They reached the town of Johnson. Scattered streetlights illuminated dark antique shops, a farm supply store, and a Chinese restaurant. They were approaching Railroad Street on the right.

"I need to piss." Dmitri said. "Five vodkas."

"Everything's closed."

"So I will piss in the woods. Sign says park is right turn. Will be deserted this time of night."

"I can pull over when we get out of town."

"Still some cars on the road. I prefer someplace more private. Are you afraid of the dark?"

"No." Kolya hit his signal and turned right. His hands were steady on the wheel. That was good. "I am not afraid of the dark."

They rattled over a wooden bridge, proceeded up a hill, past a dark and deserted building that looked like it might have been a lumberyard, and swung into a parking lot. A sign with images of pedestrians and bicycles proclaimed it to be the Lamoille Valley Trail.

Kolya parked and switched off the engine and the lights. "Go ahead."

The area was completely dark. If there were houses nearby, he couldn't tell.

Dmitri opened his door and slid into the darkness. Kolya leaned his head back and closed his eyes. His leg ached. He felt the exhaustion from the past week, but he was still calm. If he were right, this would be the moment.

Dmitri tapped on his window. Kolya cracked the door. "What?"

"I can drive."

"I thought you were drunk."

"I'm pretty sober now. You can rest your leg."

"Fine." Kolya took two deep breaths and then opened the passenger car and swung out. Dmitri pushed the muzzle of a small gun into his back, in a direct line to his heart.

"If you move, Kolya, I will shoot you. And hands up."

Kolya froze and raised his hands, feeling the urge of adrenaline and something else—regret.

Dmitri pressed the gun into his back with one hand and removed the HK .40 that Kolya had tucked into his waistband with the other. "Turn around now but keep hands up."

Kolya turned slowly. His eyes adjusted to the dim light enough to see Dmitri's shape and something metallic in Dmitri's hand. He watched Dmitri tuck the HK into his waistband.

"I didn't see you put your gun together, Kolya."

"In the bathroom."

"And your knife?"

"Still in my suitcase. Someone left you a gun in the bathroom?"

"Phone and gun." Dmitri gestured towards the trunk. "Open it. Then unzip your suitcase and step back."

Kolya did as instructed. Opening the trunk triggered the lights, and he blinked in the sudden brightness. He unzipped his case and then stepped a foot away from the car.

"Three more feet."

Kolya backed three feet. He still was in the circle of light. So was Dmitri. He watched Dmitri rummage through the suitcase and pull out the sheathed knife with a flourish. Then Dmitri tucked the knife into his own waist.

"Congratulations. Now that you have my knife, I'm totally helpless."

"You still use sarcasm as defense, Kolya. It takes me back."

"So glad to hear that. Now what?"

"Clothes off."

"What?"

Dmitri motioned with the gun. "Clothes. Underwear. Shoes. Socks. Everything. Strip."

The request was unexpected and weird. "No."

"Do you want me to shoot you?"

"You're going to kill me anyway. I'd prefer not to be found naked."

"No, Kolya. This is not about killing you—although I will if I have to. I have other plans. But there is something you should see...." Dmitri took a cell phone out, tapped a code into it, and tossed it to Kolya.

Kolya looked at the image. It was a photo of the window of the back of the vacation house in Stowe, and Alex was clearly visible. Behind her, to the right, was Tehila.

"I have snipers in position who will take them both out if you don't do exactly what I tell you," Dmitri said.

But Alex wasn't there. Or was she? He'd told her to leave the state, but he wasn't sure she had. She had a mind of her own. In fact, he'd been concerned that she'd figured out Vermont was the epicenter of his mission—and decided to stay. He should have checked back with her.

It could be true.

Yob tvoyu mat. He'd arrogantly assumed he could handle the situation. He hadn't calculated on Dmitri knowing about Alex—or threatening Alex.

Was it going to be fucking Romania all over again?

He switched the phone off. Then he hurled it at Dmitri who caught it. "Calm down, Kolya."

"I'm going to fucking kill you, Dmitri." It was one thing to be taken prisoner. He'd calculated the risks—Dmitri might kill him instead of kidnapping him—but if Dmitri had just wanted him dead, why not kill him in Russia? However, he'd counted on Alex leaving Vermont.

"I know you want to. But even if you could kill me, my people would kill her and her bodyguard. Clothes off. Everything."

Kolya stripped, tossing watch, shirt, pants, shoes, and socks into a pile. Then he stood naked in the darkness. It was more than just humiliating. He was reliving the feeling of helplessness—of hanging from chains, stripped and tortured—and that Alex was again at risk just made it worse. He'd thought he had everything under control—thought he knew what he was walking into—and he'd been wrong. He started to disassociate, and he could feel his body shaking. More deep breaths. He pushed the thoughts of Romania away and dug his nails into his palm. He forced himself to focus on the feel of the air, the heaviness of the dark. Then, back in the present, he narrowed his eyes at Dmitri. "You want a quick fuck, is that it?"

Dmitri chuckled. "It would be fair for me getting fucked in prison. But no, this is just security. Just in case you have something hidden in your clothes so they can follow you. Even maybe another weapon. It is hard to find everything—easier if you strip. And there is some justice—since it's what I had to do in prison. I have new clothes for you. There." He pointed.

Kolya turned his head. A Toyota on the opposite side of the street, next to the driveway of a dark house, was barely visible.

"Now take the Band-Aid off your arm."

"What? Why?" This changed the equation again. Kolya'd counted on the GPS tracker leading the ECA to him. He'd miscalculated on so many levels. Dmitri had just declared checkmate.

"Please, do not insult my intelligence. I know you have a GPS device underneath."

How did Dmitri know about the tracker? Or about Alex? "Fuck you."

"If I don't call within half an hour, my people will go in. Her bodyguard may be good, but they will have surprise and automatic weapons. You think I'm bluffing?"

"I think it possible."

"We can stand here for half an hour, and then I will get pictures of Alex's body. Then you will try to kill me, but I will shoot you first. Or you can do what I ask."

Losing the GPS tracker might change the equation, but was it really worth dying now rather than later? Alex would be shot, if Dmitri was telling the truth. Was Kolya willing to gamble on her life? And Novichok would still be somewhere inside the United States.

It wasn't a chess game, and it wasn't over. Maybe he could no longer count on the ECA tracking him, but he was still the only one close enough to even have a possibility of stopping Dmitri. He had to take any chance, no matter how slim, which meant cooperating—for now.

Anyway, he couldn't take the risk that Alex might actually be in the sights of a sniper.

Kolya removed the Band-Aid and let the small GPS tracker fall to the ground.

57

FRIDAY MORNING, MOSCOW, RUSSIA

THE TIMING WAS AS anticipated. Fyodor left his building on schedule. A few minutes later, he rounded the corner of his street, heading towards the Metro, followed by the black car.

On the sidewalk directly in Fyodor's path, Jonathan and Elizabeth argued animatedly in French, in increasing intensity. Just as Fyodor, followed by the black car, passed them, Elizabeth turned and slapped Jonathan hard.

"You bastard. I know you slept with my sister." The pitched argument became a scream.

"You are crazy. I never did." Jonathan shouted back.

Fyodor hurried to get by. The black car slowed, the driver peering out the window. Pedestrians halted, watching.

Elizabeth slapped him again.

Jonathan smacked her back. A woman in a designer dress shouted something in Russian about not hitting a woman. A man shouted at her to stay out of it. But a crowd was building in a circle around them, transfixed by the spectacle.

The driver of the black car rolled down his window for a better look.

Jonathan tried to grab her arms. "Stop this. You're making a scene. I didn't sleep with her."

A block ahead, Fyodor continued toward the Metro, but the black car only inched forward, the driver focused on Elizabeth and Jonathan. A block ahead, Teo strode towards them. He bumped into Fyodor, apologized, and then continued briskly. When he passed Jonathan, he nodded.

Elizabeth tried another slap, but this time Jonathan grabbed both her arms. "Stop! Why would I sleep with her when I have a woman as beautiful as you? And I love you."

"She told me... she told me...."

"She's lying. She's jealous. She wants to drive us apart."

Elizabeth burst into tears. He hugged her, and the crowd began to disperse. The black car sped up to catch Fyodor. Jonathan put his arm around Elizabeth, and the two of them walked a block in the opposite direction from the Metro stop—and Fyodor.

They then slid into the back of an idling car.

"That was quite a show." Teo glanced at them through the rear view mirror.

"Thanks." Elizabeth took out a mirror and checked her hair. "We're doing Broadway next month."

"The phone?" Jonathan asked.

"In his coat pocket."

"Good job." Jonathan turned to Elizabeth. "You didn't have to hit me that hard."

"You hit me back."

"I pulled my punch. You didn't. And you hit me twice."

"Had to make it look real. Besides, it was kind of fun."

Teo put the car into gear and pulled into traffic. Jonathan reached into his pocket, pulled out the phone he'd bought hours earlier, and dialed the number for the burner that Ted had planted on Fyodor.

Fyodor answered after two rings. "*Privyet.*" Casual, as if he hadn't just found a strange phone planted in his pocket. Then—"I'm being watched."

"We know. That's why we gave them a show. Are you planning your usual stop for pastries?"

"As I do every morning."

"Good. Buy a tea and a pastry then use the men's room. I'll be there."

* * * * *

Fyodor pushed open the door of the bathroom. Jonathan was already waiting in the small cramped space, where the café staff had a less than enthusiastic attitude towards sanitation. Teo drank tea at a table near the front window and watched for watchers. Elizabeth, having put on a hat and a jacket so as not to be easily identified as the woman who had been fighting with her boyfriend, was on her phone across the street. If the omnipresent watchers in the black car got out, they'd signal.

Fyodor looked torn between anger and fear. "Do you know how risky this is?"

"Well, obviously, since the FSB is following you—and they'd set a trap in St. Petersburg. But thank you for alerting us." Jonathan leaned against the door, blocking anyone else from entering—or Fyodor from leaving. "We need to confirm whether Yuri Bykovsky is responsible for the Novichok that was smuggled into the United States—and who the target might be."

Fyodor paled. "Do you think someone on my level would have that kind of information?"

"Then who's watching you—and why?"

"I can't help you, Jonathan. Let me go."

Jonathan pushed his back against the door. "Who raided Rzaev's compound—and why?"

"I… I…"

"We can get you both out. But you have to answer me first."

"You won't be able to get me out. I will be dead first. They are watching me." His voice dropped to a whisper. "Watching my wife. If I'm not out of here quickly, they will come for me."

"I know. Let's speed it up. Who was in charge of the raid on Rzaev's compound?"

"Tomas Orlov." Fyodor's voice remained a whisper.

Jonathan had spotted him raiding the club in St. Petersburg. "Why?"

"He wanted to know who had paid Rzaev to smuggle Novichok—and what information you were after."

Why would Orlov be so concerned if Russia had been behind the plot? Unless he wasn't in on it. "How did he know about you? About us?"

"Someone has an asset in American intelligence. Maybe Rzaev. Maybe Bykovsky. Whoever it was, knew my identity." Fyodor hesitated. "Orlov threatened my wife."

"So you told him that Kolya was meeting you."

Fyodor knew Kolya's given name but thought his last name was Semenov. In creating a legend, it's sometimes better to use the same first name. Easier to remember. Jonathan was Jonathan Smith, as far as Fyodor knew.

"He already knew about the meeting. He just didn't know the time or place. And I wore the cap. To warn Kolya. They got a picture of him by the bridge. I pretended I didn't recognize him."

"Can you get into Orlov's computer?"

"*What?* No!" The answer was whispered. "No! Do you not understand? I can't do anything unless I clear it with Tomas Orlov. The only reason I'm still alive is that he wants to use me. Please let me go. We've been too long."

Jonathan's phone vibrated, and he glanced at the text. *Someone's getting out of a car.* Maybe Orlov's desire to find out the truth about the Novichok could be used. It was the only possible play. "Tell Orlov that I contacted you. That I had questions about information we found on Rzaev's computer indicating Islamic terrorists were behind the Novichok in the United States."

"What?"

"Tell him that you agreed to confirm the information." Jonathan stepped aside from the door. "And that you've arranged a meeting with me. I'll text you the location later on the burner. And afterwards, whatever happens, we'll get you out. You and your wife."

"You are NOC, Jonathan. You could be arrested and executed for espionage."

"Yeah, I know. Now go. Your friends will be in the coffee shop in a second. Complain about your stomach at the cash register."

"Okay then." Fyodor squared his shoulders. "If I die, get my wife out."

Fyodor exited the bathroom. Jonathan stepped into a stall and watched his phone. He'd leave after Elizabeth gave the all clear.

58

FRIDAY NIGHT, STOWE, VERMONT

DMITRI DROVE THROUGH THE small town of Morrisville and then south towards Stowe, taking the road towards the mountain and the ski resort that dominated the town. Kolya, hands bound in a tight rope that had then been tied with an additional strand to the door handle, knew the roads and the direction.

"Where are we going?" They passed the turn-off for Alex's house, and he was relieved. Taking her prisoner as well did not seem to be part of the plan. At least he was dressed—in cheap oversized jeans and a flannel shirt—but dressed. Of course, a nude man in a car, even in Vermont, would draw attention.

"We need a place to hang out until morning."

"Why?" If the plan was to execute him, they could do that in the dark. If they intended to kill him with the Novichok, no reason to wait.

"Because we need light. And we need things to be open. So we are going to hide in plain sight for a few hours."

"No evil lair where you can gloat over me and wave Novichok in the air?"

"Don't be melodramatic. You know very well, it is safer not to keep all your assets together. Besides, would you be this well behaved if I took you to the Novichok? I know you. You would try something heroic and stupid."

"Me? The only stupid thing I've done recently is to start to trust you. Why do you need light?"

"That would be telling. You'll find out soon enough." Dmitri turned

246

onto the road leading up to the resort. After fifteen minutes, he navigated to a large parking lot of the year-round luxury hotel, with shops, a swimming pool, sauna, and entertainment in the off-ski season. Early June was between the two huge seasons, ski season, and summer. But even in this off-season, the parking lot was filled with cars. There was a security camera over the entrance and exit, but that looked like the extent of the security. Kolya also suspected the security camera footage would only be viewed if there was a report of a problem, which wouldn't be very often. It was Vermont.

Dmitri maneuvered into an empty spot and turned off the engine. "Get some rest, Kolya." He took out his phone, tapped a message, and then returned it to his pocket. Then he took out his gun and aimed it. "But just so you know, I slept all the way from Moscow—and I will be awake and watching."

* * * * *

The message came in over Charlie's phone. The plan was on. Dmitri had Petrov, and the next stage would occur in a few hours. He sent a text to Mickey, who would meet them at the first site with Tom and Rip, and then he sent the message on to Moscow.

A few minutes later.

After the plan succeeds—I want a video of both of them dying.

Charlie hesitated, but keeping the truth concealed would just anger Bykovsky, and Charlie did not want to anger Bykovsky. Angering Bykovsky meant that he killed you as well as your entire family. *We don't have the woman.*

But you have her address.

Yes.

Kill her afterwards. Before you kill Petrov, tell him that she's going to die too.

Do you care how I kill them?

No. As long as it's painful.

Charlie tapped his agreement. He ran the traditional mafiya killing method through his mind versus Novichok poisoning. Both would be very painful, but he was a little afraid of the Novichok, and it was no longer prepackaged. He didn't want to accidentally expose himself.

247

As far as Petrov's girlfriend went, he would contact Tom in Boston and then stop off in D.C. on his way to the islands—one last job in the United States.

Then he sent a message back to Dmitri—*all is ready. Meet as planned.*

A message came back. *Pick up coffee. One with cream and one sugar. One black, two sugars.*

59

FRIDAY MORNING, LUBYANKA, MOSCOW

HIS EYES HEAVY WITH fatigue and knowledge, Tomas signed routine papers and made calls to the families of the dead FSB agents. His secretary Natalia brought him a glass of tea and a plate of small pastries, but he didn't touch any of it.

He wished he didn't know about the Novichok. He wished he were just a low level clerk somewhere—who didn't know anything.

Natalia reentered his office. "You should at least drink the tea."

"Thank you, but no."

Maybe he could finally hire a new secretary. For now, he just wanted her out of his sight.

She picked up the tray. "Fyodor Mikailovich Dyakov has been sitting outside waiting to talk to you."

"How long has he been there?"

"Half an hour."

"And you didn't think to tell me."

"I thought you should have your tea in peace."

And undoubtedly she wanted the chance to go at him herself. Once a spy, always a spy. "Send him in."

She returned with Fyodor. Tomas dismissed her with "Close the door as you leave." The closed door wouldn't matter either. He had the place swept every day, but he didn't trust the sweepers. Someone would be listening.

Sooner or later.

Fyodor shifted from foot to foot and shook his head when Tomas motioned him to a chair.

"So?" Tomas asked.

Fyodor cleared his throat. "I want you to know that this was not my idea."

"What was not your idea?"

"I had no idea he would be there."

"Who would be where?" Tomas was generally a patient man, but today he was not in the mood for puzzles.

"I stopped at my usual bakery on my way to work today for a late breakfast. I like the almond rolls, particularly."

Tomas made a rolling motion with his hand.

Fyodor's voice rose in pitch. "When I went to the toilet, there was an American—ECA agent—waiting for me. I met him once before. Jonathan Smith."

Tomas knew that the name was an alias—but that didn't matter.

"And—what did he want?"

"He wanted me to check the files to confirm that Islamic terrorists paid Rzaev to smuggle Novichok into the United States. He says that they have evidence, but they need secondary confirmation."

"Does he suspect that you're compromised?"

"No."

Tomas didn't believe it, but he wasn't going to press the question, not with the certainty of listeners. He glanced at the phone, expecting it to ring. Or a text on his cell. Something to indicate what Yuri wanted.

Maybe they weren't tuned in at this particular moment. Maybe someone would be taking the information right now—or a little later to Yuri's office and asking for instructions. Whether they listened now or later—did it matter?

Tomas knew what Yuri would want to hear. Tomas was an idiot but not quite as much of an idiot as Yuri thought. So he told Fyodor exactly what Yuri would want him to say. "Well, then tell Smith—that you got into my files and checked, and you can confirm. Do you know how to reach him?"

He took out a pen and scribbled on a pad while he spoke.

Then he passed the pad to Fyodor, whose eyes widened. He read the few sentences, nodded, and took the pen. He scribbled a note back.

"I don't have a way to get in touch with him. He said he would contact me. He said it was safer." Fyodor's voice was calmer.

"Okay, then, you know what to do. Let me know how it goes."

After Fyodor left his office, Tomas tore the piece of paper from the pad, folded it, and put it in his pocket. He'd flush it next time he visited the toilet. Watchers might sort through garbage, but not though shit.

60

FRIDAY EARLY MORNING, ARLINGTON, VIRGINIA

HER CELL PHONE WOKE her earlier than Margaret had anticipated. Yes, it was going to be a big day, and hopefully a day of glory for her and the ECA—when thanks to Kolya Petrov, they nabbed the smuggler of the Novichok. But nothing was supposed to happen until noon. She planned to be in the office by 8 a.m. Unless something went wrong.

Which it had.

Marty Davis, heading up the ECA teams in Newport, Vermont, informed her that Petrov had not checked into his room at the local inn. No word from him or Lemonsky since they'd landed. They'd called and texted the phone he was carrying. No response.

"Well, use the GPS on his phone to locate him." She was already out of bed and choosing her outfit for the day, a blue suit with a white blouse, mindful she would most likely be in the White House within hours.

"Already tried. His phone's off." Marty lowered his voice. "Kowolsky's here, by the way, allegedly coordinating with us. He hates Kolya, and I don't trust him. I don't want him—or anyone else in the CIA—to know that Kolya's missing for as long as we can hold out."

It made sense.

She clicked off and called into the office. "Get in touch with Jonathan Egan immediately. She managed to dress and was just finishing the touches on her hair when the phone rang again.

It was Jonathan.

There was a long pause after she gave him the news.

"Kolya was worried about something happening. He taped a GPS tracker to his arm in case—so we could find him."

"Any idea what he was worried about?"

"None. He didn't seem to be worried about Lemonsky. It seemed to be just—you know—one of those feelings you get in the field."

"Have you heard from him?" Petrov was more likely contact Jonathan, whom he trusted, than the home office.

"No. But he wouldn't have been able to contact me if he'd tried. I had a problem and had to get a new phone. He doesn't have the number."

She considered asking what the problem had been, but it was not of top priority.

"Goddamnit. I should have followed them to Vermont. He's not doing that well, Margaret." Then Jonathan calmed himself. "Okay, still technical should be able to find him with the GPS tracker. Whatever you do, Margaret, don't let the CIA know what's going on."

"Don't tell me my job, Jonathan." She hung up.

FOGGY BOTTOM, WASHINGTON, D.C.

Margaret Bradford knew she could only delay calling the President and Ben Smithson for so long, especially since she had unpleasant news to convey. At a minimum, the meeting with the smuggler was not going forward. Beyond that, there were three possibilities: Petrov was dead; he was being forcibly held; or he was plotting against the United States.

She believed the first or second possibility was the most probable that he was dead or being held. He was working with someone who had reason to hate him. But her personal opinion wasn't important. Both the President and Smithson would only ask whether Petrov posed a danger to the United States. The fact that Petrov may have gone on a revenge spree in Russia would be considered evidence he'd gone rogue.

Which was why she wanted to put things into motion before alerting either of them. She owed Petrov that much.

She considered the team, headed by Marty Davis, that was waiting in Newport Vermont. Close, but so were teams from the CIA and the FBI. And the team from the CIA included Kowolsky. If she pulled anyone from the team in Newport to hunt for Petrov, Kowolsky—and Smithson—would figure it out quickly.

No, this had to be kept quiet at least for now.

She considered her list of field agents, but those not in Vermont were in D.C. or scattered around the world. No good. It would take too long to get anyone in position.

Wait. She was being stupid. Tehila Melaku was a top agent, and she was, at last count, in Vermont babysitting Alex Feinstein who had also undergone training for several weeks when she briefly worked at the ECA as counsel.

It wasn't the best solution, but it was a solution.

She called Tehila's number. "Please confirm that you are still in Vermont."

"Confirmed. We are in a hotel room in Burlington, Vermont, drinking coffee and eating pancakes with maple syrup. Is there a problem?"

"Kolya Petrov and Dmitri Lemonsky landed in Burlington Vermont at 10 o'clock last night, and no one has heard from them since. His phone is dead, but we have a location for a secondary GPS tracker that he taped to his arm—and it hasn't moved for ten hours."

"Are there vital signs?" Tehila's voice changed. No more amusement.

"It just does location. It would give the same readout if he were dead or alive."

"Not moving for ten hours is generally not a good sign."

Margaret hadn't wanted to say so out loud, but she agreed. Still, she had assumed Petrov dead on more than one occasion, and he'd surprised her. She hoped that he would surprise her again. "Maybe his car broke down, and his phone wasn't charged. Yes, it's not likely, not with an agent of Petrov's experience, but still I'd like you to check."

"Both of us?"

"Yes. You can't leave Feinstein unprotected, and she does have some training." If Petrov were in fact dead, it would be hard on Feinstein to be there when his body was discovered—but it was more important to protect her physically than to protect her sensibilities. "Mark Leslie has coordinates."

* * * * *

FRIDAY MORNING, BURLINGTON, VERMONT

Alex waited until Tehila was off the phone. "Who hasn't moved for ten hours?"

"It's not so much a who as a what."

"What hasn't moved for ten hours?"

"A GPS tracking device." Tehila was dressing and hiding weapons in various places throughout her clothes. Three guns. Two knives. Then she checked the shotgun and the Galil and stuffed them into the gym bag. "Bradford asked me to check it out."

Alex pulled on jeans, a T-shirt, and a sweater. "A tracking device on a person?"

"Yes."

Alex had a pretty good idea of the identity of the person. She wanted to scream. *Not again.* He'd promised he'd careful. She was torn between anger and fear, but that didn't matter now. Not until she knew something for sure. *Keep it* together—for *now.*

But her stomach was a hard knot, and she was finding it hard to catch her breath.

"Are you okay?" Tehila asked.

"Not really." She slid her own gun into her pocket. She only carried one, but it would have to do. "But I'll manage. Let's roll."

61

FRIDAY MORNING, STOWE, VERMONT

IT HAD BEEN AN uncomfortable night. Kolya, in the passenger's seat, rested against the door, the rope biting into his wrists. If done correctly, rope was more difficult to escape than other restraints. Still, he tried. He flexed his wrists when Dmitri wasn't watching to try to loosen the knots, but progress was minimal. It hurt his wrists and added to the discomfort. His shoulders ached from the strain of being in the same position for so long. He'd thought his shoulder had healed from a bullet wound eight months earlier, but with the forced position, his left shoulder was throbbing. His knee and right leg still ached.

Between the nightmares and fighting down the panic, he'd only dozed a little. He didn't know if Dmitri had slept.

Alex had been right. He was a fucking fool to have agreed to do this.

He woke from another brief doze at the sound of the engine starting.

"Where are we going?"

"In time, Kolya." Dmitri put the car into reverse and swung out of the parking spot. A hotel employee, arriving for the morning shift, waved a hello. Dmitri waved back. "Someone will meet us with coffee."

"I could use a bathroom."

"Few minutes." Halfway down the mountain, Dmitri pulled into a deserted parking area where signs indicated that cross-country skiers gathered in the winter. He walked around the car, opened Kolya's door, and untied the extra strand of rope holding him to the door. Then he stepped back.

Kolya maneuvered his legs and swung out of the car. His heart was racing, and his stomach in knots. Deep breaths. Outside, the air smelled of the promise of summer. It was a lovely spot, a meadow surrounded by forest, invisible to anyone passing on the road. His heart rate slowed, and his stomach eased. Not completely, just enough. He could manage.

"We need to hurry. We are meeting some people soon." Dmitri was holding *his* HK .40—to add insult to injury. He was almost close enough for Kolya to take him, bound wrists or not. Kolya considered the possibility—and discarded it. Alex was still in danger. Or was she?

He leaned back against the cool metal of the car. "I need to know that Alex is okay."

"Trust me."

Kolya raised his eyebrows.

Dmitri shrugged and took out his phone. He tapped something in and tossed the phone to Kolya.

Kolya looked at the phone. More pictures of Alex and Tehila—but from the same angle as the previous image.

"I just got this picture. My sniper is still watching but she's okay right now."

But the last Kolya'd spoken to Alex—she'd been in Burlington—and he'd urged her to leave Vermont. The pictures seemed to be the same time of day as one Dmitri had shown him the night before, judging from the way the light fell across Alex's face. It was not taken this morning. Now that he thought about it, the picture he'd seen the night before— was a day shot, not a night shot. Nothing indicated when it had been taken. In fact, all of the shots could have been taken days ago. Before he'd told Alex to leave Vermont.

He was starting to believe that this was a bluff. Maybe. Probably.

Take the risk—jump Dmitri anyway?

But there was still the Novichok. If he went along with the program, he might find out where the Novichok was—and what Dmitri planned to do. There might be a chance to do something at that point. If he took Dmitri down now, he would lose that opportunity.

Besides, what if Dmitri weren't bluffing about Alex?

He knew the odds were against him surviving if he didn't make a move now when it was only the two of them—but he'd chosen a path that meant risking his own life. Assuming that he didn't fuck everything up—which at this point was a big assumption—especially given the psychological symptoms from his last captivity, which kept surfacing at annoying times. Still,

Play it out.

He tossed the phone back. Dmitri replaced it in his pocket. "Do you need to pee or not?"

"Yes."

Dmitri stepped back and motioned with the gun.

* * * * *

Afterward, Kolya was the one driving the winding roads, with a gun against his side. He knew the area from his visits with Alex and recognized a ski shop, a pizza restaurant, an art gallery. At Dmitri's direction, he turned right onto Route 100 and passed more restaurants and shops and a sign welcoming visitors to a Renaissance Fair. Then country. On the right, a farm selling maple syrup. On the left, open fields.

"Are we stopping at the Ben & Jerry's factory?" Kolya kept his speed under the legal limit. "You like their ice cream."

"Tempting. I understand they test new flavors there. But, regrettably, no. Turn left next road." Dmitri pointed.

Kolya slid his bound hands left on the wheel so he could reach the turn signal without losing control of the car and turned onto a dirt road. They were south of Stowe, in the town of Waterbury.

Dmitri pulled out a pack of cigarettes. "You want one?"

"No." Kolya's tied hands made it a little difficult to drive and smoke, but he could have managed if he'd actually wanted a cigarette. "Open a window, please."

"You don't have to worry about lung cancer." Dmitri lit up and took a drag.

"I'm not. I just don't enjoy smoke."

"Pity. I really like smoking. I do not fucking understand why prisoners can't smoke. It's not like they give a shit about keeping us healthy." Dmitri rolled down the window. Fresh air blew in the smell of woods and fields and blew some of the smoke outside. "No reason to make this unpleasant."

"Isn't that the point?"

"Not completely." Dmitri blew smoke from his nostrils. "This is mostly business. Revenge, though, was always part. I loved you like a brother. What is that quote from Shakespeare about a serpent's tooth and gratitude?"

"Not exactly applicable."

"I could quote Dostoevsky, since we had a bonding moment in St. Petersburg near the site of one of his novels. 'Fathers and mothers, what is hell? I maintain that hell is the suffering of being unable to love.'"

"Brothers Karamazov. Does that apply to you or to me?"

"That is you, *moi droog*, or at least what I thought after you betrayed me. Then I thought, it is me as well. Although it may not apply to you after all. You apparently are capable of love, at least for Alex Feinstein. But it is all crap. Love does not matter. Money matters. And loyalty matters."

"You don't think loyalty has anything to do with love?"

"No. It has to do with honor. You disagree?"

"Maybe. It depends on who or what you are being loyal to—and why."

Dmitri inhaled smoke. "That's the question I kept asking myself about you. Why? Why did you betray me?"

"You should have figured that out why by now."

"Oh, I know. You are an American now. You love your new country. But what is a country? An abstraction. You betrayed a friend for an abstraction."

"The people in little Odessa were abstractions?"

The memories were still vivid: Arriving at Rifka's apartment and finding her, head covered in a scarf to hide the loss of hair from chemotherapy, weeping over the friend who'd been caught in a crossfire between Dmitri's gang and another gang; hearing that the local bar where he sometimes jammed with other musicians was closed because the owner had been shot for refusing to pay for protection.

"Maybe not. But is ironic. You betrayed me for America. And then America betrayed you. And here we are."

"Not exactly parallel."

"Pretty close. You sent me to prison for twenty-five years to protect people you didn't know and didn't care about. Your country sent you out to be kidnapped, tortured, and killed to protect faceless people. And yet you were willing to put yourself at risk again for that same country. You are kind of crazy, *moi droog*."

There was truth to what Dmitri was saying. But did that change anything? And how did Dmitri know what had happened to Kolya in Romania? There had to be a leak; this one was inside the ECA. Something to be dealt with later—if he were alive to do so, which was a doubtful proposition.

"Did you arrange for the assault on Alex's family?"

"Of course. I knew you had quit after what they did to you. I thought you might need extra incentive to go back to work for the United States government. So if you were worried about your fiancée… after all, given that she was used to break you… I knew you would do anything to protect her. Which is why we set up in Vermont. I have had you watched for years. I knew that you and her came here all the time to the same house, so it was better than even chance that if you sent her out of Washington to hide, that's where she would go. And you would think the Novichok was somewhere in Boston or New York, not Vermont. Clever, no?"

"Yes, clever."

Dmitri grinned, clearly pleased with himself and his planning. "Next right."

Another dirt road. Fewer houses. Black and white cows grazed in a field bordered by a white picket fence near a red barn with a silver roof.

"Good act you put on with Rzaev."

"Thank you. We were both surprised by Tomas Orlov, though. The raid was not part of the plan."

"So it was Bykovsky who arranged for the Novichok to be smuggled here?"

Dmitri took a last drag from the cigarette and exhaled smoke through his nostrils. Then he flipped the butt out the window. "Why?"

"Hate to die curious."

"I will not kill you unless you force me. I already told you that."

"You keep saying contradictory things."

"I will only kill you if you do not follow my orders. All will be revealed in time."

"Including that it was Bykovsky who was behind the Novichok?" Kolya glanced sideways. Dmitri was smiling.

"It was jihadists. That is what your ECA found in Rzaev's computer, no?"

"No, they said it was the tooth fairy."

Dmitri laughed. "What would it matter if it were Bykovsky?"

"If Americans die, the United States is going to retaliate against someone. Remember 9-11?"

"If all goes well, no one will die."

"People already died. Three people in Boston."

"They were not supposed to. The police were supposed to find the bottles first. They were too slow. Trust me."

Kolya laughed shortly and didn't answer. He was putting the pieces together and didn't like his conclusions. But he pressed forward on the main question—asking it in another way. "How can you work with Yuri Bykovsky? He's a psychopath."

"I like money. So does Bykovsky. We have much in common. Turn right again."

He finally had one answer—if he ever had the chance to pass it on. Kolya signaled and turned. The dirt road wound higher past unrelenting forest. No houses.

"This will be a subdivision eventually. All the open places will disappear soon," Dmitri said. "All around the world. Shame."

At Dmitri's direction, Kolya turned right again onto a narrow driveway. It wound up for half a mile—to a massive stone house in the middle of a field. Parked in front of a four-car garage was a white Sprinter van and a black Subaru Forester. Three men stood at the closed back of the van. Two middle-aged guys who looked like veterans and were armed with HK-91s and a man in his twenties, with a look of arrogance. One of the middle-aged men looked vaguely familiar.

"Park next to the van."

He pulled up and shut off the engine, his heart pounding. He had a mental flash of gunmen crowded around him on a street, taking him prisoner, and started to shake. He took deep breaths—focused on where he was, on what his next action would be, and the shaking eased. Dmitri motioned with the gun, and Kolya opened his door and stepped outside. He leaned against the car, keeping the weight off his bad leg.

Dmitri raised a hand in greeting. Guns were trained on Kolya while Dmitri opened a side door to the front of the van and ducked inside. He emerged with two nondescript paper cups. He removed the lid from one cup, drank, and extended the second cup to Kolya. "Black with two sugars."

Kolya accepted the cup and took a tentative sip. Lukewarm, but as advertised, sweet. Not Starbucks, but acceptable. After the first taste, he drank greedily. He didn't just need the caffeine. He was incredibly thirsty—and hungry—but he'd be okay without food. Fluids were a more immediate need.

"Everything ready, Charlie?" Dmitri asked.

The youngest man pulled a piece of paper from his pocket and handed it to Dmitri. "It's true art."

Dmitri read and nodded. "Not bad. Open up the van."

The familiar man swung open the rear doors of the van, and the motion triggered a memory of the same man running across a yard in Silver Spring. Kolya said the name he'd used when he thought of the man. "Mickey? Or whatever the fuck his real name might be."

The man glanced over his shoulder and grinned.

"We call him Mickey as well," Dmitri said. "Why he chose that particular mask."

Mickey pulled out a large backpack. He opened it and took out two steel cylinders and placed them on the ground several feet apart. Then he pulled out several blocks of a grey putty-like substance and placed them next to the cannisters. Kolya drew in a sharp breath.

"Novichok?" It wasn't really a question. "And C-4?"

"As long as the chemicals stay in separate containers, it's reasonably safe. And the C-4 needs a detonator." Dmitri finished his coffee, crumbled the cup, and tossed it into the car. "Which we also have."

"So, you're a terrorist now, *brother*?"

"I prefer to consider myself a businessman, with a very dangerous business." Dmitri handed the paper to Kolya. "You are going to perform this for us. Memorize so you can sound natural on camera."

Kolya read the paper and finally understood Dmitri's game. It was about the money he'd helped the United States take from Yuri Bykovsky. It had always been about the money. With a little revenge thrown in for dessert. Bykovsky did not forgive. Nor did Dmitri. "Fuck you. I'm not saying this."

"Do you want Alex killed?"

"If you were going to use her to pressure me, you'd have her here. But she's not. Which means you're bluffing."

Dmitri glared back. "You're willing to risk her life?"

"The pictures you showed me were not from this morning."

"You don't know that."

"I'm pretty damn sure." Besides, this was probably Dmitri's entire crew in Vermont—which meant that there was nobody watching Alex's house, if she were even there. Even if she'd stayed in Vermont, she probably would have had the sense to stay somewhere else. She hadn't explained why she was in Burlington, but he suspected that she or Tehila had spotted Dmitri's gang scouting the house.

He had his limits on what he was willing to do, either to save his own life or to find the Novichok. Declaring himself a traitor wasn't one of them.

In any event, he'd located the Novichok, hadn't he?

Dmitri sighed. "You were always too fucking smart for your own good."

62

FRIDAY AFTERNOON, MOSCOW, RUSSIA

TOMAS HAD NOT TRAINED as a spy, although with his appointment as Director of the FSB, he had learned a little tradecraft. He just hoped he knew enough.

First rule. *Trust no one.*

He had already broken that rule, by accepting Fyodor's information. Fyodor had played the double agent in the past. He could be playing it now. It could be another of Yuri's little tests—to check Tomas's loyalty.

He didn't think so. But it was possible. It was possible he would arrive at his destination—and be arrested or shot on the spot. But he had to take the chance.

He told Natalia that he was leaving to buy a present for his wife's birthday. Not a complete lie. Lyudmila's birthday was in a week. He always bought her a nice gift. As had happened the year before and the year before that, Natalie offered to go shopping for him. He declined as he always had, and she accepted it without question.

Outside the Lubyanka, he walked two blocks to a jewelry store where he had bought earrings for Lyudmila's previous birthday. Inside, the store was almost empty. A young woman, dark hair, dark complexion, attractive, set off an alarm in his head. She had followed him into the shop, but she seemed interested in a pair of diamond earrings and not in him. He tried to ignore her, asking a bored clerk to take out a braided chain of white and yellow gold necklace, explaining that he was searching for a birthday gift for his wife. He shook his head over the price, declared he needed to think about it, and left the store, alert for the young woman.

She stayed in the shop, and he breathed a sigh of relief. She hadn't been following him after all.

The Metro station at the Lubyanka was a short walk from the store.

He caught the number one line and jumped off after one stop and then meandered through the underground to the number ten line at *Strentensky Bulvar*. He stopped to buy a newspaper and glanced behind him.

No one whose face he'd previous seen.

No sight of the young woman from the store.

He boarded the train to *Trubnaya*. One stop. He waited until the doors were about to close—then jumped off. On the number nine line, he tried a new tactic. First stop, he stepped off, and then doubled back inside the car as the doors closed. No one darted back into the car with him. Then he rode to *Dmitrovskaya*.

After exiting the subway station, he strode two blocks to the Flacon Design Factory, which had been repurposed as an arts center, with restaurants, cafés, shops, and galleries. The trip had taken him twice as long as a direct route, but he was confident that he had not been followed.

At a chic outdoors restaurant, he passed diners relaxing with brightly colored drinks, and he halted in front of a window displaying hand blown glass. A young man joined him in admiring the creations.

"My mother would like that green vase." His Russian was perfect—but it was the Russian of a foreigner. American. Tomas, despite his title, had had little direct experience with Americans, even though he spoke English. "What do you think?"

"Pretty, but fragile. I am looking for a birthday gift for my wife, but one has to be so careful with fragile things."

"Probably too expensive as well." The young man's voice held regret. He leaned and spoke softly. "Very good café two doors down. Excellent coffees. Try it."

The young man turned and vanished into the crowd.

Tomas glanced again at the window display, this time looking not at the interior of the shop but at the images reflected in the glass. No one had changed position. No one even looked at him.

He could still go back. He'd done nothing but ride the Metro and look at a vase for his wife. Yuri would have nothing against him. He'd be safe—and people were going to die. He squared his shoulders and headed for the café.

It was crowded, the line long. A man stepped into line behind him. He was maybe in his early thirties—with an aura of wealth and privilege. Definitely an American.

Tomas purchased a cappuccino and carried the cup to the walled outside patio and chose a wrought iron table for two near a display of lilies and brightly painted flower pots. The American who'd been behind him in line carried his coffee over to Tomas and gestured at the empty chair. Tomas nodded, and he sat.

"The coffee here is excellent." The man spoke in English.

"I generally prefer tea." Tomas looked down at the cup, where white foam was swirled in the shape of a flower. He sipped. "It could use more sugar."

"It's an acquired taste. You are Tomas Orlov?"

"You don't know?"

The man made a gesture with his hands with Tomas took to mean yes. "I'm just confirming."

"And you are Jonathan… Smith? Just confirming."

The man nodded. "And do you know the question I asked Fyodor?"

"I do." Tomas's pulse beat rapidly. He tried to calm himself with another sip. It didn't work. "As a representative of the government, it is my duty to confirm that Islamic terrorists from Yemen paid a Russian mobster, Vladimir Rzaev, to smuggle Novichok into the United States."

"Odd that you took the time and trouble to come here and tell me what my agency already found on Rzaev's computer."

Tomas looked one last time. No one within earshot. No one paying attention to them. He thought of his family. "I said it was my duty. I didn't say it was true."

Jonathan leaned forward. "And what is true?"

"What I know to be true is that Yuri hatched a plan with Rzaev to get revenge for some American operation years ago—where you took ten billion dollars from him. It involves the Novichok, and I'm afraid that he intends to not only get his money back but to kill Americans."

"You do know that Russia killing Americans would be considered an act of aggression against the United States? That things could spin out of control?"

"I understand. Why do you think I am risking my life and the lives of my wife and children? Yuri thinks that his plan is foolproof and that your government will not see through it. I fear that sooner or later the truth will come out." He didn't think it worth mentioning that he anticipated being the fall guy if the truth did come out. "And even if the United States never sees through the deception, many innocent people will die. I hope that if your President Lewis knows that Yuri is behind the Novichok and confronts him—maybe we can avoid anything more serious. You should know that Yuri's a little crazy."

"We've had indications to that effect. Where is the Novichok?"

"In the United States, but I don't know exactly where. I just learned all this last night. No details. I also think... the two who met with Rzaev, Petrov and Lemonsky... may have something to do with it."

"Like what?"

"I don't know that either, and I don't know for a fact that they're involved. It's just an impression. I should be going. My wife will worry."

He didn't add what the American knew as well—that he was already under suspicion—and that his being gone too long would trigger alarms.

Jonathan pushed a small bag across the table. "It's a necklace. You were looking for a gift for your wife. You shouldn't go home empty handed."

Tomas opened the bag and took out the jeweler's box. Inside was the braided chain of white and yellow gold that he had examined in the jewelry store. He raised his eyes and surveyed the other tables. The young woman from the jewelry store, sporting a sparking pair of diamond earrings, caught his gaze and tipped her coffee cup in salute. "Thank you. I just hope Yuri won't kill Lyudmila along with me."

"No one will ever know what you did."

"When your President confronts Yuri with the truth, Yuri will know."

"Not necessarily. But I can arrange for you and your family to be extracted if you think there's real danger."

Tomas shook his head. "Yuri will find us. Wherever we go—he will find us. He never forgets and he never forgives." Then he finished his coffee. It was very bitter. Why did so many people love this stuff? He picked up the necklace and pushed back from the table.

63

FRIDAY MORNING, JOHNSON, VERMONT

THE SPOT WAS PRETTY typical of Vermont. Railroad Street, where there was no railroad. Wooden houses. A deserted and closed lumber yard. Lots of trees on either side of the street. So, no witnesses. Two houses farther down the road were obscured by the trees. On the right was another deserted industrial park.

In the middle of the night, the area would have been pitch dark. A perfect place for a murder or a kidnapping.

Alex's heart was pounding as they drove towards the signal that was supposed to indicate Kolya's location—except that it didn't. Tehila pulled the car into a parking lot next to a path and a park on the other side of the path. A deserted red Subaru Outback was the only other car. On the ground not far from the rear of the Subaru lay a pile of garbage. They swung out of the car.

"This is it?" Alex asked.

Tehila checked her phone. "According to Mark, it is."

Alex had braced herself to find Kolya injured or dead. But there was no sign of him.

Tehila walked over to examine the garbage pile, and Alex joined her. It wasn't garbage. It was clothes. Men's clothes. Jeans. Polo shirt. Sweater. Shoes. Socks. Socks and jeans were nondescript, but she recognized the polo shirt and sweater. She'd watched him pack both just a few days ago. Next to the clothes, a watch. She picked it up and turned it over to read his initials, a motion that was unnecessary since she'd bought it for him as a Chanukah present to replace one that had been destroyed when he was kidnapped eight months earlier.

She brought the watch to her lips and kissed it. Then she walked to the edge of the woods and threw up. She put out her hand to brace herself against a tree.

Tehila followed her. "Calm, Alex. If he were dead, his body would be here."

Now the damn tears were flowing. "Not necessarily."

"No, but since he wasn't killed immediately—they want him for something. We just need to find him in time. And we will. You okay?"

"I'm okay." She wiped her face, calmer. This was not the moment to fall apart. Not yet.

"Good. Let me check the rest of the things."

The car was unlocked with keys in the ignition. No sign of a struggle. Two suitcases in the trunk, one open. Alex flipped through the contents of the open case. Kolya's shirts. The various metal containers that hid his gun when he traveled.

Tehila scanned the nearby ground and spotted the glint of metal.

"That's the tracker?"

Tehila nodded and took out her phone. "I have to call it in. And I'll get Mark to locate the car that was driven away from your family's house two nights ago. It's pretty clear that the attempt on you is connected to Kolya's mission. We'll have surprise on our side."

"Good." Knowing that there was something they could do made all the difference.

64

A SLOPING FIELD OF tall grass and wildflowers allowed a perfect view of blue mountains—a private and beautiful spot. Kolya had a strong aesthetic sense, which was why he loved Vermont, but while he appreciated the beauty, it wasn't his focus. At the moment, his attention was on the guns trained on him. At least, focusing on the guns kept him in the present, and the flashbacks to a minimum—although he knew his hands were shaking.

Alex was safe, as he'd hoped. This time, her life wasn't on the line.

"This is a stupid reason to die, my friend," Dmitri said. "Just read the fucking script on camera—and you'll live."

"You keep saying that you won't kill me. Somehow I'm not convinced."

"Have I ever lied to you?"

"Continuously."

Dmitri shrugged. "Okay, yes, I have been lying. And yes, we were going to threaten to shoot your Alex. But she managed to get away. And you had to fucking realize it. So, either you do what I ask or Mickey will shoot you. Then we will make several bombs with Novichok to leave in populated areas. On the MTA. Or the New York subway. Maybe Penn Station. We could kill a few hundred people. Maybe a few thousand. And I know you care about unknown people dying because that was why you betrayed me in the first place. All those deaths will be on your head, because your reputation mattered more to you than human life."

"And if I do read the script?"

Dmitri smiled. "If your president returns Yuri Bykovsky's money, no one has to die. My word, Kolya. You can trust me. Maybe not completely—but on this."

He trusted Dmitri not at all. Yuri Bykovsky wanted revenge, as did Dmitri. If Bykovsky hadn't been able to find Maria Andropov and her daughter, which as far as Kolya knew was the situation, he'd take his anger out on the available targets. Kolya. And the American population.

Still—die now or later.

Later would be better. For more than the obvious reason.

The longer Kolya could stay alive, the greater the chance that Dmitri would let his guard down. Not much of a chance, but more than if he were shot now.

And in the scheme of things, what did it matter if he read a script that told a lie?

"Okay." He took a deep breath. "*Yob tvoyu mat.* I'll read it."

"Not read it. Speak it. Like it was your words," Dmitri said. "Rip is going to untie you now."

Rip, the third man in the group, set his gun on the ground and approached. Charlie, Mickey and Dmitri kept their guns on Kolya.

Rip looked nervous, obviously concerned over what Kolya might do, since both of them realized that the others would not hesitate to shoot through Rip to kill Kolya, should he pose any threat.

Kolya held out his wrists. It took Rip at least five minutes to loosen the knot, then he unwound the rope, stepped back, and picked up his gun again.

Kolya's wrists were red and raw, but it was a relief to have the rope off. He flexed his wrists, getting the stiffness out.

"Button the cuffs and your shirt," Charlie said.

Unbuttoned, the sleeves of the ill-fitting flannel shirt could flap open and show his raw wrists—evidence that he had been restrained—and was thus not acting of his free will. The unbuttoned shirt also was more in line with someone who was a prisoner.

He glanced over at Dmitri as he complied. "How much do you get to keep of the ten billion dollars?"

"Enough for a nice island estate."

"Not Florida?"

"I like Florida, but probably not wise after this. Somewhere where there is no extradition treaty with the U.S."

271

Kolya glanced at the other men.

"They will also be rich. The rest goes to Rzaev."

"And Bykovsky."

"Yes, and Bykovsky. Now take ten minutes and memorize the script. You can change a word or two—nothing of substance. Understand?"

Kolya envisioned breaking Dmitri's neck—and grit his teeth. Then he focused on the script and ran it through his mind until he had it down.

Charlie took out his phone. He gave a thumbs up, indicating that Kolya, the Novichok, and C-4 were all visible.

"With feeling, Kolya."

"*Yob tvoyu mat*, Dmitri."

He woodenly recited the words that he'd memorized that would label him as a traitor and a terrorist, pointing to the silver canisters and the C-4 as directed. Then he added the demand. The ten billion dollars that he had helped the U.S. confiscate from Yuri Bykovsky was to be deposited in an off-shore bank account or bombs spreading Novichok in confined spaces would be set off in populated areas. He related account numbers and access codes. He gave the deadline—six hours. He ended and folded his arms.

Charlie watched the video and glanced over at Dmitri. "He looks like a hostage reading a text."

Which was what he was—and what he wanted to convey.

And it had taken time. Time was his friend.

"Kolya," Dmitri's tone was remonstrative. "You are a good actor. I have seen you undercover. One more time—with feeling."

Kolya tried to shrug, but it hurt his shoulder. He raised his hands, palms out, instead. "It's hard to get into a part when I'm being held at gun point."

"I have faith in your abilities. Again."

He tapped down his anger. The point was to try to stay alive as long as possible.

Charlie focused the iPhone. Kolya began again.

"I was a dedicated agent of a secret American intelligence agency until eight months ago, when that agency betrayed me and left me and my fiancée to be tortured to death. I am doing this to expose the corrupt governments of the United States and Russia, and I am working with people justly angered by the actions of the United States in Yemen. These two canisters hold chemicals that when combined make a binary nerve agent that is deadly to touch or breathe. With these chemicals and with the C-4, we have the ability to make multiple small bombs that will combine and spread the nerve agent in populated areas. However, out of compassion for innocent people, we will accept payment of the money that I helped the American government steal from Russia instead of exploding the bombs."

He recited the cash demand and instructions to deposit the money.

This time, his performance seemed satisfactory. Charlie watched and then tossed the phone to Dmitri. Dmitri nodded approval—and then he tapped the phone, sending off the video, probably to someone in Russia—who would then forward it. To whom? Margaret Bradford? The President of the United States? YouTube?

If Lewis believed the threat, he might or might not pay the ransom, but one thing was certain: Kolya would rise to the top of the most wanted list. Unless they realized that he was a prisoner—and had been coerced. Eight months ago, he would have trusted Bradford and the President to come to the correct conclusion. Now, not so much.

Dmitri had devised an appropriate revenge for Kolya's betrayal ten years earlier—he'd be hated and hunted down by his own colleagues and friends.

At Charlie's direction, Rip stepped forward, rope in hand, to retie Kolya's wrists. Kolya ignored him. He folded his arms and turned his gaze on Dmitri. "Now what?"

"We wait to hear." Dmitri shrugged. "Then we'll see."

"You're not going to let me go, after all?"

"I never said I'd let you go. I said I wouldn't kill you. I planned for many years what to do to you. I thought about killing you—but that's fast—and then everything is over. I like this better. Once we have the money, we will leave the country, take you with us, and drop you on an island somewhere in the Caribbean. If your government finds you and does not kill you immediately, you can try to explain—but the fact that they think you killed Yelseyev and are on a revenge tour—along with three million dollars in your name in the Cayman Islands—might make explaining difficult. Or you can run. So you will have a choice: be a fugitive for the rest of your life or be caught by your friends who will kill or imprison you."

"You put three million dollars in my name?"

"Nice touch, no? It's a little expensive, but you are worth it. Not that you will have access to it. You will have to live on an island with no money and no friends, but at least you can eat coconuts. Now put your fucking wrists together, or I will shoot you now."

Kolya held out his wrists, his hands formed in fists.

Mickey loaded the backpack with the Novichok into the rear of his black Subaru Forester and took off. Two minutes later, the Sprinter rumbled into motion, Charlie driving with Rip in the seat next to him, leaving behind the Toyota that Kolya had driven to Waterbury. Dmitri sat directly behind Charlie, his captain's chair swiveled so he could keep the gun pointed at Kolya, who sat on the floor in the back of the van, his back resting against the side, bad leg outstretched, bound hands resting on his lap, again fighting down panic.

65

FRIDAY MORNING, VERMONT

ACCORDING TO THE GPS that Tehila had fixed to the car, the black Subaru Forester was about an hour ahead of them, now heading south on I-89. Before that, it had been in Waterbury, Vermont for around half an hour.

Tehila was driving at what Alex thought was an infuriatingly slow speed, ten miles over the speed limit. The Forester remained an hour or so ahead of them. At least they weren't falling behind. But they weren't gaining, either.

Tehila refused to go faster.

"If we're stopped by the police, that could put us even further behind. Because I'm not allowed to identify who I work for even to local authorities—and we have a lot of weaponry in here."

"Guns are legal in Vermont."

"Legal or not, I'm still a black woman driving with a shitload of guns. It could take hours before we're cleared."

"Fine. Whatever."

Tehila glanced sideways and then back at the road. "We have the advantage. They don't know we're following. Sooner or later, they'll stop."

"And what if sooner rather than later, they decide to kill Kolya?"

"Well, our being stopped by police won't help him. Stay calm."

FRIDAY MORNING, THE WHITE HOUSE, WASHINGTON, D.C.

Five minutes after Smithson sent her the video, Margaret Bradford

275

stepped into a black town car, and shortly after that, she was driven through the gate of the White House.

The group in the Oval was larger this time. President Lewis, his chief of staff, the DNI, the head of Homeland Security, the National Security Advisor, the head of the FBI, and Ben Smithson. Lewis dismissed everyone except Smithson and turned to Margaret.

"You have information—before we discuss the video starring your operative?"

"Yes, Mr. President. Jonathan Egan in Moscow has confirmed that this entire plot was orchestrated by Yuri Bykovsky."

"Who's his source?"

"Tomas Orlov. Director of the FSB—and brother-in-law to Yuri Bykovsky."

"Orlov is telling us this why?" Smithson asked.

"It appears he has a conscience. That he's worried people could die—and he's also worried about tension between our countries escalating out of control if Americans are poisoned by a Russian plot. Egan thinks there may be a personal motive, as well. Orlov's hoping that if you, Mr. President, make it clear you know it's not Islamic terrorists who smuggled in the Novichok that Bykovsky will back down."

"Does he know where the Novichok might be?"

"No. He only knows that Rzaev is working with Bykovsky."

"And with Petrov and Lemonsky," Smithson said.

Margaret turned to him. "Our information is that Mr. Petrov is being coerced." Jonathan had reluctantly reported that Orlov thought Petrov and Lemonsky were involved—but he had no details, and he had expressed strong doubts about the information. She felt no obligation to share that part of the conversation without further corroboration.

"Coerced." Smithson snorted. "One thing I know about Petrov—he's a stubborn son of a bitch. He was nearly tortured to death in Romania, wasn't he, without giving in? He only gave in to save his fiancée. Where is she, by the way?"

"Safe. Under ECA protection."

"Which cuts against his being coerced."

"He wouldn't leave her behind."

"She could always meet up with him in a few months, couldn't she? His prior behavior in Russia, killing an old enemy, indicates a man out to settle scores. Doesn't he have a GPS on him? They come pretty small these days."

"He was forced to change clothes, and it was left behind."

"Margaret, Margaret. He has motive. He detailed that motive in the video. Did you also know that Petrov has an off-shore account—in the same bank where he directed us to wire the ten billion dollars. There's over three million in it."

"What?" This genuinely surprised her. "When did you find this out?"

"We started looking an hour ago—after we saw the video. I don't know when you turned into Pollyanna, wanting to believe in your agent despite all evidence, but this is the situation."

"And yet you found it easily. In his name. How convenient. If nothing else, Kolya Petrov is very smart. If he were on the take, he wouldn't have money in his own name so the CIA could find it after an hour's search."

"The point now is to find Petrov and the Novichok," Lewis said. "Because if we can't, I have to decide whether to pay the ten billion in blackmail. Homeland Security and the FBI are coordinating with local police and setting up roadblocks along the highways out of Vermont as we speak, but am I correct that he disappeared ten or more hours ago?"

"That's when his phone cut out. But I do have someone assigned to the trail right now."

Smithson swung on her. "Who? Because I happen to know that most of your available agents are sitting in Newport with Kowolsky, twiddling their thumbs."

"It was my deputy who assigned the agent, so I don't have the name right now," she lied. "I will check and get back to you." She'd get back in five or six hours.

"I want the goddamn name now."

"You don't need the goddamn name now, Ben."

"Yes, I do. So we can coordinate. This is too important for petty inter-agency rivalry."

Somehow Smithson always found inter-agency rivalry to be petty when he was the one being left out of the loop.

"As I said—I will check and get back to you."

Smithson glowered, but let it drop. She hoped. Lewis did not weigh in. He was focused on Bykovsky's involvement.

"If Bykovsky is in fact responsible, then I'll need the backing of our allies to act against him and Russia. Which means it would be good to have something more than the anonymous word of an unnamed intelligence operative," Lewis said. "Margaret, get in touch with Egan. Tell him to get Tomas Orlov speaking on the record—on video—and then to call me back directly. I need something more against the findings on Rzaev's computer and a video of an American agent who is claiming to be a traitor."

"Mr. President, that would be condemning Orlov and his family. Yuri Bykovsky is not the forgiving type."

"A lot more is at stake than one man and his family. If Bykovsky is behind this—it means very serious moves against the Russian Republic. I will be involving NATO and all of our allies. Right now, Bykovsky can put out the video of Petrov—and make himself look like the victim."

"How widely was that video distributed?" Margaret asked.

"So far, it's secure. It came to me," Smithson said. "Then I forwarded it on to the President and the American intelligence community. However, we have to assume that the Russians have it as well."

Lewis nodded. "That's why I want Orlov's statement on video before I call our allies and confront Bykovsky. I need more than mumbled intelligence in a café. Get him and his family out if that's what's necessary."

Lewis acted as if an extraction of a high level official and his family from Russia was easy. "We'll do our best, Mr. President, but extractions usually require months of planning to do properly."

"You can count on getting whatever you need to get it done." Lewis turned to Smithson. "And I expect your full cooperation, Ben."

"Of course."

"Okay, we're done for now, "Lewis said. "Let me know when you have Orlov secured."

She started to rise and glanced over at Smithson. He hadn't moved. "I need to speak alone with the President, Margaret."

She looked at Smithson and then at Lewis. She could think of only one reason for the two of them to meet without her, and she didn't like it. But she left quietly.

* * * * *

Smithson gave the order over the phone while he was still in the White

House. It was pretty straightforward. Locate any ECA agents who might be in Vermont, using the list of known agents and phone data from the NSA. The report was on Smithson's desk an hour after the meeting with the President. The EC team of ten agents in Newport, led by Marty Davis, were all accounted for, but another agent, Tehila Melaku, was located in the state, heading south from Stowe.

He then made the call. Better to send one person for a wet job than a whole team. The more people involved, the more likely a leak sooner or later, and Smithson would not want it known that he'd ordered the killing and not the capture of an American intelligence operative. It could lead to the embarrassment of himself and the President that the killing was intended to prevent.

66

FRIDAY NOON, NORTHERN VERMONT

KOWOLSKY HAD BEEN ON the scene in Newport, Vermont, waiting for the meeting between Petrov and the unknown smuggler—a meeting that was never going to happen—while the ECA team froze him out of any real information. Then he got the call. He'd claimed to be going back to his hotel, because he could play the same game the ECA was playing, only better. They had no idea what Smithson had authorized. Now he was in a car on I-91 driving south at an illegal 100 mph. No, not illegal. Not for a federal officer in an emergency.

The call from Smithson was the vindication he'd hoped for. He'd suspected Petrov for years—ever since the damn Russian and his buddy had spirited a suspected member of the Taliban out of his custody in Afghanistan and then out of the country. He had thought the detainee had been involved in planting a roadside bomb. How the hell was he to know that the guy had been an ECA informer? He'd just followed protocol—take the suspect into custody, try to get some answers, and then Petrov and Egan had shown up. To add insult to injury, once back in the United States, Petrov had filed a complaint against Kowolsky, claiming he physically abused detainees.

What kind of an American files a complaint against an officer for just doing his job? That alone had made him suspicious.

Now, his judgment was confirmed. Petrov was a traitor.

Russians. Jews. He didn't trust either of them. Russians were indoctrinated at an early age. And Jews—well, Jews were loyal to each other and to Israel, not to America. And Petrov was both a Russian and a Jew. Who the fuck knew what his real loyalties might be?

The President ordered any local police who might spot Lemonsky or Petrov to hold them and to contact federal authorities. Also, it was good that local cops didn't know the truth. If the public knew that terrorists were on the road with a nerve poison, there'd be widespread panic—and the more law enforcement or government officials involved, the more likely the word would get out. It always did.

Besides, terrorists had to be handled carefully. Couldn't blow up the car—might release the poison—so a drone was no good. Humans needed to act. The right humans—at the right time.

He checked his phone. The ECA agent he was tracking was two hours ahead, but he was gaining. Hopefully, she would lead him to Petrov and Lemonsky. The Novichok had to be secured—and after that—he'd do what had to be done. What Smithson had given him license to do.

FRIDAY NOON, I-91 NEAR THE VERMONT BORDER

Traffic heading south on I-91 had slowed. The Subaru somewhere ahead of them had slowed as well. Alex checked her phone GPS. "There's a roadblock. Maybe they'll stop him."

"Maybe." Tehila did not sound confident. "Why is there a roadblock, Mark?"

Mark, on speaker, was giving them periodic updates, but there was a long silence after the question. Finally, he spoke. "Bradford hasn't told you anything?"

"If she had, would I be asking you? What's up, Mark?"

He quickly described the video that had been received by the CIA, the ECA, and the White House.

Alex took in a sharp breath. "They think Kolya's a traitor?"

"Bradford doesn't. But she thinks Smithson may have issued a kill order on him."

"A kill order? Why not capture and try him?"

"Romania. Neither Smithson nor the President wants the details of what happened there—of Kolya being set up and then their decision to abandon him—to come out. If Kolya's arrested and tried—it will. Also, the CIA also discovered an account in the Cayman Islands in Kolya's name with money from Central Europe."

"It's a set-up. Kolya's not dirty," Tehila said.

"Yeah, I don't believe it, but whatever—there's a kill order. I'm telling you. You've got to get there before anyone else. The guy you're after just got through the roadblock."

"Doesn't that mean that Kolya's not in the car?" Alex asked.

"Most likely," Tehila agreed. "The state police will have his picture even if they don't know why they are stopping him. But whoever is in that car is connected. We know that. Maybe they're meeting up later."

"Maybe." It was the only chance they had.

67

FRIDAY NOON, SOUTHERN VERMONT OR
NORTHERN MASSACHUSETTS

FROM THE SOUND OF the gravel, the lack of traffic, and the bumping over an uneven surface, they were on dirt roads. Kolya had a good sense of direction, and he'd followed the twists and turns as the van retraced its way down the mountain and then turned south. But they'd been driving for hours, and he'd been dozing off and on. When he opened his eyes which he did infrequently from his position in the back of the van, he caught only glimpses of sky and tree branches through the window near Charlie's head in the driver's seat. By now, they could be in another state. Or they could still be in Vermont, driving in circles.

Everything seemed to hurt more—his leg, his shoulder—but maybe that was because of the bumpy ride. In any event, he'd survived more intense pain.

The PTSD, though, was worse. When he was active or engaged, the PTSD was more manageable. But now, tied up in the back of the van, with long stretches of nothing to do but sleep or think, the symptoms were in full bloom. Every time he dozed, he was back in the nightmare world. He was in a cellar, not a van. Dmitri transformed into the man who'd tortured him. The sweats and shaking came and went, even when awake, as he sat with eyes closed, feigning sleep.

Grounding exercises and telling himself that it wasn't Romania did nothing to lessen the intensity. It might not be Romania, but it was close enough. He was again a prisoner, again helpless. Afraid. Angry.

He could keep his eyes closed so Dmitri didn't know he was awake, and he could direct his thoughts, but that was the extent of his control. He had been using the same survival techniques that he'd used in Romania, improvising jazz pieces in his mind, but this time it wasn't doing much to divert his mind.

He could hear the voice of his therapist. *You need to allow yourself to feel the emotions that you repressed while you were being tortured.* Well, he was fucking feeling them, and it wasn't doing a damn thing to stop the panic.

But was he really? For the past eight months, he had done everything he could to avoid thinking of his ordeal. He'd used alcohol or music to dispel the images. He'd pushed away the thoughts and refused to talk about it, even with Alex, the person he loved most. Even now, he wasn't really facing either the past—or even the present—was he?

Ironically, on the drive from St. Petersburg to Moscow, Dmitri had said something similar to what the therapist had been preaching, hadn't he? *You only get rid of the past if you face the past.*

"Hungry, Kolya?" Dmitri voice was muffled. He was eating something, or so Kolya assumed.

He had heard almost the exact same question from the man who'd tortured and starved him for days. He didn't open his eyes or respond.

"He's sleeping again." Charlie's voice. "Don't wake him. I really don't want to hear the two of you going on about your time in the damn boys' school."

"You do not have to fucking listen."

"Hard not to."

"Then turn on some fucking music."

The two of them engaged in a debate over the choice of style. Dmitri holding out for classical or jazz, Charlie for rap.

Ignoring them, Kolya returned to his thoughts. For the first time in eight months, he forced himself to remember, not just what had happened to him physically, the blows that had broken his leg, the flogging, the burns, the faces of his torturers, but the rage, the terror, the helplessness, and the despair that he'd felt at the time. Not all that dissimilar to the emotions he was experiencing now. As he remembered, the panic rose— and then it ebbed, and the shaking eased.

68

FRIDAY AFTERNOON, MOSCOW, RUSSIA

"NICE EARRINGS." JONATHAN LINKED his arm through Elizabeth's as they strolled on the banks of the Moscow River. Teo trailed behind them, snapping photos on his phone. They were scheduled to get on an Air France flight home the following morning. "Did you pay for them with my credit card?" Jonathan had a credit card in his travel name of Jonathan Smith. He paid the bills, and the government eventually reimbursed him for those expenses deemed legitimate. Since he could float the expenses better than either Teo or Elizabeth, he had given Elizabeth his card for the jewelry store expedition.

"Of course, I did." Elizabeth smiled for the benefit of the cameras placed on the walkways. "I thought I deserved a gift as much as Tomas's wife did. You'll be paid back."

"The U.S. government will pay me back for Tomas's wife's present. Your earrings, though, don't come under working expenses."

"Well, I disagree. Buying them was part of my cover. But if necessary, I'll pay you back. I should have enough saved in about ten years."

"Forget it. Happy early birthday." Jonathan's phone vibrated, and he checked the caller ID... "It's Margaret." Then he answered.

Margaret explained the president's request in a few brief sentences.

"What you're asking takes weeks of planning to be successful." Jonathan continued to stroll, pointing out sights, as he talked. "You want me to come up with and execute an exfiltration plan in a few hours?"

"That sums it up."

"Have any suggestions?"

"You'll think of something. I believe in you."

"Budget?"

"Whatever it takes."

"We'll try, but it's going to be tricky. We're all NOC. We're caught, and we're dead along with Orlov and family."

"If you're caught, we'll do whatever we can to bring you home safely."

"Not reassuring."

"I know. It's all I can do. This is urgent, Jonathan. I know it's asking a lot."

"Okay. Yeah. Like I said, we'll try. Did my friend make it home okay?"

"Your friend is missing after making a disturbing video." She described in chilling terms the video that Kolya had made. "And I believe my friend Ben sent your 'friend' Steve after him."

"Fuck it, Margaret. You know he's loyal."

"I do. And I will do what I can. But not your concern, right now, Jonathan. Focus. You have a critical job."

"Yeah, so you said. But just telling you—if you fuck him over again—I'm done." Which maybe he should have said eight months earlier—but at least he was saying it now.

"Message received." She disconnected.

Jonathan returned the phone to his pocket, took a deep breath, and smiled at Elizabeth, ever aware of passersby and cameras. "New plan."

FRIDAY EVENING, MOSCOW, RUSSIA

Smiling, Lyudmila wore her new necklace through a dinner of chicken with a feta cheese tomato sauce and a dessert of honey cakes. Tomas liked to see her happy, even if it was transitory, even if it was an illusion. He'd lied, of course, told her everything was fine with Yuri. What was the point of scaring her? He kept up the pretense, laughing at his oldest son's latest joke, promising his daughter a kitten, all the time wondering when Lewis would call Yuri and confront him over the Novichok in America.

How long after that call would Yuri conclude that Tomas had spoken to the Americans? And how long until they came for all of them?

After dinner, the children watched television in the living room. Lyudmila, still sporting the necklace, cleared the table and started on the dishes. Her gay mood dissipated with the departure of the children. Had she seen through his act? Probably. But she said nothing, and he, seated at the table with his glass of tea, said nothing.

The conspiracy of silence.

But then, what was there to say?

When he heard the knock on the front door, he shoved his chair back and resolutely rose. Lyudmila wiped her hands on her apron. "I'll tell them you're not here."

He took her hand and kissed it. "That won't help."

She trailed as he walked from the kitchen through the living room to the hallway. "Tomas, don't. Just don't open the door."

But if he didn't answer, they'd just break it down. And then what? Shoot the children? Shoot Lyudmila? Better to get it over. "Go back to the kitchen, Lyudmila."

"No." Her voice quavered, but she lifted her chin. "I'm Yuri's sister."

Maybe it would save her life and the lives of the children. Another knock, insistent but not demanding. Tomas steeled himself and slid the bolt open. Then he cracked the door and peered out.

The young man who had asked him about the vases smiled reassuringly. "*Dobry vercher*, Tomas Grigorovich. And this must be your lovely wife."

Tomas's relief lasted only a second. He pushed the young man out into the hallway. Lyudmila tried to follow, but he slammed the door in her face. "What are you doing here? You're putting my family in danger."

"President Lewis wants a statement from you on video."

"It's too dangerous."

"It's already dangerous. If President Lewis confronts your brother in law, do you think Bykovsky won't get rid of anyone who could expose the truth? We're getting you out. All of you. Then, when we're in a safe location, you can speak to Lewis directly."

Tomas shook his head. "We won't make it. And even if we get out of Russia, Yuri will find us."

"Maybe. And maybe not. We're good at hiding people. Tell your family that you have a surprise." He held out tickets.

The door opened behind him, and Lyudmila peeped out. Had she been listening? "Tomas, invite the young man in."

Behind her, Tomas heard the murmur of children's voices and the hum of the television. He could just walk away. Go back into the apartment. *And do what?* Wait for Yuri's wrath. *Maybe this was a chance, however slim.*

He reached for the tickets. "We're going out, dear. It's a special treat."
"Out?" Her voice was surprised and a little fearful. "Now?"

"It's early." He checked the tickets, and it was something his children
would like. "We're going to *Teatre Koshet.* They have a late show tonight.
I didn't tell you because I didn't know if my young friend here could get
the tickets. I wanted to surprise all of you."

The Theater of the Cats, where normally indolent house cats performed
tricks, was an attraction that his children, especially his daughter Emma,
had begged to see for the past few months.

Lyudmila made a visible effort to turn her expression from anxiety
to excitement—and she did it well. *She would have been a good spy.* In
the living room, Tomas turned off the television and announced the
expedition to squeals of excitement. Then he helped Lyudmila hustle
the three into jackets—and he selected favorite stuffed animals, one
for each child, to hug during the show. Nothing else. A lifetime of
gathering possessions, and he was leaving with nothing—just his wife
and children—so not nothing, everything.

Lyudmila gazed around the elegant living room, lingering on her
favorite chair, her grandmother's table. She folded her apron, hung it
over a rack in the kitchen, and ran a hand along the marble countertop.
Then she hugged the children. "This is going to be fun."

69

FRIDAY AFTERNOON, SOUTHERN VERMONT OR NORTHERN MASSACHUSETTS

THE MEMORY EXERCISES HAD had an effect. Kolya felt calmer and more in control, even though, by any objective means, he was in deep trouble. He was being held at gunpoint by people willing to commit mass murder with a nerve agent. By now, every intelligence agency would be looking for them. Possibly a kill order had already been issued against him personally, although hopefully Jonathan had passed on his last text which should prove that he was not acting on his own volition. Unfortunately or fortunately, neither the CIA nor the ECA had any way to track them.

Still, if Dmitri actually intended to leave Kolya on an island to be captured by American intelligence—it wasn't that terrible a prospect. He'd find a way to communicate with Washington and surrender, taking his chances with a trial. After all, one of the best trial attorneys in D.C. would defend him.

Unless, of course, it was decided to be in the national security interest to terminate him without a trial. A possibility—but one he was willing to risk.

Then he wondered what the target might be if the ransom was not paid. The subway systems in New York and Boston would be logical—but a lot of people lived in smaller cities. Albany. Portland. Springfield. Hartford. They just needed a gathering area where exploding a device containing Novichok would have maximum impact. An inside mall. Maybe a sports area.

No longer feigning sleep, Kolya watched Dmitri who in turn watched Kolya. Periodically, Dmitri turned his head sideways towards the front to speak to Charlie.

And each time Dmitri turned his head, Kolya flexed his wrists to loosen the rope. Forming fists when his wrists had been tied had allowed fractional give in the rope. Not enough, but with time and patience, he should be able to work the ropes loose. Eventually maybe he'd be able to slip his hands free.

If he had the use of his hands, he could act if an opportunity presented.

He leaned his head back against the metal. Eyes half-shut, he picked out a Bill Evans tune, *You Must Believe in Spring*, pictured his hands on the keyboard. *CM7flat 5*—and his mind swung into the melody, imagining the feel of the keys under his fingers.

"You know I am doing you a favor, Kolya." Dmitri's voice drew him out of the song. "I am saving you from life as a lawyer. You would do it to please Alex, and then you would spend your life doing something you hated."

"Yes, I so much prefer death—or being a fugitive."

"I am serious, *moi droog*. You are too much like me—you would not be happy pushing papers and begging for favors from courts."

"I am nothing like you, and you have a very limited concept of what lawyers do."

"I have dealt with many lawyers in my life, and I know exactly what they do. And be honest. You *are* like me. Neither of us would be content with an ordinary life. We are two sides of the same coin. We both have something of an adrenaline addiction."

There was truth to the description. "Perhaps. But I don't kill innocent people."

"Okay, you have a moral code that you live by. So do I. It is just different."

"A little too different." Dmitri might like to talk, but Kolya had had enough. He closed his eyes again and refused to be drawn back into conversation. For the next half hour, they rode in silence. Then, after an inaudible conversation between Dmitri and Charlie, the van stopped, and Charlie put it into park. He and Rip opened the front doors and stepped out.

Kolya shifted his position.

"Sit back, Kolya. Nothing to see."

Kolya turned his gaze towards Dmitri, whose finger was inside the trigger guard. The gun was already cocked—a round in the chamber, safety off. One twitch of Dmitri's finger—and that would be it.

"They are getting lunch. You like turkey?"

"For Thanksgiving. With stuffing and cranberry sauce."

"You are such a fucking American now."

"So you've said. Please move your finger outside the trigger guard. I'm not going to try anything."

"I know you are thinking about it." But Dmitri shifted his finger alongside the barrel of the gun. He could still shoot before Kolya could reach him, but it lowered the chances of an accidental discharge.

"I'm just thinking about jazz. And food. Nothing else. Where are we?"

"What does it matter? Nowhere important."

A minute later Kolya heard a shot. He started and felt a rush of anger.

"I prefer not to kill unnecessarily," Dmitri said. "But Charlie does not like loose ends."

Charlie got back into the driver's seat with a bag in hand, while Rip swung open the back door and leaned into the van. "Only one inside— an old guy who owned it. No other employees. We stashed him in a storeroom."

From what Kolya could see, they were in a parking lot of what appeared to be a shabby general store, with no other buildings in sights. Maybe still in Vermont. There had been no need to kill the store owner—except for the slight chance that he might remember either Charlie and Rip or the van.

"Did you get sandwiches?" Dmitri asked.

"He made the sandwiches before I shot him. There's chips, cookies, and Cokes as well." Charlie handed the bag over the seat. Dmitri fished inside and pulled out two sandwiches. He checked both. "Ham and cheese for me. And turkey for you, Kolya, because Jews do not eat ham, and I do not wish to be culturally insensitive." He tossed Kolya the sandwich, placed his own sandwich on his lap, raised his gun, and aimed at Kolya's head.

"Do you think I do not know what you are doing, Kolya?"

"I'm just sitting here."

"It would be safer to shoot him now," Rip said.

"It would be safer, would it not, old friend?" Dmitri's tone had never been anything other than friendly since that first meeting in the prison. If anything, since he'd kidnapped Kolya—his tone had grown friendlier. "But then, you will have a brief second of pain and fear, then nothing. Suffering over. Pain over. Not enough payment for ten years in prison." He looked at Rip. "Do you think it would be enough?"

"I believe in simplicity. And safety."

"That's because while you work for Charlie, and by extension Rzaev, you are not Russian. We are complicated. Maybe because of the long winters."

Charlie, in the front, was munching on his own sandwich. "I agree with you, Dmitri, and not with Rip. Shooting him would too fast and not be sufficient payback."

"And you Russians like games," Rip added.

"We do," Dmitri said. "We are playing a little game, even now."

This required an answer. "I'm not playing anything."

Dmitri chuckled softly. "You think I did not notice you loosening the ropes? Kolya, Kolya. You used to know me better. So, Rip is going to put handcuffs on you, and I know you have no wires or other tools to pick the lock. If you even twitch while he is doing so, *moi droog*, I will blow your head off, even if it is fast. *Ty panimaesh?*"

"Yes, I understand." He weighed trying anyway, but Rip was out of the line of fire. In any event, Kolya suspected that using Rip as a human shield would not deter Dmitri from emptying the magazine into both of them, and he knew the power of his own gun. Neither would survive. As long as he stayed alive, he still had a chance, however small, of stopping Dmitri.

A fool's chance.

Rip snapped the handcuffs shut on his wrists before removing the ropes. The sound and feel of the handcuffs locking brought him back to Romania. An image flashed in his head. Before torturing him, they had handcuffed and chained him to a wall. But this time, instead of pushing the images from his mind and focusing on something else, he allowed the memory—dredging up every detail of how it had felt.

"Are you okay, Kolya?" Dmitri's voice.

He envisioned the basement where he'd been held. Envisioned the handcuffs snapping on his wrists, the faces of his captors, the dampness and cold of the room, and for a moment, he let the hate and anger wash over him. His panic began to subside. He took a few deep breaths, and then he was back. "I'm fucking fine."

"Good, now you should eat. You want a Coke? Or cookies?"

It was easier to use his hands in cuffs than when tied, even though the metal bit into his wrists. Kolya unwrapped the sandwich and took a bite. Despite everything, he was hungry, and the sandwich was actually not bad. "A Coke."

70

FRIDAY NIGHT, MOSCOW, RUSSIA

A MAN IN A gray suit and a gray chauffeur's hat drove the limo through the streets of Moscow. The entire family fit comfortably in the back. The children tried the automatic windows and waved at pedestrians. The young man retrieved a box from under the seat and removed the lid to display a cornucopia of chocolates filled with coconut, raspberry, or marshmallow. Emma and the boys checked with their parents. Tomas nodded. Lyudmila, usually strict about sweets between meals, gave hesitating approval. Each child chose one chocolate.

"You can have three," the young man said. "It's a special treat."

"Papa?" Emma asked.

He nodded again, pleased that she'd ask, and sad at the deception.

A few minutes later, Emma curled up, her head resting on her father's arm. "Sleepy Papa."

He kissed the top of her head as she fell asleep. The boys, on either side of their mother, also slept.

"So, no theater of the cats?" Lyudmila sounded wistful.

"No. I'm sorry." The young man looked it, too. Tomas wondered how old he was.

"What's your name?" He'd refrained from asking earlier—spies didn't like to identify themselves—but he was trusting his family to this unknown person.

"Teo." A demonstration of trust in return.

"So where are we going, Teo?" Tomas asked.

"Vnukovo International Airport. My partner's chartered a private plane."

"They won't let us board. We need exit visas."

"Not if we're going to St. Petersburg—to catch the last of the White Nights celebrations."

Tomas had forgotten that White Nights were ongoing, but he didn't understand how taking the family to St. Petersburg would help them escape. But he'd committed to this course the moment he'd agreed to meet an American spy.

* * * * *

Yuri Bykovsky paced the gilded room that some considered in poor taste—but that he thought reflected the glory and power of the President of the Russian Republic. He was not an impatient man, not generally, but he was about to make history. No wonder he could barely restrain himself.

In few hours, the American president would accept a call from him, expressing the Russian people's sympathy for the horrific loss of American lives and the outrageous attack. He'd also have revenge for what they'd done to him—the spy who'd helped his former lover steal billions, and against the American government that had authorized it. In a few hours, he'd have back most of the money stolen from him. Yes, he'd lose half of it to Rzaev and his people, but still he'd have five billion back.

Although, why should Rzaev and his people get five billion? Maybe a billion between them. That was more than generous.

He checked the time and paced.

Maybe he needed a diversion. It would still be a few hours. He considered summoning his mistress. She was good in bed and that would be a pleasant way to spend the time, but he was a little annoyed at her. Someone else right now? He ran the images of the wives of his generals and high-ranking officials through his mind and selected the wife of the head of the GRU. She was much younger than his current mistress and much prettier. And it was fun fucking the wife of a powerful man—who could do nothing about it.

Almost as much fun as the expression on Tomas's face when he accepted that he was an idiot.

The memory of Tomas' face brought another idea to mind. Maybe he'd call his sister. He liked teasing Lyudmila. He liked that she was a little afraid of him. Not that he'd ever hurt her. She was family and he did care about family.

He picked up his phone, dialed, and waited for four rings. He tried two more times before he slammed the phone on his desk.

Why wasn't she answering? She never went out at night, and even if she did, she should have a phone on her. Given what his fucking brother-in-law knew and what he now knew of his fucking brother-in-law, Yuri needed to know where they were and what they were doing.

71

"WHETHER PETROV MADE THE video under coercion or not isn't the most important issue right now," Lewis sat in the middle of the length of the table, between the Secretary of State and the Chief of Staff. "Once we find him and the Novichok—we can sort out responsibility. What are our options?"

"Petrov's last known location was Johnson, Vermont. He could be anywhere within fourteen hours of Vermont." Margaret was at the far end of the crowded table in the situation room.

"So anywhere from New England down to Virginia?" Lewis asked.

"Or east to Ohio. We have roadblocks on all the main highways," the FBI director said. "But we can't cover every road in the whole country. We don't know what kind of vehicle. Officers have Petrov's and Lemonsky's pictures, but there's been no sightings—and without a vehicle identification—unlikely that they'd be spotted unless they're caught in a random stop."

"So, you've got nothing," Lewis said.

"Pretty much."

"Meantime, the deadline's approaching."

Margaret cleared her throat. "If—as Petrov stated in the video—Novichok is attached to small bombs and exploded in populated areas, there could be hundreds or even thousands of casualties."

"Options?" Lewis asked.

Unless federal agents stumbled upon Petrov in the next few hours, there was a real possibility that the threat could be carried out. The three positions were laid out. Those who argued that the United States should not negotiate with terrorists. There was the view that paying the money would not prevent the attack. Lewis stated the third view: that he had to do whatever he could to protect American lives.

The discussion rounded the table twice—and Lewis called for a vote. It was a tie: Margaret and Smithson voting not to pay. But the proverbial buck stopped with Lewis, and he gave the order. Pay the ten billion dollars. It wasn't taxpayer money, anyway, it was the money that had been taken from Bykovsky three years earlier.

And after the decision on the ransom, the next urgent question: confront Yuri Bykovsky on the possibility of his involvement? The Chairman of the Joint Chiefs of Staff advocated for a call to Bykovsky without waiting for concrete evidence. Homeland Security argued that a call without the evidence would just anger Bykovsky instead of defusing the situation.

Lewis looked down the table at Margaret. "When is your boy Egan getting back to us?"

"He's in transit with Tomas Orlov."

"And the plan is…?" Smithson asked.

"Ongoing." Margaret said smoothly.

"Christ, Margaret, no one here is the enemy," Smithson growled.

"The fewer who know, the better. And we're exfiltrating Orlov, his wife, and three children. It's a little delicate, given that his wife is Bykovsky's sister."

"Okay, okay," Lewis said. "We wait. And we keep trying to find the Novichok."

"Margaret, don't you have an agent guarding Petrov's fiancée?" Smithson asked.

"Yes." Margaret didn't have any incentive to share that she suspected Smithson had placed a kill order on Petrov—or what she'd directed Tehila to do to counter it.

"And has Feinstein been in contact with Petrov?" Lewis asked.

"No."

"You wouldn't know if she had," Smithson growled.

"My agent would. She's very good." She met his gaze evenly.

"Tehila Melaku, isn't it?" Smithson asked.

"Yes. How did you know?"

"I run the CIA, Margaret. I make it my business to know whatever might impact national security." He gave her his insufferable smile. "And by the way, interesting that you have a former Israeli watching Petrov's fiancee."

"How so?" She knew what direction he was heading. *Let him.*

"It's just that she and Petrov have a lot in common."

And he'd done it—walked right into an open display of bias. Margaret felt the burn of the insinuation on behalf of both her agents. Worse than that was the implication that she would understand—maybe even agree. Because after all, she'd chosen Petrov, one of only three Jews in the entire agency, for a suicide mission—and while she had vigorously resisted the suggestion that she had chosen Petrov because of his ethnicity—maybe there was something there. Something that she needed to acknowledge—and atone for. "Yes, they do have a lot in common. They are both ECA operatives who risk their lives for this country. Because I'm sure you're not referring to the fact that they are both Jews." Then she stood and left the room.

72

FRIDAY NIGHT, VNUKOVO INTERNATIONAL AIRPORT, MOSCOW

ON THE TARMAC: JONATHAN Egan waited and wished for a cigar—a drink—something. This was the moment of greatest danger. Moscow was filled with cameras and police and FSB. Two cars had to arrive safely, one carrying Teo, Tomas and his family, the other carrying Elizabeth, Fyodor and his wife. Two cars driving through the streets of Moscow doubled the danger, but the two separate cars also increased the odds that one would succeed.

He could have left Fyodor and his wife behind—they weren't part of the President's order or part of his mission—but it was ECA policy not to leave an asset in jeopardy. And Bykovsky would be conducting a purge if Tomas escaped.

He thought about his nine-year-old son and the promise of a baseball game. If he were arrested by the FSB, he wouldn't make that game. He was NOC—which meant he could be executed. Unlikely but possible. Still, it wasn't the risk to him that had him on edge. The hell of the spy game was that innocent people were endangered. If Tomas were arrested, he'd be dead. Not even a question. Would Bykovsky kill his own sister and her children as well? If he thought them disloyal—yes.

Calm. Once they were in the air, they'd be okay.

At the top of the stairs, the flight attendant—an attractive woman in her early twenties—waited, face beaming, not knowing that she and the pilot of the hired Citation XLS were assisting in an intelligence operation.

It had been a rushed and frantic operation, engaging a private plane at the last minute. But money talked, and Jonathan was perfectly happy to pay inflated prices for the privilege of flying to St. Petersburg on short notice.

Which was what he'd put on the flight request.

Headlights of a car turning onto the tarmac. Police or his people? The car pulled forward—and he recognized it as belonging to a secretary in the embassy. The back doors swung open, and Fyodor stepped out. A slender woman with short-cut blonde hair and a worried face exited the other side and circled the car to take Fyodor's arm. Elizabeth exited from the front passenger seat. The car reversed and drove slowly away.

"Hurry," Jonathan motioned. Fyodor and his wife disappeared into the plane.

One down. But Tomas Orlov, his wife, and three small children were still out there.

Elizabeth positioned herself next to him.

"Any word?"

"They're on the way."

"And Kolya?"

Jonathan shook his head.

"No, you don't have any news? Or no, he's gone over to the dark side?"

"Damn it, Elizabeth. Why do you have to always think the worst? No, I don't know anything—except that he's in trouble and I trust him. He would not betray this country."

"I wish I were as optimistic as you."

"I wish you were too."

The air was chilly. He thrust hands in his pocket, resisting the urge to check his watch or phone.

Ten minutes? Fifteen minutes?

Call? No.

A new set of headlights at the far end of the field. He watched a black limo slowly approach on the airfield. The limo pulled parallel to the Citation and stopped. He could see nothing through the darkened windows.

Teo emerged from back of the car, carrying a young boy, followed by a heavy-set middle-aged woman, struggling with the weight of a smaller child.

Jonathan strode over to the woman. "Let me." Jonathan gently took the boy. The small head rested on his shoulder. Elizabeth gestured to the woman to follow.

Tomas carried a girl of nine or ten on his shoulder. "Does Yuri know we left our apartment?"

"No idea. We'll be in the air in a few minutes, and it won't matter."

But even as he spoke, he noticed three men in suits stride towards them from the structure on the edge of the field. He'd already filled out all necessary forms, and the flight plan was filed. Last minute, but still filed.

"Get on the plane," he said to Tomas.

"Stop." One man called in English. He was close enough for Jonathan to recognize the functionary to whom he had handed his forms. Two men in uniform with guns on their belts flanked him.

Tomas froze.

The men halted five feet in front of Jonathan.

"Who are these people?" In a suit, thin faced with a look of avarice, the man in charge jerked his head at Tomas.

Jonathan had a gun hidden under his jacket, but he was holding a child—and there were three of them. Teo had a gun, but he was also holding a child.

Elizabeth, though, had her arms free and her gun was within easy reach. Still—she'd have to shoot three men. Burdened with children, neither he nor Teo could help. Jonathan shook his head slightly, and she relaxed her stance. Then he turned to the men.

"My cousin and his family. We made a last minute party to celebrate my wife's birthday at the White Nights. Is there a problem?" He decided to try a time-honored tactic. "Did I perhaps fail to pay a fee?"

The thin-faced man smiled. "There is an extra fee per passenger that you neglected to pay."

"Ah, of course." Jonathan shifted the child in his arms, reached into his pocket for his money clip. He counted out five one-hundred dollar bills and handed them over. The man spread the bills and shook his head.

"Five thousand dollars American to take off."

Jonathan carried a fair amount of cash, but five thousand was more than he had on hand. "I can write you a check." He saw an instant negative reaction. Of course. The man would want no record of his extortion.

"How much cash do you have?"

Jonathan held out the money clip. The thin-faced man took it, counted the bills, and looked up disapprovingly.

"It's only another two thousand. You are rich American who take private planes. Five thousand dollars is nothing to you." He took a step closer and leaned in. "And funny, your cousin does not look anything like you."

"It's all I've got in cash. And he favors the other side of the family."

"Then you don't leave."

"Wait." Elizabeth removed the diamond earrings she'd purchased a few hours earlier. "My husband just paid $20,000 American for these—a birthday present. Maybe you could hold them until we get back and give you the cash?" She held out her hand, the diamonds sparkling in the evening light.

The three men consulted in Russian. "Okay then." The man in the suit pocketed Jonathan's cash and the earrings. "You are going to St. Petersburg and then returning in two days?"

"Yes. As I stated in my paperwork."

"When you return, you will pay me ten thousand dollars. And I will hold your wife's earrings until then."

The price had skyrocketed, but it didn't matter. Jonathan wasn't coming back.

The little boy stirred, warm breath scented with chocolate on Jonathan's cheek, reminding him of his own son when Dylan was younger.

"Agreed."

"Good. I will be here when you land."

The thin-faced man motioned to the other two men, and they turned around and headed back to the small terminal.

"If Yuri starts asking questions, those men will remember us," Tomas said. "One of them will talk."

"Maybe. But we'll be gone."

Jonathan and Elizabeth followed Tomas and his wife as they wobbled up the stairs to the plane. Teo was last.

The seats inside the plane were leather, wide and comfortable, one either side of the aisle that ran the length of the plane. The children were eased down and buckled in, their stuffed animals placed in their arms, warm blankets tucked around them.

"How long will they sleep?" Tomas asked.

"Long enough," Jonathan said. "They may even sleep for the whole flight."

Lyudmila Orlov seated herself behind the smallest boy, and Jonathan noted the look she gave her husband. Angry or just worried? She had the right to be both. He also noticed the necklace she wore—that Elizabeth had purchased for her.

Tomas sat across the aisle from to her. Jonathan took a seat directly behind Tomas and next to Elizabeth. Teo took a seat behind Elizabeth.

"Are we going to drive from St. Petersburg to the Finish border?" Tomas turned and spoke quietly over his shoulder.

"It would take too long."

"But we're flying to St. Petersburg."

"As I said, that's where the flight plan says we're going."

"Where are we really going?"

"I won't know for sure until we're in the air."

Jonathan accepted a glass of Champaign from the flight attendant, but refrained from drinking, not wanting to jinx the operation. Teo gripped his glass with white knuckles. Fyodor and his wife accepted glasses and sipped. Lyudmila Orlov drained her glass in one long gulp and accepted a refill. Tomas refused.

Elizabeth motioned for the entire bottle and didn't bother with a glass. She took a long swig, draining a quarter of the bottle. "I'm going to need another one of these soon. Maybe two."

Jonathan felt the same, but he couldn't resist a little teasing. "You charged $20,000 on my credit card for those earrings?"

"They cost $2,000, actually, but $20,000 sounded more impressive, and those thugs wouldn't know the difference." She took another swig. "I told you that you could expense them."

The door was closed and sealed. The plane began the slow taxi to the runway, and Jonathan watched out the window. No cars racing to intercept them.

Four private planes waited ahead of them. Jonathan watched as each peeled off into the sky. Then the Citation XLS moved into position. The engines roared, and the plane sped down the runway. Jonathan felt the exhilaration as the nose lifted, and then they were in the air.

Teo and Jonathan raised glasses. Elizabeth raised her bottle. "To luck."

73

FRIDAY NIGHT, MOSCOW, RUSSIA

THEY WEREN'T AT THE apartment. A neighbor had heard a young man with a slight accent that the neighbor couldn't identify offering them tickets to the *Teatre Koshet*. The whole family had left together.

The officer on the line suggested sending men to check the theater. Yuri dismissed the idea. If Tomas and his wife had gone out with the children at night, accompanied by a stranger, almost immediately after Tomas had learned Yuri's real plans, they wouldn't be watching cats do tricks. They were running, with the help of Americans. Yuri didn't care how they'd made contact or who the Americans were. The only thing he cared about was finding them before they left Russia.

He gave orders. Check the trains and the airports. Close the borders. It hadn't been that long. They had to still be in the country somewhere.

He had been loyal to his sister. He'd given her stupid husband a big job—a job he was unqualified for—he'd given them money. They'd had status. Respect. And this was how she paid him back? They were all dead, all of them. Tomas. His sister. The kids. And whatever American spies were trying to get them out.

If Tomas was being spirited out of the country by American spies, had he already told them what he knew?

Maybe not. Wouldn't Yuri have already received an indignant call from President Lewis? Maybe Tomas had offered them information but not provided it yet.

If he stopped Tomas, there would be no evidence. Without Tomas, there was no concrete proof that Russia, and not terrorists, was responsible

305

for what would happen in America. Yuri also had the video where Kolya Petrov claimed to be working with terrorists. He hadn't planned to release it to the media—it had been meant for Lewis and the U.S. government. But that was another weapon. A disgruntled spy admitting to plotting against the U.S. made for good viewing. That had to be more persuasive than vague charges by an ungrateful brother-in-law, especially if the brother-in-law was no longer able to repeat those charges.

He was too invested in his plan to retreat. He wanted his money, and he wanted revenge.

His fucking brother-in-law wasn't going to stop him.

* * * * *

Jonathan waited until the plane reached cruising altitude. Then he unbuckled his seat belt and made his way up the aisle. He knocked on the door to the cockpit and, without waiting, opened it. The pilot glanced over his shoulder and smiled cordially. After all, Jonathan had paid a premium for a last-minute trip.

"Another hour to St. Petersburg." The pilot sounded British. That would make it easier. A Russian would have been more complicated.

"I know. But I'm requesting a change."

"A change?"

"A change in destination. Edinburgh."

"I haven't filed a flight plan for Edinburgh. It's complicated to leave Russia. There's exit visas and customs requirements."

"Yeah, I know. I'm willing to pay for you to circumvent the formalities."

"I'll have to get it okayed." The pilot reached for his radio.

"Maybe you didn't understand. I'm willing to pay a lot—but you can't call anyone."

"A lot?"

"Two hundred thousand dollars. That should compensate both you and your company for the diversion."

"Jesus Christ. Who are you?"

"Just a guy with a lot of money who wants to go to Scotland. I love haggis."

"I'm not helping you commit a crime. If you're smuggling something, you can just go back to your seat right now."

"The only thing I'm smuggling is people. The only crime will be murder—when Yuri Bykovsky gets hold of the people I'm trying to get out."

The pilot glanced towards the cabin. "The kids?"

"If we're caught, all of us are dead. Kids too. You got kids?"

"Two. Teenagers. Drive you crazy."

"The kids on the plane are nine, seven, and six."

The pilot heaved a sigh. "Okay, but you understand, there'll be hell to pay with the United Kingdom when we land. My company may not be happy with me. And I won't be able to return to Russia."

Jonathan doubted that there'd be a problem with the U.K. Information had already been sent on to the U.S. Consulate—who would have already spoken to the appropriate government entities in London and Edinburgh.

"I can throw in an extra fifty thousand just for you."

"I already agreed. But the extra money would be appreciated."

"Anyone tracking us on radar?"

"Not now—and they won't unless we pass over a major airport or military base."

"Then don't. We have enough fuel?"

"For Edinburgh, but not a lot farther."

"Edinburgh's good enough."

* * * * *

The call was from an older officer. Yuri knew him personally.

"A family matching the description took off in a private jet half an hour ago from Vnukovo International Airport, heading for St. Petersburg according to the flight plan."

"Anyone check identification?"

"No. And we have three men in custody who accepted money and a pair of diamond earrings not to check identifications."

"Shoot those men and have people on the ground when the plane lands."

Yuri hung up. It might not be Tomas and Lyudmila who'd boarded that plane—but if it were, would the plane follow the flight plan? Maybe. Maybe they thought going to St. Petersburg would throw him off. Maybe they were going to try to get out through Finland.

If that were the case, they'd be caught. No matter how they intended to get across—fake identifications—breaking them into smaller groups and separate cars—the border was closed.

But wouldn't Tomas know that he'd close the borders? After all, border security had been Tomas's job before Yuri had stupidly plucked him out and made him Director.

He'd misjudged Tomas. He'd thought the little fat idiot would never dare challenge him.

So maybe—the plane wasn't headed for St. Petersburg. Maybe it was going somewhere else. Somewhere in the E.U. or maybe even the U.K. After all, once the plane left Russian airspace, any move against it would trigger a counterattack by NATO.

There was one course of action. Order all planes down. Commercial. Private. All. Shoot down any plane that refused to comply.

74

THE SUBARU FORESTER THAT they had followed south from Vermont into Massachusetts and towards Boston had turned around and was now back on small roads in Southern Vermont. As a result, they had almost caught up. Alex navigated with Mark's directions, keeping herself calm by focusing on the task at hand. The trick was to not to get too close, just close enough that they could intercept whenever the car stopped.

They passed small towns with white churches, small towns with nothing but a name and a general store, state forests and state parks. Now they were winding up a mountain somewhere that Google maps designated as Seasonal Forest Road.

Vermont Public Radio reported that an elderly man had been found shot to death in a small country store in northern Massachusetts. The car that they were following had not been anywhere near the store. But they already suspected that there were at least two cars involved. The car they were following. And a car that they hoped held Kolya.

"How far ahead?" Alex asked.

"Ten minutes. Maybe fifteen," Mark's voice on speaker.

Tehila swerved to avoid a fox. "The good thing is that they've just been driving in circles—and that means they're not really planning to use the nerve agent. If they were, they'd be in a more populated area."

"Are you sure?" Alex asked.

"Reasonably. I've had some experience with terrorists. The bad thing is that the car appears to be headed to somewhere secluded. Two possible reasons. Maybe they're just killing time while waiting to hear whether

309

Lewis has paid the ten billion dollars."

"And the second possibility?" Alex asked. "Finish the thought. Two possible reasons—they're waiting and they're what?" She knew what Tehila wasn't saying—but she needed to hear the words. "Disposing of a body?"

"That would be another reason. If you want to ensure that a body will never be found—you need to bury it somewhere secluded. The point of the video was to extort money and to cast blame on terrorists and Kolya. If his body is found, it would make the video suspect. Which could lead to complications for Yuri Bykovsky." Tehila's voice was matter-of-fact. "It's only a possibility."

Maybe Tehila was trying to be comforting, but she sucked at it.

Alex shut her mouth around the scream that threatened to bubble up, and then took a deep breath. "Drive faster."

75

FRIDAY AFTERNOON, SOUTHERN VERMONT

ANOTHER HOUR. MAYBE TWO. Kolya again dozed despite the ache in his leg and shoulder and the tightness of the handcuffs. *Dmitri, ten years old, played Gershwin with one finger. Alex, seated next to him in constitutional law, turned and smiled. Then he was in a basement cell somewhere in Romania, hanging from* chains—and he woke from the old nightmare to the present one. But this time he was able to let go of the images from the dream.

He realized that the van was parked, and he hadn't felt movement for some time. They were waiting—most likely to find out if Lewis would give in to the demand. Dmitri was looking at his phone, but the gun didn't waver.

Kolya leaned his head back and closed his eyes again. He thought of lying in bed next to Alex. She'd be really angry that he'd knowingly walked into this. He could hear her voice, *I told you not to do anything stupid, goddamnit.* Well, he'd done something stupid, hadn't he? He thought regretfully of never having the chance to explain his rationale— or apologize for leaving her. Then he turned his thoughts to music, *Moonlight in Vermont.*

* * * * *

Tehila Melaku was less than ten minutes ahead of Kowolsky, according to her phone GPS. The fact that she'd doubled back had made it possible for him to almost catch up to her. She was heading east, and he was following on the crappy dirt road that was like so many other crappy dirt roads in this backwards place. He wanted to be close enough—but not too close. If she recognized him, she might try to lead him away from her true destination.

And she clearly had a destination. He didn't know what the destination might be but it was somewhere in these damn endless woods and mountains. She was clearly tracking Petrov—and she seemed to know where she was going.

The question was, what to do if she got there first? Maybe she'd be killed by Petrov and Lemonsky. That would be convenient. Or maybe she was in league with him. Or maybe she'd manage to take Petrov into custody.

It didn't really matter to him. He had his assignment. Whether Petrov was in custody or not, whether Tehila Melaku was in league with him or not, was all irrelevant. A trial would be politically awkward. Equally awkward, holding Petrov in a black site somewhere.

If he had to eliminate more than one person, so be it.

76

FRIDAY AFTERNOON, SOUTHERN VERMONT

KOLYA WOKE AGAIN TO a flood of blinding daylight as Rip opened the back of the van. Dmitri still sat in his captain's chair, gun still at the ready.

Was this when Dmitri killed him? The traditional death for a traitor to a Russian gang—the stomach ripped open and intestines pulled out? He calculated the distance between Dmitri and himself again. Still too far. But if he lunged, he'd force Dmitri to shoot. It would at least be fast.

But maybe Dmitri didn't really intend to kill him. It was a chance, anyway. Kolya looked at Dmitri. "Now what?"

Dmitri gestured with the gun. "Grab the C4 and the cardboard box. Place it all on the ground. It is a present."

"What?"

"Present. Gift. You know. Like Christmas. Now move."

Kolya maneuvered over to the C-4 and picked it up. Doing so in handcuffs was awkward but manageable. Then he slid to the open door at the back of the van, as Charlie stepped out of the way, his gun at the ready. Kolya stepped out of the van, injured leg straight and stiff, and deposited on the ground the bricks of C-4, and then the box with small bottles, duct tape and detonators. Everything that would be needed to make bombs.

Everything except the chemicals.

That changed. A few minutes after exiting the van, Kolya watched Mickey's car approach down the dirt driveway winding through a thicket of pine and maple trees. Mickey parked and exited the car, shooting a grin at Kolya. From the rear of the car, he retrieved the backpack with the two cannisters containing the chemicals that combined would form Novichok. All the components were together again.

At Charlie's direction, Rip, armed with the HK-91, headed back down the driveway. Kolya glanced over at Dmitri, who shrugged.

"In case anyone followed either us or Mickey. Rip will be in the woods as protection until we leave."

They were parked on a surface of hard dirt, big enough to accommodate another two or three cars. It could be a clearing in a forest, a park, or an estate. They could be in Vermont or in Massachusetts or even New York.

Did the fact that they'd unloaded everything in what appeared to be a remote area mean that he didn't need to throw away his life in a desperate act?

"You said this was a gift?"

"You can call it that," Dmitri said.

"Where are we?"

"Vermont."

"Still?"

"Yes. Still."

"We've just been driving in circles?"

"Pretty much. We went down into Massachusetts and then came back. We are two and a half hours south of Waterbury."

It was crazy. Or was it? Anyone searching for them would be looking on major roads and in major cities. No one would expect them to still be in Vermont. It was also encouraging. This wasn't exactly the population center that a terrorist would choose as a target.

"You're leaving the chemicals here?"

Dmitri smiled and tapped the side of his head. "You think I want that shit in the car while we are driving to northern Maine?"

"Northern Maine?"

"Yes. Where we have a plane meeting us. But if we got into a car accident on the way and somehow the containers spilled, I will not live to enjoy my money and my island. Also, I do not want any run-ins with police officers, who might want to check the van, and I would not want them to find either the chemicals or the C-4."

"Or me?"

"You will be asleep. We have pills for you. You will probably sleep until we are halfway to the islands."

Kolya felt both relief and regret. "Lewis paid."

"Yes, he paid. So I am leaving all this—as a present—or maybe not a present because it was paid for. When we are out of the country, your friends will get a map to find it. Your face, Kolya. You did not believe me. You thought I would kill Americans just for the hell of it. You thought I would kill you, too?"

Kolya shrugged.

"I made a deal. And I keep my word."

At least Dmitri was leaving the Novichok. Innocent people were not going to die. Apparently, honor did mean something to Dmitri. Not a lot, but something.

He had a moment when he could breathe. Not even a moment.

Charlie cleared his throat. "Actually, Dmitri, there is a slight change of plan. Petrov is going to pour the chemicals into those smaller bottles for us. The bottles in the box, Petrov. Five bottles for each of the chemicals."

Kolya glanced down at the box he'd unloaded. It held ten pint-size glass bottles as well as the tape and detonators.

Dmitri narrowed his eyes. "What are you talking about Charlie?"

"I think my words were clear."

"Why do you want the chemicals in smaller bottles?"

With a sigh and an air of patience, Charlie shrugged. "You're not a complete idiot, Dmitri, are you?"

And suddenly everything was clear. "He plans to make bombs with the chemicals, Dima. Novichok bombs," Kolya said.

"That was not the plan if Lewis paid. Which he did." Dmitri's voice showed genuine outrage, but his gun remained aimed at Kolya.

"I'm doing what I was told to do," Charlie said.

"Not by me. I run North America."

"No, not by you. And you don't run North America. Not anymore. I do. You have not been in charge of Rzaev's North America operations for the past ten years. Still, what's the problem? Americans put you in prison to rot for twenty-five years, Dmitri Andriovich. The only reason you're out after ten years is this charade. Think of this as your revenge. Why do you care if a few Americans die?"

"The *vorovsky mir* has rules and a code. As do I. And Rzaev made this my operation."

"I am taking my orders directly from Bykovsky. He wants more than money from the Americans."

"Rzaev said nothing to me about this."

"When would he have said anything? When you were in prison being watched day and night? When you were around this spy? Rzaev's letting Bykovsky call the shots. He told me, and I'm telling you. Bykovsky wants to inflict real pain on the United States—and Petrov will be the one blamed."

Rip was out of sight, down the drive. Charlie and Mickey had positioned themselves at the back of the van, ten feet away from Kolya. Dmitri was closer, directly across from Kolya, but still too far away for Kolya to jump him without being shot.

"I am a little curious." Dmitri's voice was casual. "Did Rzaev or Bykovsky tell you not to inform the police in Boston and New York after you left the bottles of Novichok in public places?"

"That was my idea." Charlie sounded proud. "I figured that American intelligence would take the threat more seriously if people actually died than if the police just found bottles of Novichok. It worked, too."

"Yes, it did work."

"Of course, Bykovsky loved the idea. And, as I said, Rzaev okayed whatever Bykovsky wanted. But don't worry. We will keep to the plan as far as Petrov goes—which seems to matter to you. We'll leave him alive on an island, as long as he behaves between now and when we get there."

Dmitri turned his gaze from Charlie to Mickey and then back.

"Whatever. If Rzaev okayed it. Kolya, do what Charlie directs or we will have to shoot you after all."

Charlie proceeded to give orders. "What you are doing to do, Petrov, is take one container at a time out of the backpack, open it, and pour the contents into five of the bottles. Close the lid on each bottle, seal it with tape, and put them in the box. Then you take out the second container and do the same thing with the next five bottles. Carefully. If you do anything other than take one cylinder out of the backpack at a time and pour, I'll shoot you. If you do exactly what I tell you to do—you'll live."

Kolya heard something in Charlie's voice, and then he identified it. Fear. Charlie was afraid of the chemicals. They all were. With justification. It was deadly stuff and death from a nerve agent was horrific, which was undoubtedly why Charlie didn't want to touch the chemicals himself.

Kolya had enough maneuverability even in handcuffs that he could perform the task. But he wasn't about to do so.

He glanced at Dmitri. Hours earlier, Dmitri had claimed that he hadn't intended to kill three people in Boston with Novichok. Kolya hadn't believed him, but it appears that Dmitri had been truthful—about his intent at least. Still, they had died. Did Dmitri realize that Charlie was lying about everything? Bykovsky wouldn't be satisfied with the comparatively gentle revenge on Kolya that Dmitri had described. But did it matter? Dmitri would go along, just as he had casually accepted Charlie murdering people in Boston or the killing of an old man at the convenience store. After Kolya poured the chemicals that Charlie did not want to touch into the bottles, Charlie would kill him.

Bykovsky would want Kolya to die—now, not later. The odds were good that shooting would be considered too quick, and that he'd suffer the more painful death generally inflicted on those who crossed the Russian mafiya. But the manner of his death wasn't his main concern right now. If he were going to die anyway, Kolya would prefer not to be responsible for innocent people dying as well.

If he simply refused to follow Charlie's orders, he just die faster. They'd kill him and then pour the chemicals themselves. Charlie would probably make the ever-expendable Rip do it.

If he complied, he'd briefly delay his own death—but at a terrible cost.

There was a simple solution, not one that would save him—but it would save others.

Kolya removed a metal cannister from the backpack. *Dump it out.* Two chemicals needed to mix to create Novichok. Pouring one out would eliminate any possibility of bombs dispersing a nerve poison. He would be killed immediately, maybe shot, maybe sliced open and his intestines pulled out, but he was willing to accept the trade.

At least he was calm. No shaking. No disassociation. No flashbacks. He felt like himself, for the brief seconds that he had left. He thought of Alex with love and regret, mentally said goodbye, and then he dismissed her image from his mind.

"Careful." Charlie's voice still showed fear.

77

FRIDAY NIGHT, THE GREAT EASTERN EUROPEAN PLAIN, WESTERN RUSSIA

"THE PILOT WOULD LIKE to speak to you." The attendant leaned over. Her face had a tinge of anxiety. Jonathan unbuckled his seat belt and followed her up the aisle.

He reached the cockpit; the pilot motioned for him to enter, and he closed the door behind him.

"I've received a message ordering all aircraft in Russian airspace to land immediately."

"Are we being targeted specifically?"

"Not that I know."

"And if we ignore the message?"

"If we're detected flying over Russia, we could be shot down."

"How much longer until we're out of Russian air space?"

"Fifteen minutes. That's a long time. The safer thing is to land."

"No, it's not. If we land, we'll all be killed. All of us." Jonathan emphasized the last few words.

"You're not going to tell me what the hell's going on, are you?"

"No, I'm afraid not."

"They won't kill me. I'm just the pilot."

"Maybe not. But just having seen our faces may be too much for them to leave you alive. Do you know what happens to Yuri Bykovsky's enemies?"

"I've heard stories."

"All true. Any way to evade radar?"

"Not at this height. The higher we fly, the greater the distance at which we can be detected."

"So go lower. What's the term—*nape of the earth*?" Jonathan knew *nape of the earth* was a technique to fly low and avoid enemy radar.

"I know it—I used to be military, but we won't be completely invisible. And it's dangerous, especially at night, especially if I fly low enough. I might not see an obstacle and we'll crash. And even if we fly low, no guarantees that we wouldn't still be seen."

"Got that. How low can you fly here?"

"We're currently over a plain and on route to Latvia. Mostly forest down there. I'll reduce speed and go down to a couple hundred feet and try not to hit a tree. Put your seatbelt on. Make sure everyone is buckled in. If there weren't kids involved, I'd put the damn plane down and take my chances."

* * * * *

Tomas watched Jonathan Egan make his way up the aisle to the cockpit. He was not fooled by Teo's words of reassurance. Something was wrong—and he had a pretty good guess what it might be. He knew Yuri. If Yuri realized they were flying out of the country, he'd issue orders to shoot down the plane.

The children still slept, while Lyudmila stared out the window. He reached across the aisle and took her hand. He wanted to tell her he was sorry for putting her and the children at risk. He wanted to tell her that he loved her and had never loved another woman. But his saying all of that might frighten her, and he'd be saying it for himself to assuage his own guilt. If they were shot down, she'd have seconds of terror, but it would be over quickly. Let her have some peace while she still could.

She turned her head, tears in her eyes. "I'm sorry, Tomas."

"You're sorry? You have nothing to be sorry for. I'm the one who should be apologizing. For putting all of you at risk."

"I'm sorry that Yuri is my brother. I'm sorry that when he wanted you to become Director, I urged you to take the job. Because I wanted a beautiful apartment in Moscow."

"I made the decision." He kissed her hand.

Jonathan Egan returned down the aisle. He paused in front of Tomas's seat. "Tighten your belts and brace yourselves."

Then he seated himself.

Tomas pulled the strap tighter as the plane plunged downwards.

78

PRESIDENT LEWIS DRUMMED FINGERS on the table as he debated his next move. Margaret Bradford sat silent at the far end of the table; Ben Smithson sat next to her—also silent.

She'd already offered information and her opinion that the President needed to confront Yuri Bykovsky—carefully. She didn't agree with the President's requirement that Tomas Orlov provide video testimony, but she'd ordered Jonathan to take whatever actions were necessary to get him out of Russia. The plan, hatched in a few short hours, was actually not a bad one. But now, all they could do was wait.

If the plane were shot down, she would only know by the silence.

If the plane were shot down—and if Kolya Petrov and Dmitri Lemonsky were not taken alive—there'd be no evidence that Bykovsky had masterminded a complex plot to attack the U.S. There might or might not be multiple casualties from a nerve agent attack. There would just be the video of Kolya Petrov—who might have been coerced, which was what she believed—confessing to treason.

If one of Smithson's people got to him first, he wouldn't live to protest his innocence. What had happened to Petrov eight months earlier in Romania would be an embarrassment for President Lewis and for Smithson if it were to come out. If he were taken alive, Petrov would have the opportunity to tell his story. Even prisoners in Guantanamo spoke to lawyers.

She took out her phone and read the encrypted message from Mark

Leslie. *Tehila on trail. More information on your request.* She'd get whatever he had for her—later. Margaret didn't want any information on Petrov's location that she might have to share with the President and Smithson.

Since Tehila hadn't requested back-up, Margaret didn't have to do anything—and didn't have to know what Tehila was doing. Margaret had faith in her abilities.

79

FRIDAY NIGHT, WESTERN RUSSIA

JONATHAN LOOKED OUT THE window. A full moon allowed him to see an endless forest of trees below. Not too far below—but far enough—he hoped. He glanced across the aisle at Teo. Teo clutched the arms of his chair. In front of Teo, Elizabeth appeared calm, but she gave Jonathan a sardonic smile, which he interpreted as either bravado or criticism.

"You okay?" Jonathan addressed Teo.

"Motion sickness, I think. How much longer?"

Jonathan checked his watch. More than fifteen minutes had passed since he had spoken to the pilot. "Not sure." They were flying slower now. If they had kept to the original speed, they would already be out of Russia.

"Hold on folks." The pilot spoke over the intercom. "We're going to do some maneuvers here. And I'm turning off the cabin lights."

The plane went dark. Jonathan peered out his window, but he saw nothing as the pilot dove closer to the trees.

"I think there's a jet above us on my side." Teo's voice registered nervousness. "Hard to be sure in the dark. But there's definitely something."

"Doesn't mean it's Russian military. Doesn't mean it's looking for us." Jonathan tried to reassure.

"It's circling."

Their plane was moving erratically, bumping lower, closer to the trees.

"I see it, too,"Tomas's voice was resigned.

"Nothing to worry about." Jonathan was a good liar. Part of the profession. Even now, he could lie with ease and confidence.

But no one believed him.

His life—the life of everyone on the plane depended on the skill of the pilot—and luck. And luck may have run out.

The presence of the children made it worse. The adults had made choices that resulted in their being here on this plane. Even Lyudmila and Fyodor's wife had had a choice in the men they married. The children had not. But at least they were sleeping. If the worst happened, they wouldn't even know it.

Jonathan thought of his own son, Dylan, and the promised ball game. He'd promised Dylan a lot of things, and he'd fallen short over and over. Dylan loved him, but Jonathan constantly disappointed. Something always came up—Jonathan had missed so many events. He hated the idea that he'd break another promise. He hated the idea that Dylan would have few memories of good times together.

"Crossing the Latvian border."The pilot's voice held celebration.

Not quite time to celebrate. The jet above them had not turned back at the border.

"There's something else coming towards us," Teo said. "I see more blinking lights."

Jonathan unbuckled his seat belt and switched to a seat behind Teo. He could see the lights but couldn't identity the aircraft.

Nothing from the pilot, but he felt the lurch as their plane increased speed. So, not good. It probably was something military. And it probably had orders to shoot down any plane that refused to land.

"More planes." Elizabeth sounded calmer than Teo, but even she had a slight quaver.

Jonathan could see the lights that indicated two more planes. Advancing side by side. So three planes. Three Russian planes meant the end. They could surrender—or they could be shot down, but the result would be the same.

He wished for x-ray vision or daylight. Some way to identify the aircraft.

He squinted, trying to make out shapes in the darkness, and realized he'd made a mistake. The three planes were not together.

Two jets were coming from the Latvian air space, not Russia. The two new jets were on a collision course with the first jet.

The lights of the first jet turned as it retreated into Russia. The lights of the two new arrivals circled back towards Latvia, and now, as the Citation climbed back to its original altitude, flanked both sides. Jonathan saw the plane just outside his window waggle its wings—a friendly greeting. It was too dark to see any identifying marks, but they had to be NATO, if not American.

Jonathan breathed again. The interior lights came on, and he turned smiling to Elizabeth. "Like I said, nothing to worry about."

"You are so fucking full of it." But she raised what was left of her Champaign bottle and saluted him.

80

MARGARET COULD FEEL THE impatience in the room rising. American forces were on the highest alert. NATO forces were on alert. But Lewis still wanted evidence before talking to Bykovsky. Lewis was wasting time waiting for a call that might never come. Meantime, the ransom had been paid. No word on the Novichok. No sign of Petrov or Lemonsky.

"Mr. President. I wouldn't advise waiting any longer to contact Bykovsky."

"We've discussed this. My decision. I'm waiting until I talk to Tomas Orlov."

She exchanged glances with Smithson. Much as she despised Smithson, now they were united in their annoyance over a too-cautious president—although she also worried that he could go too far the other way. Dealing with Bykovsky required a delicate dance in order not to trigger a catastrophe.

The clock ticked. Then the Chief of Staff lifted a phone and handed it to Lewis. Margaret couldn't hear the words, but she could see Lewis' face.

"Jonathan Egan?" she asked.

Lewis nodded. "I just spoke to him and to Tomas Orlov. They've cleared Russian air space and are being escorted to Scotland." He hung up. "Contact Bykovsky. Time to end this."

"Mr. President." Margaret had waited to see if anyone else would issue a warning. No one did. It was on her. "Do be careful how you handle Bykovsky."

The attention of the entire table shifted in her direction.

The computer screen in front of the president brought up the image of his Russian counterpart. Yuri Bykovsky in a skin-tight shirt, smiled at the screen, the translator, a middle-aged man in a suit, frozen at attention, behind his shoulder. Even farther back were the shapes of two bodyguards.

"President Bykovsky." Lewis's face was grim.

The smile never left his face. The gracious leader. "Thomas, why so formal. We are friends. Russia and America, you and me."

"I am not calling out of friendship."

He continued as if he hadn't heard the translation. "I assure you that Russia will deal firmly with the jihadists who threatened your country."

"I have irrefutable evidence that you are responsible for allowing Novichok to be smuggled into the United States in a scheme to blackmail the United States."

Bykovsky spoke rapid and angry words in Russian. The translator, visibly disturbed, recited the words with emotion.

"Are you insane? Russia has nothing to do with this."

"I am not going to debate facts with you. I have proof provided by your brother-in-law."

"My brother-in-law is a criminal who knew he was going to be arrested for corruption. And I have proof, too—a video of an American agent claiming responsibility. I can put it out on the Internet and let the world decide."

"The world has already decided and will back the United States. If Americans die from the Novichok that you had smuggled into this country, there will be serious consequences."

"Are you threatening ME? ME?" Bykovsky's face turned purple. The translator's, white. "Do you understand who you are dealing with?"

"I understand perfectly. You've been warned. Contact your people immediately before this goes any further. You also need to tell me where to find the Novichok."

Yuri spoke slowly. "Even if you had any basis to your wild accusations, I would not necessarily be able to contact an agent in your country. Do your agents stay in touch with you?

"You have to have a way."

Yuri shrugged. "Not necessarily, even if it were true. And it's not. It's a lie created by your intelligence agencies to slander Russia—when it is one of your own attacking your country to get back at you for what you did to him. And I take threats against my nation very seriously. Very. Seriously."

"You've been warned."

"Are you going to threaten me again, President Lewis?" The translator spoke in an emotionless monotone. "Thank you for this enlightening conversation." And Bykovsky was gone.

81

FRIDAY AFTERNOON, SOUTHERN VERMONT

THE DIRT DRIVE ON the right disappearing into woods would have been easy to miss, but Alex had been counting down the distance on her phone. From satellite images, she knew that the drive was about a half mile in distance. She also knew that there was a clearing at the end, large enough for several cars to park. And while the satellite hadn't updated recently enough to give them images, they both knew from the GPS signal that the car they had been following all day was there.

Tehila slowed the car as they passed the drive but didn't turn. As they had discussed. She rounded a bend, where the car would be invisible to anyone near the driveway entrance and pulled off and parked.

She handed Alex the shotgun and picked up the Galil.

"Be careful going through the woods. Stay low and go straight through the brush towards the clearing." Tehila pointed.

"And you?"

"I'll take the drive."

"Do you really think it's necessary for us to approach separately?"

"Absolutely. And Alex, if you should get to the clearing before me—and you see Kolya —don't do anything until I get there."

"Unless I have to."

"Unless you do. Just be careful. On three then. One, two."

Tehila spoke the word three, and Alex swung the door wide and dove for the ground, flopping on her belly into the dirt, and crawling forward.

* * * * *

Kowolsky was less than five minutes behind Tehila Melaku's car, which had come to a stop. Somewhere on the road ahead. He slowed and then pulled off the road. Maybe a hundred feet ahead was an opening in the woods—a driveway maybe. He took out his phone to check for satellite images. Yes, it was a drive, and there was a clearing ahead. So that was where she was headed.

He checked his Glock and returned it to his holster. Not the best weapon for what he needed to do. On the seat in the back, he had a Crazy Horse rifle under a blanket—a precision weapon, good for the purpose. He reached back and pulled it out, checking the ammunition, and then opened the car door. Then, he cautiously moved slowly into the woods.

82

FRIDAY AFTERNOON, SOUTHERN VERMONT

THERE WAS A SINGLE shot from the woods, in the direction of the road, where Rip had headed a few minutes earlier. The shot startled everyone. Charlie and Mickey turned their eyes in the direction of the shot, attention momentarily wavering from Kolya. And Kolya seized the moment. Why simply pour the chemicals on the ground when they could be better used?

Kolya hurled the open canister of chemicals at Mickey's face. Reflectively, Mickey threw his arms up to protect his face. The liquid splashed against his arms and then into his eyes, and he screamed. Despite the protestations of pain from his leg, Kolya charged ten feet and tackled Charlie, hitting with his shoulder. Charlie, surprised and off balance, toppled to the ground.

Kolya seized Charlie's wrist, trying to wrestle the gun loose. He tried to deliver a knockout blow with an elbow, but the handcuffs on his wrists reduced the power, and Charlie easily blocked it. He smashed Kolya in the face with his left hand and tried to free the gun.

"Shoot him, Dmitri! Now! Shoot him, Mickey!"

Kolya had seconds. A fraction of a second.

"I can't fucking see. I can't fucking see." Mickey partially blinded from the chemicals, was still screaming. But he raised his gun, firing wildly towards Kolya and Charlie.

Charlie struggled to raise his gun, his finger inside the trigger guard. Kolya gripped his forearm. They rolled over on the ground as a bullet plowed into the earth inches from Kolya's head.

A second bullet went through the fleshy part of Kolya's arm.

A third hit Charlie in the left shoulder.

"Shoot HIM not me!"

Dmitri still stood in his original position, maybe ten feet away—just watching, gun raised, but not shooting.

"I'm coming." Mickey closed the gap between the two men struggling on the ground, aiming at Kolya. If he got close enough, he wouldn't miss, even if his vision was impaired.

Kolya shifted his grip from Charlie's wrist to his hand. He inserted his right index finger over Charlie's finger inside the trigger guard. Charlie struggled to regain control, but Kolya, with two hands on the weapon, had the advantage. Kolya adjusted the angle. Then his index finger pushed down on Charlie's finger and fired the gun.

The round hit Mickey in the chest as he in turn fired his own gun. Kolya thought he heard a third shot, and then Mickey fell. The round from Mickey's gun missed by inches.

Charlie struck at Kolya's eyes with his left hand. Kolya jerked back and but kept his grip on the gun and hand. Charlie stabbed two fingers at Kolya's face. Kolya dodged again.

The handcuffs limited options. If he lost control of the gun, it was over.

He tried to jam his good knee into Charlie's balls. Not the right angle or the right speed to do any damage. He slammed a shoulder into Charlie, which did nothing.

"Shoot him, Dmitri." Charlie shouted again. "You idiot. You fucking idiot. Shoot him."

Nothing.

The few seconds that they had been struggling felt like an hour.

Charlie slammed his left hand down on Kolya's wrists, once, twice. The blows loosened Kolya's grip. Charlie head butted Kolya. He ripped his hand free and rolled away, holding the gun. Then he pushed himself to his feet and aimed at Kolya's chest.

A single shot reverberated.

The bullet plowed into the side of Charlie's head and blew out the opposite side, and he crumbled back to the ground.

"Whoops," Dmitri said.

Kolya dove for the gun and pried it from Charlie's limp fingers. He stood and turned his attention back to Dmitri. They faced each other, guns raised and aimed. "Thank you," Kolya said.

"You're welcome." But he didn't lower his gun. Neither did Kolya.

"Did you shoot him because you didn't like him taking over?" The adrenaline ebbing, Kolya felt his injuries, the old competing with the new. He knew without looking that the wound to his arm was bleeding though the flannel shirt. It hurt to keep his arms raised.

"Maybe. And maybe I shot Charlie because years ago, you wrote me a letter that I didn't read. Are you at all sorry that you put me in prison?"

"Perhaps a little. Perhaps more than a little. But you were killing people, Dimi."

"I would not have killed anyone you liked if I'd known."

"That's not the point."

"It is to me." Dmitri glanced sideways at the car that Mickey had driven.

"If you go for the car, I'll have to shoot you." The gun was growing heavier, but he forced himself to hold it steady. He blocked the protests from his leg.

"After I just saved you? What kind of dick are you?"

"A dick you kidnapped and set up to be the fall guy." He could have listed all the offenses—all the schemes that he knew Dmitri had engaged in—starting with the attack on Alex's family. But now there was something on the other side of the ledger.

"I have a gun, too, *moi droog*. Maybe we will shoot each other. That would be a poetic end. Two brothers locked in love and hate. Worthy of Dostoyevsky."

"I'm not that fond of Dostoyevsky." Kolya added dizziness to his other complaints, but at least, there were no flashbacks. No shaking.

Dmitri had just conned the American government out of ten billion dollars, and because of Dmitri, Kolya had spent an unpleasant day as a prisoner. Innocent people had died, and Dmitri was part of the conspiracy that resulted in their death.

"You were willing to let Charlie kill a lot of innocent people."

"No, Kolya. I was not. But it was two against one. They would have killed me if I had not pretended to go along with them. I know that they intended to kill you as well, instead of honoring what I wanted. You think I didn't understand what was going on? But I'm not interested in futile heroic gestures. I was waiting for you to give me cover with one of your ridiculously stupid stunts so I could shoot them. And you did."

Kolya was tempted to let him go. It was absurd and sentimental.

Anyway, he didn't know how much longer he could continue the stand-off. He wanted desperately to lie down. "If you surrender, I'll do my best to get you a deal. I'll testify on your behalf. Maybe you won't have to serve any more time."

"And my money?"

"I don't personally give a shit, but if you want a deal, I suspect you'll have to give it back."

Dmitri shook his head. "No deal. So we have an impasse. Except… you don't look so good. You are bleeding, and I think your arm hurts. Your leg, too? Maybe I will just wait until you pass out and walk away. And there is Rip. Sooner or later, he will show up—and then we will have to deal with it. Or you will. I might simply walk away."

"Maybe. There was a shot. It might not be Rip showing up."

"So we play poker now? Except if I remember right, you don't like poker."

"Sometimes you have to play."

83

KOLYA KEPT HIS GAZE and the gun firmly on Dmitri. Just out of sight, hidden behind trees, someone was moving in the woods. Twigs were snapping. Leaves crunching. Someone—maybe more than one person—was approaching. Rip—or maybe, possibly, someone on his side.

It could go either way.

Whoever it was emerged from the woods to his right. He couldn't identify the person without turning his head away from Dmitri, which would be dangerous. However, Dmitri had a full view, and Kolya had a view of Dmitri's face. Dmitri was surprised.

Kolya risked a glance sideways. Hair and clothes disheveled. Alex had never looked more beautiful. She stood with arms raised and a shotgun pointed at Dmitri. There were so many things he wanted to say to her, but not now, not in front of Dmitri. He said what was essential. "Don't shoot him."

"He's pointing a gun at you." The sound of her voice was better than the best jazz.

"He just saved my life."

"Really?"

"Yes. Really."

"Then why are you pointing a gun at him—and he at you?"

"It's complicated."

It was too long an explanation. It would require hours. He wasn't even sure he could articulate it.

Dmitri remained silent, letting the argument play out between them.

335

"So we're going to just stand here until someone shoots or someone gives up?"

"That's about it."

"Goddamn it, Kolya. You're bleeding. Again. You need medical care."

"I'll live. Are you okay? I told you to leave Vermont."

"I'm fine, and I don't obey your orders."

She took a step toward Kolya, but he shook his head at her—for her to stay where she was. If she came too close, it would be easier for Dmitri to shoot them both.

Dmitri smiled at Alex, displaying the charm that had been his hallmark. "Alex, I have wanted to meet you for more than ten years, since Kolya first described you. You are as beautiful as he said you were."

"Dmitri? He's mentioned you."

"He said good things I hope."

"Actually, he's said very little, but that's Kolya."

"Drop the gun, Dmitri," Kolya said. "There are two of us."

"They have shit ice cream in prison. I am not fucking going back." Dmitri shifted the aim of his gun from Kolya to Alex. "I don't want to shoot her or you. But if you force me, I will."

"Where's Tehila?" Kolya asked Alex.

"In the woods somewhere. Moving into position. I think she shot someone." Alex glanced at Kolya. "Dmitri was your best friend in the *dyskeii dom*, wasn't he?"

"He was."

She turned to Dmitri. "Maybe you could agree to leave the country?"

"It is what I want to do—go enjoy my money on an island somewhere. No more criminal shit. Kolya, you have the remaining chemical canister. Your government will believe you were coerced, and you can explain that I got away after you were injured. You can return to your life, whatever you choose it to be. Trust me."

"But not completely."

"No," Dmitri agreed. "Not completely. But if I break my word, you can come after me."

Kolya felt Alex's gaze on him, willing him to agree. She was a defense lawyer, not a prosecutor, and she would lean towards mercy. But beyond whatever she wanted, what did he want? Without Dmitri, he would not have made it through the hell of the *dyskeii dom*. Without Dmitri, he'd be dead now. On the other side was everything that Dmitri had done, and everything else that Dmitri might do in the future. Still, there was a chance that Dmitri really would settle on an island somewhere and stay the hell away from criminality. Maybe a small chance, but still a chance.

However, it was more than just a weighing up of what Dmitri had done for him or against him—more than what Dmitri might or might not do in the future. If their opportunities in life had been reversed, would Kolya be the one who'd become a criminal? Dmitri had described them as two sides of the same coin. It was not inaccurate. He felt a bond of kinship for the person Dmitri was—a bond that went beyond the mere transactional.

"I can't stop my agency or other agencies from hunting you down," Kolya said. "You have ten billion dollars that you coerced out of the American government."

"Bykovsky and Rzaev have most of it. I only get a couple hundred million."

"You were involved in a plot where people died. That will keep you on a wanted list."

"I understand that, too. And I'm sorry they died. Still, your government will have to find me. And I understand if you decide to work with them to find me. I am done with this revenge shit. You and me, we are okay."

Were they? Kolya didn't trust that either. But he'd put Dmitri in prison once. Maybe Dmitri should be in prison, but Kolya didn't have to be the person putting him inside. Not this time.

Kolya lowered his gun. "Do you have a key to the handcuffs?"

"Here, Alex." Dmitri lowered his gun in turn, tucked it into his waist, and tossed her the key. She unlocked the cuffs.

Kolya flexed his hands and wrists, feeling the circulation returning, and looked over at Dmitri. "*Idi*. Go. Before someone else shows up who is not your childhood friend."

"You are okay?"

"Not really. But I'll live."

Dmitri grinned. "Which is what matters. And Kolya, you should know. Someone is selling your agency's information to Rzaev."

He already knew. It was the only way Dmitri could have known so much. "Who?"

"Rzaev doesn't tell me everything. For you to find out."

* * * * *

It took Kowolsky fifteen minutes to wind his way through the trees and underbrush, paralleling the dirt road, moving steadily towards the dim sound of voices. He tripped on roots, and stickers from a wild bush with trailing branches and white flowers tore his pants. He'd twisted his knee. All of which had just served to make him more determined.

And now, that determination had led him to a clearing where he had an imperfect view of three people. From his position, he could identify them: Kolya Petrov, Petrov's fiancée, and Dmitri Lemonsky. A white van obscured part of his vision, but that wasn't a bad thing. It also obscured him from their view.

He angled himself so he could make out a backpack and a metal cylinder lying on the ground, along with two bodies.

He had no doubt what he had found. That there had been a falling out among the terrorists that resulted in two dead—didn't change the evidence.

He'd been right. Everyone else who'd belittled him as paranoid, as prejudiced because of Petrov's nationality and religion, they were idiots. The proof was in front of him—and there was Petrov's fiancée, safe and sound. Petrov wasn't being pressured to do anything. Of his own free will, Petrov was a traitor who'd blackmailed the United States.

Any question that Petrov's actions had been involuntary disappeared with the realization that both Petrov and Feinstein had guns.

And Petrov was his first target. Petrov was known to be an excellent shot and was therefore the greatest danger. Petrov, Lemonsky, then the woman. He'd take them out in that order.

He watched every step, avoiding snapping twigs, or crunching leaves. He halted, judged that he was close enough for a kill shot. His rifle had a round in the chamber. He raised, aimed for Petrov's head, took a deep breath, and moved his finger inside the trigger guard.

84

FRIDAY AFTERNOON, SOUTHERN VERMONT

ALL GOOD SPIES HAVE a sixth sense—a highly developed ability to sense something wrong despite the lack of other information. The spies who survive any length of time in the field not only have it but pay attention to it.

Kolya had been a field agent for most of his adult life. He'd had mishaps and injuries, but he'd survived: one part luck, one part skill, and one part listening to the whisper of that sixth sense. As Alex freed his hands, Kolya's sixth sense was whispering.

He heard and saw nothing, but his skin prickled, and he felt the gaze of someone hostile. Something was about to go terribly wrong. Something—or someone—was in the woods, near the van. He spun and saw Kowolsky in firing position a fraction of a second before Kowolsky pulled the trigger.

He dove for Alex just before the explosive sound of a shot rang out. Not one shot. Three shots, so close together that they sounded like one. She turned a startled face towards him, as he tackled her, and they fell together, hitting the ground hard. His hands and arms and her back took the brunt of it. For a second, she looked like she couldn't breathe. Had she hit her head? He maneuvered himself between her and Kowolsky and checked her again.

"Don't move." He braced for more shots. It was harder to hit a person on the ground, but not impossible. He lifted his head and shifted his position, aiming his gun towards the spot where he'd seen Kowolsky.

* * * * *

Kowolsky cursed at the miss. Both of them were on the ground and from where he stood, he was unlikely to make the shot. He had to finish things quickly. He maneuvered for a better angle. Aimed.

Then he froze as the barrel of a rifle pressed against his skull.

"Drop the gun, or you will be very dead." A melodic voice with a hint of an accent.

Tehila Melaku.

"Petrov's a traitor," he said through gritted teeth. "You know it. And I would think a Mossad agent would be fine with an extrajudicial elimination of a problem."

"Ex-Mossad. And you thought wrong, asshole."

"Should have known. Fucking Jews stick together."

"Well, this fucking Jew is going to blow your skull off unless you comply."

He did, dropping the gun and raising his hands. He had missed his chance, and Petrov would probably be exonerated. Hell, the bastard might even be acclaimed a hero—again. He knew the truth, but he would be ignored. Still, it wasn't worth dying. He'd wait. Sooner or later, he could prove what he knew.

In the meantime, he let the bitch march him back to his car, handcuff him to the steering wheel, and remove the keys.

* * * * *

Tehila appeared at the edge of the woods. "All clear."

Kolya suddenly felt every injury—the knee, the shoulder and the new wounds. He had to fight the impulse to stretch out on the ground and close his eyes. He could let go. It was over, really over. And Dmitri?

Dmitri was gone. So was Mickey's car.

Alex stood first. She offered a hand and helped pull him up. When he put weight on his right leg, it buckled. He hadn't felt any pain when he'd tackled Alex, but it was the last in a long line of indignities. He draped his arm around Alex's shoulder and steadied himself.

Tehila slung her gun over her shoulder and took out her phone.

"Why didn't you come out earlier?" he asked.

She held up a hand, signaling him to wait. She checked the message on her phone and tapped a message back. Then she gave a nod of satisfaction and returned the phone to her jeans. "I had to shoot one guy in the woods, and I wanted to be sure there were no other threats. You didn't need my help—until the asshole started shooting at you. You're welcome, by the way. Who is that schmuck?"

"Stephen Kowolsky. We don't get along."

"That would seem to be an understatement. Made some cute comments about Jews, by the way. He's handcuffed in his car. Reinforcements are coming. And an ambulance."

Then the three of them turned to look at the bodies. Charlie had been shot in the shoulder by Mickey and in the head by Dmitri. Mickey, though, had also been shot twice. The bullet that Kolya had fired had hit his chest. Another round had hit him in the head as well.

Kolya had only fired once.

Another debt to Dmitri.

Then he turned to Tehila. "You let Dmitri go?" How much had she seen or heard?

"Kowolsky's fault for shooting at you. It gave Dmitri a chance to run. Someone will find him eventually." Except she also had made the decision to hold off. The three of them were bound together now, in a conspiracy of silence. "And we can't go after him right now. We are babysitting this stuff." Tehila walked around the backpack. "Do you think there's any danger?"

"Two different chemicals have to mix together to form Novichok, and I threw a canister with one of the chemicals at Mickey. So no."

"But the C-4 is real?"

"Yes. And the remaining chemical is not completely safe, either, just not as deadly as Novichok."

"There you are. We cannot just leave C-4 and a dangerous chemical in the middle of the woods. What if a child found either? Someone else can chase your friend." She exchanged glances with Alex, who smiled in return, and that triggered a question.

How had Alex and Tehila found him? The timing was interesting—they must have been right behind Mickey—because he and the van had been sitting in the clearing for more than an hour before Mickey showed up. So they must have had some way to track Mickey. Or Mickey's car,

341

the car that Dmitri was now driving. He assumed that Dmitri would come to the same conclusion as he had and either change cars or check for tracking devices.

But that also raised the question of why they had left Stowe for Burlington—as well as why they had not left the state after his call.

He'd ask Alex about it later. He didn't need to know right now.

Alex's shoulder was no longer enough support. "I need to sit." He needed more than that, but he'd be home soon. All he wanted was a week in bed, lying next to Alex. He leaned heavily on her as she steered him towards the front seat of the van, where he collapsed in gratitude.

85

PRESIDENT YURI BYKOVSKY WAS hunched over his laptop at his ridiculously ornate desk when Rzaev entered. Was he muttering to himself? Rzaev wasn't sure. But he was sure of the look in Yuri's eyes. At best Yuri had been borderline sane—but now he'd gone over the edge. Still, Russia had had its share of madmen and survived.

"What has happened, Yuri?" Rzaev seated himself directly across from the President, his tone conversational. The best way to keep a crazy person calm was not to acknowledge that he was crazy.

Pavel had followed Rzaev and positioned himself behind Rzaev's chair. Rzaev never went outside his own compounds without Pavel. Yuri, however, was alone. The guards, his private secretary, dismissed by Yuri, hid in the outer rooms. So it was just the three of them.

"My fucking brother-in-law told Lewis I'm behind the attempt to poison Americans with a nerve agent."

"Do you care?"

"I care that Lewis will impose sanctions and otherwise harm my reputation."

"So? We still have ten billion dollars. Not a total loss."

Yuri pulled the laptop back and slammed the lid. "Lewis threatened me if Americans were killed."

"It no longer matters. It's over."

"He threatened me. It's not over."

"It is, although I have a question: did you tell my people to explode Novichok in American cities even after Lewis paid?"

343

"I did."

"And you were planning to kill Petrov?"

"After what he did, of course. And his girlfriend too."

"Without asking me?"

"You only operate your 'business' because I allow you to do so. I don't have to ask you anything."

"I see," Rzaev said.

"That pompous idiot Lewis thought he could threaten me. Me. And he wants his money back. He could start a war."

"He won't go to war over money. He will bluster and threaten sanctions—maybe even impose sanctions—but he won't go further."

"I am going to kill Tomas. This is his fault. All of it. And my sister. And their brats. All of them. Then I'm going to kill the American spies who helped him, as well as Petrov and his girlfriend. I'm putting out the order with the SVR tomorrow morning, since your people fucked it up."

Rzaev waited out the rambling tirade. In theory, he didn't care if Yuri killed his sister and her family or some American spies. He did, however, care if Yuri took actions that could impact his business or his travel. The Americans tended to respond strongly when people were assassinated on their turf. "You need to calm down, Yuri. We gambled. We won in what matters. We got the money, even if Lewis now knows the truth."

"That reminds me. Where is the money?"

"In the Cayman Islands. Five billion has been transferred into your account."

"For what you did, I don't think you deserve half."

"It was what we agreed."

"I didn't agree to anything of the kind."

"Actually, you did."

"I don't care if I did. Five hundred million is more than enough for what and your people did."

"You're going back on our arrangement?"

"It was my money. The Americans stole it from me. You just performed some minor services. You understand?"

"I understand." Rzaev had had no choice but to cooperate with Yuri for the past five years, but he hadn't particularly liked it. He was liking it less and less. "But I don't think assassinations of American agents are a good idea."

Yuri continued to rave. "The Americans think they've gotten away with it. They think they made a fool of me. Killing their agents will show them otherwise." Instead of calming down, Yuri was just sounding more insane.

"This was never supposed to lead to a showdown with the United States," Rzaev said. "That was why it was important to put the blame on Petrov and to have him corroborate the false information in my computer. Now we just have to wait it out."

"And how do I know that Lewis isn't planning a first strike against us? Don't you think that's possible?"

It was a wild statement, but Rzaev took it seriously. "No. Because—no matter whatever you think of him—he's not crazy."

"How do you know? How do you know that he doesn't have ambitions on Eastern Europe? On Russia. But I'm ready." Yuri leaned forward, conspiratorially. "Stalin built a bomb shelter under the Kremlin in case of nuclear war with the United States. Did you know that?"

"Everyone knows that. It was abandoned after Stalin died."

"Abandoned but not destroyed. I had it updated. A few months ago. Just needed some work on the air filters and updated electronics."

"So, there you are. You will be safe if America strikes. And they won't. They know it is mutually assured destruction."

"No, not if we surprise them."

This conversation was just getting crazier. Rzaev didn't like the direction. He didn't like the look on Yuri's face.

"They have satellites. How could you surprise them?"

"Submarines. We strike by submarine. Then follow with missiles."

"Do you know how many people would die?"

"Enough of us will survive. Then we will be the rulers of the world."

Rzaev was not a military expert. He knew very little of the effects of nuclear winter, but he'd heard the term. He didn't know how far radiation could travel or how long it would last. He knew that nuclear war was unthinkable and anyone who thought it was anything other than unthinkable—and was in a position to launch missiles—was a dangerous maniac. He thought of the gardens he'd cultivated and loved. Of his homes in Peredelkino, St. Petersburg, Miami, and on the coast of Italy.

"Tell me you are not serious."

Yuri leaned back in his chair. "I haven't ordered it yet. But doesn't it make sense to do it? Before Lewis attacks us? Preemptive action is always better, isn't it?"

"Of course. Preemptive action is always better." Rzaev looked up over his left shoulder where Pavel stood unmoving. "Don't you agree, Pavel?" Pavel always understood what Rzaev needed, even without words.

Pavel stood unmoving. "I agree. Now?"

"Now."

Pavel raised his right arm, which held a Tokarev. Yuri gaped at him, and Pavel smiled back. Then he shot Yuri Bykovsky in the eye. Yuri fell forward on his face. Pavel walked around the desk, wiped the handle of the gun, slid it under Yuri's hand and closed the fingers around the butt. Then he pushed Yuri aside and opened up the laptop. It took him five minutes. Then he turned off the computer, wiped the keyboard with a sleeve, and brushed off his pants as if there might be invisible flecks of blood.

"I went into the security system and erased the video of the past half hour in this room."

"Good." Rzaev did not allow anyone to cheat him, no one, from the lowest member of his gang to the President of the Russian Federation. He also believed in keeping his agreements. All quite apart from his concern that Yuri might have become crazy enough to actually launch an attack on the West. "And the other?"

"That too."

That was also good. Rzaev was genuinely fond of Dima and pleased about the money that the operation had put into his pocket. Doing a small favor in return was fair enough.

Rzaev walked to the door and called for help from Yuri's assistant.

"There has been a tragedy." Rzaev spoke with the gravity and sorrow that would be expected on such an occasion. "President Yuri Bykovsky took leave of his senses, was talking about ordering a strike on the United States, and now has taken his own life."

86

TWO DAYS LATER
SUNDAY, DAYTON, OHIO

FEDERAL MARSHALS HAD MET them at the airport, where Tomas said goodbye to the three ECA agents and to Fyodor. Fyodor and his wife went in one direction, Tomas, Lyudmila, and children, accompanied by the marshals, had boarded a flight to Dayton, Ohio. On landing they were driven to a house with four bedrooms, a large kitchen and a small fenced backyard. A marshal handed Tomas documents with their new identities, the keys to the house, and a three-year-old Toyota Highlander that stood in the driveway.

The children scooted through the house, approving of the bedrooms and the yard. Emma threw her arms around Tomas in a hug. "Kitten? Can we have a kitten?" He glanced over at Lyudmila. Wearing the necklace that he'd given her for her birthday, thanks to Jonathan Egan, she beamed her approval. If a cat could ease the transition, so be it.

FIVE DAYS LATER
SAVAII, SAMOA

The house sat on the top of a cliff, a contemporary masterpiece that included a waterfall cascading down into the immaculate swimming pool, a marble patio surrounding the pool, and floor to ceiling windows of unbreakable glass facing the Pacific, fifty feet below. Stone stairs carved into the side of the cliff allowed for easy access to the beach. The house and the surrounding one hundred acres offered luxury and privacy and had cost four million dollars when Dmitri had bought it twelve years earlier from a guy going bankrupt. One of the many properties that the United States government had failed to find after arresting him. A fund had paid for upkeep, and caretakers had preserved the property while Dmitri had been in prison.

He'd netted five hundred million from the Novichok business, apart from the other two hundred million that he'd previously hidden in Swiss banks. In Samoa, with no extradition treaties with the United States, he could live like a fucking king. Until he got bored—but he had a way to go before then.

On the pool's edge, Dmitri stretched out on a lounge chair, a bottle of lemon pepper vodka on the table next to him while he cradled a glass of the same vodka over ice. In Russia, he would never have drunk vodka with ice, but here, in this heat, it tasted damn good. The cool tones of Coltrane's saxophone floated out from the loudspeakers next to the pool house. He had Ben and Jerry's Cherry Garcia waiting in the freezer. Not a bad life.

He drank more vodka, feeling the warmth infuse his body. His phone vibrated and he picked it up. One word. *Done.* He typed a message on his phone and hit send. He smiled thinking of the reaction on the other end. Then he refilled his glass and carried it into the pool, where a young woman in a bikini waited for him. *Not fucking bad at all.*

FOGGY BOTTOM, WASHINGTON, D.C.

The team, Jonathan, Teo, and Elizabeth, along with Tehila, were back in the ECA conference room for a farewell Friday afternoon luncheon of Thai food, wine, and beer which beat the hell out of the soggy sandwiches they'd eaten before leaving for Russia. Kolya had spent a week resting and visiting doctors. He'd had a series of shots in his knee, and he was back on crutches for another two weeks. He'd start physical therapy as soon as he was off the crutches, and his various minor wounds were bandaged. His PTSD symptoms were in abeyance. All things considered, he was feeling reasonably decent.

This was his first—and last—day back. He was here to turn in his identification card and was due back at the law firm on Monday. He dreaded the thought of the stacks of documents, but he put that out of his mind.

"What's the information on who's taking over in Russia?" he asked Jonathan.

Jonathan shrugged. "The deputy secretary, I think, but it looks like there may be a power struggle before things settle out. I suspect various contenders will be killing each other for a few months."

"It's the Russian way. Rzaev is staying out of it?"

"So I understand. Although I suspect he'll have strong influence with whoever comes out on top."

"Unless someone kills him as well," Elizabeth added.

"Unlikely." Kolya said. "He has dirt on too many people that would go public if anyone were stupid enough to try to kill him."

"Well, here's to Rzaev—or Bykovsky—not killing us." Jonathan raised his wine glass. "And to a successful operation."

They raised glasses, drank, and returned to their food.

"This worked well." Teo dug into a plate of shrimp in red curry sauce. "We should keep the team together going forward."

Elizabeth rolled her eyes. "I'll put up with you and Jonathan when I have to. But I'm not interested in forming a band."

"Forming a band generally requires skill on an instrument." Kolya reached for a spring roll.

"I play violin," Teo said.

"I bet Elizabeth does great vocals," Jonathan said. "I play the guitar."

"You know three chords. That's not actually playing," Kolya said.

"Oh, shut up," Jonathan said. "Just because you're a goddamn genius on the piano, doesn't mean you get to dump on our musical abilities. What do you do, Tehila?"

Tehila swallowed a bite of vegetable curry before answering. "I make a great challah. And I kill people." Then she turned to Kolya. "Would you and Alex be available for Shabbat dinner tonight? Emma is making extra."

"You know we're not religious."

"I know, but I'm working on it. Ask Alex."

"I'll ask." Kolya returned to his lunch, and the banter continued: Jonathan teasing Elizabeth about a pair of diamond earrings she was wearing, Teo joking with Tehila. It was the familiar release after the successful end of an operation, and he had missed the camaraderie as much as he'd missed the action.

His phone buzzed with an incoming message. He thumbed it on: *All the videos of you in Russia have been destroyed. You will have to find the leak yourself. Sorry. And sorry I never read your letters.*

"What?" Jonathan asked.

"Just a friend saying hello." Kolya returned the phone to his pocket.

"Speaking of saying hello," Jonathan served himself Thai noodles, "Margaret would like to see you before you turn everything in—if you think you can resist the urge to break her neck."

"I'll try my best."

* * * * *

The *Vanity Fair* prints of 19th century writers on the wall were the same as the last time he'd been in the office, but it had only been a week and a half—so not yet time to rotate. Everything else was the same as well. Bradford was again behind her desk and he was again on crutches. He maneuvered himself into the chair directly opposite her. Same chair.

No, not everything was the same. He wasn't quite the same.

"You are planning to resign again, Mr. Petrov?"

"I understood it was a temporary position."

"Only if you want it to be. I would be delighted to have you back on a permanent basis, assuming that you are up for it. What do your doctors say?"

"Once I'm through physical therapy, I should be fine." Then, because he knew that his leg wasn't her only concern, he added. "Everything else is under control."

"Pleased to hear it." She paused. "For what it's worth, I never thought you were a traitor."

"I am aware." He knew from Tehila and Alex that Bradford had sent them to rescue him and to protect him against Kowolsky. Her recent actions didn't erase the past but did soften it.

"All the copies of that video you were forced to make self-destroyed, by the way. Do you know if there are still copies in Russia?"

"My understanding is that there are not, although I don't completely trust the source. My source also indicates that you have a mole."

"I believe your source—at least with regard to both matters. The news about the video is good. Your identity is protected, should you have any desire to return to field work. And I have people on the hunt for the mole."

"Good people I hope."

"I hope so as well. By the way, you should also know that your source is still wanted for his part in the Novichok plot, even though he did help in the end. Low priority, though, as long as he stays out of the United States and out of sight."

"I assumed as much. I am not interested in going after him."

"I assumed as much as well. There's a different matter that has come to my attention—that I think you would be both appropriate for and interested in should you decide to remain."

"I'm listening."

"It involves neo-Nazi activity. My counterpart in the intelligence service of one of our closest allies contacted me. He is very concerned about the possibility that neo-Nazi groups may be operating across borders—and inside government agencies—and wants to coordinate with us."

It was exactly the type of matter he would have wanted to take on. If he were still an agent.

"It could be a long assignment and most likely would involve travel outside the country. You would be able to spend some weekends with Ms. Feinstein, but it would be a separation. And it will be dangerous. Especially for you, given that..." she hesitated.

"Given that I'm Jewish?"

"Yes."

"Although it does give me somewhat more incentive."

"That too. My counterpart thinks that neo-Nazis are organizing and planning mass murders. Which of course is what Nazis do. They would have no hesitation at brutally murdering an American intelligence agent. They would especially enjoy killing a Jewish American agent."

"You make it sound so appealing."

"I don't want to mislead you about the nature of the assignment."

He raised eyebrows.

She sighed. "Yes, I recognize that previous history might make it hard for you to trust me. For what it is worth, I recognize that I do owe you an apology. You were correct. I should have asked you to volunteer in the Romanian matter instead of deceiving you, and I should not have put Ms. Feinstein into harm's way. I am sorry."

"Thank you for that."

He might never completely forgive her betrayal, but the apology coupled with her recent opposition to Smithson's kill order made the idea of working for her again more acceptable. But was it any guarantee she wouldn't do something equally underhanded in future? No. It was the nature of the business if he decided to stay. There were few people in his life whom he trusted absolutely, and Bradford was not one of them.

Still, the opportunity to take down Nazis was hard to resist.

"Take the weekend to decide. And of course, you will have as much time as you need to recuperate before you return to field work. Unfortunately, neo-Nazis are not going anywhere."

"I will let you know." It wasn't just his decision, which Bradford seemed to appreciate. "Now if you'll excuse me, I am due at Shabbat dinner."

87

FRIDAY NIGHT, GEORGETOWN, WASHINGTON D.C.

THEY LAY SIDE-BY-SIDE, LEGS entwined, while a recording of the Bill Evans trio played "Emily." The love making had required interesting positions, but it had been very good. If he turned his head, he could see the full moon framed in the window of their townhouse. It was an almost perfect moment. He drifted into a doze, content. But life doesn't permit more than a moment of perfection.

"I liked Emma." Alex's voice woke him. "And Tehila does make a hell of a good challah."

"I thought you would like Emma. I agree on the challah."

"But you don't want to celebrate Shabbat every week?"

"Not especially. Do you?"

"Not every week. Sometimes maybe. And, no, I'm not becoming religious or going to keep kosher. But there's a warmth to honoring our heritage, at least sometimes."

"I generally prefer cold to warm. But if you want to have Shabbat dinner on occasion, I have no objection. Maybe you could get Tehila's challah recipe?"

"You know I'm a disaster in the kitchen."

"I'll make it. It'll be my contribution."

"I'm fine with that. Next question: Are you planning to go to work Monday?" Alex rose up on an elbow. That was nice. He had a better view of her breasts.

He ran his hand down her body to her thigh.

"Are you listening to me?"

"Always."

"Then answer the question."

"We need to talk."

"That's my line, Kolya."

"Sometimes, it helps a relationship to alternate roles." He slid his hand to a more delicate spot in a slow movement he knew she enjoyed.

"Stop that. You said we should talk, so... talk."

He took a deep breath and returned the hand to its previous position on her thigh. "I met with Bradford today."

"Don't you still want to shoot her?"

"To some extent but not enough to actually do it. Anyway, she's asked me if I would consider coming back for a new assignment after I finish rehab. That she believed in me and assigned Tehila to protect me from a kill order—doesn't erase the past—but does make palatable the idea of working for her—temporarily."

"Temporarily?" She pushed his hand away and sat all the way up, positioning herself cross-legged to face him. "You realize, I *do* know you. I know you're miserable practicing law."

"It's that obvious?"

"You weren't trying hard to hide it."

"Will you be miserable if I accepted? The new mission will involve travel, if I take it."

"Where? No, I know. You can't say. How long will you be gone?"

"Hard to say."

She raised his hand to her lips and kissed it. "I can deal with the fact that you have a risky job. I can deal with the separations. Both of which are preferable to you being miserable. What concerns me is—you have a weakness that has been used against you twice. And could be used against you again."

"You're referring to yourself?"

"Your feelings for me make you vulnerable."

"I would have died on several occasions but for you."

"I know. But tell me that you didn't put yourself at risk this time because you thought I was in danger."

"I did. But I would have done it anyway. Because I thought I could stop Dmitri and find the Novichok."

"Arrogant much?"

"Sometimes."

"You did something goddamn stupid. You were lucky to get out alive. And you won't be lucky every time. You still have PTSD."

"Manageable."

"Until it isn't."

"Trust me."

"This isn't a question of trust. I'm worried about you getting hurt."

"I know that, too. I won't accept Bradford's proposal unless you're okay with it."

She leaned over to kiss him, a cascade of dark hair falling on his face. He pulled her back down against him for a deeper and longer kiss that turned into something even better as she positioned herself on top of him.

"If I hurt anything, tell me." But she knew what areas to avoid and what not to avoid. This time was slow and tender, and the opposite of hurting.

Afterward, he murmured in her ear. "I love you."

"And I love you. Accept Bradford's offer."

"Are you sure?" He stroked her hair, and she snuggled into his chest. With her head nestled beneath his chin, he couldn't see her face.

"No, but I'll live with it. By the way, I've been asked to help out in a class action case in New Jersey. It could take a year or so. Lots of discovery. If you're going to be traveling anyway...."

"When would you go?"

"I have some cases to tie up here first. And the matter hasn't been filed yet. So, I'll be here to cheer you through physical therapy."

It made sense—and he liked that she wasn't going to be brooding over his leaving. He also liked her being out of town while he was gone—somewhere where her connection to him wasn't such public knowledge. "You sure you're okay with this?"

"Are you? I may be gone longer than you."

He thought about coming back to Washington with her gone and knew he'd hate the emptiness. But he could hardly ask her to put up with his absences and not do the same. Not if they were going to work for the long term. "Yes, of course. Maybe I can join you in New Jersey on occasion."

"Maybe I'll let you."

It was not a perfect solution, but few things in life were perfect. For the first time in a very long time, he fell into a nightmare-free sleep, arms around Alex, dreaming of snow falling on the Nevskii Prospeckt while Ellis Marsalis played in the background.

About the Author

S. LEE MANNING spent two years as the managing editor of *Law Enforcement Communications* before realizing that lawyers make a lot more money. A subsequent career as an attorney spanned from a first-tier New York law firm—Cravath, Swaine & Moore—to working for the State of New Jersey, to solo practice. In 2001, Manning agreed to chair New Jerseyans for Alternatives to the Death Penalty (NJADP), writing articles on the risk of wrongful execution, and arguing against the death penalty on radio and television in the years leading up to its abolition in the state in 2007.

An award-winning short story writer, Manning is the author of international thrillers. Her life-long interests in Russia and espionage are reflected in her Kolya Petrov thrillers, *Trojan Horse* and *Nerve Attack* (Encircle Publications, 2020 and 2021). Manning is currently working on the third thriller in the Kolya Petrov series.

Manning lives in Vermont with her husband and two cats, but frequently visits her daughter in California and her son in New Jersey.

If you enjoyed reading this book,
please consider writing your honest review
and sharing it with other readers.

Many of our Authors are happy to participate in
Book Club and Reader Group discussions.
For more information, contact us at info@encirclepub.com.

Thank you,
Encircle Publications

For news about more exciting new fiction, join us at:

Facebook: www.facebook.com/encirclepub

Twitter: twitter.com/encirclepub

Instagram: www.instagram.com/encirclepublications

Sign up for Encircle Publications newsletter and specials:
eepurl.com/cs8taP